P9-DUB-687

HOUSE
LIGHTS

HOUSE
LIGHTS

Leah Hager Cohen

W. W. NORTON & COMPANY
New York London

"On Having Mis-identified a Wild Flower" from *New and Collected Poems*,
copyright ©1988 by Richard Wilbur, reprinted by
permission of Harcourt, Inc.

Manufacturing by Courier Westford
Book design by Anna Oler

Library of Congress Cataloging-in-Publication Data

Cohen, Leah Hager.
House lights / Leah Hager Cohen. — 1st ed.
p. cm.
ISBN 978-0-393-06451-3
1. Family secrets—Fiction. I. Title.
PS3553.O42445H77 2007
813'.54—dc22   2007006910

W. W. Norton & Company, Inc.
500 Fifth Avenue, New York, N.Y. 10110
www.wwnorton.com

W. W. Norton & Company Ltd.
Castle House, 75/76 Wells Street, London W1T 3QT

1 2 3 4 5 6 7 8 9 0

To Samuel G. Freedman

Who has not sat nervously before his own heart's curtain?
Up it goes: the scene is set for saying farewell.

—RAINER MARIA RILKE
from *The Duino Elegies*,
the Fourth Elegy
(translated by William H. Gass)

HOUSE
LIGHTS

My dream is to act.

That is how I started the letter I sent my grandmother on the sly, late in the winter of my twentieth year.

> *I know you will be surprised to hear from me. It has been more than three years since we last saw each other. You may not realize that I am out of school now and "at loose" in the world.*
>
> *I would very much like to talk with you about becoming an actress. I have always been fascinated by you, your amazing career and life.*
>
> *I have never known the reason why you and my mother do not get along. She does not talk about it. But I don't believe that should prevent us from knowing each other.*
>
> *My parents do not approve of my becoming an actress. (I have not told them that I am writing you.) I am eager for any advice you can give me. Please write me back and let me know ~~when~~ if when we can meet.*
>
>

Your granddaughter,
Beatrice Fisher-Hart

ONE

The Salon

N EAR THE END of the time that I still thought the world of him, my father and I took a walk along Memorial Drive. We took many walks here, the two of us, on Sunday mornings when it was closed to traffic and became a promenade instead for pedestrians, baby carriages, cyclists, and skaters. We would start by the Weeks Footbridge and follow the road, which follows the curves of the Charles River, all the way down to Mount Auburn Hospital, where I had been born. It was a kind of ritual that one or the other of us would mention this fact when we came within sight of the institution's brick buildings. Just before this part of the walk, we'd pass under a great canopy of sycamore trees. I loved these trees, with their mottled gray and yellow bark, their massive trunks and huge, spreading branches. In late autumn, they littered the ground with their seedpods—fat, bristly brown balls.

What makes this particular day stand out among so many like it was that my parents had been fighting. In their case this meant becoming soft-spoken and icily vague with each other; an austere chivalry permeated their interactions. That might not sound very bad, but it happened rarely enough to unsettle me when it did. This time it had been going on for several days.

It was November, a morning of frail gold, and once we'd reached the boulevard of sycamores, my father made the casual, lighthearted suggestion that I collect their seedpods, gather up as many of the bristly balls as I could hold in the lap of my poncho. "We can bring them back to your mother. She'll put them in a bowl, make a decoration of them," he said. "Don't you think she'd like that?"

I was twelve at the time, and felt old for this activity, but being anxious to mollify my mother, I agreed. I was anxious, too, to rescue my father, whom I somehow recognized as being the cause of her mood, her anger. I think we both knew that if I could charm her out of it, we would all find relief. Not only that, I think we knew that I was the *only* one who could charm her out of it. And so I set about filling the lap of my turquoise poncho with sycamore balls. Tree gonads, my father called them. The sex organs of the tree, he added, in case I didn't understand.

He didn't join in, but stood there with his hands clasped behind his back, his chin jutting forward, the November sunlight reflecting off the Charles and spangling the short curls that ringed his head. He stood there like a portrait of a man watching his daughter at play by the river. He stood there, lovingly observing me, but I knew if this *were* a painting, it was he who would have been its subject. When I'd gathered a few dozen balls, I went to show him, holding my poncho out like an apron, and he placed a hand on top of my head and said, "That's fine." Two racing shells glided along the river then, coxless and silent and swift, and I imagined (absurdly) the rowers taking note of us, being struck by the unusually fine image we made, standing there on the bank in the chilly golden light.

When we got home, my mother did allow herself to be won over by our gift. She let my father put his arm around her waist and kiss the side of her head; she moved into him almost imperceptibly when he did so. It turned out the magic was strong. It had actually begun working from afar, because she had baked maple syrup bread pudding and squeezed fresh orange juice while we were out on our walk. And she did in fact put the seedpods in a wide glass bowl at the center of the dining room table, which she had already set for our breakfast.

ABOUT TWO WEEKS after I'd secretly contacted my grand-mother by mail, I was stealing up the front stairs of our house when my mother stepped out of her office and halted me with her voice: "Bebe, love." Having given me one of literature's most romantic names, my parents promptly lopped it off at the first syllable, doubled it, and forevermore called me by the nurseryish result. "I have a patient coming any minute, but just quickly: reservations for the Pudding tonight, two or three?"

My parents ate in good restaurants several times a week. I often came. When we ate at home we ate well, too. Even if it was only eggs, they'd throw in chopped scallion, grated Asiago, a spoonful of Dijon.

"Um, I guess three."

If I had said no, I would have been spared a frightening sight, one that haunted me for a long time after. But I rarely said no. As much as it makes me cringe to admit, I loved being with them, had long preferred my parents' company to that of anyone else. I cherished the feeling of being indispensable within our threesome.

I had another, more strategic reason for saying yes on this occasion: I had just, finally, gotten a reply from my grandmother. Her letter was in my hand, in fact, when my mother came out of her office:

a simple ecru correspondence card suggesting we meet at a Back
Bay tea shop the following week. I wasn't sure whether to share the
news with my parents yet or savor it secretly a while longer. But
certainly part of me was eager to spring it on them without delay,
and I had an idea the Pudding might provide the perfect setting for
what was sure to be a boldly disturbing announcement.

The strange fact is that although my grandmother lived just across
the Charles on Beacon Hill, only two stops away on the T, I saw her
hardly ever, something less than annually, and then in the strained
company of my mother, or (more rarely) my mother and father. As
I had said in my letter, I did not know the reason for the estrangement, but its existence was and had always been part of my most basic
understanding of how our family functioned. The fact that I had
now breached this boundary, unarmed with any good understanding of why it had been drawn, was as scary as it was invigorating.

My parents were psychologists, Dr. and Dr. Fisher-Hart. They had
faculty positions at the university, as well as a shared private practice
whose offices occupied an addition to our house. We lived in an old
Federal Revival on the fringe of a desirable Cambridge neighborhood, with a separate entrance for patients around the side. Although
the addition had been built expressly for my parents' purpose, the
soundproofing had been badly done. Ever since I was small I had
understood I must close doors gently, tread lightly on the stair.

My grandmother was Margaret Fourcey, the legendary actress.
She had retired from performance more than a decade earlier, and
because her most memorable performances had been on the stage,
few people of my generation were familiar with her work outside
of a couple of cameos in what had turned out to be airy Hollywood
embarrassments. But among theater people she was still revered. I
knew from having read in various periodicals that she was still
actively involved, in a behind-the-scenes fashion. Supposedly she

held a weekly salon for a select cast of theater dignitaries, at which ideas for new projects were hatched and collaborations formed. Getting myself invited to this salon was my prime objective.

I had a single memory of having seen her on stage. I had been eight; she must have been near sixty. We'd been out in western Massachusetts, my parents and I, out in the hilly green: some arts festival in the summertime. I remember my grandmother made the people in the audience laugh very hard, and although I didn't understand the humor, I was excited by their laughter and proud of her power to summon it. She wore a dark blue evening cape; every time she swirled around I caught a glimpse of the sky blue lining, and I remember how teased I'd felt, even punished, by how fleeting and few these opportunities were.

My parents didn't approve of theater. They would have balked at this charge and moved to qualify it, pointing out among the volumes on their shelves those that contained plays, admitting freely, of course, that these tended to bear copyrights earlier than the twentieth century, and from countries other than America. *However,* they might have added, *sadly, the contemporary business of popular commercial theater contributes so little to—even, more often, impinges on—individual human development and society's greater good.* Not that either of them had ever put it in precisely those terms, but that was the beauty of the Fisher-Harts: our talent for intuiting that which had not been said.

Privately, I had incubated the fantasy of becoming an actress ever since seeing my grandmother perform. I had surprised everyone, including myself, by declaring the intention publicly in my last year of high school. My parents, unaccustomed to my diverging from their will, were initially kind but resolute in their refusal to endorse this goal. I surprised everyone again by insisting I would pursue it, with or without support, and in the end they relented.

Given their predilections, my parents were being wonderful, they maintained, letting me defer admission to college for a year, enabling me to "court my dreams," as my father put it repeatedly to friends and colleagues at holiday parties and various brunches and dinners. They had agreed to let me live at home while they footed the bill for acting classes, asking only that I take one fully transferable college credit class each semester, leaving me time to go out on auditions and attend, in theory, rehearsals—two things I hadn't actually wound up doing. Assuming, as they did, that my acting bid would fail, I could the following year either enroll in a full-time degree program at my parents' expense or support myself in whatever else I endeavored. "Wonderful options," my father had pointed out, earnestly, lest I think myself unlucky. I did not.

Upstairs in my room now I lay on my bed, which dipped severely in the middle, and reread my grandmother's brief note.

Beatrice—

   I can meet you next Friday the nineteenth. If this is convenient, you may find me at the Sweet Alyssum Tea Shop on Chestnut Street at four o'clock. I am intrigued.

M.F.

Why the initials, I wondered? Did they signify coldness, impersonality? Or was it her way of acknowledging, even winking at, playing along with, the clandestine atmosphere I had established? I gazed at the ceiling, mulling this over to no great satisfaction: I simply did not know her well enough to hazard a guess.

My bedroom was the single finished room on the third floor. The rest of the attic was hulking and dark, with exposed beams and boards, and occasional cracks of light where the roof met up unevenly with the walls of the house. I passed through a corner of that murky storage space every time I entered my room. This had the effect of rendering my room, with its buttermilk-hued walls, its cornflower blue carpet, its yellow curtains and lampshade—all of the myriad civilizing details my mother and I had chosen together— slightly irregular, or fraudulent.

I liked my room, though. I'd asked to move up here when I was thirteen, and cherished the irregularity of it as well as the privacy. Also the view. From my current position on the bed, lying under the low-sloping ceiling, I couldn't see much, only a bit of bird's nest poking messily from the eaves, lengths of twig and straw hanging haphazardly at the upper corner of my window, whose panes were wavy and warped the tops of the trees. But I had lived here my whole life, in this obdurately right-angled house wedged between Harvard and Central squares, and I knew if I were to go look out the window, I'd see to the right the brick order of university blocks. And if I were to lean forward at the waist and look out to the left, I'd be rewarded with the denser sprawl of multifamilies, public service agencies, discount shops, community murals: more color, more litter, more stuff.

We Fisher-Harts were oriented, crucially, toward the right. The point had been made in the correct, which is to say subtle, fashion from the time I was first aware. It was made in the way my parents fenced and landscaped our compact lawn, in the sort of mail that got pushed through the brass letter slot on our front door, in the routes of our evening strolls, in the particular grocery and liquor and flower shops they went out of their way to patronize. Certain shabbinesses about the house had been well masked, and those which couldn't be concealed were mitigated, at least, by the blue oval plaque my mother had managed to secure from the historical society, mounted outside the front door and painted with the date

1818. But flaws in my own bedroom had been left relatively alone, and I catalogued them with care, almost jealously. Some of them, certain marks and cracks and holes, I had actually created: a dent in the closet door where I had once in anger put my fist; discolored scrabbly patches on the wall beside my desk where I had stuck up pictures of pop stars with chewing gum, only to find out years later that gum did not scrape off as well as tape. Lying on my back now, I noticed with idle interest that the old kidney-shaped water stain on the ceiling had begun to bulge.

I could hear a patient walking along the peastone path my parents had laid: hurried, hard-soled footsteps. To me they sounded both anxious and full of propriety. In a minute my mother would open the outer door of her office into the tiny waiting room, and with a modulated smile invite the patient into her private enclave. It was always a stretch to imagine the welcome or warmth or even love the patient might feel at that moment.

Sometimes when I was younger, although I knew it was very wrong, I used to stand at the bottom of the stairs, outside my mother's office door, and eavesdrop on the private world unfolding inside. I could never do that with my father's office. Like my mother's, his had a door opening into the waiting room, where a white-noise machine sat on the floor beside a potted tree and generated its hissing surf sounds all day long. His office, however, did not communicate with the rest of the house.

I toyed with the prospect of telling my parents at dinner that night about my upcoming date with my grandmother. I imagined saying it with casual cheer, and then my mother's face drawing tight, going cold, my father reaching out to touch her arm. I would do it, I decided. I would tell them tonight. It wasn't the idea of hurting them that motivated me, but the idea of shocking them, knocking them off-balance, they who were always supremely well balanced.

At nineteen, I'd begun finally, belatedly, to question their unremitting self-assuredness—the very quality I'd once treasured in our family above all. Now I found I liked the idea of provoking them to speak, to act, outside their usual realm.

But at dinner that night my father was irritable, which was unlike him, and my mother placating, which was unlike her. We were shown to the table directly in front of the Pudding's stone fireplace, something that had happened only a few times before, and which had on those occasions clearly pleased my parents, so that I understood it as a privilege reserved for esteemed customers. But tonight my father complained that he was hot. "Take off your sweater, Jer," my mother suggested, and he ignored her. "Shall we change places?" she offered. Her chair was farther from the fire. "Then *you'll* be hot," he groused.

The disgusting thing about us Fisher-Harts was that there were only three of us in the world, and we had mythologized ourselves preciously. Before Sarah Fisher wed Jeremy Hart, they had decided they wanted to share a last name. They contemplated becoming the Fishers, and they contemplated becoming the Harts, but rejected these options as too eclipsing. The hyphenated route at first struck them as cumbersome and aesthetically inferior. So they toyed with being Fisharts and they toyed with being Harshers and they toyed with tossing the Fisher and Hart right out and choosing a new surname entirely. Then one Sunday, strolling along Memorial Drive, they watched a couple up ahead under the sycamore trees lofting a little boy by the hands between them every three steps, and my father had said, "*He's* a little hyphen," and my mother had had a quick fantasy of me, or some child, anyway, one day linking the two of them together like that, and suddenly having all three of us be the Fisher-Harts felt exactly right to them both.

What I didn't know then was that while being specially linked and loved was an important part of the myth, being isolated—set apart and incomprehensible to anyone else save the other two Fisher-Harts—was at least as important. Or, I should say, I *felt* it without comprehending it. Because I did receive the unvoiced message, and respond to it. My response was there in my rejection of close friendships with peers; in my easy assumption that few beyond my parents' choicest colleagues and friends were in our league morally and intellectually; in my remarkable lack of interest in venturing out into the world on my own, at least up until this point.

That night at the Pudding, although my parents' off-kilter behavior continued, with my father acting oddly strained, and my mother solicitous, I did not trouble myself too much about it. There was no reason to. Dr. and Dr. Fisher-Hart were famously brilliant at deciphering riddles and smoothing muddles, and I was more than willing to entrust the current one to them. Whatever was wrong, they would, between them, fix. I had grown up with this fundamental assurance, and it had always proved true. Not only could they work repairs on themselves, but when other people ailed, when other families fell apart, my parents were summoned for their ability to heal.

My father did not eat his salad, but after the plates were cleared my mother laid her palm over the back of his hand and he seemed to perk up, asking me about work.

The closest I had come to finding theatrical employment was as a tour guide at the Conway Jimerson Homestead, a restoration of a station on the Underground Railroad. Whenever I said "tour guide," my parents were unable to prevent themselves from murmuring "docent," at which point I would correct *them* with the title officially used by the Homestead (and which I otherwise found absurd and pompous), "historical interpreter." At any rate, I had this job giving tours, in period dress. Three or four days a week I'd ride

the bus from Harvard Square to Watertown, don the costume of
Constance Jimerson, maiden sister of bachelor brother Conway—
ardent abolitionists both; wed, as we were supposed to say, to the
cause of antislavery—and give tours of the premises: a farmhouse
and its smattering of outbuildings. I was not employed to act the
part of Constance per se; too little was known about her personal
life to allow a performance that could be both richly informed and
historically accurate. (A pity, I thought, when this was explained to
me at the interview; I would have much preferred the job the other
way.) Our costumes were meant simply to suggest what the Jimersons would have worn. Mine was a faded green print cotton dress
over a hooped petticoat, and brown high-button boots.

My parents liked it when I told stories about the local school
groups we received, and the tourists from afar. Children were often
disappointed to learn that "underground railroad" was a metaphor.
"Where are the tracks?" they wanted to know. "How did they climb
down to them?" I was amazed at how little their teachers prepared
them. But then, the pull to believe in underground passageways was
strong for me, too. Sometimes, even though I knew better, I
couldn't help studying the woodwork and floorboards for signs of
a trap door. Sometimes when I closed my eyes I imagined a net-
work of tunnels dug deep under the damp soil.

"Well," I said now, splitting a roll and spreading some of the special herbed butter they always served at the Pudding, "there was a
little boy yesterday who had all these personal questions. About *me,*
I mean."

Despite the fact that I wasn't meant to portray Constance Jimerson, many visitors to the Homestead, especially young ones, tended
to relate to me as though I were her, and expressed far more interest in the particulars of her story than in the more general history
I'd been trained to impart. The grown-ups conveyed their ques-

tions with a certain knowledgeable distance. "How would the fugitive slaves make contact with the Jimersons?" "Was Constance involved in women's suffrage?" "Why didn't she marry? Did she ever have a suitor?"

The children's questions had a much more immediate quality, sometimes phrased in the present tense, sometimes in the second person. As in, "Aren't you scared what'll happen to you if you get caught?" And, "What's your favorite color?" And, "If you really go to the bathroom in that bowl there, don't it make your room smell nasty?" I took gladly to their attentions and worked to cultivate their fascination. So long as none of my fellow guides were around, I felt free to improvise.

To me it was all a wonderful acting exercise. I thought about posture and the way she would have carried her hands. I tried to avoid contractions in my speech, and to pronounce my words with a certain care, almost as though I were a foreigner. I wore my hair very short then, and was dying it platinum, but hid those facts with a bonnet, and my boots clacked neatly over the wide pine boards as I gathered my skirts and led the groups from room to room. And when addressed as Constance, I never corrected the questioner, but always responded in the first person. "I fear only what might befall the people we are helping; they are the ones who face real danger," I would say. And, "My favorite color is the pink of primroses." And, "Yes, I suppose sometimes the smell can be a bit offensive, but of course we empty and wash out the pots first thing in the morning, just as I'm sure you must do, at your own homes." Then my inquisitors would giggle. Visitors were invited to sign a big leather-bound guest book, kept next to the cash register in the gift shop, before they left, and many times in this book I was singled out for glowing notices.

The thing that had made the little boy the day before stand out was that his questions had been directed past Constance Jimerson, toward me. "Are you white?" he'd wanted to know. My first thought was that he was asking, was the real Constance Jimerson white? But no, he meant me, the actual present-day girl there in the frayed green dress.

"...Yes," I responded. It had never occurred to me there could be any question about this.

He was black, and wore a shiny silver parka with an index card safety-pinned to it reading PHILIPPE GOODE, GRADE 2—MS. WEINBURG. "How come you working here, then?" he asked.

It threw me, having him break the fourth wall, as they would have said in my acting class, having him crack everyone's willing suspension of disbelief. It was as if someone had switched on the house lights in the middle of a dramatic performance, suddenly illuminating the larger reality in which a play was being staged. I felt nailed by this little boy with the metallic parka and the soft eyes. We were standing in Constance's bedroom, under the eaves. The two main things to talk about in this room were the rope bed—a nice oddity, authentic to the period but not the house; you would tighten the ropes beneath the feather mattress to make the bed more firm—and the large needlepoint on the wall, authentic to the house, though whether it had been crafted by Constance herself had not been verified. It spelled out a William Lloyd Garrison quote:

I WILL BE AS HARSH AS TRUTH AND AS UNCOMPROMISING AS JUSTICE.

"Why you want to work here?" The little boy persisted with his question.

His teacher said, "Philippe," in a way that made it apparent he was the class troublemaker. "Questions about *history,* please." And I, off the hook, had given her a duly thankful look and conducted the class down the narrow back stair into the kitchen. ("Please hold the handrail as you go.") But in the intervening day I had thought several times about this boy and felt unnerved, as though I had barely escaped being exposed—and at the same time oddly regretful, as though being exposed were something I might want.

I related a few anecdotes for my parents as we waited for our entrées, telling about the boy without telling them about my lingering reaction; telling them about one of the other guides who always wore nail polish even though it wasn't allowed and who then went to comical lengths to hide this from the site supervisor; telling them about the site supervisor, a narcissist with muttonchops whose devotion to period accuracy was rivaled only by his devotion to his own appearance. I knew how to tailor a story to please them. Keep each tale brief, salt it with just a few dashes of idiosyncratic detail, land lightly on the punch line. I was warming them up, feeling my wattage increase proportionate to their amusement. I was prepping them for my big number, the announcement that I was going to meet with my grandmother, that I was hoping to become—I had earlier searched for and settled upon this word—her protégée.

But our waiter came and as he set down our plates, my father's stuffed pork chop slid onto his lap, an unlikely event in any case but extraordinary at the Pudding, where such an occurrence was unthinkable. Amid the profound apologies and genteel scramblings to put things right, my father bent his head very low and kept it steadfastly down. I thought at first that he must be attending to a stain, and then, with a confused and frightened lurch, that he must somehow have gotten hurt, burned perhaps. From the peculiar way he slumped, I even entertained a flash of fear that he'd suffered a mild heart attack. But within seconds it became impossible not to realize, along with a queer, creeping sensation of terror and shame, that he was crying.

MY MOTHER'S ABILITY to take command during a crisis was breathtaking. One might almost think she welcomed the opportunity. Later that night, after having discreetly managed our smooth exit from the Pudding, and guided my father competently to bed, she heated milk for the two of us in the kitchen and poured a shot of something into each mug, some liqueur. She had never given me hard alcohol before. It stung my mouth warmly and brought to mind the color mahogany. Neither of us had had any dinner that night, but I wasn't hungry and evidently neither was she. The kitchen was the largest room in the house, and had had the most work done on it. It was hung with copper pots and a variety of woven baskets we never used. On the counter stood a vase overflowing with what looked like buttered popcorn: forsythia cut from the bushes along the driveway. My mother knew exactly when each spring it would be possible to force the blooms.

"Dad's down about something at work," she told me. "Let's sit."

A Queen Anne chair, upholstered in eggnog brocade scattered with blue hydrangeas, filled a corner of the kitchen. She gestured for me to take it; for herself she pulled up a wooden barstool. "The university is reviewing a complaint that's been made. By a student," she added quickly. "Not a patient. It's an allegation of misconduct."

"Oh. What kind?"

"Remarks of a sexual nature."

I pictured my father as he'd looked at the Pudding, bent over a plate still smeared with the remnants of haricots verts and red juice from the chop that had landed in his lap. I could see, too precisely, the way his back, covered in mustard brown merino wool, had shaken with silent sobs while the restaurant staff had moved about him, pretending not to notice, murmuring apologies, retrieving the ruined food. Only after my father had regained control did my mother beckon our waiter back over. "My husband's not feeling well," she'd said in a low voice. "Could we please get the check?" Naturally the manager refused to charge us and begged us to send him the dry-cleaning bill. He wanted to wrap up our entrées, but my mother demurred, so we simply left—my father, as if in obedience, performing the role my mother had assigned him: that of patient.

On the sidewalk he'd hunched his shoulders and tucked his chin inside his coat as my mother stood on the curb and hailed a cab. When it came, he'd slumped into the front seat while my mother and I slid into the back and she gave the driver our address. My father coughed several times on the way home. In the front hall he allowed my mother to hang up his coat. Then he shuffled off for aspirin while she made him tea. His posture, as he mounted the stairs to bed, had served as a kind of armor against any inquiries I might have made.

But now my mother had taken it upon herself to offer the story, or a fragment of it. Although her words made the room tilt, I remained superbly still. I was sitting cross-legged in the big flowered chair, holding the mug of doctored milk against my stomach. "Not to be stupid," I said, "but so? How is this different than before?"

I had been in middle school the other time, and found out by accident. I don't think they'd planned to tell me, but I overheard them whispering and confronted them. They'd sat me down. My mother had done most of the talking. That time the complainant had been a patient. A girl only a little bit older than I. I knew what she looked like, had seen her out my bedroom window going to and from the office.

That time I had been extremely upset—had missed days of school over it—and my parents had gone to careful, considered lengths to put it into context, explaining that to a certain extent it came with the territory, that in their field, the likelihood of coming under some kind of accusation during the span of one's entire career, especially for a male therapist, was perhaps greater than it never happening. They made it sound more or less par for the course. I had often heard my parents refer to friends or colleagues as "quality people," and the implication seemed to be that the family of the complainant—the patient—was not of the same ilk. But it was confusing, because at the same time they took care to absolve her, instructing me that this girl was neither evil nor bad; they framed for me how a young woman, struggling in her own life, engaged in an intense relationship with her therapist, might confuse fantasy and fact. In the end, as my parents had assured me it would, the review board found that my father had acted appropriately toward her, well within the guidelines of the profession. The matter had ended without any loss of standing to my father, and had left me with the lasting impression of my parents' joint forbearance.

"I mean, why should he let himself get *so* down about it?" I asked my mother now. There was some petulance in my voice. I didn't know how to be more direct, how to voice the fear that if he was this upset, the charge might be legitimate.

My mother looked at me without blinking. "He's tired. And he's hurt."

"Do you know the student?"

"Yes."

"Is she—basically a fruitcake?"

"She is—was—one of his supervisees." In other words, no; we both knew how selective my father was about supervision. My mother supervised doctoral candidates in clinical psychology on occasion, but my father, because of his standing in the department and his general reputation, was in greater demand; sometimes students would try to arrange for him to be their supervisor even before they'd enrolled in the program. He'd implemented firm limits: only two supervisees per year, selected by him after interviewing the entire pool of hopefuls.

I had met several of the chosen over the years. Rarely, he would invite a special favorite over for dinner. More often, they were included in larger holiday gatherings at our house, bearing bottles of scotch or armfuls of flowers, and an air of reverence and gratitude that was unmistakable to me even when I was quite little. He would never have accepted someone he didn't think was "quality" as a supervisee.

"When did you find out?" I asked.

"Today."

"Before or after you made reservations for dinner?"

She paused. She sat high above me on the stool, darkly outlined, almost silhouetted, by the recessed lighting behind her. "Before."

"Would you be telling me now if he hadn't lost it at supper?"

The look in her eye was cool. I knew she wouldn't have.

"I don't know when I would have told you," she hedged.

I was not supposed to ask her such a pointed question. We both understood it was full of implication, judgment—when after all here she was, attending first to my father and now to me, exercising her particular competence, seeing the family through crisis, and wasn't she filling me in, giving me the straight story? What did it matter how much time had elapsed between when she had heard it and when she chose to tell? The lines around her mouth were hard. They read like a chronicle of what it cost her to hold things together.

I backed off. "Is there anything I'm supposed to do?"

"Just—if you could be *kind,* Bebe. And discreet."

"Yeah."

"I'm going to finish up some things in my office before bed." She rose and yawned. The yawn felt staged. It signaled an end to solemnity. She had told me; I had heard; now we were to go act normal. I got it; I was not a Fisher-Hart for nothing. My mother's long body, in its decorous clothing—a straight black skirt falling to mid-calf, a sleek burgundy cardigan grazing her knees—hovered above me, backlit. She leaned in for a moment and her fingers swept my chin. *Good girl,* I understood this to mean. I managed a small smile. She turned and walked toward the door.

"Oh—Mom."

Halfway across the kitchen, she turned.

"I meant to tell you. You won't like this, but. I contacted Grandmother. We have a date to meet. Next week. To talk about acting. So. I think that's good."

Her brow creased slightly. Nothing else. She squinted at me like that. At some length she gave a nod and went to her office.

I remained where I was, savoring the sharp-tasting milk.

ON THE APPOINTED afternoon my grandmother waited for me in the tea shop she had named. It was just off Charles Street, below street level, and I passed by several times before realizing it was the place. Arranging this meeting entirely by mail had lent it a clandestine feeling. And although I enjoyed the sense of drama this conjured and knew full well I was its architect, at the same time I was genuinely nervous. For the first time in my life, I cared about impressing my grandmother. What's more, I realized that while she had agreed to meet me because I was Dr. Sarah Fisher-Hart's daughter, I would have to impress her in spite of this fact.

Now, having finally located the shop, and my grandmother in it, I sat facing her across a round, marble-topped table. I thought she looked appraising. In my letter I'd said I wanted her advice; I wondered whether it was obvious that I wanted her contacts, too.

It was the first week of spring. Inches of gray slush coated the sidewalks and streets. I had worn stockings and impractical shoes, inside of which my toes clumped up wetly. The waitress, graceful and long-nosed, brought our things on a tray. I had asked for a rose hip tisane—having recently read of such a thing in a book—and it came in the thinnest-walled glass mug I had ever seen. My grandmother had a pot of hot chocolate, which I would have much preferred had I not given my order first and then been embarrassed to amend it. "Here you are, Ms. Fourcey," added the waitress, setting down a plate of madeleines which I had not heard my grandmother order.

She thanked the waitress and offered me a cookie, then took one herself and dipped it, disarmingly, into her cocoa. The radio, tuned to the classical station my parents listened to, played something low and full of symmetry. I sipped at my drink; it tasted abominably of hot perfume.

"So. You want to be on the boards," stated my grandmother. I didn't know her well enough to gauge whether this stilted delivery was offered archly or humorously, to put me at ease. I tried to read her face. A prestigious magazine had published a profile of her several years back, alongside the Hirschfeld portrait that captured precisely what the article referred to as her "increasing and not unflattering resemblance to a Roman senator" as she aged. Sitting across from her, I could appreciate the aptness of the description. Something about her pewtery bangs suggested it, and of course the remarkable nose and chin for which she was famous, but also the mixture of hauteur and righteousness she exuded. I tried to find in her appearance the reason my mother continued to hate her.

"Yes."

"Why?"

I had anticipated the question, and was a little proud of my answer. "I want to deliver beauty into people's lives."

She sat very still. At that time I supposed she was never not performing, and I imagined her performance as a test that I, her audience of one, must pass. I sat equally still. "I don't know what that means," she said.

A bead of sweat sank like mercury from my armpit to my ribs. Neither did I. I had been counting on her to know. The words, when they had come to me, simply struck me as perfect. I had envisioned that perhaps she'd nod, and without further ado embark on what would become the quietly epic journey of educating me as to how to become a great actress. I mean I actually sort of believed I had come up with *the* phrase that would set in motion an explicit series of events that had been scripted—by me or by fate, I couldn't make up my mind which would be preferable—to unfold between us. "I . . . I want to be an instrument," I stammered, ". . . of . . . of . . ." —casting about—". . . beauty."

Her eyebrows rose skeptically. I thought that was the end of our meeting right there, and I was ashamed of failing so early in the game, and I filled with a swift, concentrated rage toward my mother.

But we were not done. The Fisher-Hart telepathy worked only, perhaps, within my nuclear family. I had misread my grandmother. Rolling her spoon between her palms, she seemed really to puzzle over what I had said. "Is that different," she mused, "from being an *object* of beauty?" And then she laughed, at what I did not know, but it was a bright tumble of sound that caused the long-nosed waitress to look around from her task behind the counter and smile.

"—I don't know," I said.

"I was once called a famous beauty."

"I know." It was in all the press clips I'd ever read about her. Truthfully, I couldn't see it.

"It may be worth less than you suppose."

"What?"

"Beauty, Beatrice." She set the spoon down. "You put me in a difficult position."

"I'm sorry."

"Not undeserved."

"Oh, I'm sorry! Please don't think I'm—"

"What?"

"Trying to take advantage."

She shrugged. "Aren't you?"

I blushed. I was liking her ridiculously more than planned.

And who was she, this cipher of my bloodline? The bulk of what I knew at the time came from *Who's Who* and *The New Yorker* and *Vanity Fair;* from footnotes in other people's biographies and obituaries; from old reviews I'd dug up at the library; from Internet searches I had conducted in my attic room at home, always with an ear out for my parents' footsteps on the stairs. It would be easy—and wrong—to say that I sought information only indirectly, through secondary sources, as either an act of solidarity with or sensitivity toward my mother. I knew my discreet researches were really delicate acts of aggression. Conducting them, I transgressed against my mother's clear—though never stated—wishes.

This is some of what my research turned up. In 1954 Margaret Fourcey, Boston Brahmin, age twenty, had married my grandfather, Neil Fisher, German-born Jewish playwright, then thirty-nine, in New York City. In 1955 she gave birth to my mother. The same year, Neil Fisher was called before the House Un-American Activities Committee; three months after giving testimony he died in a hotel room of a drug overdose. In 1957 Margaret Fourcey won her first Tony nomination making her Broadway debut as the female lead in *Pyramus and Thisbe,* the last play Neil Fisher ever wrote. In

1959 my mother, then four, went to live with her Fourcey grand-parents in Boston, under whose roof she remained until she left for college. In 1968 Margaret Fourcey won the Tony for reprising her signature role in the revival of *Pyramus and Thisbe,* this time with an interracial cast. In 1969 she married the actor playing Pyramus, Maynard Clinkscale, and gave birth to their daughter, Ida.

The stuff of soaps. And at the same time ancient history. Fasci-nating, yet with a postmortem quality: artifacts preserved under glass. That's what I thought at nineteen. The bones of the story possessed glamour and fine, arcing drama. My ability to imagine the rest—the inevitable tissue and sinew—was impaired, largely, I suppose now, by adolescent solipsism. But by something else, too, something I was only then, that year, beginning to notice: the silence I'd grown up with, a governing silence so seamless it was like the air I breathed. Now when I try to distill its manifestations, I can hardly think of any. My parents never issued any directive against speech; nor were there explicitly taboo topics in our house. I do not remember any time my parents refused to answer, or even deflected, a question I put to them. It's more as though they sent me unspoken messages not to inquire about certain things, and I heeded and complied so flawlessly that there was never any need for them to say *hush.*

But now I wanted to understand my family better. That was my other reason for seeking out my grandmother, although I had not included it in my letter and did not dare mention it now. Certain omissions had finally struck me as odd, certain explanations as inad-equate, and I thought my comprehension would profit from hear-ing our story related by someone other than my parents.

My grandmother sat waiting for an answer to her question.

"Well," I admitted carefully, "it's true I am taking advantage of—*being related* to you." I was determined to be frank. I had decided real candor was rare, and therefore charming, and I also had an idea it could work to incite event, to speed life up, hasten movement—all of which at that point in my life was desirable. "But I don't mean to play on your, you know, guilt."

"Guilt!"

I thought she was going to—not hit me exactly, but throw her cocoa at me or something, tip the table over: I was afraid. And it was a rush, a thrill. Animal and intoxicating. The Roman senator gave way for a moment to terrifying beauty. Things coursed into my bloodstream; my heart slammed; I had to open my mouth to breathe.

And where my carefully composed line about delivering beauty had failed, my cloddish remark assuming her guilt succeeded. She *couldn't* dismiss me after that, couldn't let me return empty-handed to the house where that assumption—that she must be burdened by guilt for having chosen her career over her daughter—had been passively or actively allowed to form. I didn't grasp all this then. But when in the next breath she recommended I come by her house the following Tuesday at seven-thirty, I understood that somehow during the preceding few minutes I had gained power in our relationship, and that this shift had determined the outcome of what, if life were a play, might have been the scene titled: Beatrice's Audition.

WE HAD IN OUR family a tradition of great men. Great figures of men.

There was Neil Fisher, long dead. My grandmother's first husband, the very definition of integrity, courage, conviction. He hadn't named names. Hadn't caused any to be inscribed on the blacklist alongside his own. He'd merely shielded his wife, and when it seemed to him hopeless, taken his life, in the swift privacy of a hotel bathroom. His own name, in death, rarely came up. That and the scarcity of photographs of him seemed to confirm his tragic status. My mother had a few pictures in an album whose pages were brittle and scarred with discolored smears of glue. A black-and-white print showed him in an undershirt, straddling a chair backwards, cigarette smoke obscuring half his face. A faded color snapshot showed him standing next to a park bench wearing a red and black plaid flannel shirt and glasses with heavy frames. And in the last picture he peered, crinkle-eyed and craggy, down at what might have been a sack of sugar—my mother—cradled in his arms.

There was Maynard Clinkscale, ten years gone. More than impressions of the man himself, my thoughts about my grandmother's second husband were founded on my understanding of how everyone else had loved him. He remained for me like something in science, one of those particles that can't be seen but only detected by its impact on the environment. Maynard Clinkscale left trace elements with everyone he'd touched. He couldn't always have been simply adored; certainly in 1969, the year he married a white woman, he must have been the target of much hatred. But everything I had heard of him pointed to a man widely and justly beloved. I had dim memories of his girth and warmth; a big, almost baggy face, freckled like a banana; a laugh like tires going slowly over gravel. I had been at his funeral, nine years old in a dress that didn't cover my knees. My memories of that day were frozen images, movie stills. Thickets of people back at my grandparents' Beacon Hill townhouse, and every one of them in tears. Not simply in tears but sodden with grief. My grandmother, just her face, as if in close-up, glistening wet. My Aunt Ida—only child of Maynard and Margaret—at the center of a knot of people in the garden, convulsed. And my mother—so improbably—alone in the dark nook of the kitchen pantry, where I'd come upon her bent at the waist, both hands gripping a shelf, heaving with silent sobs. Who Maynard had been to her, what she had been crying for, I did not understand.

Then there was my own father, born Jeremy Bernard Hart, now
Jeremy Fisher-Hart, as beneficent as the day was long. As a child, I'd
thought him unusually tall and robust. During our Sunday morning walks on Memorial Drive, he'd often retell, at my bidding,
Greek myths, or our favorite bits from the *Odyssey,* all spun out in
his rich, professorial voice. And it was ridiculously easy for me, a little girl walking alongside him, taking two steps to his one, to con-
flate him with the very heroes and gods he described. His hands
seemed to me huge, his chest broad as a bull's. The morning light
on those walks, filtered through the canopy of sycamore trees,
would bronze his brownish curls, gloss the high pink dome of his
forehead where his hairline was receding. When, much later, I came
to realize that my father was not an especially large man, I experienced a profound sense of disorientation.

We took these walks, just the two of us, not every Sunday but
many, and at every time of year. In winter we'd throw sharp little
rocks onto the frozen Charles and listen to the various sounds they
made, skittering over the ice. In summer we'd stop by the Longfel-
low Bridge and he'd buy me a bomb pop from the ice cream truck.
Often these walks were framed as a service we offered my mother.
We would be, as my father put it while zipping up my jacket in the
front hall, giving her "some time." Occasionally she would say—he
would tell me she had said—that she had a headache and needed to
close her eyes. At any rate, I understood that he and I were joined
in providing her a wide berth, which was fine with me; they were
the only times I ever had him to myself.

Beyond the house my father's duties and authority ranged far
and wide; he bore the titles president and chair and director over
and over again, on academic committees, in professional organiza-
tions, on research teams. When people called the house and asked
for Dr. Fisher-Hart, I knew nine times out of ten it was my father

they wanted. And I never sensed jealousy from my mother; on the contrary, she seemed not only to admire but to insist on his superior professional standing. Even the way their positions were reversed within the house seemed further evidence of his supreme decency. For while he always deferred to her at home, I managed to mistake this behavior for kindness, rather than the paying of a debt.

These three men—three figures of men—were talismanic for me, an unlikely trinity I liked to keep in mind. I was not indifferent to the particular strengths of the women in our family: my grandmother's artistic reach and bohemian courage, my mother's professional stature and domestic proficiency. But their virtues seemed glittering and cold contrasted with those of the men. The men's attributes were marked by warmth and compassion. Perhaps because I grew up amid a weakness for mythologizing; perhaps because two of the men in my pantheon were already dead and the one who remained had always seemed elevated beyond other mortals, it was natural for me to attribute magical meaning to their lives, to braid the individual strands of their accomplishments together. Neil, Maynard, Jeremy. Their finer qualities informed one another until they all three dripped with goodness, selflessness; they were so beautifully, effortlessly moral.

ON TUESDAY EVENING I was all set to walk to the T for my grandmother's salon when my mother intercepted me and offered to drive. I hesitated, wondering if she meant then to come inside my grandmother's house with me. But the weather, after a brief thaw over the weekend, had suddenly turned cold again, and I was wearing foolish shoes again, and I thought about how on Beacon Hill there was never any available parking anyway, so I was probably safe. "If you want to," I said ungraciously.

We sailed along easily to Storrow Drive and there immediately
hit traffic. The sun had gone down but the sky held a lavender after-
glow. It, and the lights of Cambridge and Boston beginning to prick
up through it on either side of the indigo river, which was still cluttered with pale fingers of ice along its banks, made me ache with an
unspecified impatience. Somehow the traffic seemed my mother's
fault. If I'd taken the T, I'd have been there already. She didn't want
me to make it.

I looked over at her sideways. She'd switched on public radio and,
oblivious to my internal accusations, was listening to the newscast-
ers offer their erudite summations of the day's events. Her long camel
coat seemed homely and wilted, as though exhausted from the long
winter. We crept along. She handled the car with dogged patience,
no whisper of complaint. I wondered why she had volunteered to
chauffeur me this night. I wondered whether she was jealous.

Once, years ago, she'd lain on the couch with a sick headache,
and I'd been driving my toy cars along the cushions, and then cautiously along her limbs and through her hair, and to my surprise she
didn't snap but whispered, "Ah, Bebe, that feels good," and then it
became my duty. For a long time after that, whenever she had one
of her terrible headaches, I would minister to her with my toy cars.
It was a strange job. I had to play at being childlike in order to carry
out the adult role of caring for her. She never asked me explicitly
to do it, but when she lay on the couch with a wet washcloth folded
across her brow, I understood. "Oh Bebe, love," she'd murmur, with
a kind of gratitude that made me feel conscripted.

Now, on Storrow, she shifted into neutral and we idled in the choke
of cars. Perhaps because it was obvious to me that I was in the process
of leaving her, she suddenly looked innocent, unleavable.

"Sorry," I said.

"About what?"

I waved my hand vaguely toward all the congestion.

"The traffic?"

"No. Though I should have taken the T."

She lowered the radio. "What are you sorry about?"

"I don't know. Nothing."

"Bebe."

"About—doing something you'd rather I not."

"You mean going to your grandmother's."

"Yeah."

She shook her head dismissively. I didn't know whether she meant it wasn't true that she didn't want me to go, or that I didn't need to apologize for it.

Traffic let up. When we were nearly there I said, "How's Dad?"

Our family's silence on the matter over the past several days had been concerted, as had been his cheerful demeanor. As usual, my parents had closed ranks and joined forces to send a persuasive message that all was well. Sunday had felt almost scripted. It dawned cold and gray. My parents had put on their parkas and wool hats and gone off to hike the Fells. They arrived home in the early afternoon with a carload of grocery bags from Whole Foods, which I had helped to carry in. Then my father had napped while my mother prepared lamb stew, and my mother had done work in her office while my father made strudel, and in the evening we all sat down to supper together with Aaron Copland playing on the stereo and four white candles lit in the center of the table. It was like a thousand other fine Sundays in my life, only I noticed it differently this time. The artfulness of it, the careful presentation we all made to one another.

"How's he doing?" I asked again, and my mother turned down the car radio, and put on the blinker, and turned left onto Revere, but when she had finished all of this and turned to me she only said, "He's okay."

"Really?"

"I think he's feeling better. Doesn't it seem that way to you?"

I looked out the window and laughed a little rude laugh.

"What?"

"Nothing. 'Seem,' that's all."

I had been to my grandmother's townhouse so few times that it held a kind of fixed quality in my mind, less a living house than a sublimely colored plate in an old children's book. I was surprised when my mother found it easily in the maze of one-way streets up on Beacon Hill. It was as though it were a regular destination for her. There was, it gratified me to see, no hope of finding a parking space. My mother let me out in front of the entrance.

"What?" I said, turning back with one foot on the sidewalk, because somehow—with an indrawn breath, a clearing of the throat, something—she had pulled the invisible thread strung between us.

"Just—give her my regards."

"Thanks," I said, "for the ride," and got out.

I watched my mother drive away. It was important to wait until she disappeared entirely from sight. I didn't want to enter my grandmother's house tainted. Once her car vanished around the corner, I was free to see how beautiful the evening was: trees and stoops lit by lamps, the sky still holding its dose of purple. The scene looked sufficiently unrelated to the rest of the world, my home across the Charles. I approached my grandmother's door.

The knocker was shaped like the head of a lion. Its call was answered by a diminutive elderly woman in a green wool cap, a worn tweed jacket, opaque stockings, and blocky shoes. It was all I could do not to say, "Alice B. Toklas, I presume?" In spite of that reference, I was disappointed with the general look of her, so devoid of glamour, and I thought that if the salon was composed of others like her, old and dowdy, I was wasting my time. But she smiled at me with surpassing warmth and said, in a voice tinged with Old Europe, a curling-at-the-edges sort of accent, "Beatrice. How wonderful." She ushered me in and showed me where to hang my coat and said, "I'm Silke," offering her hand, which was blue-veined and strong. "A very old friend."

"Oh," I said, curious, but shy to ask, and followed her down the hall.

"In here," directed Silke, showing me into the parlor, which looked different than I remembered: backwards, like a slide viewed from the wrong side. There was an enormous gold brocade couch, and before it, arranged on a long, low wooden table, half a dozen wooden bowls filled with cashews, olives, purple grapes, hummus, water crackers, and chocolate-dipped figs, all in a row. There was a fireplace, with a fire lit, and a large bay window at the far end of the room, draped with swags of blue-green velvet and flanked by floor-to-ceiling bookshelves. Standing before one of these was the only other person in the room, a tall man with his hands clasped behind his back, his head, with its fringe of thick, gingery waves, tilted sideways to read the books' spines. He turned when he heard us. He had the look of a former athlete, a buoyancy that seemed to counter the slight paunch, the pleats on his brow. He seemed to be around the same age as my father. He wore a pair of eyeglasses pushed up like sunglasses on his head. His coloring tended toward pink, and he had a rather boyish smattering of freckles.

It is tempting to say that I recognized the moment, that I knew then my life would be altered by this person, that there was a sign, a response within me, a latent knowledge that stirred when we met. But that would be making a myth of it, which is the last thing I want to do.

"Hale, this is Beatrice," said Silke, gesturing, and turning to me:

"And this gentleman is Hale Rubin." I could tell from the way she said it that I was supposed to know who that was.

"How do you do?"

"Hi," he returned with a nod, in a way that shamed me—without coolness but also without the least aspiration to charm. He said it just *regular*.

Then in my nervousness I looked helplessly around the room and breathed out a thin laugh, aware as I was of my deficit: I could hardly start a conversation with someone I was expected to know but didn't. I had no point of orientation, no framework or instructions with which to approach the scene, and my life had not prepared me simply to *be*. Silke apparently suffered from no such difficulty. She reached into a bowl and helped herself to an olive, licking forefinger and thumb rather impishly. Her cap was some kind of boiled wool; knobby and green, it looked oddly like a pickle, at an angle, on her head. She caught me looking at her and beamed back, comfortably.

Hale Rubin gave a second slight nod, excusing himself, and turned back to the bookshelves. Hale Rubin, Hale Rubin. The name *was* familiar. Somewhere in the house footsteps sounded, and simultaneously the doorbell rang and Silke said she'd go see who it was.

As she left, two little boys came barreling past her into the room, the littler one dressed in nothing but an undershirt, the bigger one in pajamas printed all over with bugs. "Pax! *Paxton!*" yelled the bigger, in evident pursuit. "Get back and get your jammies on. Grammy's going to fry your butt," he added, which made the littler one yelp happily. Seeing Hale Rubin and me, the bigger one then skidded to a stop, but the littler kept going, giggling hard, apparently infected with the dual thrills of naughtiness and nakedness, until he got to the fireplace, where he scrambled onto a chair in order to reach a wooden box on the mantel. He still wasn't tall enough.

"Get it for me, Teej," he said, bouncing.

Teej looked at me, shook his head, and sighed. "I'm not going to get it until you get dressed."

"*Get* it! Tee-*jay!*"

Then a beautiful woman strode into the room, scooped the little naked child off the chair, saying adoringly, "Come on, devil," and, securing him on her hip, turned to me. She wore a short scarlet and orange Chinese silk dress and knee-high black boots. Her hair was a cloud of black ringlets, her eyes were rimmed in smoky liner, and she shared the same unmistakable nose and chin as my mother and grandmother. "Hello, I'm Ida," she said. "You're Beatrice, right?"

I shook hands with my aunt. I hadn't seen her since her father's funeral, ten years past. Maybe I'd heard she'd had children. I thought she lived in San Diego. Thought she was a singer, some kind of recording artist? But I didn't know.

"This is Paxton. That's Thomas James. And we are going to get this guy ready for bed now."

"No, Mommy, no! I want the army!"

"Teej, you bring it, all right?" She was already walking out of the room.

Teej, giving me a look that assumed my full commiseration with his plight, climbed up on the chair and retrieved the wooden box from the mantel. On the way out, he stopped before me. "Do you know what a praying mantis is?"

"A kind of insect?"

He pointed to his shoulder. "It's that, and . . ."—he searched the stomach of his pajama top—"that."

"Cool."

"You're my cousin?"

"I think so, yeah."

"How old are you?"

"Nineteen—nearly twenty."

"I'm six and my brother's three."

"Teej!" His mother's voice carried down the hall, and he hurried out, bare feet padding, toy soldiers, presumably, rattling in the box.

Then Hale Rubin, whose presence I'd nearly forgotten, so quiet had he been over by the bookshelves, came over and poked at the fire (I had an idea he was amused), and Silke came back with more people, all of whom had obviously been there before, and a moment later my grandmother entered the room, and everybody was saying hello. I saw it all as through a sheet of glassine. The brightest details shone: my grandmother's heliotrope smile, at once so public and so genuine; the new arrivals, their voices raised as if still speaking over street traffic; the flat glint of light on Hale Rubin's eyeglasses as he turned: brief wafers of white.

Seated we were: Hale, Silke, my grandmother and me, and then John, Javier, and Nina. John, who looked nearest my age, was around thirty, drop-dead gorgeous, and plainly, affectingly, in love with Javier. Javier, it emerged, was just back from London, where his new play was being staged in a theater that Nina, who had performed there years earlier, was saying had the best Ethiopian restaurant just around the block from it; yes, yes, agreed John, but the worst acoustics. The theater or the restaurant, Hale wanted to know. "Both!" cried Nina. They tossed that ball around for a while and then John said, "Who's the whippersnapper?" and they all turned to look at me.

I was at the far end of the couch, in heels and a gray skirt and pink ballet-neck sweater, and I knew I must have looked fresh and inexperienced; it almost excited me to think they were thinking this of me. The reason I kept my hair clipped short was that I was vain about the length of my neck, which I could now feel growing mottled with heat. I was too caught in headlights, or too caught up in playing that I had been caught in headlights, to do more than smile breathlessly. Or maybe the breathlessness was affectation. That was just it: I was much too mired in the importance of presentation to *know* always whether a behavior of mine was authentic or not. In any case, I felt a great, warm headiness, a spun-sugar sort of feeling, which insulated me from speech.

Nor was it my grandmother who answered John's question, but Silke, in her sepia-toned accent, who spoke. "This is Beatrice. Margaret's granddaughter."

"Oh!" said Javier.

"Are you visiting?" demanded John. "Where from? How old are you? Have you done anything?"—eyeing me up and down as if jealous, but then breaking into a laugh to show he was playing.

"Oh, are you—you're *Sarah's* daughter," said Nina. She was in the neighborhood of fifty, and had a kind of reformed air, as though she'd given up something, cigarettes or alcohol or religion. Her hair was sleek; I bet the package called the color aubergine. She wore a necklace made of linked silver O's, and she touched it now. No one looked at my grandmother. A general embarrassment, like cake flour, sifted upon us. I didn't mind it; I felt it heightened my presence, trained a powerful spotlight on me. "It's nice to meet you," added Nina.

"It's nice to meet *you*," I said, and heard my words come out as little round pearls. I was excited by their attentions; the flush in my cheeks was real.

Years later, Hale would tell me that in that moment he related to me as a problem to be solved.

Only in hindsight can I fill in what I was blind to at the time: my grandmother's almost certain discomfort, and the awkward sympathy everyone else in the room must have been feeling for her. It shames me now to think that at the time I was so in love with the idea of myself, and the success I believed I was having in that moment, that I was oblivious to my grandmother, sitting quietly in her chair by the fire, enduring with grace—indeed *sponsoring*—my coming-out, my debut in her world, where she had so much to lose, where she might yet be judged for past actions.

The silence lasted until Hale Rubin broke it. His voice sounded low and easy. "What role, Beatrice, would you most like to play?"

Who I was at that time was concentrated in my fantasy of how I was perceived by others. So Hale's question undid me. It was simultaneously devastating and thrilling. It held echoes of the little boy's question: "Are you white?" He seemed to be speaking past the self I had on display.

What role would you like *me to play?* I felt like saying. *Direct me,* I felt like saying, because of course that's who Hale Rubin was; that's why Silke had assumed I'd recognize the name, which I finally at that moment did. It was as though his name were a quarter inserted in a slot, but which had fallen into place only after some delay. Hale Rubin was the one who had directed my grandmother in the play I'd seen as a child, the one in which she'd worn the blue cape, out in western Mass. He'd gone on to direct her several more times; they'd both won Tony Awards for projects on which they'd collaborated. I should have remembered his name from the famous magazine profile. He'd been interviewed for it, I was pretty sure now; I would have to reread it when I got home. I scrambled to answer correctly—not truthfully; I had too little sense of my own desire to approach whatever the true answer might be—but to come up with something he might deem correct, worthy.

"Thisbe," fell from my lips.

A ripple. Because my answer was seen as an affront, or an homage? I didn't know, but now people did look toward my grandmother, and back at me, and there were smiles of a confused nature. I had again managed unwittingly to make myself an entity that required some reckoning; I could tell from the charge in the air.

Footsteps came down the passageway. Into the room stepped my aunt in her high-heeled boots, and my star instantly dimmed. The boys were not with her this time. A chorus of "Ida!" went up, and Javier rose, and Nina and John, and from this I guessed that she did not frequent my grandmother's salon, but that her attendance was a special event. I gleaned bits of information from the questions they showered her with. "Are you recording now?" "How did Tokyo go?" "How are the boys dealing with the move?" Another chair was pulled up near the fire and she sat and crossed her legs with casual magnificence.

As the salon got under way I saw that I had not been wrong to seek the privilege of attendance. Growing up, I had spent a lot of time around academics, who had their own brand of glamour, though it was brittle and dry. Perhaps this was a result of being pressed into the service of rightness. For it struck me that always, among my parents' colleagues, there was that—underlying every conversation or friendly dispute: the scramble to discern and articulate the *right* position, and align oneself accordingly. So that every intellectual debate became a moral one.

My father possessed this kind of glamour. It made people turn to him at dinner parties and brunches, in the midst of spirited debate, and say, "Let's hear Jeremy's position on it." It was always surprising to hear people call him Jeremy, less formal than the Dr. Fisher-Hart most people used, less intimate than the Jer to which my mother always shortened his name. "Professor," someone would say, prompting and announcing him at once. My father would take a beat, as though collecting his thoughts before speaking. Really, it was in order to give everyone a moment to finish shushing one another up and down the table. Then he'd come into the silence, speaking slowly at first, and low enough that people would grow even more still in order not to miss what he had to say.

I used to love it. I'd been aware of it from the time I was very small, eating at the children's table, or playing with my cars and mat in a corner of the room. I'd hear my father's name and feel the room grow hushed and poised for him. Then he'd say something full of the sound of turning pages, the odor of chalk dust, a speech peppered with *ology*'s and *ism*'s, and always one or two things that made everyone chuckle, and when he was done, although the conversation would continue, often with greater enthusiasm than before, sometimes even strident with voices of dissent, it was nevertheless somehow understood that he'd given what would stand as the final word on the matter. And I would continue to eat my tart or race my tiny ambulance along drawn roads with an almost wicked sense of well-being, conferred on me by his unquestioned status.

At my grandmother's salon I was again the child, absorbing the talk of the grown-ups, much of which was again greatly, almost pleasurably, beyond my reach. While some words sounded vaguely familiar, *Brechtian* and *Brandoesque*, many floated over my head and did not lodge. But the talk was very free, the words bandied about with a certain ease, and ideas put forth as if experimentally, to be as easily retracted or reworked moments later. Every now and then someone tossed me a bone—"What do you think, Beatrice?" asked Javier at one point, my name three distinct syllables in his accent, "Is skill at lying or skill at truth-telling an actor's greater asset?"—and I'd gnaw it in a puppyish, ineffectual way before fumbling. But still, I made sure to get my teeth in. The longer the night wore on, the more I cared about having a standing with this group, and it also

became clear to me that this would require something more—
something other—than being an effective interpreter and compli-
ant actor, playing the part of whomever they wished me to be. I
would have to bring something to the table.

Around ten-thirty the gathering broke up. A man came for Ida—
I only heard his voice in the hall—and she went out; so the night
was young for her! John, Javier, and Nina departed as they had
come, en masse, with offers to see me to the T or into a cab, but I
insisted I was all right on my own. Silke went off into the kitchen
with a stack of empty bowls. I was beginning to wonder if she lived
here, or was even a kind of employee, a longtime personal assistant,
perhaps? Hale Rubin showed no sign of leaving, either, but settled
deeper into the couch cushions and propped his shoes on the coffee table.

I went to my grandmother. "Thank you so much for having me."

"Beatrice: you are welcome."

"Oh. *Thanks.*"

"If you'd like, come back next week."

"I would. I mean I will!" I blushed with victory, the feeling of
having pulled something off.

Now, looking back, I don't suppose my grandmother's second
invitation was extended in honor of anything I had done right, nor
as a kindness, but because my presence had struck her as being
potentially useful. Her relationship with me might turn out to be a
way of communicating something to my mother. I think later still
my grandmother's designs changed. I think as we grew more inti-
mately involved, her relationship with me turned out to be a way
of communicating something to herself. And there was love for me,
too, I know. That came in time. But that night I experienced only
the selfish elation of having won a prize.

"Well, good night." I turned to Hale. "Good night."

He smiled and gave a nod, again not at all coolly, but without extending himself. I noticed this. All the rest of the evening I'd noticed him fairly little. He had listened more than spoken, sometimes with his eyes shut, although this detail I'd been able to observe only when John was leaning forward on the couch. Because of the way we'd all been sitting, my view of Hale had been obscured much of the time. Now, standing before him, I found his quietness arresting. It did not correspond to lack, or want; on the contrary. It seemed dense enough to exert its own gravitational pull.

"Good night," I said a third time, flustered, already exiting as my grandmother bade me the same. In the hall I found my coat and let myself out. The moment I closed the door behind me I wept.

WHEN I WAS in middle school and my father had that first allegation made against him, the girl had been a student of my same music teacher and I had stopped playing cello. Something like that. I don't remember the specific chain of events. I know that I had been sick of playing anyway, had become so bad about practicing that my parents set up an explicit system of bribes, or incentives, as they called them: little gifts at first—a charm for my charm bracelet, a book, a sundae—and later on, more conveniently for them, money: two dollars for every hour of practice. I had begun playing in third grade. When all my peers were taking up violin and flute, I had chosen the cello, knowing my parents would approve the cheek of this: a small girl with a large instrument. When our school's music program was cut, they sent me for private instruction.

And even though by the time I was thirteen I had become bored with music lessons, and all the practicing, I remember thinking it was unfair that I had to quit when it was the other girl who'd been bad. Not bad, of course, as my parents united in telling me, but confused. I never had a proper final lesson. My mother just mentioned to me that I wouldn't be going anymore. By then I'd been playing a three-quarter size instrument, and for some reason it had never been sold or passed along, but still languished, as though forgotten, upright and voluptuous in its scaled-down way, leaning against the shadowy back of my bedroom closet.

I thought of my old instrument when I came into the kitchen the night following my grandmother's salon. My mother had put on the Bach cello suites, loud. Rain showed under the streetlamp out the side window and made a background din against a broken drainpipe that had lain on the ground, hidden between the hedges and the side of the house, for months. Ingredients simmered on the stove, a pan of olive oil and tomatoes and onions and sage and wine. I loved being in the kitchen when my mother was there to animate it. Her hair, the color of a cello, it occurred to me that night, swelled out from where it was cinched at her nape. Always about my mother there were visual clues that she was not necessarily the woman she might have been.

As for my father, I hadn't seen him much during the previous week. He had been out a few nights, as had I a few others. My old crowd from high school was all away at college, and none of the black-clad existentialists I'd met in acting class had particularly aroused my interest, but there was one kid at work I'd become friendly with. Kid: Ezra was twenty, but with the kind of build and features that meant he'd get carded for another decade, at least.

Pale, with a wolfish scruff of black hair, Ezra had seemed, when he first started working there, as quiet and intense as a character who winds up getting consumption in a nineteenth-century Russian novel. But then his sense of humor began to leak out, in wicked little spurts, and I saw that he was really sharp and even slightly friendly, though in a scathing sort of way. So I liked him, and this made me realize I hadn't particularly liked anyone in a long time. Like me, Ezra wasn't in school. Unlike me, he was still trying to figure out what he wanted to do. Lately, he'd said this might turn out to be the postal service or paleontology. Clearly he felt no rush to decide. Although as far as I knew he didn't smoke or drink, he gave off a terrific aura of vice, which I figured was mostly an act, and I somehow respected him all the more for it.

"What did you do?" my mother would ask, the morning after I'd come home late from spending an evening with Ezra.

"Not much," I'd say. "Saw a movie. Had tea." The funny thing was, it was always true—we had fallen into the routine of going to a movie at a second-run house, then hitting a late-night diner where we'd always order the same thing: yellow cake with chocolate frosting and iced tea—but I was careful to tell it in a way that left the impression I might be covering for some seriously less tame activity.

As far as whether something romantic might be developing between Ezra and me, I privately thought this an interesting possibility, but maintaining a certain ambiguity around it suited me fine, at least for the moment. Not knowing how much I trusted my feelings in such matters, I was in no hurry to pose the question, not to Ezra nor to myself, and certainly in no hurry to air the idea before anyone else, least of all my parents.

"I met my cousins last night," I told my mother now. She was rubbing raw chicken parts with a cut lemon, and showed no sign of having heard me. "They're pretty cute. Paxton and T.J. Did you know about them?"

"About them? Yes." She embodied preoccupation, eyeglasses perched near the end of her nose, frowning at the large, beautifully illustrated cookbook with her damp hands, like liabilities, held far from the pages.

"Well why don't we ever see them? What's the matter between you and Ida?"

"The matter? Nothing, I . . ." She interrupted herself to read aloud in swift monotone, "*Half a cup (three ounces) chopped lean salt pork (green bacon) or pancetta.* Shit. Shoot. I forgot that. I wonder if we have regular bacon."

"Is it because she's black?"

"Bebe! Of course not! What a terrible thing to say."

"It was a joke."

"Well it was in poor taste."

"No it wasn't."

"Look in the freezer please, tell me if there's any bacon."

I went to hand her the package, but she gestured irritably with her raw chicken juice hands, so I set it on the counter with an icy thunk. She went to scrub, rather surgically.

"She *is* your sister."

"I was fifteen when she was born. And living in a different city. Her half sister."

"She must have idolized you. The older sister she heard about but never got to see."

My mother programmed the microwave, inserted the frozen block. "That's interesting," she mused, pressing START. "Ida-lize."

Occupational hazard. I was too accustomed to hearing my parents make more meaning of my words than I intended to be impressed with this bit of cleverness. But it struck me that fifteen must also be about the number of years between her and me. She would make a ripe figure for idolizing. Might I have been projecting my own feelings onto Ida? I thought of her as I had last seen her the night before, turning away from us all in that brief scarlet sheath, going off to meet whoever stood waiting for her in the hall. A throaty gust of laughter, her boots clacking, a baritone response, then the shutting of the door. I had gleaned that she and the boys had been staying there, in Boston, at my grandmother's, for some weeks already, in an apparently open-ended visit. No mention of a husband.

"Why don't we have them over for dinner?" I suggested.

"Them?"

"Ida and the boys."

Silence, in which there was the poking of the bacon, sighing, more punching of microwave buttons.

"Oh Mother?"

"*What,* Bebe?"

"I don't get it."

"Bebe. Can we talk about this some other time? I don't even really know her."

"Whose fault is that? You're the big sister."

"Who was sent to live somewhere else."

"But you even said that's because Grandmother couldn't have her career and take care of you as a single mother. You said it was the best thing she could have done to take care of you."

My mother laughed dryly. "Yes, I said that."

"Well, hello: you're my source of information. If you want me to know something different, say it."

"I can't get *into* it now, Bebe." Her voice took on an almost pleading whine, which was grossly out of character. Even during the worst of her headaches, my mother's demeanor was controlled. She remained elegant in pain, was almost *made* elegant by her pain, and the brittle, pale composure with which she met it. That she would allow herself to whine jarred me. "I'm trying a new recipe," she continued, plunking cans on the counter with harried movements, in concert with her voice. "... I don't have all the ingredients, she probably wouldn't come anyway, it would be uncomfortable, Dad's on his way ..." Her voice trailed off.

The music had ended. The rain flung itself down against the broken drainpipe. I stirred the mixture on the stove; it spat at me.

"How's his thing?" I asked.

A beat. "He's fairly down."

"Oh." For her to be this succinct was not unusual, but for her to be this blunt, about anything like a weakness in him, was. It made me scared in a way I wasn't used to being scared.

"Although I'm sure he wouldn't want you to know."

"No." The image of him in the Pudding, bent over his soiled lap, crying, came vividly into my mind before I could prevent it. The mixture in the pan spat again.

"Would you turn that down a hair, Bebe, love?"

I lowered the gas flame.

"Mom, what did he say? That got him in trouble?"

She took a long breath in, blew a long breath out. I stirred in slow motion, focusing on the translucence of the onions. She kept at her task while recounting, in a near-monotone, "He was talking about clinical work, about the roles of therapist and patient. He said something about needing to be the right tool for the job. About how if you're a hammer, everything starts to look like a nail."

She paused long enough, as she poured two cans of diced tomatoes into a pot, that I said, ". . . And?"

"And the student said, am I the hammer or the nail? And he said, you're the hole."

It made me go cold in the legs to hear that. "What did he mean?"

I watched her carefully. She stirred with a wooden spoon, her movements constant and smooth. "He was making the point that if you have a variety of psychoanalytic tools at your disposal, you're better able not only to meet the needs of individual patients, but to recognize their needs, rather than treating each similar-looking symptom with a single solution."

"But what did he mean about—what he said she was?" The base of my skull felt tight.

My mother neither hesitated nor made eye contact. "It was a quip—you know Daddy. A rather thoughtless witticism. But apparently it was also part of a longer conversation that was experienced by the student as containing several double entendres." She closed her eyes, tilting her head sideways, and held up her left hand in what could have been a dismissive motion.

We would make nothing of it, I understood her to mean. We Fisher-Harts, with our superior understanding of the complications and pitfalls of communication, would regard this as simple foolishness on the part of the student. A mismatch of sophisticated, unchecked wit and sophomoric hypersensitivity.

But a voice deep within me insisted that such a mistake would not have been possible, that my father would have been in command of his remarks. I did "know Daddy"; we both did, and both knew full well he was not capable of "a rather thoughtless witticism." He had an extraordinary ability to tune in to what others were feeling; he would have known precisely how such a remark would have sounded to this student. In a way, it was the same gift that made both him and my grandmother luminaries in their disparate fields: the gift of empathic expression.

Once, when I was much younger, in grade school, I'd gone with him to his office at the university, and I'd had to wait out in the hall for part of the time while he met with someone, a young woman with curly red hair and big red-framed glasses and cherry red lips and enormous wedge sandals. I'd been rather impressed by how teetery she was on them. And when they were done meeting, they'd stood in the open doorway of his office for a moment. I'd been sitting there on the floor outside his door with its window of frosted glass that had his name stenciled on it. I'd been reading the library book I'd brought, but I put my finger in my place and got to my feet when my father introduced me to the young woman. "My daughter, Bebe." She had widened her eyes behind her huge eyeglasses and leaned forward from the great height of her sandals to shake my hand, and she'd said, with a heavy Boston accent, "Your father is a very, very special man!"

I had been enormously embarrassed, on her behalf, but then I noticed my father, leaning against the doorframe in his rumpled tweed jacket, arms crossed, smiling: he was well at ease, enjoying the moment. Here he was, this man of the academy, this great thinker, esteemed by all—and yet he had the time, and the equanimity, the great democratic heart, to feel without judging, to feel for and with her, this wobbly cherry-lipped woman. And immediately I'd felt chastened, and full of wonder at the largeness, the generosity of spirit of my father. I had sworn to make myself more like him, open to all.

He was, irrefutably, a special man. Alas for the mediocre-minded supervisee who couldn't grasp the goodness, the moral strength and depth that earned him his easy way with words and wordplay. Perhaps she might be pitied for it, even excused, but certainly she was in error. I shut up that little voice inside me in this way. My mother stirred the pungent sauce on the stove without a further glance at me. The very straightness of her back issued a directive. We knew who we were, it seemed to say. We owed no one an apology.

And yet.

"Mom? What was it that girl, the violin student, back when I was in eighth grade, you know—what was the thing she said Dad did?"

If my mother was surprised that I had finally, after so many years, asked her to tell me the details of that incident, she didn't show it. She didn't even turn around. "My God, Bebe. I don't remember the specifics of that! So long ago."

I said no more. But the odd thing was that I *did*—I remembered something specific about it, something I'd never told anyone, something I myself thought I'd forgotten, until this past week.

A school friend had given me a spy kit for my birthday that year. Just junk from a toy shop—it had included a periscope, a motion sensor, fingerprinting supplies, a wallet with secret compartments, a remote listening device. And with this last item I had done something terrifically naughty, something really shamefully bad. As I have said, when I was much younger I occasionally listened outside my mother's office door while she was with a patient, but because my father's office connected only to the waiting room (where I was not allowed) and not to the rest of the house, I'd never been able to eavesdrop on him. And so, when I received the spy kit for my birthday, I knew right away that I would try to bug his office. I had no particular reason for doing so except that his office had always been so utterly off-limits. The plan struck me as devilishly funny and clever, almost a perfect lark.

It became clear right away that most of the stuff in the kit didn't even really work that well; I'm not sure I ever thought I'd truly be able to make out what anyone was saying. But I went ahead and planted the listening device under his office couch, and as it happened, it was the one thing in the kit that was pretty functional. The reception didn't work as far away as my attic bedroom, but from a hiding spot behind the stairs I found I was able to listen in. I only ever did it once, briefly, on an afternoon when the violin girl was there, and I wound up catching a snippet of what I am now fairly certain turned out to be their final session. This is what I heard:

MY FATHER: You don't have to do it here in front of me. You could
      just visualize it while I talk you through it, and then you

could practice it when you're alone, and tell me how it went next week.

THE GIRL: (*something unintelligible*)

MY FATHER: Of course, it is fine, if you want, for you actually to try it now. That might even make the most sense, because then if it's not feeling right, I could help out.

THE GIRL: (*a sharp burst of sound that might have been a laugh*)

MY FATHER: I mean that I can help by watching, and by offering suggestions. You know, I hope you know, that I only want you to feel comfortable. I want nothing more than for you to believe, to really believe, that there is nothing wrong or dirty about giving yourself pleasure.

And then, for some reason I didn't understand, I switched off the amplifier. That was the extent of what I had heard, an auditory memory that had come back to me with inexplicable clarity during that week after the Pudding. Of course I couldn't be sure of the accuracy of this memory; it could hardly be verbatim, six years having passed. But it came to me as if word for word, and in my gut I believed now what I had then: that something was off about the exchange. I couldn't know what they had been talking about, but I felt sure this memory was connected to the current situation.

I stood near my mother at the stove, wanting to tell her about this bad thing I'd done years earlier, and what I'd heard as a result. But I could not. I was afraid of what would happen if I did. I was afraid that something enormous would change irrevocably.

"Are you going out tonight?" my mother asked, getting tongs from the crock of utensils.

"I don't know." I had no plans to. It was so cold and wet. But, "I might," I said, and then, fabricating this outright, "Ezra had said something about doing something." I guess I said this to annoy her, or to try to get her to express disappointment. I had the idea she missed my being around more, missed the old trio of her, my father, and me. Perhaps it was I who was really missing it.

She began to set pieces of chicken in the hot oil: a crescendo of fry noises. "Well that works out, then," she said lightly. "I think Daddy and I will eat alone tonight."

How strange, how disproportionate, the reaction I had! I felt stung. My nose got the ripe, swollen feeling of wanting not to cry.

"I'll set some aside for you, though," she added. "In case you don't eat out."

"No, thanks," I said with careful disdain, and retreated to my room under the eaves, where the rain kicked up its assault and the kidney-shaped water stain glistened freshly, the color of weak tea.

Later that night when I did steal down to the kitchen to fix myself a plate, I was taken aback, upon removing the foil from the serving dish into which the food had been neatly transferred, to find that the entire dinner remained untouched.

I BECAME A regular at my grandmother's salon. I dressed well and said little. When I did inject an opinion or observation, I strove for a tone of winning candor, but I was not unthinkingly candid. I couldn't allow myself that level of unregulated expression, since I continued to regard the salon as one giant audition. To that end, I had to monitor myself, be on continuous watch. I would be judged, as at a regular audition, not only by the content of my speech, but by the quality of my voice, by my physical appearance, and by the way I moved. Nina, who had starred on daytime television decades ago, once reminisced about the odd doubleness, during her years on the soap, of glimpsing herself on the monitors while in the midst of doing a scene, and I had thought, *But I do that all the time.* Mostly I found it easiest to sit quietly on the edge of the brocade couch, projecting rapt interest and significant inner depth.

Bit by bit, I learned more about them all. Nina, after her long stint on the soap, eventually left in order to cofound an experimental theater troupe; it had broken up a few years later, but won her lasting respect from her peers. Javier's stage and radio dramas had been much produced and honored in Argentina. John had been scooped up from one of the rare master classes my grandmother gave; he and Javier lived together in Jamaica Plain. Ida, it emerged, was a classically trained singer, and had performed German lieder and opera in San Francisco before having the boys.

Silke, most astonishingly, turned out to have been a cabaret dancer in postwar Paris. She had known my grandfather, Neil Fisher, in Berlin before the war. They'd met up again in New York City around the time my grandmother had come on the scene: an ingénue with her hair held back by a blue satin ribbon, Silke once said, like Tenniel's Alice, and I couldn't tell whether or not she was joking. Thinking about the timing, I realized Silke might have—must have— known my mother as a toddler. When she first got to New York, she told me, she'd danced a bit, then settled into piecemeal jobs in theater: dance coach, dresser, script mistress. She'd moved to Boston, at my grandmother's urging, when Maynard Clinkscale died. During salons, I'd steal incredulous glances at her atrophied calves in their dark, heavy stockings, and think: *How marvelous, how tragic!*

All of this, their stories. How they filled me with longing. How they stirred in me a sense of joyful possibility, shot through with hopelessness. I despaired of ever being able to relate so offhandedly, with such confidence and ownership, an equally fabulous story while reaching for a handful of almonds on someone else's coffee table. But it was almost all I could think about—possessing such a story of my own, reaching a point where I would be able to offer it as casually, when asked (as I would surely often be asked), "How did you get where you are now?" And there would be no paucity of fascinating detail for me to supply, and I could pick and choose among anecdotes, and still my interviewer would want more, would want to know how I'd managed to cram in so much experience at such a young age, and how I'd handled fame so gracefully, and how I'd then transcended my early success to achieve even greater heights in midlife.

The specifics of my imagined career eluded me. I only knew that it had to be luminous. My want was so fierce and pure it was humbling. It made my fingers hurt, as though they literally ached for what they could not grasp.

Hale's story was less readily available than those of the others. I was conscious of him as an enigma. I found it hard to look at him directly, and I confused this, during those early months, with an aversion. Because he didn't talk much to begin with, and was even less garrulous on the subject of himself, I had to rely on what came out in conversation, and it was a few months before I was able to string together the following facts about his past. After directing several highly acclaimed plays during the eighties, he had surprised everyone by abandoning Broadway. He'd directed an avant-garde company in the East Village called Fire Escape Theater, then abandoned that to do theater work with inmates and gang members. He was just now, apparently (but this was mentioned in whispers and asides), contemplating a return to commercial theater.

As for my grandmother, her story was at once the most public and the most obscure. It was not lost on me that nearly everyone at the salon had some sort of political edge to his or her artistic identity. In spite of her blue-blooded lineage and home address, my grandmother's bona fides topped the list, beginning with her being the widow of Neil Fisher—what more impressive credential on the left than having been widowed, in effect, by Joseph McCarthy?—

continuing with her civil-rights-era marriage to Maynard Clinkscale, and cemented, it turned out, by work she had done with South African actors and musicians before the end of apartheid.

And yet. I sensed a tiptoeing ethic around mention of my grandmother's past. This puzzled me; I could not account for why it should be so. There was a way in which she seemed actively to deflect attention from her early years in theater, to discourage questions about that time in her life.

One rare Tuesday night when the group broke up, Ida was still with us, not whisked off earlier by the man who never came inside past the front hall, and she leaned toward me and said in her amazing voice, which managed to be clear as a tuning fork and husky all at once, "Beatrice, do you have a minute?"

I thought: *This is it.* I was ready for my anointing. I expected her to say, *I think you have it, girl. Let me make you an appointment with the guy who does my hair on Newbury Street. Let me front you for a pair of high leather boots. Let me take you out this weekend to hear some jazz. Then there's somebody I'm dying to introduce you to.*

"Sure," I said, sitting back down.

The others were already out in the hall, putting on coats or carrying glasses back to the kitchen, making noises of departure. Ida sank into the empty spot beside me on the couch. She was less decked-out than usual this night, but even her stay-at-home gear was striking: a red velour sweat suit and two-tone suede sneakers.

"What do you think of the salon?" she asked.

"It's wonderful. I feel so privileged to come."

"Yeah. They're special, these people. In a way, I think you must recognize how special even more than I do. I mean, it's not like I didn't know it, growing up, but on the other hand, that's *all* I knew, growing up. You know? You come in with fresh eyes, it must really hit you. I kind of envy that."

I bristled at the implied slight. But I did not think she intended it as such. She was smiling at me, dazzling. Up close, her eyes showed flecks of topaz. I was so ready for her invitation. Not wanting to sound defensive, I stowed my winning candor and brought out instead a self-deprecating little laugh. "I guess I grew up around a different *kind* of special."

"Mm, right, right. Everybody has their own 'special.' " And she winked, expertly, a thoroughly charming gesture; it was as though I'd been kissed.

It did pain me that she had no idea what I meant, probably did not even believe me. I wished I could show her then and there evidence of *my* special home. I wished I could whip out a picture of my mother, whom she had not even seen since Maynard Clinkscale's funeral. Ida couldn't know how smart my mother was, how serene in the face of crisis. I wished I could show her footage of my father, his colleagues and students milling about him during a gathering, hanging on his every word. Ida couldn't know how esteemed my father was, or of his numerous affiliations, his long list of titles, his publications, his stature, his charisma.

"Well, listen, Beatrice, the reason I wanted to talk with you is I've been wondering if you ever like to babysit?"

"Sure! That is, you mean for the boys?" I felt a fool for having thought she might want to spend time with me herself and fought to keep the disappointment out of my voice.

"Yes, sometimes I need a sitter when Mom can't do it, or I just hate to ask her too often, and I haven't found anybody since we moved here. I know you haven't spent too much time with them"—several nights, they'd made brief appearances at the beginning of the salon—"but they're good kids. Teej practically takes care of Pax by himself."

"Oh, well. Yeah, they're great kids. I'd be happy to."

"You would? Oh, that's fantastic. You are fabulous. You have no idea."

We stood and she gave me a hug. Her curls brushed stiffly against my ear and smelled of some ethereal, intricate perfume.

"I'll pay you, of course," she added as we separated. "What do you charge?"

"Oh, no. That's all right," I felt compelled to respond.

"Don't be silly," she said, already taking a step toward the door.

"No, I couldn't accept your money," I insisted, and she took me at my word.

ARRIVING HOME THAT night, I saw that a piece of paper had been attached to the front door. In the milky porch light, under whose beam moths flitted, it looked like some kind of advertisement, printed on brilliant orange paper in a large font size. An ad for housecleaning services, or a restaurant opening. But such flyers were generally folded in thirds and pushed through the mail slot, not plastered flat to the door. Then I thought it must be a personal message intended for me, since I was the one returning at this late hour. I mounted the brick steps and peeled the paper from the door, absently noting the loops of scotch tape that had held it there. Batting away a moth, I began to read:

* STOP SEXUAL HARASSMENT *
* EXPOSE PERPETRATORS *

My heart seized up. I had spotted my father's name as well. I shoved the sheet of incriminatingly orange paper into my bag and fumbled for my key. In the front hall, I shut the door behind me, turned the deadbolt, and peered through the rectangle of glass at the street. The night was moonless. The streetlamp on our block guttered and dimmed. Headlights swung slowly toward me and then away: a car turning in stately fashion down another side street. Far off, an ambulance siren traced a thin line of sound. Barely illuminated, the new small leaves on the trees shimmied like horses shaking out their manes.

My parents generally locked up around ten. Now it was eleven. Had the paper been stuck up within the past hour? Might it have happened within the past fifteen minutes, within the past five? Or earlier? My parents, locking up, would likely not have spotted something fixed to the *outside* of the door. I thought back to when I'd left the house, around six-thirty. Surely I would have noticed the paper, so brazen-colored, if it had been there then.

I switched off the porch light. The wall sconce at the bottom of the stairs had been left on low for me, but other than that the house was dark. A perverse impatience, a fear, perhaps, that delaying inspection might somehow heighten the destructive potential of my findings, made me sit down at the bottom of the stairs and retrieve the paper from my shoulder bag. Quietly, minimizing my rustlings, I spread it on my lap and examined it in the darkish hall. But even then, rather than ingest the flyer's content, I busied my mind with more clinical observations, musing over the implications of timing and font and the choice of such a fierce shade of orange. The Scotch tape had been rolled into tight, scrimping cylinders and placed on the diagonal, with notable regularity, behind each corner. In the lower right-hand corner of the paper were the initials U.A.H.C., over which I puzzled. They looked at once familiar and not. A certain graininess to the heavy, zigzagging border revealed that this was not an original document but a reproduction, and what that implied—the existence of an untold number of other such photocopies—brought a slow, dull pain to the base of my skull.

Even as I staved off thought about the document's content, its outward characteristics painted a worrisome picture.

U.A.H.C. I let my mind play over those initials while I rose, turned off the light, and tiptoed upstairs. On the second-floor landing I saw a yellow stripe under my parents' door and heard classical music playing low: quick and mellow piano trinklings, like colored candies in a box. I pictured them each sitting up in bed, leaning against the padded headboard, wearing pajamas and the bifocals to which they had both recently graduated, reading or possibly marking papers or editing journal articles side by side. My mother with the lap desk my father had given her one Mother's Day propped against her drawn-up thighs. My father with the remote control for the slim Bose stereo my mother had given him for his birthday resting beside him. Glasses of water on their respective bedside tables. A yellow legal pad on my father's side. A floral-print journal on my mother's. Box of tissues, bottle of hand cream. Books and articles piled on every flat surface around them.

I paused, listening, stilling my breath and looking at the item I held between my thumb and index finger, observing with peculiar detachment the way it trembled there.

"Hi, Bebe, love," called my mother.

"Hey."

"You all right?" asked my father.

"Yup. 'Night."

"Good night, sweetheart."

Up to the third floor, through the rough bit of raw attic, and into the fabricated haven of my room. I turned on the lamp, shut the door, and flopped across my bed. Although it was only May, it had been sunny all day and my room up under the roof held the heat. I leaned over and switched on the air conditioner, which had been installed at the wrong angle and immediately started to gurgle and wheeze. After a few minutes, it would begin to emit a steady drip onto the floorboards. I kept a folded-up towel beneath it for this reason.

I rolled onto my back, feeling the cold air pour across my face. The flaming orange paper shivered in my fingers as I lay there and held it above me, at last taking in what it said:

* STOP SEXUAL HARASSMENT *
* EXPOSE PERPETRATORS *
BOYCOTT PSYCHOLOGY PROFESSOR
JEREMY FISHER-HART!
OF COMPLAINTS AGAINST HIM: 5
OF ACTIONS TAKEN BY THE UNIVERSITY: 0
SAY **NO** TO CAMPUS COVER-UPS
U.A.H.C.

Over and over I read it, as though it were written in a code that might be cracked through repetition, as though eventually the face value of the words would fall away and reveal their true, benign meaning. Of course, this was folly. All that happened was that I committed it to memory. Even after I crumpled the paper and threw it into the trash, I could not stop replaying fragments of the text. *# of complaints against him: 5.* Around that single line my mind reeled. There was no way *into* it, no way to parse it or react. How meaningless the number in the absence of context, in the absence of a less opaque description than the word *complaints.* And the numeral *5*— what did *5* mean? Five complaints lodged by a single student, a lunatic in a slithery skirt and low-cut blouse? But even as I conjured the picture of such a woman, a competing image nosed into my mind: a line of five. Five different women lined up with their complaints written out on yellow sheets of legal-sized paper. The first in line wore a long braid and held a violin by the neck. Midway through teetered a curly-haired woman in high heels, dressed head to toe in cherry red. Last in line, feet stoutly planted, an angry, proud figure clasped to her chest not only a personal statement, but an entire orange ream.

I dragged my fingernails down the side of my face. They left pulsing tracks. I turned my face to the pillow. Though the air conditioner droned, the room still felt stifling. The need for air seemed urgent. I threw a book at the tan bulge in my ceiling, wishing to split its center crack wider, wishing to send the book straight through the roof, to leave a breach in the ceiling through which nighttime coolness might filter, and starlight might shine. The book missed, and I could tell from the sound it made upon landing that I had damaged its binding instead.

They had lied to me, my mother and my father, about everything. Our status, our position, our rightness. The irreproachability of our triumvirate. Our wholesome enjoyment of thoughtfully chosen, expensive meals. Their beneficent wisdom in letting me continue to live at home this year. And all our trappings of *quality*—the armloads of flowers fresh from the garden, the eleven-year-old maroon Saab in the drive, the classical music on the stereo, the *1818* plaque on the front of the house—resonated with me then as sham.

An easy bit of wordplay, from *sham* to *shambles*. Only wordplay was *their* stock in trade; I wanted no part of it. I wanted something new, action. I threw a shoe at the water stain, and this time gouged a small hole in the plaster, and a fine dust rained down.

They had lied to me, then left me to find evidence of their lies taped to the front door. That evidence I retrieved now, plucking it from my wastebasket and bringing it back to my bed, where I smoothed it flat. My hand shook with anger, the bitterest pitch of which was reserved for myself. I was a liar, too, long complicit by inaction, by keeping up their silence, our silence, our act.

"SARAH." MY FATHER came into the kitchen thinking I was my mother. "What is this?"

I straightened from behind the refrigerator door. It was my hindquarters he had mistaken. Embarrassing for us both.

He blinked. "Oh!"

I had grown to what would remain my full height that year, and was wearing, that day, a longish skirt. I had once heard someone describe my mother as a tall drink of water. So his error made me feel, confusingly, pleased as well as mortified. He held out an object on his palm.

"It's a doorknob," I said, closing the fridge. I'd found a little tub of pâté; I'd been going to take it up to my room with some crackers.

"Oh, Bebe. Sorry." He blinked again, shook his head, said something about allergy medicine. "I thought you were Mom. Do you know why this was on my desk?" He looked down at the brass knob. It belonged to our front door.

"She wants you to fix it." He showed no sign of comprehension. I sighed. "It keeps falling out."

"It does?" He regarded it a little stupidly.

"You haven't noticed?"

It had been a fortnight since I'd come home to find the orange flyer. In all that time I had mentioned it to no one, a fact that disturbed me, but I could no more articulate the reason for retaining my silence than I could bring myself to break it. Really, ever since the night he'd cried at the Pudding, my father and I had been tiptoeing around each other with dreadful gentleness. We'd greet each other in the thinnest approximation of upbeat tones, make smiles in each other's direction rather than directly at each other, and carry on through the rooms of the house without pause, as though by coincidence we each happened to be very busy whenever we chanced to cross paths.

During the last two weeks I'd extended this behavior to my mother as well, and intensified it almost to the level of parody, hoping to force one of them to say something. But my behavior went unremarked, which had the effect on my anger of water thrown on a cooking fire. Outwardly, I maintained composure. Was I playing a game, toying with them? Seeing how taut the smooth surface could be stretched without rupture? Was it that I needed one of them to name it, to *see* the rupture first? It is a fact that since finding the flyer, I'd made a nightly ritual of throwing an object against the crack in my bedroom ceiling. And at work I was lying more freely.

"Well, why does she put it on *my* desk?" my father griped now under his breath. He slipped the knob into the pocket of his yellowish brown cardigan. Then he smiled at me, full of sad humor, as though we were in cahoots against her madness. In fact, we all knew that my mother was far handier with a screwdriver than my father, but in this instance I sided with her, at least insofar as wanting him to take notice of, if not actual responsibility for, what needed fixing. Angry as I was at my mother, I suppose I still held higher hopes that she might become an ally in cutting through the fog; he, it became clearer and clearer, was hopeless. I did not return his smile, then, but looked at him coldly. He might have been sent over by central casting to play the part of the shrink, in that mustardy cardigan with the brown elbow patches. His eyebrows were getting bristly, I noticed, bristly and gray, and the way he'd habitually arch them in empathy seemed a therapist's cheap trick, like bad acting, what my acting class would call "indicating." But as soon as

I thought that, I ached with remorse and even with a terrible surge of helpless love.

"All right," he said, noticing none of this, despite the famous Fisher-Hart sensitivity. "What's that, honey? Making yourself a snack? Great. Well. I have a three o'clock." He took the doorknob back out of his pocket and fondled it absently as he headed from the kitchen.

"Dad."

He turned with a kindly, vacant smile.

"What's the U.A.H.C.?"

"Sorry?"

"The U.A.H.C. Some club or something at the university?"

"I don't know. It might be. Why do you ask?"

"I saw a flyer."

"Yes?" The eyebrows rose; a faint smile creased the corners of his lips. It was an automatic expression, meant to convey his polite, obliging interest.

I felt as if I'd swallowed a stone.

I felt as if I'd been led into the woods without bread crumbs.

Was it truly possible he had not seen the flyer himself? That in the past two weeks it had not, although it had presumably been posted in more places than just our front door, come to his attention?

"Forget it," I managed.

He shuffled out. When had he begun to shuffle?

I grabbed a box of crackers and a knife and ran upstairs, where I watched from my bedroom window to see his patient arrive. A minute later a figure came crunching over the peastones. Not a woman, not a girl, but a man, heavyset and bald. The relief that occasioned was itself further cause for dismay. But I climbed up onto my bed and arranged the delicacies I'd brought, making a fairy circle of rice crackers around the tub of pâté. I spread and ate them one at a time, clockwise, while taking inventory of my list of unaskable questions. *How many women total had lodged complaints against my father? What was the purported content of his remarks? Why had he uttered them? What did my mother know of it? For how long had she colluded in silence? Why had she? What would happen now?* The air inside my room was stagnant, but outside the window a breeze caught and tugged at the nest which sagged, unraveling, from the eaves, and a few bits of twig and straw blew loose.

In an hour I would go to work. Not at the Homestead, but at my grandmother's house, doing what had become my other regular job. Ida's request, although humiliating in the moment, compared to the speech my imagination had composed, had proved, in light of things, not without appeal. Anyway, she had taken my response seriously and begun to avail herself of my services immediately and immoderately, two or three nights a week. Suddenly I had a legitimate reason not to spend all my evenings at home. And I had a new foothold in the world of my grandmother.

I liked the babysitting. My cousins were generous purveyors of sometimes dubious information. Their father's name was Thomas James Prince Jr., which made them Princes, too. He was variously a musician and a "seller," possibly of ships (thought Paxton) or furniture (thought Teej). He lived in "San Diego, Los Angeles," and they saw him sometimes but not very much, although both boys assured me they would be moving back there eventually.

Before I tucked them in, Paxton would ask for the wooden box from the mantel, the one he had clamored for the night of my first salon, and I would get it down for him. Then, while I sat by the double bed they shared and read to Teej, Pax would empty the contents, dozens of lead soldiers, one at a time and arrange them on his patchwork spread. He breathed through his mouth while he did this and did not get impatient when invariably some fell over and knocked others down with dull clinks. He could identify each one as hussar or dragoon, grenadier or pikeman. I was unfamiliar with any of these terms, a fact he quickly apprehended and attempted to remedy with great concern and patience, winning my amused awe.

The boys said the soldiers had belonged to their grandfather, which brought to mind an absurd picture of Maynard Clinkscale, big as he was, prone on the parlor carpet, setting up the little men in rows. But that night, replacing the wooden box after they had fallen asleep, I noticed that N. FISHER, BERLIN, 1929 had been carefully burned into the bottom.

So they had belonged to *my* grandfather. I stood by the mantelpiece in the dark parlor, before the cold fireplace that smelled of stale ashes, rubbing my fingers over the letters burned into the wood so dark and soft with age. It didn't help that I understood no one had been hiding the box, contriving to keep it from me. The fact that it was simple neglect made it somehow worse.

My habit, once the boys were asleep, was to select a book from the parlor shelves. They contained a surprising mishmash. There were juvenilia: leather-bound, beautifully illustrated editions of *Peter Pan, Alice in Wonderland,* collections of the Brothers Grimm, Hans Christian Andersen, Greek myths. There were echoes of my parents' bookshelves: Plato, Shakespeare, Dickens, Freud, Jung, Sontag, A. S. Neill. And then there was everything else: Man Ray and Beckett, Borges and Rube Goldberg, books on cockfighting, footbinding, mushrooms, murder. Each night I browsed, I stumbled across fresh evidence of an unremittingly catholic appetite. I played a game with myself that I could learn more about my grandmother from her bookshelves than if I let myself prowl the rooms of her house—which, incidentally, no one had forbidden me to do. Still, after selecting a book I would confine myself to the kitchen for the rest of the evening.

My grandmother always got back from wherever she had been by ten. She'd find me sitting in one of the captain's chairs at the kitchen table, which was a great, thick farmhouse thing, and she'd take care to notice whatever I was reading and to ask a question or two about it. That night I asked her a question instead. I asked her where Ida went all these evenings.

My grandmother sat at the table opposite me. She wore a lavender pullover and tiny garnet earrings. She ran a hand back and forth over the top of her close-cropped hair, which struck me as the gesture of a young man. "She is seeing someone," my grandmother told me. "Although she doesn't want the boys to know, at this point. She doesn't want them becoming attached if it isn't going to work out."

I nodded, as though I had already sussed this out. I hadn't even thought about it, but it did make sense. "Are they staying here, then? I mean, are they going to stay in Boston?"

"That is, so far, unclear."

I nodded again, as though this were natural, when really I was feeling a stab of sorrow for the boys, for the uncertainty of their family's future, for the fact that they didn't even know how uncertain it was. Maybe it was because our words had made room, however obliquely, for the fact of the boys' father, that I found myself saying next, "Grandmother, do you know about my father?"

At the time I was conscious only of my desire for information; the question seemed a natural part of my ongoing reconnaissance mission. These decades later, I see that my asking served a double purpose. I was seeking to offer information, also. To enlighten her as to how far I was willing to go. I believed my mother had effectively shut her out of our family, and that any entry I could provide would hold value. I wanted to feel myself of value to her.

"What about him, Beatrice?"

"That he's charged with sexual harassment."

"At this moment, you mean?"

"Yes."

"No. I did not." She hesitated, ran her knuckles over the surface of the farmhouse table. "I had known—previously."

"Previously?"

"Two other times, I had known of, when some question came up about his conduct."

"Two? With students?"

She looked confused. "With patients. Clients. Years ago. Before you were born."

I must have looked sick.

"Both times resolved favorably."

Still, I couldn't—my throat was completely dry. I wanted to get some saliva together so I could swallow. I felt her move and had the sudden, unbearable thought that she was about to heat me some milk. "I don't want anything," I said very fast, and she looked bewildered; apparently she'd only been shifting in her chair.

The math, the math. My mind bucked at the confusion of numbers. Two before I was born. The violin girl. The number five on the orange flyer. I couldn't compute, couldn't tally them up. Was the number five inclusive of or in addition to the past? Now the kitchen seemed to grow enormous, dark at the edges, with light pooling on the thick slab of table. The refrigerator made its noise. I felt I should go but was no match for inertia.

"Beatrice, I'm sorry. I shouldn't have spoken about what's long done. I didn't think."

"No, it's . . . It's not that."

"What is it?"

I looked at her, the unimpeachable sweep of her nose and jaw, softened but not lessened by the wrinkles around her mouth and eyes, the gentle draping of the skin along her neck. "People love my father. They look up to him. A lot do. A lot of really respected people, I mean."

"They probably have excellent reason to."

"But—!" *How can they?* I was thinking. *How can they and not be as fraudulent as he, or as flawed?* And now I was crying, quietly, but blinded by tears, which trembled in my eyes and then fell, one after the other, with fat, silent splashes onto the table.

"Beatrice, you don't need to hear it from me to know that people are complex. People are full of contradiction, of paradox. You are. I am. There isn't one good part, one good role, I mean, in the history of theater that doesn't hinge on that fact."

I pulled my sleeve over my fist and wiped the wetness from the tabletop.

"Why *do* you want to be an actress?" my grandmother asked, almost abruptly.

I looked up, surprised. "I don't know," I said honestly. "Do you know why you wanted to be one?"

She looked up over my head and yawned. "There's a line in *Lear:* 'Speak what we feel, not what we ought to say.' In my upbringing, this idea was anathema. I think I was sort of frantic to find a venue for speaking truth. It seemed like this was possible in the theater as nowhere else. Remember, this was a different time. A different era.

"Acting," she continued, "just seemed like the most wonderfully subversive way of getting at unallowable truths."

With a jolt I pictured the Homestead, all at once understanding my wayward behavior there. What my boss might call my compulsion to falsify felt to me, honestly, like the very opposite, like a refusal to capitulate to myth. As Constance I breached the boundaries of the allowable story. But it wasn't really the story of the Underground Railroad I wanted to challenge—that was just practice for a more formidable task, the illumination of a different sort of underground. What I was able to pull off as Constance at the Homestead, I might one day enact as Beatrice on the home front.

"And did it turn out to be true?" I asked. "*Is* there more truth in theater than in the world at large?"

My grandmother laughed. "Some of the time, there is," she said. "Sometimes the theater is as full of fakery as anyplace else."

IT TURNED OUT that whatever improper remarks my father was accused of making had been caught on tape. I learned this by accident—although that hardly seems possible. The amount of childhood knowledge I would once have characterized this way, as having been learned by accident, seems to me now improbably large and wrongly dismissive of the extent to which my parents allowed themselves to be overheard. I will never know for sure, but when I consider how often, how routinely, even, I gleaned information by eavesdropping, it doesn't make sense that my parents weren't aware of it. That they could have been so bunglingly cloddish at discretion meshes neither with what I know of their personalities, nor indeed with their very job descriptions. They knew enough to have that white-noise machine in the waiting room between their offices; why then did they never take an equivalent measure to protect me from overhearing them? It leaves room to consider that they wanted me to learn things without having to assume responsibility for telling me.

Not that I thought about this at the time. Then I thought the responsibility for listening in on their conversation was all on my shoulders, all my fault. It was a night or two after my grandmother's and my talk, and I was what my mother called skulking around. As a child, I used to like to come up behind her at some party or soiree and dig the knobbiness of my nose and chin into the small of her back. I'd feel her start—sometimes she'd even emit a shriek—and then she'd reach around and grab my arm and bring me forward, out into the open. "She's a great skulker, Bebe is," she would tell people, laughing, and the other adults would smile down as if charmed at the prospect of a child skulker. Thus designated, I cultivated the art. I used to make-believe I was a cat burglar or spy, and half convinced myself I had special powers of slinking about in shadows, gathering information undetected.

On this night I had been reading in bed but, restless, cast my book aside around midnight. I felt suddenly parched. Or had something alerted me? A sound, a glow in the trees outside my window that meant someone downstairs had switched on a light? I thought I would get a glass of water, and stole downstairs, keeping to the side of each tread so as not to creak. This was something I did in any case, day or night, from long force of habit.

I was surprised to see, at this hour, a light on downstairs. The pocket doors that led from the hall into the living room were partway closed, but they framed a tall rectangle of light. Crouching low on the stairs, I looked through the spindles of the railing and saw a slice of couch, a sliver of bookshelf, a length of window revealing blackness. I heard my mother's voice. By the sound of it, she was traveling around the room. "You mean you knew it was being recorded? Jesus, Jer." It was not uncommon for some supervisory sessions to be taped, at the student's request, for learning purposes. "You told me it occurred outside the course of supervisory sessions. I thought you said it took place at a coffee shop."

I couldn't make out his response to my mother.

But she returned, loud and clear, "So there are *two* conversations, then? *Jer?*"

I sat on the bottom step and wrapped my arms around my legs, my teeth clenched to keep from chattering. I wore what I often wore to bed: one of my father's old undershirts and a pair of underpants. I had shaved my legs the day before, but in the chill, a fine stubble rose and pricked against the inside of my arms.

His answer, again, was too muffled for me to hear.

"*God.*" Her voice carried easily.

Then there was silence, and I sat shivering. My mind went to the girl who had made the complaint against him when I was in middle school. I could picture her as she had looked from my bedroom window, a long dark braid going down her back. Sometimes she had carried her violin case to therapy. Her feet crunching over the peastones. I couldn't picture her face, only the top of her head as seen from above. *You know, I hope you know, that I only want you to feel comfortable.* I had heard him saying that from my hiding spot under the stairs. To how many others had he spoken those words?

I wondered who they were, the others. I wondered about the two instances that my grandmother said had occurred before I'd been born. *It's almost inevitable, in this field, over the course of a long career, that a complaint will at some point arise. It's a kind of occupational hazard.* They had told me that and I had believed them. I could believe it of a single instance. But two, three, five, eight? What was the final tally? How could my father be purely innocent in the face of so many different "instances"? And what was my mother's role in it all, standing tall by his side in her long dark skirts and sweaters, her sober garments, her eternal air of reproach and forgiveness? I had a quick image of leaving her alone on the couch with a wet washcloth across her brow, and then of my father and me coming in from a walk on Memorial Drive, me with my poncho held out like an apron, conveying a score of bristly brown balls. Tree gonads, that was the consolation prize, the gift of atonement he offered her through me.

I thought of my recently acquired knowledge: that my mother had told her mother about the earliest complaints, the two that had been made before I was born. She had apparently told her of no complaint since. What to do with this new piece of information? All those years, I had supposed that the reason for their estrangement lay wholly within the fact that my mother had been sent away, at age four, to live with her grandparents. For the first time now, as I huddled at the bottom of the stairs, I imagined that their break had something more to do with my father's conduct; my mother's decision to stand by him; my grandmother's possible warning against him, or her disparaging of my mother's decision to stay.

I had forgotten why I came downstairs in the first place. My thirst had evaporated, my shivering abated, and I sat as stone. I had no thought, no volition. After a bit my father spoke again, still too low for me to understand but with rising intonation. New goose bumps flecked my arms and legs.

My mother's voice came softer now. "No," she said wearily. "Don't ask that. I would never want that, Jer. Do you? Do you at all love me?"

"Sarah, Sarah," my father said, his voice finally audible but wretched-sounding. "I know, I have no right—but if you could believe me—oh, please: I never stopped."

I knew that should make me feel good, and I guess in a way it did.

THE NEXT DAY I got caught embellishing at work. I had just come off a tour and was descending the stairs to the "crypt," the basement of the Conway Jimerson Homestead, where the historical interpreters bided our time between tours. Calling it the crypt was an inside joke, the basement being the one part of the house that had been remodeled. Not remotely sepulchral, it had a fluorescent-lit kitchen area with Formica countertops and a dinette where we ate

our lunches from home, and a sitting area furnished with comfortable chairs and a large couch. An intercom let us communicate with
the gift shop, a hundred yards away, where visitors bought their tickets to the house. In this manner we were informed the moment a
group was discharged from the gift shop; then whichever one of us
was up next would go receive the visitors at the front door. On slow
days an hour or more could elapse between tours. But when we
were busy—weekends, holidays, summer—I might find myself
hard-pressed to pee, swig a little Coke, and straighten my bonnet
before heading back up.

On this day, one of the other guides was hurrying up as I came
down. The stair was very narrow; we each clutched our skirts and
petticoats close to our bodies, and I turned sideways to let her get
by. There were three of us on that day, the third being Ezra, and I
was glad of the chance to hang out with him before the next tour.
As she squeezed past, the other guide hissed in my ear, "Beware the
Brunt." I took this to mean only that our foppish boss, Brant, was
making one of his rare visits from his office above the gift shop
down to the Old Homestead (every now and then he'd descend on
us for some kind of inspection, get a whiff, as it were, and withdraw,
always with a faint air of unexpressed disapproval)—and not that I,
personally, was in trouble.

But, "Ah, Beatrice," said Brant, turning at the clack of my period
shoes on the stairs as I came down. "Just the person I wanted to see."

Ezra, reading on the couch, smirked at me behind Brant's back.
I bit the inside of my mouth to keep from smiling. "Brant, hi!"

"Let's sit down over here." He lowered his voice to give us a semblance of privacy, and gestured toward the dinette. Palm flat, fingers
together. His gathered muslin sleeve draping gracefully. Although
Brant himself did not usually give tours, he always wore nineteenth-
century dress on the job, in order to help "preserve the integrity of

the historical interpretation." Ezra emitted a cough. I flipped him the bird behind my back and sat.

"I wanted to talk with you about a serious inaccuracy in your presentation, Beatrice. Apparently you have been telling visitors that Constance had numerous lovers?"

A fit of coughing erupted behind me. For a long time after, Ezra would be able to make me laugh simply by dropping the word *numerous,* inflected a certain way, into a sentence.

"Um . . . I'm not really—What? Sorry, what was the question?"

He gave me a *Come, come* look. "You told at least one group of visitors, this very morning, didn't you, that Constance was in the habit of inviting into her bed the single men who passed through this station on their way to freedom."

"Ohh."

I heard Ezra, evidently anticipating a new round of coughing, get up and hurry into the bathroom.

I made myself stammer fetchingly. "I-I didn't mean to imply that they *did* anything in bed. But . . . I'm pretty sure I read that? Somewhere. Wasn't it in the material . . . ?"

Brant gave me a look of patient concern. "We have no documentation of any kind to support that theory."

"Really?" I tried to say this in a way that sounded both meek and mystified, and I squinted at the ceiling, as though *certain* I remembered having read something to this effect.

"Beatrice," he said sadly, "I must tell you that any fabrication on tour is not simply a disservice to the people who come here to learn about our nation's history. It's a disservice to the memory of the Jimersons and those they helped. If you are asked a question and are unsure of the answer, you may always refer the visitor to me." He leaned forward confidingly and put his hand on my wrist. "Some things even I don't know. And then I simply say, 'Hm. I don't know!'"

Behind the bathroom door, water ran furiously in the sink. I withdrew my hand, on the premise I had an itch on my chin.

Brant edified me for several minutes more before consulting his pocket watch, which he wore on a chain clipped to his vest. "Well, I can't give any more time to this now. But you do understand the importance of this, don't you?"

"Yes," I agreed, careful still to look puzzled and vexed. "I'm sorry. I must have mixed up something else I was reading . . ."

"That's all right." A quick smile. Brant had very regular teeth, the front ones oddly tapered at the ends. "No harm done."

He bounded up the stairs in the manner in which he must have supposed a strapping and morally courageous forty-year-old farmer would have taken the stairs in the mid-1800s. Ezra, who'd deemed it safe to emerge from the bathroom moments earlier, quietly resumed his seat and book. "Slut," he said peaceably, turning a page.

I flashed him a smile and went to the fridge to get my lunch: vanilla yogurt and an orange. Sitting at the dinette, licking the inside of the yogurt lid, I pictured Constance sweaty and righteous up there on the rope bed, transgressing beneath the needlepoint: I WILL BE AS HARSH AS TRUTH AND AS UNCOMPROMISING AS JUSTICE. It felt corrective, redemptive, and despite my apology to Brant, I could not summon the least remorse; on the contrary. In my mind I'd unshackled her from myth, freed her to ride on top, hair hanging loose, flouting the social compact, her bare back rounding and bucking up under the dark eaves.

MY GRANDMOTHER'S SALON served increasingly as my anchor that spring, and also as the window through which I believed I might ultimately be transported from the grim and undiscussed unraveling at home. At her salon I felt both highly visible and liberatingly unknown, a tabula rasa, luminous and smooth. I hoped to come across as winsome, smart, and willing, but most essentially as innocent—a quality I thought likely to prompt intervention, to fan their collective urge to mold and instruct me.

All I wanted was to make them want this.

There I was—*am,* still, etched in my own memory—legs crossed at the ankle, looking from Nina to Ida, from Silke to John, from Javier to my grandmother to Hale, slowly swiveling my brief platinum tresses on a neck I was careful to keep extended, drinking in their words through clear eyes, pressing my glossed lips together in bemused thought, laughing moderately on occasions when I got the joke, frowning thoughtfully on occasions when asked to contribute my opinion, always slightly watching myself, holding myself in controlled readiness lest I miss a cue.

Now, from the vantage point of twenty years later, I see that the role of innocent served another purpose as well, one that had as much to do with what was going on at home as with the salon and my dream of breaking into theater. By presenting myself as a blank slate to my would-be mentors on Beacon Hill, I was also enacting a desire to erase the stains and fissures that had materialized on the smooth surface of our family's image. I felt sullied by what I was learning about my father, about my mother's complicity, and, worst of all, what felt like my own complicity, too. Not because I had known; I hadn't. Simply because I had loved him, and us, had believed in, and had buttressed by my ready belief, the story of us Fisher-Harts being nobler and smarter and finer than average. *Quality people,* whatever that meant.

So I was, that spring, singularly driven to wipe my slate clean and begin anew. And while there did burn in me a desire to start sketching fresh with my own hand, to claim authorship of myself, this desire lay at odds with what I was accustomed to and could not help pining for: being informed of who I was from without, by a source greater than myself. And this is the state I was in when the salon became the centerpiece of my weeks, and it colored how I regarded the other attendees. It lent their words and gestures an oracular quality, since I was at that time so particularly hungry for signs, for direction.

All the while I felt as though I were poised, waiting, biding my time under a great weight. I still had not said anything, to anyone, about the orange flyer, or the conversation I'd eavesdropped on at the bottom of the stairs, or my grandmother's revelation that my father's troubles predated my birth.

My dream is to act, I had written back in the dark, slush-marked days of late winter. The inciting event: writing to my grandmother at my desk in the attic, a thin light spilling through the wavy windowpanes as I scripted my words with the fountain pen I'd been given as a graduation present.

I knew nothing then of the charge that would soon be leveled against my father, or of the effect that this charge, as none of the earlier ones, would have on our family. I knew only that I was committing a deliciously secretive infraction, by breaching the silence between our threesome and Margaret Fourcey. It seemed merely a fittingly romantic beginning to a romantic career. The branches of our crab apple tree had looked black as licorice, interlocked as lace that afternoon, through my high window, and the sepia ink gleamed darkly on the page before drying a paler shade of brown.

My dream is to act, I had written, and I believed I meant acting as in theater.

The words sound different to me now, as I look back at who I was then, fast approaching my twentieth birthday, still living at home, playing the same role I had performed all my life, and all the while so critically unable to *act.*

———

THEN IN ONE AFTERNOON two important things happened.

First, I found out my father's other supervisee in clinical psychology had requested reassignment. My mother intercepted me on my way to the kitchen to tell me this. I had just come down from my room and was on the bottom step when she opened the door to her office. Quiet as I'd trained myself to be, she seemed always to know just when I was passing by.

I tried to preempt whatever she might say. "I'm on my way out," I invented.

"Where to?" She leaned against the doorframe, long and slim, hands behind her back. Her glasses hung around her neck on a beaded chain; I'd been disappointed when she started doing the whole glasses-on-a-chain thing, which felt contrived, and like another in a series of wrong choices. Regarding her now, it was impossible not to be aware of her physical similarity to my grandmother, as well as certain marked, and rather layered-on, differences. The differences were all stylistic—the tightly cinched hair, the somber earth tones, the absence of jewelry other than wedding band—and collectively signaled a constrained, reined-in sensibility. I wondered if they were undertaken as part of a conscious effort to distance herself from Margaret Fourcey. My mother was then just forty-nine, but I couldn't help thinking that in some respects she came across as older than my grandmother.

"Library," I answered, making quick use of the fact that I happened to have an overdue book in hand.

It was an aesthetically pleasing volume—at once slim and heavy, and bound in jade green cloth—and this was the main reason I'd kept it out so long, since I had found it effectively unreadable. Aristotle's *Poetics*. It had been mentioned a few times at the salon, and I

had developed a suspicion that the book itself might be a shibbo-
leth, or at any rate a signpost I ought to follow, so I had checked it
out, only to find it suffocatingly boring. But I kept feeling, almost
superstitiously, that to crack its code would hasten my progress in
the salon, and in the world of theater more generally, and so every
few days I found myself scooping it up once more and struggling
through a few of its thin, rustling pages.

Now, although I had in fact been on my way to fix myself a cup
of mint tea (having determined that tackling Aristotle required
refreshment), I set the book on the bottom stair and took my raincoat from the hall closet.

"Well, Bebe. Love, I wanted to talk with you a little about Dad."

"Does it have to be now?" Jamming sock-feet hurriedly into my
rain boots.

She sighed. "Do you have just a minute? This . . . complaint is
looking more serious for him. Not the complaint, of course, but
the manner in which the university is dealing with it." She spoke
in her professional voice, rational and comforting: comforting by
its very adherence to rationalism. "The current political climate
on campus is such that the department feels the need to give the
student perhaps more . . . oh, benefit of the doubt. One result of
this is that it's all being handled with less discretion, more of an
open forum. So word of mouth has . . . *swayed* . . . Well, the thing
is, two days ago, Dad's other supervisee requested to work with
someone else."

"Oh."

"I wasn't sure whether or not to lay this on you. But I thought
. . . if you're going to hear it, it would be better if you hear it from
me."

Pearly light shone through the window above the door, casting
a lozenge on the wall behind her. In it, the rain traced sinuous

shadows. "Um. Okay." I snapped up my raincoat and bent to retrieve the book.

"The thing is, you might hear it elsewhere." Her voice sounded fraught.

"Why?" I asked, straightening slowly.

"Well, there's a campus group trying to turn it into a . . . cause célèbre!" She gauged my reaction as if to see whether we might share a rueful smile here, but I gave her no glimmer.

"What campus group?"

Another sigh. "They call themselves the University Anti-Harassment Committee. It's a new group, I never heard of it before this year. I don't think they have a lot of credibility, a lot of weight, but. In this age of the chat room. And institutions' being so easily cowed. 'Mea culpa, mea culpa.' The whole climate." She shook her head, sighed again. The sighs, I thought, were meant to convey ennui, but the uncharacteristic disjointedness of her speech betrayed her: she was upset.

"U.A.H.C.," I said.

"Yes." Then, "You've heard of them?"

I looked at her hard. Her oval face was framed twice. Once by hair, pulled back in a dark twist, and then again on the wall behind her, by the lunatic shadows of rivulets. A trembling cameo. I wanted to rail at her, to insist she take responsibility for once again having doled out information only when I was likely to learn it elsewhere. I wanted to make her tell me the honest reason she didn't have contact with her mother. I wanted to ask her why we weren't talking about the *thing,* my father's behavior and apparent pattern of behavior—I wanted to make her tell me about all the other times. I wanted to insist on a full accounting.

I could not act on any of it. "Look," I said, "maybe we can do this later. I have to go."

"I see." Her tone held censure.

"What?"

"Nothing." She shifted her weight from the doorframe. "You're right. Go. Take an umbrella."

I slid an umbrella from the stand and turned the doorknob. It came off in my hand. I gusted out a sigh, thrust it back in the hole, turned it while jamming it *in,* and made my exit without looking back. I knew she would be watching me, though, and so made myself stride broadly and with confidence down the front walk, but underneath I felt swimmy and faltering, a taste like aspirin in the back of my throat.

A block or so beyond our house, I slowed. The air smelled of grass and mud, clean and barely sweet. Walking, drawing the warm, wet air in through my mouth, I took in that everything was wet and white and gray and black, and here and there bursts of color: an azalea bush, the odd red car. I felt I was walking through a shifting kaleidoscope, and my thoughts were turning, the colors and patterns coming in and out of focus. I was thinking, *University Anti-Harassment Committee,* and *House Un-American Activities Committee;* and I was thinking of cellos and violins; mother and grandmother; of wives standing by and not standing by their accused husbands. I was thinking of Brant, in his muslin shirt, touching my wrist and speaking of my duty to history. I was thinking about Aristotle, saying there within the pages tucked under my arm that history describes the thing that has been, and poetry the thing that might come to be.

And then my mind went to Silke and something she had said at the last salon, just days earlier, when people were still arriving and she and I had been alone in my grandmother's kitchen. She had asked me to retrieve a tin of sardines that was too high for her on the shelf—whatever else her role in my grandmother's life might be, she appeared, minimally, to be in charge of snacks—and while I was kneeling on the counter she had clapped her hands together and cried, "*Ach so!* I see. You *are* like your grandfather." I had turned, pricking with curiosity. She had never mentioned him. No one had. So few alive had ever met him, and although I'd known that Silke knew him, first in Berlin and then in New York, she had not volunteered anything about this or about him; I'd the sense the subject was taboo. But there was something about the way she said this now, about my being like him, that made me think it had been on her mind all this time, as if her utterance were concluding a protracted argument she'd been having with herself.

"I am?" I asked. "How?"

She stood there with a funny smile on her face, twinkling at me.

"What?" I was hungry for some portent of my character.

She proclaimed heartily, one finger in the air, "In the caboose!" and briefly grabbed her own rear to demonstrate.

I blushed—being more generously endowed in this arena than I would have liked—and slid down off the counter, sardine tin in hand.

"Shame, Silke." She tsk-tsked herself. "No tact."

I laughed. "Did you know him well?"

"Sure!"

"Do I seem like him in any other ways?" I felt greedy, asking.

She cocked her head at me, laid a gnarled finger alongside her mouth, and muttered to herself. *"Die Augen? Nein. Das Kinn? Nein. Die Schultern? Ach, ja, Vielleicht."*

I wondered what she was saying, what she was seeing.

She finished her appraisal without delivering a verdict, only a benediction. "Let's hope you are like him a fighter for justice, and not like him weak in the heart."

I will be as harsh as truth, as uncompromising as justice.

"He had a weak heart?" I asked.

"Sure!" She shrugged, as if to say, *Obviously.*

"You mean like a heart condition? I didn't know that."

"No. I mean that he died from a broken heart," she pronounced, and with a slow, philosophical nod, picked up a wooden bowl of dried apple slices and led the way back toward the parlor, where people were gathering for the salon. I had trailed behind her with crackers and sardines, confused, wondering whether she meant he had died of a heart problem and not an overdose; also, whether she meant that his heart had been broken by the H.U.A.C. ordeal, or something else. The exchange seemed to me full of the promise that I would learn more from Silke as time wore on, that this warm and foxy old German woman would become my secondary mentor, not in the theater world, but in the theater of family lore.

Now as I walked farther and farther from my parents' house, mulling over this interaction with Silke, amid myriad other fragmented bits, I saw how splintered, how incoherent my life had become—in so short a time! Only this past winter it had been for me a whole, seamless tapestry. Now, in early May, it had revealed itself as frayed and particulate, a fabric shot through with holes. I felt as though my very skin were pocked, and only then realized the storm had begun in earnest.

The sky had darkened and taken on a greenish cast. Fresh gusts cut in and whipped the rain stingingly against my face while I struggled to open my umbrella. I was by now on Mass Ave, and decided I'd cross the street to a coffee shop and dry out with a corn muffin and Aristotle. Lightning flashed and a pain coursed through me, a quick, acute longing for home, coupled with the certainty that home did not exist.

That was when the second thing happened. Continuing on my way across Mass Ave, with the DON'T WALK palm already flashing its red warning, I spotted, several paces in front of me, a woman who so much resembled my grandmother that it made me do a double take. In all these years of living just across the river from each other, there had never been a chance encounter, and I knew the likelihood of her simply happening to be here, on this particular block between Central and Harvard squares, at this hour, in the rain, was far-fetched. But I could not help playing pretend, and so I followed this woman who shared my grandmother's distinctive stature and her crisp-cut pewtery hair. I was careful not to steal a glimpse of her face and thereby ruin the illusion. And as I tailed her, this faceless woman, safe in the knowledge that it was all a fabrication, I tried to imagine what the meaning of such a coincidence might be, were it actually happening in real life. I tried to think of it in narrative terms.

Wedging the Aristotle more completely under my arm, so as to protect it from the rain, I groped to remember what he'd said (and I'd half followed) about simple and complex plots, reversals and recognitions, the plausible and the probable. In this way I managed to loose myself within a labyrinth of thought, and it was from within this abstracted state that I saw the woman, whom I'd been trailing for several blocks now, turn and go into a building, and as she turned I saw her profile. And it *was* Margaret Fourcey, in fact. I didn't try to call out to her, but followed her inside.

The building was old, more shabby than charming. Its lobby was yellow-gray and narrow, and by the time I entered it, empty. On the right was an elevator with an almost Art Deco ashtray beside it. Inside the ashtray were sand and a wad of gray gum. I folded my umbrella and shook it. Drops spattered all over the black-and-white tile floor. I could hear the elevator's cables straining, so I tried the old detective-novel trick of watching to see where the floor indicator stopped—it was a semicircle of Roman numerals going from one to eight—but determined that the arrow was permanently stuck between three and four. Then I noticed the directory mounted on the wall behind me, and I began to read it, floor by floor, until among the tenants of the seventh floor I saw the simple, unadorned: H. RUBIN. Aware that I was being brazen, yet somehow insulated by the absurd impression that none of this was real, I rode the elevator up.

There were no markings on the doors apart from numbers, and as I had forgotten to notice the number, had there even been one, on the directory, I was forced to skulk, my forte, down the hall, pausing outside each door to listen. It was the strangest sensation: I could feel my heart beating rapidly, reverberating in my throat, yet at the same time I was detached, as though the drab hallway were filled with some soporific ether, and I glided smoothly through it. I could smell the rubber of my green rain boots.

In that definitive magazine profile of my grandmother, the one I'd gone back and reread after the salon, it turned out that Hale Rubin had been quoted as saying, "All the critics who call Maggie the bravest actress of her generation have got it wrong. It isn't bravery. That she makes you *think* it is, that's the marvel of her: that's her craft." One reason the quote interested me was that it seemed so dubious a compliment. The other reason was that I thought to be brave must be very good, but to have the ability to *play* brave must be even better. It made me admire my grandmother the more, and feel somehow—unreasonably, perhaps—aligned with her.

In my current stupor, however, bravery was irrelevant. I crept down the hall with pounding heart, containing yawns in the hollow of my throat. Behind closed doors I detected the sounds of filing cabinet; keyboard; telephone; nothing; and then, behind the one at the end of the hall, my grandmother's voice. I knocked, harder than I'd meant to, and the door, not latched, swung wide.

"Beatrice Fisher-Hart," announced my grandmother after a second, rather drolly. There was surprise in her voice, but not as much as seemed warranted. So that I half expected her to say, *We were just talking about you.* She was sitting on the edge of a large messy desk, her stocking feet dangling a foot off the floor. Hale sat behind the desk, in a brown leather chair, and he smiled at me. It was a narrow, cramped room, strewn with loose papers and what I took to be bound scripts piled on shelves and stacked thickly on a worn Oriental carpet. A few framed theatrical posters decorated the walls, including one of *Pyramus and Thisbe* with my grandmother's and Maynard Clinkscale's names above the title. Behind the desk a single window looked onto an airshaft and the brick wall of the adjacent building. The rain continued determinedly. Lightning flashed; thunder rumbled. All very stage-set, it occurred to me. That thought proved my palliative, the antidote to my racing heart. *Play it like a scene.*

"I saw you outside." I heard my voice and it sounded perfectly breathless, as though the direction for my line in the script read (*breathlessly*). "At least someone who looked like you, but I didn't think it really was. So I followed them in—I mean, you." Hale's office worked on me like a kind of charm. From the moment I stepped inside, despite the general mess and packing-container dimensions, I wanted to be there. It was still and dry, and smelled of something profoundly good (ginger snaps, I later learned). A desk lamp with an amber-colored glass shade glowed against the dark storminess outside and made Hale, seated behind it, the warm center of the room.

"What a coincidence," said my grandmother, pleasantly.

"I know!"

"Suddenly you're everywhere."

"I *know*!" I laughed and it was as though the sound of my laughter shook me out of my sleepwalking delusion. Embarrassment

came crashing down. I felt the extreme awkwardness, the prepos-
terousness, of my being there. "Oh: well, sorry. Sorry—bye! I guess
I just couldn't help seeing if it was you."

They returned the laugh politely, and I offered one last mugging,
madcap smile to exit by, and then I was hurrying down the hall
toward the elevator, practically sticky with mortification.

"Beatrice." My grandmother called to me just as I pressed the
DOWN button. I turned. She stood in Hale Rubin's office doorway
in her stocking feet, elegant and long, the same—the identical!—
confident-casual stance of my mother standing in her own office
doorway, arresting my progress up or down the stairs of our house
on any given afternoon, to inquire about dinner reservations, perhaps, or whether I'd remembered to roll the garbage cans in from
the curb. Or as earlier that very afternoon, to deliver bad news
about the reverberations still making themselves felt in the after-
math of my father's latest grotesquery. But—and I shook my head
as I reminded myself—this was not Sarah Fisher-Hart. This was
Margaret Fourcey. Whose power to affect me was both lesser and
greater than my mother's.

"Would you mind coming back a minute?" she commanded
amiably.

Behind me the elevator door opened.

I believed she was about to disinvite me from the next salon.
Never mind the moments of intimacy at her kitchen table a few
nights earlier. Never mind the fact that I thought I'd begun to
endear myself to her, the way all the other members of the salon
were plainly endeared to her. *It's really a gathering for more mature
artists,* she would say, nicely. *More accomplished, those with real experience in theater. And in life.* I had the wild thought that if I were to flee
now, she couldn't lower the ax; I could at least postpone the terrible moment when she would, pleasantly but firmly, sever ties.

Behind me the elevator door closed. She stood waiting. Already, as I retraced my steps down the hallway toward her, I was rehearsing the way I would react to her disappointing news, the graceful way I would nod, broadcasting maturity even as I accepted her judgment, thereby causing her to doubt it. *We don't really have a place for little girls with nothing better to do than loiter pathetically outside people's offices, spying.* Or what if our talk at the kitchen table had cooled her on the idea of allowing me into her home? What if she had decided that night to turn me out, and was seizing this fortuitous opportunity to say what she'd already rehearsed? *We are products of our environments. In light of what I now know about your father, I regret to say your presence is no longer welcome at the salon.* I knew on some level these thoughts were ridiculous, but they were powerful nonetheless.

"Please," she said, once I had come back, indicating that I should sit. I did, on the small chair opposite Hale's desk, as did she, again up on the corner of it. I sat straight and tense, unable to contain the nervous smile that played about my lips. "Speaking of coincidence," my grandmother began, and with a look turned the floor over to Hale.

"Yes, as it happens," he explained, and cleared his throat, and continued, "I've been asked to workshop a staged anthology of sorts, an experimental production drawing upon some of the Greek myths."

At this point he stuck a finger behind his glasses and rubbed at one eye, then the other, then removed the glasses altogether as the project of assuaging his itch required more vigor. It seemed indelicate of him, yet I was captivated by the action—by the fact that he had the full attention of two women, yet cared so little for vanity, was so self-assured, that he could be content to let us wait and watch him rub at his eyes. I don't mean that he was being selfish or rude; it didn't feel like that. Only that he was free to act on an impulse as basic as scratching an itch—yet somehow it touched me, all out of proportion to the event.

If there is such a thing, then, absurd as it sounds, that was it: the moment I began to fall for Hale Rubin.

Eventually satisfied, he replaced the glasses and blinked at me. "Anyway, if you like, we might try you for the part of Thisbe."

TWO

The Rehearsals

B Y M I D - J U N E we were in rehearsal. Although my classes had ended, more abundant summer hours had kicked in at the Conway Jimerson Homestead ("Now that we're in High Season," Brent liked to go around saying), and I was still babysitting for Ida's kids two or three nights a week, so that suddenly, after a year of hanging about the house far too much, I was out nearly all the time.

I arrived early for our first read-through, on a Saturday afternoon. Through the affiliations of the musical director, rehearsals would be held in an empty classroom at the university. The directions I'd been given led me to one of the long, low buildings flanking the Old Yard. The day was unseasonably warm and humid, and even though I'd worn a sleeveless dress, I was damp by the time I reached the room, a kind of mini-lecture hall on the third floor. Hale was the only one there. He was going along the far wall, opening windows with some effort. Without speaking, I joined in, working from the opposite end. They took a lot of muscle. We met on the last one, hefting it open together. His pink oxford showed a circle of magenta under each arm. He gave me a nod. "Thank you."

"Sure."

Others began to trickle in, about a dozen in all, some familiar to me from the salon (my grandmother, John, Ida), most not. We arranged ourselves in the first couple rows of chairs. My grandmother greeted me with a warm hand on my shoulder and a smile, but the seat she chose was away by the windows, next to Ida. I wound up on the far right of the group, replicating the marginal, watchful position I always assumed at my grandmother's. It was stifling in the room. I crossed my legs and within seconds they were slippery-slidey with sweat. Some of the actors fanned themselves or extracted water bottles from their bags. I wondered who would be playing Pyramus. To my disappointment, the only really leading-man-looking types were a strapping blond guy who I heard say was going to be Cupid, and John, who I knew hadn't been cast as Pyramus. But maybe, I reassured myself, not everyone was there yet. As I gazed about, surreptitiously searching for a definite type, someone with the right virile-but-dreamy look, I became interested in noticing how varied the group was—in age, color, body type, sartorial sense—we were a motley crew, a far cry from the uniform assemblages of my parents' world. Once we were all present, Hale took up the stool at the front of the room, and everyone fell quiet.

"Sorry about the heat in here," he said. "We have this space, such as it is, through June. After that, it may cheer you to know, we'll have to find other quarters."

"Any idea yet where?" asked someone behind me.

"We're working on it. Keep you posted," Hale promised, and he thanked us all for coming. He was unfailingly courteous, yet there was nothing overwrought in his courtesies. As he made announcements about the production, he unbuttoned the cuffs and rolled up the sleeves of his oxford. He wore khakis, sneakers, no socks, no wristwatch. A few times someone interrupted with a question. He listened carefully, without impatience, responded, and went on.

The play, he explained, would comprise interlaced scenes of pairs of mythical lovers: Cupid and Psyche, Orpheus and Eurydice, Daphne and Apollo, Pyramus and Thisbe. The approach would be nonliteral. Some of the characters might be represented by puppet figures; some of the props by human actors. "There's so much shifting in these stories," Hale remarked, "between the animate and inanimate. The possibility of metamorphosis has to be always hovering, pregnant. The line between thing and mortal is constantly porous."

I tried to fit what he was saying into Aristotle's rule book, to locate his words in the context of the *Poetics,* but my mental ability shrank at the task even as my admiration for Hale swelled.

There would be a Greek chorus singing in the style of a barbershop quartet, he informed us, with a smile I thought signaled his own amusement at the idea. But—and he sobered right up as he explained this—we would not be bound to the traditionally absolute separation between the chorus commenting on the action and the actors themselves. He would be asking each of us, he said, to think about pairs of lovers, and about pairings in general. The pairing of gods and mortals. Of things and beings. Of art and reality. Of witness to the action and agent of the action. "Every presumably rigid barrier might be subverted," he proposed, looking around the room. "Might"—he made a fluid gesture with his fingers—"melt."

I sat up higher in my seat, feeling everything as if with heightened sensitivity: the sweat pearling along my hairline and soaking the back of my dress. My heart going about its rhythm in my chest. A slight shallowness of breath.

"I would ask each one of you to think about transgression," Hale went on. "Transgression, defiance, noncompliance. Each one of these myths contains a crucial act of contravention. What do we mean by that?"

"Contra-vention." An older woman named Jean pronounced the syllables slowly, as though she were working it out in her head, "that's 'against coming together.' "

A woman with a long gray braid, named Gracie, picked up the thread. Their generation must have all had Latin in school, I thought, rather cowed, too aware that this was all over my head. "*Society,* that's the coming together of people in an organized fashion. Convening. It's like an agreement about how we're all going to act together. So contravention's like breaking that compact. Going against society."

"Against convention," said John. "Contravention as opposed to convention."

"Okay." Hale was off his perch now, roaming a little, hands in pockets. I sat right at the edge of my seat. "So we have four sets of lovers, all acting in some way *against the social compact.* Are there costs for their transgressions? Are there benefits? I ask each of you to begin to think about how these questions play out for your character—really for all the characters."

My scalp was aprickle. I wasn't remotely doing what Hale had just asked: thinking about my character, Thisbe. Instead I was thinking about the two individuals who sprung instantly to mind when I heard the word *convention*: my parents. I was thinking about my father's own secret problem with transgression, and the questions Hale had raised about cost and benefit. I was thinking about my presence here, amid these people in this room, how my being here might be said to constitute an act of contravention in itself.

I realized Hale was still talking, and I had missed some of what he had said. He was back on his stool now, consulting an index card: it seemed he'd moved on to more pragmatic stuff. Scenes had been scripted, he was saying, but the overall form of the piece would emerge largely via the rehearsal process. As a "workshop," the whole thing would legally fly below the radar of Actors' Equity; nobody would be paid. Although there was a possibility of the play becoming a commercial production down the road, the focus would be on the creative process rather than outcome.

"I don't particularly care whether or not it ever gets mounted publicly," Hale disclosed, with a shrug. It occurred to me that the shrug was intended somehow to include everyone in the room, to assume our camaraderie on this issue, and in fact, I saw, as I stole a glace around the room, everyone else did seem to be in agreement. It seemed to speak volumes about Hale's reputation that all these real artists were willing to give up pay and exposure for the opportunity to work with him.

After about an hour of discussion, we broke for ten minutes before beginning the actual read-through, and during this break my insecurity mounted. Everyone spilled out into the little hallway. A few people, fishing out cigarette packages, tramped off downstairs. Another handful headed for the bathrooms and vending machines down the hall. The rest sprawled on window seats and on the floor. The heat, combined with their own actorly sensibilities, made for markedly relaxed poses: legs out, shoes off, heads lolling against the wall. Randy, the guy playing Cupid, removed his T-shirt and wore it like a turban. A sylphlike young woman removed her cardigan and fanned Ida with it, playfully. Everyone seemed to have landed within a small cluster of intimates. I stood just outside the door to the classroom and wondered what I was doing here.

Then I felt something cold against my arm; it was John's soda can; he was being funny. "You can have some," he offered, and my

"Thank you" must have taken him by surprise, being too earnest, as though he'd offered rescue rather than mere refreshment. We sat in tandem and leaned against the wall.

It was the first time we had ever really talked as the two of us and not as part of the salon. He was nice. Hale, he said, had invited him to play Daphne in drag. I was pretty sure he was joking, but not sure enough to laugh or to ask what part he was really playing. He took a big gulp of orange soda. "Are you thrilled to be doing Thisbe?" he asked. "I saw your grandmother do it on Broadway. Not that I was born yet. On videotape. She was amazing. I wanted to fall down and cry. God, you're lucky. Your lineage. Your skin. How old are you?"

"Nearly twenty."

He sighed. "*Baby*. When's your birthday?"

"Two weeks."

"Cancer?"

"Gemini."

"Man. To be working with Hale Rubin at your age." He handed me the can again. "Is there no air in this hallway? I'm sweating like a mother." He plucked at his collar a few times and sighed. "So what was it like?"

"—What?"

"Growing up *chez* Fourcey."

"Well . . . I didn't. I grew up in Cambridge."

"But I mean *around* that whole milieu. At the feet of Dame Margaret."

"I didn't really. I've seen her more in the past four months than in the whole rest of my life put together."

He raised an eyebrow at me, pursed his lips. "Why? Do I sense a saga?"

I squinted back at him. How much did he already know? That was always a confusing question for me, since at least part of our family's story had been laid bare in the public domain. "Well, my mother and my grandmother don't really get along," I said slowly, searching his face to see whether he registered surprise or know-ingness. He just cocked his head and nodded, as if to say, *Go on.* "Well, basically, my grandmother sent my mother to live with her parents from the time she was four. So." I shrugged. "And I guess my mother never forgave her."

He reached out for the soda can. I passed it back. "So your mother kept you and Maggie apart?"

"Yeah." I knew those close to her called her Maggie, but that John, so young, was in that league, gave me a pang. Of course, being Javier's partner, perhaps he enjoyed certain entitlements he wouldn't have otherwise.

"So how does she feel about this, your mother I mean, you know, about your doing this play?"

"Not psyched." This was more conjecture than anything my mother had actually expressed. "But," I added, "it *is* my life." As soon as I heard these words I was aghast, as though I'd committed the most flagrant betrayal.

AROUND THIS TIME it became clear that the present complaint against my father wasn't going to disappear. Classes had ended, so the fact that my father was at home more was not in and of itself notable. But while summers normally meant he redoubled his efforts to organize whatever upcoming conference he was in charge of; or poured himself into finishing whatever article he'd promised some journal; or finalized, with my mother, amid colorful piles of travel brochures and guidebooks, the details of their annual August vacation, this June he was uncharacteristically idle. I kept running into him at hours when he would normally have been at the university or in his home office, and he would be doing things like making himself toast, or perusing a back issue of *National Geographic,* or trying to germinate morning glory seeds. I found him occupied in this last endeavor one day around noon. He sat at the kitchen table in shorts and socks and a yellow polo shirt, scowling through his bifocals at the instructions on the packet, then making a little cut in each seed with a paring knife. I was so worried, for no reason, that he was going to cut his finger, I had to leave the room without doing whatever it was I'd come in for.

My worry, actually, was not completely irrational. There were signs of unprecedented fragility about him. He seemed distant, distracted, as if mentally ensconced in a hedge maze of gigantic proportions, through which he was determined to fumble on his own. At first I thought his distance was a symptom of mortification, but whenever he did relate to me, the look in his eye was less mortified than wounded—and *baffled,* as though try as he might, he could discern no justification for the wound.

It made me afraid to interact with him—afraid as much of being confronted by more evidence of this new fragility, as of confronting the truth about whatever it was he'd done or said to bring him to this state. So I avoided him more than ever, him and my mother both.

And I found myself lonely in a way I had never in my whole life been. I was cutting myself off from them, and in spite of everything I missed them. I hadn't let myself join them at a restaurant in ages, and that was what I missed, perhaps, the most, or most emblematically: the comfort of all the minor luxuries we were in the habit of enjoying together—the curved salad forks, the baskets of crusty sourdough, the chilled plates bearing scallop-shaped pieces of butter. The steady procession of such artifacts had always symbolized both what my parents had achieved and that to which they continually aspired.

The means to attain and the sophistication to appreciate. It was part of what I now think of as the unspoken Fisher-Hart credo. As long as we ate at the Pudding or Trieste or Le Ciel d'Or every week, then the leak in my ceiling, the rot in the garage, the cracks in the foundation didn't matter. We directed our energies *outward,* positioned ourselves to impress and attract the world beyond our yard. Excellence in maintaining appearances could compensate for, even be a means of transcending, internal faults and failings.

It is true that I was particularly well primed, just then, to *notice* the split between outward appearances and inner life, because of my grandmother's salon. There, heated discussions took place over the best way for an actor to prepare. Did he build a character on externals: clap on a fedora, affix a mustache with spirit gum, affect a limp, a swagger, an accent, *et voilà?* Or did he reach into his own psyche, disinter some element stored there, and use that as the basis for concocting persona?

A more concrete sign that the complaint against my father was serious emerged in late June. I came home from work one day to find an unfamiliar man in the front hall, bending over to slip a manila envelope into a briefcase that sat on the deacon bench. My mother was standing at the foot of the stairs in a long denim sundress, arms folded across her chest. "Thank you for coming by the house, Allan," she said.

"No problem. You're right on my way home," he replied, straightening. He was youngish, but I knew by his dress that he wasn't a student. He wore rather mod eyeglasses, with rectangular lime green frames, and a crisp lavender sports shirt. Nor was he a patient; they didn't use the front entrance.

"This is my daughter, Bebe. Mr. Watanabe."

"Allan," he corrected.

"Beatrice." I corrected her, too.

We shook hands. His was slim and hard. He turned back to my mother. "All right, have a good evening, Sarah. Try not to worry. I'll give you a call tomorrow."

Once he'd gone I raised my eyebrows at her and pointed over my shoulder with my thumb.

"A lawyer," she answered. "He's helping out with some advice about Dad's hearing."

"Dad's *hearing*?"

"Not a court hearing. He just has to go before the review board at the university. It's how they do it. It's part of the process."

"So you hired a lawyer?"

"It's the prudent thing." All at once her face seemed unstable, as though she was gripping her muscles to keep it from sliding, and I thought her eyes looked red and sort of full, charged with emotion. But the light in the hall was coming in flat and burnished from the south where the sun squatted low in the sky, and perhaps it was just that. When she spoke again, she sounded normal. "Anyway, he seems very good. Smart. And he's gay and a minority."

"What does that have to do with it?"

"Think, Bebe. You don't ask a straight white man to represent you on a sexual harassment charge."

"In other words, appearances."

"It's the way it's done."

"You know a lot about it," I said, but in a whisper calculated not to carry. I was looking back out through the screen door, where Allan Watanabe was getting into a Porsche across the street. He looked so clean, so burden-free. His car shone glossy and black. Although I was dismayed to hear we needed a lawyer, I felt relieved that he would be the one representing my father. I could still feel his handshake, smooth and firm as sandalwood, confidence-inspiring. Certainly that was something in short order around here lately.

The next morning my dismay grew. It was June 21st, my birthday, and although I had looked forward to this day, to all the promise contained in the notion of officially entering my twenties, becoming an adult, I awoke out of sorts, not for any reason I could put my finger on, but as if in premonition of a sinking heart. The air hung muggy and dirtyish, like rinse water for paintbrushes.

My mother was already seeing patients by the time I got downstairs; I had heard one come up the peastone path while I was dressing. When I entered the kitchen, however, my father was there to greet me. He was wearing an undershirt and frayed khakis, and leaning both palms on the counter by the coffeemaker, gazing abstractedly out the window, his lower jaw jutting forward. He broke from this pose to say, "Happy birthday, darling," and try to kiss the side of my hair as I went to the fridge. "Thanks, Dad," I said, ducking.

I didn't have rehearsal that night, and my mother had made reservations for us to try a new Afghani restaurant in Boston. In honor of my birthday, we would all go out together. It would be the first time in nearly three months.

I slung cereal and milk in a bowl, sat at the table, opened my book. Having at last paid the overdue fine and renewed the *Poetics* for another month, I had fallen into the habit of carrying it with me almost everywhere. It was still a struggle to comprehend, but easy to tote around, being the size of a clutch purse, and it made a fine prop at rehearsals and the salon—where I was still mindful of establishing my seriousness in people's eyes—and doubled as something I could hide behind when I didn't want to be approached, whether at home by my parents, or at the Homestead, by the Brunt or one of my fellow guides. Ezra, noting its omnipresence, had begun referring to the book as my "boyfriend."

I read the part now dealing with characters. I had slogged

through this before to little avail, but, thinking familiarity might breed understanding, I began to reread. "In the Characters, there are four points to aim at. First and foremost, that they shall be good." Immediately, I hit a wall. What was that supposed to mean? It seemed so reductive. I didn't understand how an intellect like Aristotle's could be hung up on that kind of kindergarten morality. What, you couldn't have bad guys in theater? How boring, and more important, what a blow to realism.

A radical thought asserted itself: What if Aristotle wasn't, by modern standards, an enormous intellect after all? What if his works' value lay more in the fact of their existence, their survival through the centuries, and because it was a comfort to us today to know that men then had puzzled over the same sorts of questions about humanity? What if his important status derived not so much from intrinsic worth as from context, even happenstance? I would have to ask my grandmother and the others about it at the next salon.

I found Aristotle dreadfully prescriptive and hierarchical, obsessed with breaking things down into their composite parts and itemizing them one by one. The *Poetics,* I decided, was really more of a rule book than anything else. Actually, there was a way in which Aristotle reminded me of my parents: absolutely certain of what they imparted. And devoted to the appearance of goodness. There again, Aristotle chimed in neatly with their views. Even men with "infirmities of character," he stated, should be portrayed by the poet as being, at the same time, "good men."

I was at precisely this point in the text—I remember because of the irony—when my father cried out: an unnatural, almost womanly scream.

I, starting, flipped a spoonful of milk and cereal all over the thin, tallow-colored pages before me. My father was standing by the toaster, holding his left wrist and looking at his hand as though it were a foreign object. He began to palpate his palm and then squeeze his forearm, his elbow, all the way up to his bicep, kneading and gaping and making no sound at all to break the silence that followed his scream.

"Dad? What's wrong?" It looked precisely the way heart attacks are always described as looking. Oh, my father! My good, strong father. Yes, of course he was good, beneath his "infirmities." I would concede it in a flash! I would testify to it, if asked—anything, only let him not fulfill my brain's hysterical expectation that he would within the moment topple to the slate floor.

He did not. He pawed strangely at his left arm. Under the skin that had loosened with age, the clear shape of his muscles showed. I had a daughter's intimate knowledge of those muscles, from the countless times I'd been lifted and carried by their power, all the instances I'd ridden safe in the high basket of those encircling arms. "Dad!"

"I'm okay." He yanked the toaster cord out of the wall. "Just stupid." He shook his arm out, rubbed it some more. He had a look almost of wonder on his face, like a child. "Got shocked."

"Dad!" In fresh alarm I half rose. Wasn't that serious? "Did you get electrocuted?" Maybe his heart *had* stopped for a moment. "Are you—?"

"No, no, I'm okay." And giving a sigh, and a final shake to his wrist, he resumed what he'd been doing: working a stuck piece of bread out of the slot with a fork.

At that sight, at the realization of what had happened, all my terror, all my tenderness, congealed in anger. At least from the time I was five I had known never, ever, to stick anything besides bread into a plugged-in toaster.

I saw that I was shaking with anger as I wiped the book's pages with a napkin. I left the *Poetics* splayed open to dry while I returned to my bedroom; milk had also spattered my shirt and pants; I would have to change.

What's wrong with him? The words were wallpaper in my mind as I pulled off the soiled clothes. *Fathers don't stick forks in toasters. Fathers know better than that.* The most basic rules were being flouted. It gave me a feeling of vertigo, as though the very house were listing on its foundation. I sat on my bed, half-dressed. Footsteps on peastones, receding: my mother's client. So the forty-five-minute hour was up. I would have to hurry to get to work on time. But I didn't move. I had slipped; I'd let my mind travel to forbidden territory: to that earlier patient from six years back, my father's accuser. I'd never known her name, never seen her face. I'd never even heard her voice, during that snatch of her therapy session I'd invaded. All I really knew of *her* was the long brown braid and the violin case. From which I used to dream that she would remove a rifle and gun the three of us down.

When that earlier incident had occurred, I'd been finishing up eighth grade, and that same dream had come to me night after night. The worst part of the dream, the crazy part, was that in it she was right, she was justified. We—my father, but my mother and I, too—all deserved to die. In the dream my mother and I were as guilty as my father of whatever wrong had been done her.

In the end, I'd missed three and a half weeks of school during this time. I developed migraines. My mother got me an appointment with her neurologist, who wrote me a prescription. The medicine made the pain in my head manageable; it let me sleep, dreamless.

When I returned to school they had whispered, "Her father's a pervert." "I feel sorry for Beatrice. Did you know her father's a sex maniac?" At the perimeter of the playground they had whispered and elbowed each other, gestured with their sharp chins, eyes averted, hands shoved deep into the pockets of their nylon windbreakers, the bold colors of ice pops lined up against the fence. That windy spring, the wind had made my eyes water whenever I went out. "Are you crying?" people would say. "No, it's the wind."

And all the while I would hear, as if carried by the wind, their sibilant whispers: "I feel sorry for her." As the weather warmed up, the headaches worsened and other symptoms emerged. I had no energy, little appetite. My throat swelled so that I could barely swallow. The pediatrician diagnosed me with mono and for another six weeks, then, through the end of the school year, I was officially allowed to do what I wanted: stay in bed all day.

That fall I didn't enter Cambridge Rindge and Latin, the public high school most of my old classmates would attend. Nor did I repeat eighth grade at my old middle school, something the faculty recommended in light of all the classes I'd missed the previous spring, more than two month's worth. I enrolled instead at Bowers Academy, a very small, private secondary school a few blocks from the Public Garden, whose tuition my parents somehow managed to scrape up for each of the five full years it took me to graduate, always making quietly clear the fact that this was something of a strain on our resources. The restaurants, flowers, fancy cheeses and wines—minor everyday luxuries in which our family indulged— were necessary to project the Fisher-Hart trait of highly discriminating taste. Private school, on the other hand, was a big-ticket item that also made it difficult for my parents to speak credibly about their firm belief in public education.

Now I heard the crunch of little stones again: my mother's next patient. I had to be at the Homestead in less than an hour. Speed descended like a kind of muse. I scrambled from the edge of my bed, plucked clean clothes from their drawers, and sprung into them so quickly I scratched my cheek with the tiny prong on the buckle of my wristwatch. In the mirror I gazed as a small seam

opened up, and two or three drops of blood welled from it. Hissing
a curse, I pressed a bit of tissue to the spot, like a man who has cut
himself shaving.

And it was that, the scrap of tissue clinging to my cheek as I
rode the bus to work, that cast me back into a memory of dark
winter mornings when I'd sit on the bathroom hamper watching
my father shave. I'd cherished those times, the underripened feeling of the predawn hour when only he and I were up. The cold
house seemed to confess its faults in the low moaning and rustling
sounds that were really—I knew, because he'd explained it—water
banging through old pipes and mice in the walls. My father was
mine alone then, and I was mesmerized by the clinical way he
regarded himself while he worked; the slight, expert contortions of
his face; the bands of pink skin emerging beneath the blade as his
face was slowly revealed, as though by his own hand he created
himself anew each day. How godlike he seemed in this task. Infrequently, his hand would slip. Then a humbling thread of scarlet
would unfurl and spread through the mantle of white cream; I
remembered that, too.

EZRA CAME DOWN the stairs into the crypt, having just come off
tour. "Why, Constance, you con. You inconstant old con artist, you.
Connie, conner, you sly slut of a liar. How the hell are ya, where the
hell have ya been?" He thought he was being funny.

"Hello, Ezra." I was just crossing to the stove, where the kettle
was shrilling. I turned off the gas. A communal tin of instant coffee
was kept available in the crypt. "Want any?" I asked, spooning crys-
tals into my mug.

"Dishwater? Thanks, I'll pass." He went and stretched himself
lengthwise on the green plaid couch, his legs extending over two

cushions, his feet in their period boots propped on the frayed arm. His own arms he crossed behind his head, framing his lupine ruff of hair. He looked self-satisfied and indolent.

I had arrived late to work, borne the Brunt's condescending, smiling rebuke, and descended to the crypt with a slamming headache. I'd neither eaten breakfast nor packed a lunch. The instant coffee would be my sustenance for the day, and I'd been loading it heavily with powdered creamer, which had the effect of coating the interior of my mouth with chalky grit. Nevertheless, I'd spent the better part of the last hour sitting there drinking away, listening to the footsteps of tour groups overhead, and trying to cheer myself a little by thinking dastardly thoughts about Aristotle as I read. Meg, one of the other guides, came into the crypt just then. She was about my age, a shy mouse of a girl with apologetic posture. She went to the fridge, removed a paper bag labeled with her name, sat at the dinette, and unwrapped a sandwich, which she proceeded to dispatch in neat little bites, doing her best all the while to ignore Ezra's and my back-and-forth, which went like this:

"How's the rope bed? Will you be giving a demo?"

"Shut up, Ezra."

"Bet you'll have *numerous* volunteers."

"Shut up, Ezra."

"Constance, my darling."

"Ezra . . ."

"Yes?"

"Shut up."

"Cocky Connie. Cocky Connie concocted coffee. Cocky Connie wasn't coital, was she?"

"Jesus, Ezra, you're not even funny!" I slung my stirring spoon hard into the sink. Poor Meg, her back to me, jumped but went on eating. At the sight of her jumping I thought of me, upsetting my cereal bowl earlier that morning, and my headache leaned forward against my brow.

"Bea," said Ezra, differently.

"*What?*" Pressing the heel of my hand into my forehead. "You're so less cute than you think."

"Sorry." He swung his legs around and sat up properly.

"My *God,* Ezra, you don't even know me." The truth is that given the things I was learning about my family, I was afraid he might not *want* to know me. Bringing my coffee over to sit on the couch, I saw that he looked injured. "Well, sorry. But you *don't* know me that well."

"What's up with you?" He said it very softly, as if we could have a private conversation.

I shook my head.

"What's going on? What are you doing after work?" I could barely hear him. Poor Meg, without finishing her sandwich, slipped politely into the bathroom and shut the door.

"I'm supposed to have dinner with my parents."

"Get out of it."

"I can't."

"Yes you can. Tell them you have other plans."

"Maybe." I had told Ezra nothing of the troubles with my father, but all at once I found myself fighting off an urge to tell him everything.

"No maybe."

The intercom sounded. This would be the Brunt up in the gift shop telling us another tour was on its way down to the house. I was up next.

"Meet me at the diner," he persisted.

The intercom sounded again. It was indeed the Brunt, but telling us to go on stations. That meant it had become too busy for individual guides to lead separate tours. Instead, we were each to take a part of the house and a steady stream of visitors would be sent through it.

If there was one part of the house I felt was mine, it was the bedrooms. Conway's was the grander, with a barrel-vaulted ceiling, a sleigh bed, and a nice oddity displayed on a chair by the doorway: an old medicine case, with little corked vials that had once held nineteenth-century remedies. I loved their names—belladonna and laudanum, asafoetida and nitrate of silver, jalap and catechu and ele- campane—penned on age-dark paper in minute, effortful curlicues. There was no telling who had written the labels, Conway or Con- stance or someone else, a doctor or an apothecary. In fact, the med- icine case was another of the artifacts whose provenance was unknown; it might not even have been original to the house. But sometimes I embellished. When asked.

"What did they have all those drugs for?"

I was supposed to say, "We don't know for sure that the Jimer- sons owned these, but there are household accounts that show they purchased certain medicines and medicinal herbs. Many people at that time would have kept such items as household remedies."

Instead, I liked to say, "The Jimersons thought of themselves not only as social healers, but as ministers to all kinds of pain."

I had learned to be more circumspect, not craft any tale so fasci- nating or finely detailed that visitors would be moved to mention its particulars to Brant, while he rang up their post-tour purchases of sealing wax or faux-antique paper dolls or ceramic "corncob" pipes. But I could not help painting a more evocative portrait than the one I had been trained to relate.

Brant had said my embellishing constituted a disservice to his- tory and its players. But I believed the opposite. Marooning them on the forlorn island of Only What We Know, a place whose boundaries were determined by the scant information provided by a handful of surviving documents, seemed the greater disservice. I paid homage with my imagination, and hoped I might get visitors to do the same.

Ezra and I had argued about it.

"You don't think it's important to distinguish between fact and fiction?" he'd challenged me. He was the only person who knew that I continued to make things up on tour.

"I can't believe you're taking the Brunt's side!"

"But leaving him out of this—you really don't?"

"Look, the Underground Railroad is the one part of our country's race history that America can feel good about, proud of. We love to tell this story, right? There's a whole mythology built up around it."

"You think it's a myth?"

"I didn't say that. But it is mythologized. Or canonized, or something."

"Hm."

"I just mean why should one person, one institution, get to hold the keys to the family mythology?"

"What?"

"Or I mean the national mythology."

"Where are you getting this stuff? Have you joined a radical student group?"

"I just don't happen to believe fact is a synonym for truth."

"You have a promising future in bumper stickers."

"You're just afraid of ideas."

"I'm just not used to your espousing them."

In spite of our belligerent tones, or what might sound like belligerence to a third party, I found it exhilarating to banter like this. Ezra's mental toughness and rough edge emboldened me to aban-

don my usual limits of expression. But whether I ought to trust such
boldness, whether that meant I could safely unburden myself to him
about personal matters, the family laundry, I was less sure. Lately I'd
found myself doubting how strong he really was, how much he'd be
able to tolerate. Tough as he pretended to be, he was like a baby,
really. I was beginning to think he was easily injured. I looked over
at him on the couch now, stole a glance at his pale boyish profile.
He barely even had to shave, I thought. And this caused me quite
unexpectedly to picture Hale's jaw, and the heavy, gingery stubble
he'd allow free rein for days on end.

Abruptly, with the question of that evening still unresolved, I put
down my mug, cried, "I call the upstairs!" gathered my skirts, and
hurried to the second floor. Interpreter of the bedrooms. A minute
later, I heard the front door heave open and Meg greet a group of
visitors in her reedy voice. From another part of the house came
sounds of Ramona's group, still shuffling through the kitchen. Ezra
came softly upstairs behind me, sort of indicating with his head that
he'd slip down the back stairs to take the kitchen station, just as soon
as it was vacated. I could hear his breathing, and my own, and the
creak of his shoe and the whisper of my dress as it brushed the wall.

"What's going on?" whispered Ezra, his mouth the height of my
ear. "What's up with you?"

I shook my head helplessly. Downstairs, Meg was delivering her
introductory spiel. She was on the Fugitive Slave Act of 1850.

"What are you thinking?"

I was thinking of Hale. I said, "Today's my birthday."

"Happy birthday," said Ezra.

"There should be a word," I said suddenly, "that means both
happy and sad."

"Bittersweet."

"A better word."

"Beatrice." He said it in a passable Italian accent.

"That's actually Latin for 'bringer of joy.'"

"That's funny. My name's Latin for 'bringer of jello salad.'"

"Ha ha."

"So that's why you're moody? Depressed about aging?"

"No. That's why you should be nice to me, though."

"I'm too nice to you."

"Okay."

"I'll buy you cake tonight. At the diner."

"Okay."

"Fire in the hatch."

This last was in reference to the batch of visitors Meg had just dismissed; they were beginning to ascend to the second floor. Ezra exited down the hall, leaving me alone at the top of the stairs. I took a breath and turned to greet them with a polished mien.

IN THE END I spent the evening of my birthday with neither my parents nor Ezra. The phone was ringing when I got home from work; it was Ida, desperate for a sitter. Of course I could have turned her down, but I was grateful for the out.

By then I had grown fairly close to my little cousins. I was sitting for them, minimally, every Thursday and Sunday evening, and also saw them briefly at the beginning of Tuesday night salons. From them I had learned that Ida didn't limit her evenings out to Thursdays and Sundays; these were simply the nights my grandmother was unavailable to stay with the boys. It seemed Ida managed to get out nearly every night of the week. Still, I told her I would come. "Baby!" she said. "You're a lifesaver."

I broke the news to my mother, who replied with characteristic restraint, "If that's your choice," and called Ezra, who said, "You

suck, sucker," and pleased me by trying (in vain) to talk me into calling Ida back and reneging. My father was not around; I left my
mother the job of informing him about the change in plan. I had
just enough time to shower and change before leaving the house
again for the T.

It was about six-thirty when I set out, warm and breezy, gold
and blue, with a dusty, almost pixilated quality to the air. A splendid
evening, the longest day of the year. I felt young and old and very
alone and on the cusp of all things. I was glad not to be going to
dinner with my parents, and glad in a way, too, not to be seeing
Ezra, even though we would undoubtedly have had a good time
eating diner cake and trading clever, scathing remarks. But I was
unsettled by my earlier impulse to spill everything out to him. I
couldn't imagine the weight of my father's story not upsetting our
balance—and we were all about balance, Ezra and me. We were like
a couple of beginners trying to navigate a tightrope while also
attempting, laughingly, to knock one another off. Rightly or
wrongly, the situation with my father had made me feel the neces-
sity of pulling back from Ezra; I no longer felt light enough for our
high-wire act.

I caught the Red Line at Central Square. It shuttled through
darkness and then rose and went over the Charles, which was peri-
winkle and dotted with sailboats like so many folded handkerchiefs.
I got off at the next stop and walked to my grandmother's street,
arrived on her doorstep, clacked the lion-head knocker.

This night it seemed to take longer than usual for someone to
answer the door, and then it was both boys at once, tussling over
who'd gotten there first. It seemed Pax had, but while he was struggling to pull the heavy door open himself, Teej had pushed past and
done it. Now Pax, in a fury, punched his older brother on the arm,
and Teej shoved Pax to the ground and began to wail, clutching his

arm with more drama than I supposed was warranted. And so this was what I stepped into, out of the magical evening. I sat on the floor in the foyer with them until they stopped crying, and then I said, "You guys want to take a walk?" and they looked at me as though I'd proposed a bank heist.

"But we're in pajamas," Pax pointed out.

"That's okay. You can just put on sneakers," I told them. "It's my birthday. After your mother leaves I'll buy you an ice cream."

Ida's suitor had by then become enough of a fixture that she had introduced him to the boys. His name was Lawton Shumway; he was an attorney. He was tall, broad-shouldered, always impeccably dressed. Sometimes Ida went out to meet him someplace, but on those evenings when he picked her up at the house, he'd step inside for a few minutes, kiss her neck, say hello to me (never failing to address me by name), and produce from his pockets small presents for the boys (invariably things found at the counter of a convenience store: individually wrapped chocolate-covered cherries, horoscope scrolls, Red Sox key chains, scratch tickets), before whisking their mother away.

Tonight, however, he did not come to the house. Ida went off to him in a swirl of perfume and translucent gold trousers, and then the boys and I headed out for the ice cream shop. It took a long time to get there because Pax had to pick up every bottle cap and scrap of paper and drinking straw and bit of plastic thing he spied, and Teej had to pause to announce the make of every car. He was pretty savvy, but I liked it when there was a kind he didn't know, and he'd scrunch up his lips and think and say, gravely, "Well this one here's a Tortilla, I think. A Toyota Tortilla."

After ice cream, as we walked back to our grandmother's house, it was still light up in the sky. But it had grown dark enough down low that the streetlamps had come on, and the lights inside people's houses. Pax got tired and I had to carry him up the steep incline, his left sneaker bumping against my thigh so that later I would find pale blue bruises there.

After I'd put the boys to bed, I was standing in my grandmother's parlor perusing the bookshelves when I heard the dull anvil sound of the door knocker. Which made no sense. It was too early for Ida to be back, and she wouldn't knock in any case; she would have her key. Ditto my grandmother. The knock sounded again. Ezra, I thought. It would be like him to sleuth out the address and dazzle me with rudeness, showing up unasked. I went down the hall barefoot and swung back the heavy door.

Hale stood under the porch light with a bouquet of roses and asters and lilies in his left hand. For a split second I had the idea they were for me. I hadn't received anything for my birthday, from anyone.

Looking nonplussed, Hale glanced over my shoulder, as if someone else might be coming along. "Beatrice. I didn't realize I'd see you here."

"Ida asked me to babysit. Last-minute."

"Oh. Is Maggie—?"

"She's not here. Ida didn't say where she was." Some color even yet lingered in the sky, the long lavender dusk of summer solstice. A moth batted against the porch light and fluttered down between us. He lowered the bouquet, almost absently, so the blooms were pointing toward the ground. "Do you want to come in?"

"Maybe I should." He came through the doorway. "Maggie'd asked me for dinner. Unless I got the date wrong."

"It's the twenty-first."

"It is, right?"

"Yes." We were back in the parlor by now, having drifted there, and I was somewhat amused to see Hale take up his regular position on the far end of the couch next to my grandmother's chair, just as if this were a Tuesday night salon. "I'm sure it is," I added, "because it's my birthday."

"Today? Happy birthday. Twenty-one?"

"Twenty."

"Just twenty," he said, and sighed—not with the nostalgic sorrow people affect to show how they regret having aged; a kind of false compliment to the young person for having managed a shorter time thus far on earth—but more of a considering sigh, as though he were having to rethink a prior conclusion. He consulted his watch. "I wonder if we should be worried."

"Oh!"

"I don't know. It's unlike her. When do you expect Ida back?"

"She never says. Usually, it's Grandmother who comes home first. Tenish, ten-thirty."

"It's nine now." He stroked the side of his face. "I think I should—would you mind if I waited?" My grandmother refused to own a cell phone, and short of calling up her various friends, it seemed there was little to do for the moment besides wait for her to surface.

"No, of course not." I blushed: his question seemed unduly gracious. Although I'd managed over the past months to insinuate myself into the household, we both knew he was on much closer terms both with my grandmother and with her house. His question served almost as a reminder of how thin my own claim still was. "Maybe I could—do you want to put those in water?"

He looked at the bouquet, still upside down in his hand. "A good idea," he agreed. We went to the kitchen together, and he was the one who knew where to find a vase, though I filled it with water and trimmed the stems. I was nervous for a reason I couldn't name. Hale, whistling in such a way that I wondered whether he could be nervous, too, put on the kettle. "I'll make some tea," he said.

"Are you worried about her?" I was trying to get a bead on whether *I* ought to worry.

"A bit," he admitted. "This has never happened before. With us. On the other hand, it's not like it *never* happens, in general, people getting the days confused . . ."

"Yeah." I remembered he'd been invited for supper. "Are you hungry?"

He grinned. "I *am* pretty hungry."

So he went to the fridge, and I to the pantry, and we came up with cheese and pears and ginger snaps and sat at the great slab of a table with these.

"How are rehearsals for you?" he asked.

"Good," I lied.

On that first hot, heavy afternoon, once we'd regathered for the read-through, Hale had explained that the actor engaged to play the part of Pyramus had dropped out because of a scheduling conflict. "For today, could I prevail upon you, Maggie, to read Pyramus's lines?" he asked. My grandmother had said, "All right." She sounded game, if surprised. I was mortified.

The myth of Pyramus and Thisbe had long been fixed in my head as the quintessential romantic tale—not only was it the template for Romeo and Juliet, but it held a pivotally romantic spot within our family lore. In the story, Pyramus and Thisbe are neighbors whose parents have forbidden their love. They meet in secret on opposite sides of a common wall that joins their two families' houses, and speak to one another through a chink in that wall, until the night when they at last disobey their parents. They agree to meet beneath a mulberry tree. Thisbe arrives first, but is frightened off by a lioness. She flees, accidentally dropping her cloak as she does. The lioness, her jaws bloody from a recent kill, mouths the cloak. When Pyramus arrives soon after and finds Thisbe's garment ripped and bloodied, he believes his beloved is dead. He stabs himself with his own sword. Thisbe returns, takes in the scene, and uses the same sword to end her own life. Their blood spatters the white fruit of the mulberry tree, which forever after bears reddish purple berries.

I had been eager to throw myself into the pathos of this role. But now, to have to read love scenes with my grandmother! I wished Hale might have chosen someone else. I said nothing, however, and when we got to our first scene together, her line readings were so nimble and immediate they jolted me. It was as though she was thinking thoughts and expressing them in real time. There was something almost indecent, something profane, about my grandmother's acting. It had to do with the discrepancy between my knowledge, on the one hand, that these were only lines in a script, and my experience, on the other hand, of her voice reaching into my body. The sound waves she generated affected me viscerally. Here she was so obviously not a beautiful young man, not my forbidden love, and yet her words made my stomach quiver.

Taken by surprise, I had stammered Thisbe's lines back awkwardly, but even so they felt realer, more pared and interesting, than any lines I'd performed on the high school stage or in acting class. No matter how many centuries old the lines, the sound waves created as we uttered them back and forth were fresh-hatched, a sensory reality with their own unique force. I understood this for the first time at that rehearsal. The shock of it was beautiful and altering.

I had to admit that as an exercise it had been valuable, illuminating, to read with my grandmother. The trouble was, in the weeks since, she had continued to stand in as my scene partner. The longer I kept waiting in vain for Hale to announce he'd found a replacement for the part, the more I began to feel the victim of a practical joke. What if he decided to keep her in the role? I had the awful feeling that he'd become intrigued, watching us rehearse, by the way this particular casting choice pushed the whole notion of breaking taboos that much further.

Sitting at my grandmother's table with Hale, having just lied to him, I was disgusted to find myself in danger of tears. Hale must have read it on my face because after a moment, he said simply, "Rehearsals *not* going so well for you, then?"

And for some reason, with no more bidding than that, I began to spill out my true feelings at length, in a most un-Fisher-Hart way. I told him how I really felt about doing the scenes with my grandmother, how it both inspired and dismayed me. I told him about my mother and her strangeness around my grandmother. I told him my memory of Maynard Clinkscale's funeral, and how I'd found my normally composed mother in the pantry, sobbing, holding on to the shelves for support. I told him about my father, and the charges against him, and about collecting seed balls from the sycamore trees when I was small, and driving toy cars over my mother's forehead, and about stopping cello lessons when I was thirteen. At some point during all of this, the kettle whistled and he rose and made tea, though I was hardly aware of him doing it. I told him about the flyer calling for a boycott of my father's classes, with the initials U.A.H.C. on it, and how I'd finally put it together how that was eerily similar to H.U.A.C., my grandfather's persecutor. I told him about the Jimerson Homestead, how I'd been lying to visitors, making up stories about Constance. And I told him what I had not, until that moment, admitted even to myself: "I think about you, like, not even thinking, you're just in my head all the time, I know I shouldn't be, I know it's very stupid, but I can't stop it, it's like I just *have* you, constantly, in my head all day and all night."

Finally I was quiet, and kitchen was quiet, and my face was burning and I was looking at the table.

Hale said, "So much, Beatrice."

"I know, I mean, I know it's terrible. You're probably almost as old as my father. I know—my God, growing up in that house—Oedipus and Electra and everything, I know. I'm sure if you were looking on from outside, you could easily say, Oh, this is a classic case of . . . *whatever*."

"You mean, a person could easily dismiss your feelings as not real. As a mere syndrome. Or symptom."

"I guess, yeah."

"Why do you put me in that category?" he asked softly. "What makes you think that would be *my* reaction?"

Between us on the table, his tea smelled spicy. The kitchen clock ticked.

"Oh, *God*," I cried, "you're not even surprised. Have you known? Did you know—has it been obvious?"

His eyeglasses were pushed up on top of his head, and his eyes, a lively gray, were clear and steady. He spoke slowly. "I didn't know you were feeling this way. But it's true"—he waved a hand, as if gesturing at the words I had lain out—"I don't feel enormously surprised, just now." He smiled, then cast his eyes downward, and I thought in that swift severing of contact he revealed himself.

The phone rang. I hesitated, unsure which one of us ought to get it, then rose and picked up the receiver. It was a wall phone, with an old-fashioned rotary dial, and it felt heavy in my hand.

"Hello?"

"—Beatrice?"

"Grandmother! Yes, I'm babysitting. Hale Rubin's here, he said you had—"

"Oh good. Put him on, dear."

I handed the phone to Hale.

He said, "Maggie." Then he listened for over a minute. I actually studied the second hand on the clock. Finally he spoke again. "And what are they saying now?" He was sort of frowning at the phone. "Right . . . I'm sorry you were alone for all that . . . Is there a room number? . . . Okay, let me hang up so I can get over there." He stood and replaced the receiver in its cradle on the wall, then said to me, "Your grandmother is fine. She's with Silke, who collapsed this afternoon. They're at Mass General; I'm going to go there now."

"She collapsed? But—why? How is she?"

"Conscious. Listed as stable. Other than that, they're not sure. I guess they're still running tests. Beatrice, I'm sorry to—just leave."

"Of course, that's okay."

"Will you be all right?"

"Yeah. Yeah. Please tell Silke, you know, I hope she feels better. I hope she's okay. I'll visit her tomorrow, if that's all right."

We were walking briskly down the hallway now.

"Are you worried?" I asked him for the second time that evening.

"Well," he said. "Yeah. I'd like to learn more what's going on."

I held the door open for him. Now the sky was black, the sidewalk illuminated at intervals by streetlamps. On the front step he paused, standing sideways, appearing to give thought.

"I'm forty-eight," he said, with a rueful little smile. "In response to your earlier speculation."

Then with both hands in his pockets, he took a backward, rather dancerly step down onto the sidewalk, before turning and hurrying down the hill toward Charles Street.

TEN YEARS EARLIER, at Maynard Clinkscale's funeral, when I had found my mother sobbing in the shadows of the pantry, I had slipped quietly over the threshold, making myself share the darkness but not daring to speak or touch her. After a few seconds she had half turned and put a hand on the side of my face. Her fingers were wet. Despite the dim, I could see that her face was uneven in both color and swollenness, and I experienced a rush of anxiety that my father might ever glimpse her this way. I had the notion that we must collude to hide from him any knowledge that she could look this unattractive.

Wrestling her sobs to an end, she had said, "He wasn't *my* father," with a bitterness so biting it almost made me back up. And yet I had the sense her words weren't directed toward me. It was more as if she was using me as the audience for a soliloquy that had been going on inside her head.

Nor had I quite understood her words' meaning, or the reason for speaking them with such bile. Was it scorn at herself for allowing this degree of feeling over a man not her father, or—and this seemed graver—was it an expression of anguish that he was not hers? Inevitably, then, my thoughts had flown to my beautiful young aunt, Maynard's own daughter, as I'd last seen her in the garden: on her knees in grief, surrounded by a knot of people reaching out to stroke her wild hair, offer solace.

As if sensing that my attention had wandered, my mother had choked out another sob. "She didn't love *my* father." It was a child's complaint, thick with accusation. I studied her face again. She looked blotchy, inelegant, her mouth set in unrecognizable petulance. Her tears elicited not my sympathy but my distaste. Her hair had come partly undone from its clip; the long strands hanging loose looked for all the world like broken bow strings. I remember that I did not really want to, but I'd gone on tiptoe to tuck the loose hairs back in. And as if this was what she wanted from me, she had bent to allow it.

She'd never cried in front of me before nor had she since, until the day after my twentieth birthday.

I'd gotten home quite late the night before. Ida returned well past midnight. My grandmother had still not come back from the hospital. I'd taken a taxi home, where I'd floated upstairs and into bed feeling glass-limbed, fairly insensible with exhaustion. So it was late the next morning when I finally rose and wandered down to the kitchen, where I found my mother sitting at the table, half hidden behind a huge vase of wilting pink freesia. Between her elbows sat a tissue box; spread around her lay a harvest of used tissues. She was crying steadily, almost dispassionately, as though it had been her chore these past few hours to keep it up, to pace herself. I didn't detect any of the crackling, high-voltage loss of control that had made such an impression on me a decade earlier in my grandmother's pantry. It was instead as though she had found a comfortable rhythm, had reached a plateau of emotion and could afford to be thorough, even assiduous, in playing it out. That said, it was still only the second time I had seen my mother cry, and it took me aback.

"Mom, what happened? Is it Dad? Is it the university?" I slid onto the chair opposite her. I had on one of my father's old undershirts, which I'd slept in, and a pair of cut-off jeans I'd pulled on before coming downstairs. I raked my fingers back and forth through my scrappy locks, working out a few tangles, yanking my mind out of its Hale-reverie and into the present moment.

My mother blew her nose and said stuffily, "Silke died. Your grandmother called early this morning. Asking for *you*. She gave me the *message*." Fresh tears welled, rolled down her cheeks, and dripped copiously from her chin, but she did nothing to sop them up. Her voice stayed flat. "They determined the reason she collapsed yesterday afternoon was a small heart attack. She had another, massive one, around four this morning."

"And died?"

She nodded.

But—that can't be right, I thought, *we never got our chance to talk.* Silke was supposed to tell me more about my grandfather and his weak heart, and how it had been broken. She had been going to shed light for me on old riddles and secrets—not that she'd said this, but it had been my plan. I could tell she was fond of me; we'd been warming to each other more and more.

I sat looking dumbly at the table. Sunlight was streaming in, full of itself and lovely, turning the blond wood to honey. It illuminated, inside the glass vase of wilting freesia, a furry mold growing on the stems. I thought I could smell a bad odor coming from them. My mother sniffled and blew her nose as if exhausted. "Why are *you* so upset?" I thought to ask.

She raised her head, looked at me with hard eyes. "You think you came on the scene—you think you arrived—what, from nowhere? Like Venus on the half-shell? No mother, no history, you just— emerged? In all your splendor." She gave a dry, withering laugh. Then: "I knew Silke," she said, and that was all, but the implication was that, relative to her knowledge of the woman, *my* acquaintance with Silke barely deserved mention. She pressed her lips together; they trembled.

Ire robbed me momentarily of speech. When I did find words, they came haltingly, as I struggled not to lose control completely. "I never said I just emerged. You—that's totally unfair. You never . . . *supplied* me with . . . any history. *I* had to find my way across the river myself. I was making connections in *spite* of you. And you don't know anything about what Silke's told me."

"What did she tell you?"

This came back at me so rapidly, and with an utter change of affect, that I was again rendered speechless.

"Well?"

"She said I have the same ass as your father." And then in spite of myself I started laughing.

Across my mother's face flickered a smile—against which she seemed to be warring—but it spread and grew until she began laughing, too, helplessly, and as if it hurt. "Did she—did—did she say 'ass'?" my mother queried, barely getting the words out.

"No." My own mirth redoubled as I pictured her face, and her accent, and the mixture of shyness and satisfaction with which she'd delivered her verdict, so that my sides were heaving with laughter as I gasped out: "Caboose!"

My father came into the kitchen to find us both in fits. He smiled in the dim way he seemed generally to have about him lately. "What's funny?" he asked.

"Nothing," my mother managed to get out through her hilarity. On a shrill of laughter: "Silke died!"

My father cocked his head, looked from one of us to the other and back. He wore a look of hopeful amusement, as though at any moment he might be let in on the joke. "Who's Silke?"

"Fa . . . fa . . . fam . . . family friend!" my mother shrieked. She covered her face with her fingers, and then with a tissue, fairly dissolving with laughter.

My father's smile lingered rather pathetically while he shook his head: no, he seemed to decide regretfully, he didn't get the joke. He took a can of ginger ale from the fridge and shuffled from the room. At the sight of this—his new gait, his unprotesting defeat, his abandoning us even as we excluded him—the laughter died abruptly in my throat.

I thought of Silke as I had last seen her—just over a week ago at the salon. "I don't understand death," I said, and even as the words left my lips I was embarrassed by the idiocy of the declaration, its obviousness. It was the utterance of a little girl. But perhaps I longed for my mother to see me as a little girl just then. I do not know the extent to which it prompted what followed, but after I said it, her manner toward me softened. Her hilarity—hysteria—gone, she began, in a voice that was stripped and rough with all that crying and laughing, to volunteer a story I had never heard.

"Bebe, love"—a deep sigh—"you know, I didn't have real god-parents, but Silke was like a godmother to me. One of my earliest memories—maybe *the* earliest—is of being in my mother's dress-ing room, on Broadway or off-Broadway somewhere, and playing with Silke on the floor. There was a blanket spread out for me, by a radiator which clanked. I didn't mind the clanking, it was very cozy by the radiator. Silke was sitting on the floor with me, and we were arranging toy soldiers on the blanket, making up stories about them. We made them have a picnic, and we colored the food on paper and cut it out and arranged it on the blanket. It was blue and green and yellow. Silke must have done the cutting. I was about three."

"Where was Grandmother?"

"On stage." My mother slid her finger down the hourglass side of the vase. The flowers were definitely emanating something rank. I wondered whether she was noticing the fur growing on the stems of the wilting freesia. But her eyes seemed not to take it in. "After I came to Boston to live, I saw Silke much less often. I don't know, a couple of times a year, I guess. Tops. In New York, I saw her every day. We moved in with her, into her little apartment, after my father died, I don't know if you knew that. And even after we got our own place, Mother and I, she took care of me a lot of the time. Silke, I mean. Mother would have—not only rehearsals and performances and things, but she would go out a lot, too. Socially."

I felt the last word dangle, not with bitterness but with rue. It made my mind go to Ida, and the delicately perfumed zephyr on which she would sail off into the summer evening with her suitor. Always, then, I'd experience a moment of palpable silence, or absence, really. That moment after the door had closed behind her, leaving me and the boys in the relative dimness of the front hall. I brought my bare legs up onto the chair and wrapped my arms around them.

"Were the soldiers lead?" I asked.

"What?"

"The toy soldiers."

"I don't know. They were little, metal. They might have been lead. I remember they nestled in their own wooden box. Why do you ask?"

"They were your father's."

"What are you talking about?"

"I know the soldiers you mean. Paxton and T.J. play with them. They live in a wooden box on Grandmother's mantel, and on the bottom it says N. FISHER, BERLIN, 1929."

"That's incredible." She sucked in a breath. "I didn't know."

"What?"

"Anything. That they were his. That they were from Germany. That she still had them."

It was the first time it ever occurred to me that my mother's understanding of her own history might be impoverished. I was so accustomed to thinking of her as the withholder of information.

"They should be mine," she said. She gathered all the used tissues, wadded them up in one hand. "They're mine."

"Pax adores them," I said, not to contradict her, but because I couldn't help it. The soldiers' meaning, for me, was so tied up in the mileage he got out of them. "You should hear him," I began, smiling. "He knows every lit—"

"They're mine," she repeated flatly, though it was unlike her to interrupt. She balled the tissues more tightly in her hands. "Listen. I was fourteen when my mother remarried. I wasn't invited to the wedding—they had a civil ceremony, at City Hall. Then they told me and my grandparents, after it was done. They had a big dinner in a fancy restaurant for all their friends, a couple of weeks later. They invited us, but my grandparents didn't go. I think they refused. So they put me on a train to New York by myself. Silke met me at Grand Central Station, and we went right to the restaurant, to the party. Someplace in the West Fifties. I had my suitcase in my hand."

The sun slipped between branches of the crab apple tree and struck her full in the face. She grimaced and angled her chair. The smell of decaying flowers was powerful.

"I was really shy, really angry, and completely starstruck. By my own mother, even. She was gorgeous, Maynard was gorgeous, it was this roomful of gorgeous, elegant, crazy theater people, and I was this tall, slouching teenager from Boston, in a long-sleeved brown velveteen dress. Jesus. It had an empire waist. My grandmother and I went shopping especially for the occasion." She shook her head over the apparently unexpected memory of that dress.

"Anyway. I don't know what made Silke do it. She might have been tipsy. It might have been a kind of misplaced act of solidarity. Although she loved Maynard, too. Everyone did. I don't know. But at some point during the party, she came and sat beside me, and she told me that my father didn't really kill himself because his name appeared in *Red Channels*."

"What's that?"

"It was like being blacklisted. His suicide happened just a few days after his name got added to the list. That was supposedly the reason he checked himself into the hotel and swallowed all the pills. But Silke told me that wasn't really why. She said it was because my mother had told him she was going to leave him."

I noticed she had lowered her voice as the story went on, although there was no one else in the room.

"She benefited from it, you see."

"No, I don't see."

"His suicide. It helped her career. She'd been going to leave him anyway, and his death came like a bonus. She got this tragic-heroic status, the bereaved widow of a principled man. And at the same time she was safe from being linked too directly, too uncomfortably to Communism. She was cleansed and elevated. In one fell swoop."

I didn't know what to say. The shock of my mother's spontaneously divulging all this required nearly as much processing as did the conclusions she had reached. I rose, carried the flowers to the garbage, dumped them out, and ran hot water into the vase. I let it overflow for several seconds before shutting the tap. I turned back to face my mother. "Do you mean to say she wanted him to kill himself? My *God,* Mom." I didn't know which seemed more shocking in the moment: that my mother could believe such evil, or that my grandmother could have committed it.

"No . . . I don't mean she *encouraged* him to do it. But she must have felt—freed by it. It was a perfect solution for her. She must have been . . . glad . . . secretly grateful."

"Did Silke say as much?"

"No."

"Well, do you blame her for it? Do you hold her responsible?"

"Who? For what?"

"Grandmother. For his death."

Another long sigh. She shook her head and looked out the window, where tent caterpillars had spun their thick webs into the forks of the crab apple tree. "There are many things," she said obscurely. "Too many things. It wouldn't be fair to burden you." And she gath-

ered up all the used tissues and threw them away and said nothing
more on the subject.

This was the mother I knew.

MANY YEARS EARLIER, back in middle school, before the violin girl accused my father, before I'd had to give up the cello, I'd
been in a recital.

Even though, as I have said, I had by this time in my cello-
playing career become somewhat resistant to practicing, the truth
is that I was excited for this event. I had been chosen by the music
teacher for a special honor: to participate in the chamber music
portion of the recital, which included two violins, a viola, and me.
Of all the cellists in middle school, the teacher had picked me. In
fact, sometimes when I think about the circumstances around my
giving up the cello, I suspect a bit of Fisher-Hart family spin might
have been applied to the story about my dwindling interest in
studying music. Sometimes I think I went along with that story in
spite of a real desire to keep playing.

At any rate, on the evening of the recital, only my father sat in
the audience. I could see from the stage that he was alone. Afterward, in the hallway of the school, he explained to me that my
mother had had to meet with a patient. I knew she hadn't had any
scheduled appointments that evening, and was furious. It was an
emergency session, my father said. I was still furious; I didn't believe
any emergency could justify her absence from my recital. When we
got home, I was horrible to her, cold and imperious and unforgiv-
ing. Such was my anger that my mother did something she would
never ordinarily have done: she discussed details of the case with
me. She explained that she was treating a young woman whose
father had just killed himself.

In my anger, I must have retorted with a dismissive crack.

I remember my mother's face drew absolutely taut then; before my eyes it became a plaster casting of her face. She said, controlling her voice so that it sounded as though she were reading from a textbook, that the suicide of a parent inflicts irreparable harm on a child, is a trauma from which a child may never fully recover. It inflicts hopelessness and despair. Because it is a form of abandonment that annihilates the possibility of resolution.

Her voice was a terrible thing, lacerating.

There I stood in my long, black concert skirt, my hair pulled back like hers in honor of the evening—pulled back in a borrowed clip of hers, in fact—hating her absolutely.

It was my father who stepped in then and made the peace, laying a hand on my mother's head and stroking, with great tenderness, the length of her hair, while saying to me cajolingly, "Go look in the kitchen, Bebe. Your mother got you something special, to celebrate."

And on the counter I'd found an exquisite cake, which I recognized as being from our favorite upscale bakery over in Brookline. Its chocolate glacé icing was smooth as silk, and on top, molded in white chocolate, was a cello.

SILKE'S MEMORIAL SERVICE was planned for the end of that week, on Saturday afternoon. I was scheduled to work, but informed the Brunt I would have to leave early that day. It started out overcast; by lunchtime it was pouring rain. The tour schedule was sluggish as a result. Even in the windowless crypt we could hear the rain. Ezra, miserable with a summer cold, sat hunched, breathing through his mouth, over the mug of instant soup he held in both hands.

"Why don't you eat some?" I suggested, coming to sit beside him on the couch.

He shook his head rather pathetically. "I just like how it's keeping my hands warm."

"You should go home."

He closed his eyes, shook his head. "I need the money."

"Well, at least take these." I held forward the aspirin I'd dug out of the crypt's little medicine cupboard, and he accepted them feebly, washing them down with the glass of water I'd also brought.

Certainly he was overplaying it. Nevertheless, I found myself catering to him out of what I was sure was an unwarranted but overwhelming sense of guilt. Things had turned rotten between us that week.

I had heard his invitation to go out on my birthday as a casual suggestion, impromptu and offhand. But the next day he called and asked whether he could take me out that night, instead. I demurred, citing Silke's death. He persisted, saying in that case, could he drop by the house briefly, since there was something he wanted to give me? An hour later he'd shown up on the doorstep with a flat box wrapped in dark blue paper and tied with a length of purple grosgrain ribbon. It contained a silver bracelet etched with vines and berries. "It's beautiful," I'd said, my stomach twirling confusedly: where was the irony in this gift? Why was he giving me jewelry?

"I got it because they kind of look like mulberries," he'd explained, in all earnestness, and with a kind of poorly concealed pride at having selected something so perfect. I had recently filled him in all about Pyramus and Thisbe and the bloodstained fruit of the mulberry tree. Standing on the doorstep squinting in the bright sunlight, his smile had been uncharacteristically shy. He looked freshly showered, too, and was wearing a clean shirt with a collar.

"Oh," I'd responded, in a terrible lukewarm way, as his hopes and intentions suddenly came into focus. How stupid of me, I hadn't seen this coming.

"Happy birthday, Beatrice."

"Thanks. I—I better go." I'd hurried to close the door, cringing at his blunder, or my blunder, whoever's it was.

All those months I had believed we were both happy with the platonic nature of our relationship. Sure, there'd been some chemistry, a little tantalizing edge to our friendship, but it hadn't seemed either of us wanted to take it any further. To think I had misread him was disturbing. Worse was the thought that *he* had misread *me*, as seemed evident from his sullenness the next few days at work. He treated me as though I'd been unfaithful to him, or a tease. It was as if he were holding me accountable for something I'd never done, never intended to convey. But in the absence of any outright accusation, I couldn't defend myself, couldn't do anything except tiptoe around being overly solicitous, until I was behaving exactly as though I were, indeed, responsible for some grievous offense. The knowledge that I *had* been on the verge of unburdening myself to him—if we'd gone out the night of my birthday, I surely would have told him about all the terrible charges against my father, inevitably deepening the intimacy between us—only made me feel more culpable.

As Ezra took the aspirin and drained the glass of water, I looked down at the faded green folds of my antebellum skirt, guiltily awash in relief that such an evening had never occurred. But glancing up at his profile then as he swallowed, his Adam's apple pressing tight against the collar of his period shirt, his dark lashes lighting for an instant on his pale cheek as he closed his eyes, I committed what seemed an illicit act: I imagined that we had gone out as agreed, and that he might have touched or kissed me, even professed love. Something about our both being in costume lent this fleeting fantasy a banal, syrupy falseness. Blushing, I looked back at my lap, as stricken as though he could tell what I'd been up to in my mind. A sour weight seemed to spread through my body.

He held the empty glass back out toward me, with a congested, self-pitying snuffle. I kept my hands in my lap. "Forget it, Ezra. I quit. I'm not your maidservant, or your nurse."

He looked at me in surprise, hangdog and heavy-lidded. "Two stock characters in porn films, by the way."

"You're acting like I did you some wrong. It's bullshit. You're acting all freaking *aggrieved*."

He took a beat. "It must really be hard being a girl and having to deal with all those hormones and mood swings all the time."

"It must really suck being an asshole and knowing you treat your friends like shit." I was surprised by my vehemence, the great, reckless anger that seemed to have sprung up full-grown from nowhere.

It must have surprised Ezra, too: he lifted an eyebrow, which caused him to look momentarily rakish, even through the fog of his cold. The words came huskily stinging out of his mouth. "You're a sorry little poseur bitch if you think *I* treat *you* like shit."

"But you have been," I insisted, after a moment's honest consideration. "You've been acting like I did something to you, and I've been walking around *letting* you, I've just been obligingly *acting* like the guilty party, and I will not do it, I'm telling you now. I'm not going to go along with that story."

"You were cold," he said, but now his voice was stripped of bitterness. It was flat and defeated. "You were so totally cold on Wednesday, when I came over. You didn't even ask me in."

"Silke had just *died*!"

"You didn't even ask me in. I was so . . . I was really excited to see you"—he said it softly, a confession—"to see you at your house, and see your reaction to the—the bracelet."

"God Almighty." I leaned my head back heavily against the top of the couch. The ceiling dangled cobwebs and, here and there, gray clinging clumps of dust. I felt pinned under the weight of my own plight, but also Ezra's now, as I imagined how it must have felt for him that afternoon, as he'd stood there all showered in his clean shirt and hadn't even gotten past my doorstep. I'd been caught up in grieving for Silke; that wasn't a lie. But it wasn't the whole truth, and it wasn't what had kept me from receiving Ezra. I was caught up in love and longing for someone else, someone infinitely vaster than this boy, someone who might actually be big enough to bear the weight of me and my terrible, cumbersome family history. That was the real explanation, but it wasn't one I could very well offer Ezra.

I thought of Hale as he had been the last time I saw him, stepping magically backwards off my grandmother's doorstep, hands deep in his pockets, buoyant as the breeze in the moment before gravity delivered him to the sidewalk. "I'm forty-eight," he'd revealed, such beautiful words, because I'd known, I'd understood, by the bemused squint in his eye and the flush on his neck, that it was also a way of saying, *I think I could love you.*

Ezra spoke quite flatly in the direction of his shoes. "You don't want to be with me."

I turned to him in exasperation, feeling once more guilty and at the same time falsely accused. It was a trapped feeling, and baffling: how could a person be simultaneously innocent and culpable? "You're the only person, practically, I've even wanted to be friends with this whole year!"

"No. What I'm saying is, you don't want to *be with* me."

Of course I had known that's what he meant. I *was* a little poseur bitch. "Oh. *With* you with you. I—no. I'm sorry."

He sighed—it was almost a laugh—and rested his head back where mine had been a minute earlier.

"Do you want me to return the bracelet?"

"No, just—shut up—just—don't mention it, ever. And just—don't blame me if I hate you for a little while."

"Okay," I agreed. Perhaps I would be cleansed by his hatred, and then we could be friends again. "Like, for how long?"

He shook his head, eyes closed.

"I'm just asking, do you have any idea? A week? Two?"

A sigh. "You are a pushy broad."

He sounded half serious, but I wasn't too unhappy about that. It sounded like the beginning of my penance and therefore the hastening of his forgiveness. I felt some relief, as though we'd gotten through the worst of it and were already on the mend. Then I wanted to say, *I love you,* but obviously that would have been the wrong thing, so I thought of saying something else, something that would contain my gratitude and affection without offering any unintended promises, but I couldn't think of anything that would safely accomplish this. I thought of, *My father has been charged with sexual harassment,* or *My grandmother profited from driving her husband to suicide,* or *My mother is a world-class enabler so full of resentment she can barely breathe,* or, *I'm in love with a man as old as my dad,* something that would expose me as terribly as he had exposed himself when he'd stood on the doorstep with his hopeful grin and his dark scruff of hair still damp from the shower. But I didn't say anything, except when the intercom buzzed, and then I said, even though Ezra was up next, "I'll take it," and bounded up the crypt stairs, the clack of my boots on cement even louder than the rain, and unlatched the Homestead's front door in time to greet the next batch of visitors.

I DIDN'T REALLY miss Silke until after the memorial service. Only once my mother had dropped me off (she said she'd look for a parking space), and I had let myself into my grandmother's front hall, where I stood wondering what to do with my dripping umbrella—for there were already so many of these spilling out of the stand and piled in a heap along the wall—did it hit me that Silke was not there to greet me. She was not going to materialize in a moment and ask me to accompany her to the kitchen, and she was not going to set me to the task of climbing up on the counters to seek things out in high cupboards. Not until then did I even realize how much of a custom this had become, for her and me to be there early in the kitchen every Tuesday evening, deciding which things to set out in the shallow wooden bowls that week. Silke would stand in the center of the kitchen, hands on hips, feet apart, hat tilted back, looking for all the world like a little old cross-dressing Germanic Peter Pan, and command, "Dig in the back! Try to find some of those seaweed rice crackers. And that chocolate-hazelnut spread—my favorite. Look behind the soup. No, no, behind *Der, was ist das? Yah, yah,* tomatoes. Your grandmother likes hiding from us the good stuff, eh? We gotta outsmart her, you and me." Of course, it was all make-believe; my grandmother was pleased for us to put out whatever we could find. I half suspected Silke of burying certain delicacies in the back herself, in order to make a game of rooting them out with me later on.

I was lost in this reverie when John came up and kissed me. "Your grandmother asked me to move a bunch of these out back," he explained, stooping to gather a wet armload of umbrellas.

"Oh, okay." It was strange to see him in a tie. Taking his words as an invitation, I knelt to gather up a half dozen more and followed him down the hall and out the garden door, where we tossed them onto a bench. Then John ran his fingers through his hair, glanced at me, glanced over his shoulder into the bustling beehive of a kitchen, and withdrew a single cigarette from his shirt pocket. He lit it, exhaled a long spume of smoke, and shrugged at me. "Javier would have my hide."

I nodded.

He held out the cigarette.

"No, thanks," I said. We stood in companionable silence.

I thought of my mother as she was at this moment, circling and criss-crossing the neighborhood in the old Saab, navigating all the impossible one-ways and dead ends in search of a parking space. Wipers going, headlights on, roads slick. She had worn a black shirt with three-quarter length sleeves to the service, and I could picture her with both hands on the wheel, her bare forearms strong and untanned, the undersides as smooth and pale as the inside of an almond. I had timed leaving work too close; by the time I'd gotten off the bus I was already running late. Despite my half running home and scrambling to change as fast as I could, my mother and I had arrived at the memorial service just after it began; we'd taken a couple of the only remaining empty seats, in the back, where we had not encountered anyone we knew. Even as we sat down, an elderly man I did not recognize was introducing my grandmother to give the eulogy. She had risen and turned to face the assembled mourners.

I had not had an interaction with her since my mother's kitchen-table revelations. During the past weeks of rehearsal, uncomfortable as I was at the thought of playing Thisbe to my grandmother's Pyramus, I had also been more drawn to her, and had felt more admitted *by* her, than ever. Her talent as an actress seemed to transcend the stage; the qualities it contained—intimacy, immediacy, truthfulness, being alert to the moment and to the presence of another—were the mark of a great human, the mark of someone who is good not only at acting but at *life*. I'd believed there was love growing between us.

Now, everything my mother had divulged seemed to threaten

that. Had Margaret Fourcey really built a career on the ashes of her first husband? He had written her signature role. She had played it and left him—or would have, if he hadn't relieved her of the need by killing himself. And for the rest of her days she had reaped the glory of being associated with his perceived martyrdom; reaped the benefits of being disassociated from his radical politics; and all the while she'd enjoyed herself with a new husband and daughter, discarding the old daughter as surely as she'd shrugged off the inconvenience of the old husband. Was that the true story? Which was Maggie Fourcey's greater asset: skill at lying, or skill at truthtelling?

Now in the garden John put out his cigarette on the heel of his shoe, wrapped it in a leaf he plucked from the wisteria, and slipped it into his pocket. He looked at me and gave a funny, small smile, then stepped out from under the terra-cotta roof and began tapping out a soft-shoe, airy as angel food cake, on the wet granite. "Come, Bea!" he prompted, holding out a hand. I smiled and shook my head. John shrugged and closed his eyes, his face tilted up toward the sky, dancing around the garden. As he circled back, his soft-shoe sent tiny sprays of water up from the patio bricks. "Beatrice!" he commanded, again extending his hand.

I stepped out of my sandals and crossed to him, followed him over watery stones. When I smiled, rain came inside my mouth. I placed my hand in his open palm, and he caught me around the waist and began to waltz me along the circular path. I had never in my life waltzed, and I was laughing.

"What charming children." We turned toward the voice: Javier's. He stood regarding us with a mixture of reproach and affection from under the terra-cotta tiles.

I felt a flurry of contrition: we'd been caught being naughty! But John laughed delightedly, and strode toward his partner. I trailed along.

"Baby," John said as he reached the little patio, and he leaned his sodden face forward to kiss Javier's cheek.

"Oh no you don't." Javier leaned back lithely and held up a single restraining finger.

"Dance with me," beseeched John. He gave a tiny bow and extended his hand as he'd done earlier to me. Water dripped from his eyebrows onto his prominent cheekbones. His grin was enormous, a slice of watermelon.

"Very becoming, this behavior. Very becoming. And at a funeral," chided Javier. "Tsk tsk tsk. What shall I do with him, Beatrice, eh?"

I smiled and raised my shoulders, though Javier continued to look only at John.

"Silke," John retorted, "wouldn't give two figs. Silke's beaming down on us right now."

"Most probably," Javier allowed. Then they kissed, very tenderly, and I was embarrassed and went back inside. Only once I was among all the dry people did I realize how drenched I was, inappropriately so, and I ducked into the boys' room to hide myself. A bath towel had been left draped across Maynard's old easy chair. I used it to pat dry my arms and legs, rub at my hair. There was a black metal fan on Maynard's old desk. I switched it on and stood with it blowing on my stomach. After a bit I rotated and let it blow on my back. I was standing this way when my grandmother came in.

"Beatrice."

"Oh."

"I didn't realize you were here."

"I'm sorry, I just came in to—"

"Not here in the room, I mean here in the house. I saw you at the service, but I didn't know you'd come to the house." She shut the door behind her, sat on the bed, removed her shoes, straightened the covers a little, and lay back against the pillows.

"Do you want privacy? I'm sorry." I started toward the door.

"Don't go."

I halted.

"Your mother won't set foot inside my house," she stated. "I saw her with you at the service."

"She's just looking for parking," I explained, but even as the words left my mouth I realized a fair amount of time had passed. It did indeed appear she'd changed her mind and gone home. How funny that my grandmother seemed to know what had happened before it had even hit me.

"Silke forgave me."

I knew it was not a non sequitur. It was a thread, and I seized it. "Forgave you for what?"

But my grandmother had closed her eyes as if in pain. This was not the time to press. She looked old. Her crepey neck, her blue-veined ankles. Her lips were pressed together hard, radiating vertical lines. Her skin gleamed with perspiration, and I went over and angled the desk fan so that it would blow across the foot of the bed. She didn't speak or open her eyes. I thought she might be crying, in a way, behind her eyelids and shuttered face.

"Grandmother. I'm going to leave you to rest." I hesitated. "Is there anything I can bring you?"

"Hale." She did not open her eyes.

"Okay." I closed the door gently behind me.

The house was somewhat less packed than it had been earlier. I went down the hallway, peeked into the kitchen. Someone had propped open the garden door, and the rain beat a musical tattoo that filled the room. More people sat and stood smoking now out on the patio. I could see Ida's curly head out there, leaning against Lawton Shumway's broad shoulder.

The parlor seemed to have been staked out by the young and

beautiful set, people in their late teens and early twenties, and although I was no older, I found their presence trying. Who were they and how could they have possibly known Silke? Were they relatives? Or the children of old friends? It bothered me that they should have appropriated what I thought of as the territory of our salon, in which they were taking no pains to hide the fact that they were not mourners but partiers. They were rather chic and lively, bonded in the manner of young people at a gathering dominated by elders. Through the parlor was a little solarium, and I decided to check in there.

"Excuse me," I said, to a couple standing in front of the door.

The girl, whose blue-black hair angled to frame her narrow face, studied me curiously over the top of her plastic wineglass. "Are you Margaret Fourcey's granddaughter?" There was a pointedness to the way she asked it that made me for some reason wary.

"Yes."

"I thought so. Keeley Tate," she said, holding out her hand. "You have a part in Hale's new play, don't you?"

"Yes." I shook her hand, which was slim and wiry.

"*What's* your name?" Her voice went up at the end, as though she ought to have known it but couldn't quite recall.

"Beatrice."

"That's right."

All this while we were still shaking hands. I was torn between pleasure at being recognized (as an actress, no less!), and irritation at being delayed—not to mention self-consciousness over my wet dress, which I could see her discreetly appraising. Our hands slipped apart.

"Hale's my father," she explained.

My first thought was that she had spoken in error. I hadn't known Hale to be married, currently or ever. Not, of course, that paternity required marriage. But this girl, this young woman—I guessed she was a few years older than I—bore no physical resemblance to him that I could see. Besides, the idea of her being his daughter seemed to usurp, violently, the place I'd projected for myself in his life. It was disturbing to think of her, this Keeley person, with her severe, faultless haircut and fine, sharp chin, having a prior and much greater claim, a history complete with filial intimacy.

"Nice to meet you." The flatness of my tone might be ascribed to the solemnity of the occasion. "Is he in there?" I pointed at the solarium door.

Keeley raised her eyebrows. She stood a little shorter than I, though she wore heels and I was barefoot. "I don't think so. I haven't seen him since we arrived, practically. And Warren and I have been standing here for what, fifteen minutes?" she asked the young man, who spilled crumbs from his plate as he consulted his watch.

"About that," he concurred.

"I'll check for you," she offered, and this riled me, too, that she would presume to put herself in the role of interlocutor. She knocked on the door with two knuckles, looked at me as she cocked her head for a response, and, not hearing one, tried the knob. It turned. Within the privacy of this tiny, abundantly windowed room, awash in pearly gray daylight, almost hidden by the array of pots with their spreading profusions of leaf and vine, two men conversed in white wicker chairs. I recognized the one facing us as the elderly man who'd introduced my grandmother at the service. The other turned around at the sound of the door; this was Hale. I took obscure satisfaction in the fact that Keeley had not known his whereabouts. The smile that grazed his lips was qualified, and went through some minor transformations as he took in first the black-haired girl, then me in the doorway behind her.

"Sorry!" she said brightly. "Didn't realize you were in here. Hm, what's this room?" Glancing around pertly at the flora and the great vertical lengths of rain-speckled glass. "Beatrice was looking for you."

"Grandmother," I said quietly, as discreetly as possible, "is asking for you."

Hale rose from his chair. The older gentleman began to get up as well, with effort; Hale offered his arm. "I'm sorry to cut this short, Jacob," he said.

"Not at all. Not at all. I've been indulging my memories," said the other. "Or rather, you have been indulging me!" On his feet, he smiled rather sweetly, pulled a cloth handkerchief from his pocket, and wiped his neck, first one side, then the other. It was a humid little room.

"Thank you again. It's really been good to see you." Hale clasped the man's shoulder and they steered a path out of the solarium, Keeley and me backing up to make room. As the white-haired man made his way out of the parlor, Hale turned to me and asked quietly, as though matching my discretion, "Where is she?"

I was reluctant to talk in front of Keeley. She was tilting her chin up at Hale with a kind of tensed charm, as though waiting to be filled in on the mysterious conference that had been taking place in the solarium. But he did not see it, or did not reveal that he saw it, and she, with a little shrug, tossed her black hair and drifted back over to the rugbyish fellow. I waited until she was reengaged in conversation before I murmured, "Maynard's study." I expected Hale to head off solo then. But he turned to me and indicated with the smallest of gestures that I was to accompany him. Out in the hall, he asked, "She all right?"

"I don't know. I guess she seems worn."

He nodded. We were moving down the corridor slowly. He said, "There hasn't been a time for us to talk."

Blood rushed to my neck and face. "I know."

Then I waited for him to go on, my every molecule an antenna for what he might say next. But he said nothing next, so that I wondered whether I had heard him correctly, or misunderstood his meaning. When he'd spoken, I'd understood him to be referring to us, to him and me, and the time since our talk at my grandmother's kitchen table. But in the absence of elaboration, I tried to think whether his comment could have been about him and that older man, or my grandmother, or Keeley, or anyone, really, anybody else but me.

"I didn't know you had a daughter," I said. What I really meant was, *I didn't know that no one, not even you, is guiltless when it comes to keeping secret histories.* That wasn't fair, of course, since I could hardly accuse Hale of having *kept* this from me; after all, who was I to him?

Hale stopped walking. He tilted his head at me, frowning slightly. "I don't."

"But the girl—"

He cut me off with a sigh. "Keeley's not my daughter. Did she tell you that? I was married to her mother, briefly. About twenty years ago. So I was her stepfather for a short time."

"Oh." Two sensations swept through me concurrently. One was relief. The other was embarrassment. I had been born about twenty years ago. The thought of infant me, wet and mewling, coming into the world just as Hale was taking a woman to wife, felt awkward. I wanted to ask why Keeley was here then; had she known Silke; had her mother known Silke; was her mother here, too? But I had no right to grill him. I bit the inside of my lip.

Hale's glance left my face and flickered down the length of me to travel back up, slowly, in critical, tallying fashion. He regarded my bare feet, with blades of grass still stuck to them, and the bits of dried mud specking my shins, and my blue dress all wet against me, and then my face again. He said nothing, but asked with a look, *What happened to you?*

"John and I were waltzing in the garden. He said Silke would approve."

Hale smiled, not really at me, but as if he was smiling at the conjured image of John and me in the garden, and at what John had said. It was, again, a qualified smile, his lips closed, as though he were locating something tiny, a poppy seed perhaps, between his front teeth. Much later I would come to associate that look—characterized by the faintest crinkling around the eyes, and by the fact that behind his lips you could tell he was lining up his front teeth, feeling their edges touch—with a kind of cherishing contemplation of the minute and ineffable. It was a way of pausing to consider, a way of honoring, even, something so small and indescribable as to lie not only beyond speech but also, ordinarily, beyond a person's conscious notice. My parents, of course, were skillful noticers as well, but had a tendency to mark what they noticed with speech, and somehow also, inescapably, with judgment. In Hale, the sense of *taking things in* was not compounded by further analysis or evaluation. With him, the act of bearing witness seemed to exist in its own right, for its own sake.

We resumed walking down the hall until we stood outside the door to the study. Hale paused there and squinted at a wall sconce, seeming to weigh his thoughts before he spoke. When he did, it was nothing about Keeley, and nothing about the unexplored subject of him and me. "By the way," he said, "some good news. Looks like I've found a Pyramus. And, Bea. I guess there's no reason not to tell you this also: that was Jacob Freundlich back there, the man in the sunroom. A very old friend of Silke's. I haven't—obviously!—had a chance to tell anyone else yet, but he is offering us a place to do the show, out in the Berkshires. A performance space as well as living accommodations. Any objection if we move rehearsals out there for the rest of the summer?"

"Objection?"

"Would you be free to relocate?"

"Yes."

He nodded. And entered the room where my grandmother lay, closing the door softly behind him.

I WAS IN A HURRY to get home and announce the news of my imminent departure. This was momentous, not only because, at twenty, I had never lived anywhere else than under my parents' roof. It also meant that I would be making good on my goal of moving out into the world as a legitimate actress, and just before the time allotted by my parents ran out. Even though there was no indication of being paid a salary, to earn room and board through stage-craft was no small accomplishment. I imagined the accolades my parents would offer when I divulged the news. As sweet, I imagined their disguised chagrin.

I took the T home, and arrived a little past six to find the screen door closed as usual, but the front door beyond it gaping open. My first thought was that my father might finally be fixing the broken doorknob, but when I tested it, it came out easily in my hand. I slid it back in. Against the wall leaned two unfamiliar umbrellas: one of those ubiquitous collapsible black ones and the other fancier, lime green, with a wicker handle. A smooth male voice from within sounded like the lawyer, Allan Watanabe. But if it was he, what of the other strange umbrella? Had he brought a second attorney along with him? That seemed a grim sign. I sidled over toward the pocket doors, which had been drawn nearly shut. Through the slit I could make out my father, sitting on the taffy-colored leather armchair, bent forward, his elbows resting on his knees, listening intently, almost earnestly; he looked less like himself than like one of his students. Also, he looked in need of a haircut and shave.

Peering through the slit from another angle, I confirmed my earlier guess: Allan Watanabe was indeed sitting comfortably at the roll-top desk. An ankle rested on the opposing knee. He looked breezily gallant in a marigold sports shirt and olive green trousers. A tall glass of what looked like iced tea sat untouched on a coaster beside him. I couldn't determine the content of his speech, as a couple of window fans were blowing loudly. Angle myself as I might, I was also unable to make out anyone else in the room, neither another attorney nor my mother. I was just wondering whether she could, in fact, still be on Beacon Hill, trolling for a parking space, when her voice rang out from behind: "Bebe, whatever are you skulking around for?" and it was as though she'd bested me again, in a game we'd been playing my whole life.

I straightened and turned. She'd pulled a fast costume change. Gone were her funeral clothes, the black blouse and skirt. Now she wore a lavender jumper and white blouse and descended the staircase as a handsome woman of leisure on a beautiful summer evening. Although she did wear a crease between her brows. Also coming down the stairs was a woman about her age, no one I recognized, made up and accessorized in a way that suggested she was neither friend nor colleague. This woman carried a clipboard and pen. She projected an air that managed to be both bureaucratic and deferential, and I was confused; it seemed unlikely she was here in the capacity of co-attorney, but who was she?

"My daughter," my mother explained to her. And to me, "Mrs. Ellefsen." And with no further elaboration, she led—hustled?—the other woman toward the kitchen, saying, "The stairs to the basement are right through here."

It was the night at the Pudding all over again, when my plan to unveil news had been preempted by my father's breakdown. Only now my proclamation was being upstaged not by one arcane parental drama but two. I had half a mind to go upstairs, pack a suitcase, and leave. Never mind the practical hitch in this plan, that I had no place to go *to* just yet. The theatrics of it appealed. Also—this part I see in retrospect—it would have been a way of communicating to my parents *in kind*. A way of forcing them to experience what it was like for me to be kept in the dark, then roughly jarred by a moment of crisis, and only later offered an accounting—a partial, stinting one—of what had precipitated the event.

After a moment's hesitation, during which I ran through a few possibilities (stay at my grandmother's? at Ezra's? at Hale's?), curiosity won out. That and a new recourse to candor. Not the old "winning candor," the calibrated, circumspect version I'd been so pleased with myself for selecting back when I first attempted to insinuate myself in my grandmother's salon. What the hell. I had a foot out the door, and a house coming down around my ears. I could afford real candor, blunt and fearless—or more accurately, I had little to lose by it. I thought of Silke crying out triumphantly, "In the caboose!" I thought of her assertion, indecorous and emphatic, that my grandfather had died of a broken heart. I thought of the guttural sound she would have made if she thought I was going to use her death as reason to resign myself to not speaking, not inquiring, not knowing. Until, bolstered by all of this, I pried open the pocket doors, strode into the living room, and plunked down on the couch.

Allan Watanabe and my father looked so identically nonplussed I nearly laughed out loud. The lawyer, who had broken off midsentence when I barged in, flashed me a polite smile, glanced at my father questioningly, and took momentary refuge in sipping his iced tea. A leaf, frozen in an ice cube, floated around in it: my mother's unmistakable touch. She grew her own mint, and during the summer months would always devote one ice cube tray to this purpose. My father's earnest attention, which he had been directing to the lawyer, faltered as he gazed at me and was replaced by a stricken look, ashen and full of rue. Then over this he managed a thin layer of cheer. "Bebe! Hello, sweetheart. Uh, this is Allan Watanabe, our attorney. Allan, my daughter."

"We met," I said.

"Nice to see you again," he said.

"How do things look?" I knew my tone was brazen.

He laughed appreciatively, as though he found nothing so charming. "I'll let your dad fill you in."

"He won't, though."

"Bebe, please," my father chided.

"Really, he won't," I told Allan Watanabe. "I realize you probably have attorney-client privilege or something, but I am his daughter and I am twenty, and I think I have a right to know. So if you won't fill me in, I guess I should just track down the woman who's made the complaint and ask her to tell me. Or should I say the women who have made the complaints?" I gave the final *s* extra sibilance.

Allan shot a sharp glance at my father, then cleared his throat and spoke evenly to me. "The worst thing you could do for your father would be to establish contact with the plaintiff."

"Then I guess you better hope I care." I looked at my father when I said that. I had a train-wreck-y feeling, was scaring myself, but couldn't stop. The fear, though sickening, was mingled with elation.

I could sense Alan Watanabe looking at my father, expecting him to say something, and for that moment I, too, ached for him to respond, to reproach, make clear he would not tolerate my disrespect. But my father was peering down at his fingers, interlaced between his knees, as intently as though contemplating the Gordian knot.

The lawyer slid some papers into his briefcase and shut the clasps. He rose and spoke with surprising gentleness. "Jeremy. I'll call you tomorrow."

"Thanks, Allan." My father, still looking down, shook his head slowly.

The lawyer touched his shoulder. "Good night."

Their rapport shamed me. I understood that I had misfired; this was not Silke's brand of candor, but something entirely more bratty. I understood Mr. Watanabe must think very ill of me, and this made me even more sorry, because the truth is he seemed like an intelligent and admirable person. Worse, I realized that my behavior, although prompted by a desire for everyone's cards to be laid on the table at last, could hardly have encouraged my father in this direction. There seemed, however, no way to undo the damage. Even if I'd wanted to retract my implied threat, I'm not sure I could have mustered the energy to break through the iciness that had clamped down inside me.

Allan Watanabe left the room without further acknowledgment of my existence, disregarding me as completely as if I were a scrap of evidence that had been declared inadmissible at trial. A moment later came the sound of the screen door closing. I said nothing. I was feeling lethal, thinking with some terror about what I might say next, and with even greater terror about the possibility that I would not be able to choke a single word past my frozen throat, when my father glanced up at last from his fingers, trotted out a ghost of a smile for me, let it die on his face, then stood and walked from the room.

The clarity of his action stunned me. He could not have communicated any more precisely his abdication of the role *father*. When he walked out on me without a word, an offer, a fight—it seemed a confession of the worst failure, of not only his guilt but also his impotence and defeat. A grave chill took hold in my body, and as it did I had the impression of something else moving out—I don't know what to call it, not *warmth* or *innocence* or *trust,* exactly—but the sense of something vital being physically displaced by that chill was quite real to me, and I was beyond grief.

Sometime later I heard voices in the hall, my mother bidding the clipboard woman farewell, the screen door opening and hinging shut again, then the heavy front door being closed and the deadbolt locked into place. My mother pushed the pocket doors all the way back open, a corrective motion, setting things to right. She slid out of her shoes and crossed the room, now crosshatched with evening shadow, in order to shut off the fans. Only then, as she turned to head out, did she notice me sitting there and give a start.

"Oh, Bebe!" She put a hand on her chest. "For pity's sake!" She sounded breathless, as though she'd been caught red-handed. "I'm sorry I didn't come in the house earlier, after the funeral."

I said nothing.

"When I dropped you off, I really did mean to come in as soon as I could find a space. But the more I drove around, looking, the more impossible it seemed." I wasn't sure what she meant by "it"—finding a space, or coming inside her mother's house. "I tried calling you, to let you know at least not to expect me, but the phone just rang and rang; I couldn't get a person."

Still I said nothing.

She paused and sat on the edge of the ottoman that went with my father's leather chair. With the fans off, the evening song of birds and insects came freely through the window screens. "I wouldn't have been able to come in for long, in any case. Since I had to keep an appointment."

"You don't see patients on Saturdays."

"Not with a patient. The woman I introduced you to, Mrs. Ellefsen. She's a real estate broker." Her voice was the softest thing in the world, like warm milk, or new grass, or baby hair. That voice must be very effective with her patients, I thought. They must relax at the sound of it, gravitate toward the safety of its source. "We are putting the house on the market."

"Is Dad fired?"

"—No. We're settling his case. Part of the settlement involves his resignation." Her voice, in contrast with the news it brought, offered profound solace. I wanted to let myself be lulled by it. But I was determined we should speak truth to one another.

"So then he's fired."

She chose her words carefully, something she was expert at doing. "He won't be affiliated with the university any longer. But he won't lose his license. Mr. Watanabe is helping us determine the possible options around maintaining a private practice. It appears it may help to relocate."

"Relocate?"

"Out of state. Maine and New Hampshire are possibilities."

"It's such exquisite timing!" I cried, the blood rushing to my temples. "Because I'm moving out."

She shook her head. "Sorry?" The fading light behind her grew grayer by the second. It was like light reflected in a pot lid, opaque, nearly useless. I strained to make out her face, which receded every moment further into shadow. The brightest thing about her was one bare shoulder, opalescent in the dull light. She was bent toward me; her hair in its clip had swung forward and fanned out across the other shoulder. She looked young. Maybe when I was born she looked like that. Bare-shouldered, round-shouldered, less sure of her rightness, less vertical. "Oh, Bebe, that isn't—please don't think that you need to—or that you should—"

"But I really am. I am anyway. Hale Rubin's taking us, the whole ensemble, we got offered a place in western Mass."

A bird was calling from someone else's yard, its short song stirring and sweet.

A time passed.

"I'm *sorry,*" my mother said then.

"I don't know what that means," I replied, but I do not think I said it unkindly.

THREE

The Farm

QUITTING MY JOB at the Homestead was an undeniable pleasure. Saying goodbye to Ezra was harder. When I went down the steps into the crypt I found him not reclining on the couch, brooding over a book, nor nursing his cold in bleak fashion over a mug of herb tea, but on his feet, cheerful, healthy, and trading quips with two other guides: Meg, looking uncharacteristically lit from within, and Vivica, a relatively new hire who was now flashing bewitching dimples. When he saw me in my street clothes, Ezra tossed me a casual nod and a hello, as if I were just another worker, and went on charming the pair of girls in their hooped skirts. So I had to stand there waiting patiently, and then, when it became clear Ezra had no plans to acknowledge me any further, I had to say, "Excuse me," and then, "Sorry, but Ezra, can I see you for a minute outside?"

He followed me woodenly up out of the crypt and through the back door into the kitchen yard. I'd never been with him before when one of us was in costume and the other in street clothes, and it was displacing. Normally we were almost equal in height, but with me in sneakers and Ezra in boots, he stood a trifle taller, and I had to squint a bit, looking up at his face with the sunlight behind him. I told him I was leaving town, and why, and he nodded with dead eyes and said, "Fine."

"Ezra. You're the best friend I've had all year. I would've been totally lonely without you. Don't be an idiot."

"You're the idiot, Con."

"Why am I the idiot?"

A tour spilled out through the back door, a half dozen white people wearing shorts, cameras dangling around their necks. Ramona, their guide, followed and began describing the sort of work that would have been done in the various outbuildings. Ezra grabbed my wrist and steered us swiftly toward the privacy of the icehouse; rough as he was, I was grateful, because it seemed an important concession. Once inside, he shut the heavy wooden door, immediately plunging us into cool and pungent semidarkness.

"You're an idiot," he explained flatly, "for expecting me not to feel hurt."

That was fair, I thought. But my crime was one of thoughtlessness, not malice; I wanted that established, at least. "I never conned you, though. Nicknames aside. I didn't, Ezra."

"It feels like you did."

"I never, never meant—"

"I didn't say you *meant* to," he spat. "It doesn't matter what you meant. It *feels* like you did."

I scowled. I was glad we were in the icehouse, in the dark and the cool. No ice got stored here anymore, of course, but there was still the large pit dug out in the center of the structure, filled with insulating hay, which gave the air its sweet and homely odor. What Ezra said worried me beyond the scope of him and me—the whole idea of injury not requiring intent. Why wouldn't he just tell me he didn't hold me responsible for his feelings? What could I do to get him to say that, to absolve me? I felt as if I were in a jail from which only he could release me, by renouncing the notion of my guilt.

For a moment, then, I was united in compassion with everyone who might suffer under a burden of perceived culpability—which is to say that I wondered whether my father felt jailed, too, desperate for the warden—his former supervisee—to grant him a reprieve. And my grandmother, despite her insistence that Silke had forgiven her: did a part of her nevertheless remain imprisoned? And if so, who was it that held the key, my mother?

I felt helpless to convince Ezra of my innocence. And I didn't see how I could leave—the icehouse, him, Boston—without first obtaining such a release.

"I told you I was going to hate you for a while," he reminded me.

"You didn't mean real hate." I stated rather than asked it. "You are my *friend*. I want you to come and visit me. I want you to come out when we do the show. Will you?"

"Maybe."

"No maybe."

I felt, more than saw, him smile at this.

"Quoth you," he said. "You're a wily bitch."

"You should curse less," I said, and gave him a shove that caught him off guard, sending him backwards into the cold pit. There was the muffled crash of him landing in the hay.

"That was pretty good," he conceded in a low voice.

I loved him greatly then. How relieved I was to have been given absolution, even if I'd had to wrestle it from him. Flecks of hay whisked up into the air. They made my nose itch. I flung open the icehouse door and light streamed in and showed Ezra, blinking and grinning, sitting up and brushing golden dried bits out of his dark, ruffed hair.

Saying goodbye to my parents proved undoable.

Sunday morning after Silke's memorial service I went into the atticky part of the attic, took the largest suitcase I could find, and packed everything of mine I could fit inside it. I could not have supplied any justification for such rash behavior. True, as it turned out, arrangements for relocating the cast moved quickly; the first group of us would head out later that week. But I didn't know that would happen when I awoke that morning, and even if I had, there was no reason I couldn't have passed the next four days at my parents' house. I packed and left impulsively, even before securing my grandmother's permission to stay at her house, which is where I wound up that night.

Nor did I plan to leave without saying goodbye. It just—happened. While I packed, I could hear my parents moving around in other parts of the house, and I imagined running into at least one of them on my way out. After I had hung up my towel and opened my curtains and made my bed, I gave a last glance around my room. The bright orange U.A.H.C. flyer, still hidden in plain view among various books and papers on my desk, happened to catch my eye. And I thought of a gesture that might accomplish what I had not been able to the night before—that is, put the truth on the table without resorting to meanness.

I folded the incriminating flyer in thirds, tucked it discreetly inside an envelope, and carried it and my suitcase downstairs, not taking any great care to prevent the latter from bumping down the steps. I envisioned the noise might bring at least one parent into the hall, and that my parting act would be to surrender the envelope, thereby communicating that I'd known more than they had been willing to tell me, but was not inclined to use this information spitefully. However, I got through the front door without either parent intercepting me. I stood there on the step, the sunshine warm on my head, at a loss—shaken, really, at the prospect of leaving my parents' house without saying goodbye. But by then I felt I had to go through with it, so I closed the door behind me, sticking the knob back on when it came off in my hand. Then I bent over, put the envelope through the mail slot, and heaved my suitcase down the steps.

I SPENT THREE of the subsequent four nights under my grandmother's roof. The fourth, I spent at Hale's.

It was the Wednesday after Silke's funeral gathering, the day before the first batch of actors was due to head out to Jacob Freundlich's Farm. I wasn't leaving until Friday, because there was room in Ida's car for me and she wasn't going until then. At any rate, I was alone in my grandmother's house, listless, bored, in limbo. It was late afternoon, and dim inside, because the shades were pulled to keep out the heat. My grandmother was out somewhere; I did not know when to expect her back. Ida and Lawton Shumway had taken the boys down to the Public Garden for a Swan Boat ride; I had been invited, but felt my presence was not really wanted—it was to be the boys' farewell outing with their mother's suitor. But as the hours went by, and no one returned, I found myself drifting about the rooms uncomfortably. I had never been all alone in that house before.

My grandmother had been really wonderful, kind and generous, when I'd materialized on her doorstep Sunday with my fat suitcase in tow. She'd struck me as being fairly robed in sadness, and surely she could see that all was not well with me, either; perhaps apprehension of our mutual suffering softened the barrier between us, because she hadn't asked many questions about my sudden appearance, insisting only that I call my parents so they wouldn't worry. I called at an hour when I knew they would not pick up, and left word on the machine. The boys, already excited at the prospect of going to spend the summer on a farm, were that much more tickled to have me move in with them for several days beforehand, and treated my presence like that of the first guest to arrive for a long-awaited party.

But on this afternoon, with everyone out, I found myself afflicted with that particular strain of restlessness that comes from the total absence of anyone wanting or needing or expecting anything of you, indeed, of people not even knowing where to find you if they did. Of course the latter was not literally true, but such a small handful of people knew my whereabouts, and it was the first time in my life I'd ever existed in the kind of anonymity that comes with such displacement. I was feeling fundamentally off-kilter. I wandered into the parlor, my temporary bedroom, with my suitcase stowed discreetly behind the couch.

I opened the wooden box on the mantel. The lead soldiers, wounded and well alike, had been tucked away with infinite care, as usual, by Pax: all lined up in neat rows. I latched the lid again and turned the box over, ran my finger over the gouged markings, blocky and dark with age: N. FISHER, BERLIN, 1929. My mother had been right to say the box and its contents were hers. I regretted having told her how much the boys enjoyed playing with the soldiers. I knew of nothing she owned that had belonged to her father. I thought of her at home, in the kitchen at this hour, drinking iced tea, perhaps, and reading a journal article, or turning the pages of a cookbook. The radio on low, tuned to classical. As I imagined it, she had already acclimated herself to my absence, just as she seemed to have lost no time acclimating herself, and then applying the full force of her considerable managerial skills, to selling the family house. Of course, that was her specialty: coping impressively with loss.

I picked up the phone and dialed. If she had answered, I don't know what I would have said. I half think I might have gone home to her then, the box of lead soldiers under my arm. The telephone rang and rang. No one picked up, not even the machine.

Then the loneliness of being in my grandmother's empty house became unbearable, and I dialed another number, not one I knew by heart, not one I had any history dialing. I found it penciled in my grandmother's curling, elegant hand among a list of numbers written on the inside front cover of the address book next to the phone. Hale answered before the second ring.

"It's Beatrice," I said. We spoke a few sentences and he invited me over.

He was only over on Marlborough Street. His place was small, comfortable, cluttered. We sat on the couch and drank tall, sweaty glasses of juice. At first, in my nervousness, I was overcome by the same soporific, druggy feeling that had afflicted me in the hallway of his office building, a kind of trancelike impression that none of it was really real. I felt out of my skin, distanced from myself, not Bea, nor Beatrice, nor Bebe, nor Thisbe, nor Constance. I had on black jeans and a tank top the color of coffee ice cream and pink flip-flops, which I kept sliding on and off. I also kept running my fingers through my short pale hair, still damp from the walk over.

We played chess, which helped. I was not a big chess player, but when he went to the bathroom, I spotted the set on his shelves, and had laid out the pieces by the time he came back. It smelled good. The white pieces were poplar, and the red, cedar. I arranged the board so that he was white. When he came back, Hale acknowledged what I'd done with a tilt of his head and a smile. He sat down and word-lessly moved his first pawn. He won four games in ten minutes, each lasting no more than five moves, until I was beside myself with a kind of vexed elation—and somehow simultaneously knocked back into myself, so that I was no longer regarding from a distance the poor lovelorn girl on the theater director's couch; I was me, Bea, with Hale, in the moment.

"How do you *do* that?" I cried.

He laughed and taught me the queen's gambit.

At some point we noticed it had grown dark. Hale turned on lamps and ordered Thai. I shed my flip-flops once and for all, and sat cross-legged on the couch to eat. We drank ice water. The brittle, translucent tails of shrimp accumulated in a small pile on top of the newspapers on his coffee table.

"I think there's jazz on the esplanade tonight," he mentioned. "If you want to take a walk later."

"Sure."

But we never made it out of the apartment.

After eating, Hale gathered up our takeout containers and brought them to the can in the alley. I did the few dishes in his little galley kitchen, which had a window that looked onto the living room. I did them as slowly as I could, touching his things with voracious mindfulness. He came back inside and put on a flamenco album—through the cutout window, I watched him slide it from the paper sleeve, place it on his old-fashioned turntable, lower the needle onto the groove. I wiped my hands on his dish towel, then filled the empty ice cube tray sitting by the sink. When I put it in the freezer, I saw he had a big piece of driftwood sitting on top of the fridge. It was at least three feet long, gnarled and sun-bleached. The sight made me absurdly happy. I was so happy! And sad in equal measure. It was the suffering of knowing that I could do nothing to prolong this feeling forever.

We talked till late.

He told me just a little about Keeley's mother. She had been an actress. He said she'd been "very troubled," that now she lived in Belize, that he had helped Keeley out with college. I assumed he meant financially.

I told him how my father had been forced to resign, that my parents were selling our house, that I didn't know where they would end up.

"How long have you lived there?" he asked.

"Always."

When next I looked, his expression was inscrutable. I didn't know if this was what he was thinking, but I suddenly became self-conscious about the fact that my "always" was laughable beside his. Or not laughable—Hale would never laugh at another person's experience; I knew that even then—but paltry.

"Did you ever know my grandfather?" I asked, perhaps wishing to remind him that in spite of my youth, I had lineage, a history long and complicated enough to make me interesting to him.

He shook his head and his eyes crinkled. "I was still an untutor'd youth in Poughkeepsie when he died."

"Really?"

He laughed. "Really."

"No, but I mean—really, you're from Poughkeepsie?"

He laughed again, more of a roar this time, and although I didn't quite get the joke, I felt pleased with myself for having amused him.

The record we'd been listening to ended but continued to spin, emitting a scratchy whisper.

"When I first laid eyes on you," said Hale, "I thought you were going to be trouble."

From the way he said it, I wasn't sure whether he meant to imply how far off that early impression had been, or that it was now confirmed. I met his gaze steadily.

"I thought you meant to make trouble for Maggie," he said. "No. I guess I didn't think you meant to. I just thought you were bound to."

I continued to meet his gaze. I felt suspended by it, as though I were dangling over an abyss and our eye contact was the thread keeping me from falling. For some reason, my mind went to the great twisted length of driftwood I'd seen in the kitchen. I could take only shallow breaths.

"I think I was projecting Keeley-stuff onto you," Hale went on. "Unfairly." He was regarding me intently, his head, his whole body, perfectly still. "I am glad I met you." A banal phrase, but the way he said it, it was not banal; it was a delicately considered confession.

The record went round and round, producing no music. It sounded like tires going through a puddle.

I said, "I don't think I can kiss you."

"I don't think I can kiss you," he agreed.

I was crushed and relieved and aroused.

We found an old black-and-white movie on TV, and I fell asleep sometime during it, awaking several hours later fully dressed and alone on his couch in the viscous gray light of predawn. I let myself out and walked back to my grandmother's, discovering by degree, as I covered the deserted handful of blocks, that all the unruly happiness was still intact within me.

JACOB FREUNDLICH'S FARM was an idyll. Sprawled between an untended apple orchard and a dammed-up stream, it comprised a barn that had been converted into a theater, a stable that had been converted into a dormitory, and a farmhouse that appeared to have been little interfered with since the mid-twentieth century. Beyond the farm rose a gently cleft hill, and beyond this spread the luxurious sky, smoky with lilac-dusk when we arrived there on Friday, the second day of July.

My head prickled strangely as Ida, the boys, and I came rumbling up the rutted dirt lane in Ida's secondhand station wagon. The feeling intensified when I got out of the car and turned around, smelling the air, spotting the barn where we would perform, and the pine trees ringing the meadow. This had to be the place, I thought excitedly, where I'd seen my grandmother perform all those years ago! That single night from my childhood had made such a lasting impression: my grandmother's wit, the audience's delight, the flashes of sky blue silk as she spun around in her marvelous cape. To think I'd come full circle, arrived back on this spot, only this time I would be acting alongside her on that very stage. As soon as my grandmother came out of the farmhouse to greet us, I asked her about it and she confirmed my guess: this was indeed the place.

She filled me in on the history of the Farm. Jacob Freundlich, who'd been an old friend of Silke's, and of Neil Fisher's, for that matter, had bought the property from an alfalfa and apple farmer in the 1970s. He converted it into a kind of extremely off-Broadway venue, and it had served as a great petri dish for the avant-garde for many years. Then it got sort of reinvented in the eighties, when, for several summers in a row, an exhaustive supply of movie stars would traipse out from Hollywood for a few weeks at a time and perform in this or that improbable vehicle, while their entourages and hangers-on, the journalists and paparazzi, pitched tents, literally, in the surrounding fields. Eventually the Farm fell into financial straits and by the late nineties was in disrepair and finally disuse. The theater had been dark, the property unoccupied, for three years when Hale first began talking with Jacob Freundlich about starting things up again.

After Ida, the boys, and I had unloaded the car, my grandmother led us into the kitchen, where we found a dozen people still lingering after dinner. Several of the group had come the day before, but from the comfortable way they inhabited the space it was as

though they'd been here a month. Hale was there, and the woman
with the gray braid, Gracie, and also John and Randy, who was the
guy playing Cupid, and the married couple whose names were
Hendrik and Jean. Last, I saw Maeve, the sylphlike woman I'd
noticed at our first read-through. I'd felt jealous of her that day;
she'd seemed to be taking the ingénue spot I envisioned for myself.
But in the subsequent weeks of rehearsals back in Cambridge, I had
grown, begrudgingly at first and then more freely, to like and
admire her. Now she greeted us all and informed me that she and I
were to be roommates for the summer; she promised to take me to
the room we'd been assigned, in the old stable that had been made
into a dormitory, in a little while.

Everyone was sprawled on a few rough-hewn benches at an
impressively long, weathered table, which made my grandmother's
great slab of a table back in her Beacon Hill kitchen look petite,
and which now bore the remnants of a communal dinner. Some
French bread and a little dish of blueberries were all that was left
by the time our carload arrived, and although we'd stopped for
burgers on the Pike, the boys pounced upon these scraps as if they
were ravenous.

I'd been reeling over the discovery that this was the very place
where I'd seen my grandmother perform so many years ago, but
from the moment I entered the kitchen, although I managed to
greet the others normally, my attention was occupied almost exclusively with Hale and with the considerable effort of neutralizing
any outward sign of this fact. Not that I was trying to hide my feelings from him (which would in any case have been closing the barn
door after the horse), but I did think it prudent to hide them from
the others in the ensemble, my grandmother chief among them.
Not only prudent, I thought it requisite.

This was hardly surprising, considering the only precedent I had for affections (if that is the word) between an older, venerated man, and a much younger woman with something like apprentice status within the field. How could I help but see this, see us, against the scaffolding my father had built? As lovely as our evening of chess-and-Thai had been, how could I help but believe that if I were to refer to it publicly, it would bring shame to and bear consequences for Hale? I would never traffic in orange flyers, but I feared the least sign of acknowledgment from me might amount to such. I would rather err in the opposite extreme; silence and denial seemed to be in order.

So I was thrown when, just after I'd found a perch on a wooden step stool tucked into a corner of the kitchen, Hale leaned way back on the bench, holding on to the table to keep from falling over backwards, singled me out with a smile and said, "Hello, Bea," in a voice full of warmth and tinged with amusement, not caring a jot who noticed.

WE SPENT THAT first weekend at the Farm largely on our knees. We scrubbed floors, scoured tubs, made up beds (ten of them in the house, another seven in the stable), washed windows, dusted, disinfected, and picked flowers: chicory and purple clover and wild lilies.

Maeve and I were great roommates. Our room was tiny—literally an old horse's stall that had been appointed with two cots and two dressers. Given such close proximity, we fell into a kind of intimacy that felt like sisters or cousins. She was five years older than I, and laughed at herself easily. She'd blurt random minor confessions that revealed her to be perfectly, ploddingly human, and then she would redden (her complexion hid nothing), and dissolve in helpless chortles. The very helplessness of her laughter was what made it so endearing.

She'd ask me questions about my job at the Homestead, and I was interested to notice how fascinated she seemed, how dreamy-eyed it made her to hear about my costume and role as a historical interpreter. She wanted to hear all about us, my mother and father, Ida and the boys, Maynard and my grandmother. If my own knowledge of most of the family was rather impoverished, I tried not to let it show. And if I fell back on some of my Homestead habits, embellishing here and there, perhaps I might be forgiven. I'd tell her stories about us all, and Maeve would sigh and say, "What a *family!*" And in the wistfulness of her tone, in the falseness of my own portrayal, I realized at last how lonely I was, how lonely I must have been all along, for the idea of family contained in the way I described us to her.

If I had grown up within the estimable gleam of a qualified kind of family radiance, generated by our highly exclusive assemblage of three, a certain dullness had always clouded the picture, an insularity that canceled out real intimacy. Mine was the lonesomeness of a princess in a tower, me in my attic bedroom, watching the patients, like poor subjects, trod over the peastone path, coming and going in an endless procession while I stood at my window, level with the treetops, buoyed by the prideful mythology of a father and mother who bore the power to heal. I only now understood that I wanted a family that was not simply admirable, but thick and layered, full of misunderstanding and connection, warmth and mess. I only now understood it because only now, on the Farm, did I glimpse such a thing was possible.

On the farmhouse's front porch in the evenings, all of us sitting around a few citronella candles, my grandmother herself could sometimes be prevailed upon to tell anecdotes about the Farm's early years, and then I could feel every one of the ensemble pressing forward to hear her, to drink in not only her stories, it seemed, but the luxury of being associated with their characters and with this place. I would look around at us at such times; it was truly wondrous to me, how we were a bunch of strangers who had knit together into a kind of family. We'd all be rather dirty at the end of the day, barefoot, in torn jeans and things, swatting mosquitoes, peaceful.

In the stories she told about those first few summers out here, my grandmother would have been in her mid-forties: a wife and mother; a Broadway star with a tragic past and an untouchable reputation (reviews even of her few flops would single her out for approbation); a flouter of racial barriers and a fearless spokesperson for liberal causes; an actress with enough clout to get critics from the *New York Times* schlepping out to the lesser shires of western Mass. I tried to picture her as she'd been then. Photos from the period showed her long-haired, loose-limbed, wearing the gauzy skirts and patterned head scarves of the time.

My own mother had just turned forty-nine, but it was hard to imagine Margaret Fourcey and Sarah Fisher-Hart being anything like each other at that—or any—age. There was my mother, sedate and refined, with a tendency to steel herself inwardly in her assumption of too many burdens and secrets. I thought of her as she was at that precise moment in her life: adjusting to a daughter who'd just flown the nest, a husband who'd just fallen from the pedestal he'd long occupied, and a house that had been crumbling around her and which she was now relinquishing altogether.

From the distance of the Farm, over a hundred miles away, it felt possible to *regard* my mother. Living with her, I'd been too preoccupied with my own symptoms, the chafing and suffocating of which I had become increasingly aware and resentful. So that toward the end, living with her had been like driving in the car with her, stuck in traffic on Storrow Drive. It was as though I'd been seated smack beside her but unable, in my own misery, to bring myself to turn my head in order to take her in and imagine her position, her plight. Fury and fear overtook me if I tried. Now, from the calm cradle of the Berkshire mountains, I could think of her and feel pity, and also, sometimes, just sad.

CHORUS	Gracie, Jean, Hendrik
DAPHNE	Ida
APOLLO	John
PSYCHE	Maeve
CUPID	Randy
THISBE	Bea
PYRAMUS	Kaliq
EURYDICE	Margaret
ORPHEUS	Phil

A cast list went up outside the barn. Although we had been in rehearsal a few weeks already back in Cambridge, Hale had continued to try various people in different roles, and the final distribution of parts had not been made firm. Then in the move to the Farm some shuffling of actors had occurred. We lost some along the way, and picked up a couple of new ones. So the posting of the cast list felt momentous, and contained some surprises. I of course was thrilled to see a name, in ink, of the actor who would be my Pyramus—I had yet to meet him; the last two actors to join the cast would be coming by train from New York. John, it turned out, really had lobbied Hale to play Daphne in drag, but seemed happy enough to take on the god of music instead. My grandmother gracefully accepted the assignment of Eurydice, which the smallest of all the main parts. What came as the biggest surprise to everyone, including Maeve, who had been engaged for the lesser part of one of Psyche's sisters, was that she had been bumped up to the role of Psyche herself (the original actress having a commitment in Boston that could not be left). I experienced a fleeting spark of jealousy over this.

For all that Maeve seemed jealous of my lineage, I envied her her honest route to this production. And I found the account of her odyssey as fascinating as she had found my descriptions of working at the Homestead. Originally from suburban Connecticut, she'd graduated from Emerson College with a degree in drama, then plunged herself into performing in everything she could, taking any role in any production, no matter how pitiful, she claimed. In five years she'd racked up acting credentials in and out of Boston proper, Cambridge, Somerville, Newburyport, Providence, Worcester, Northampton, Truro, New Haven, Portsmouth, Brattleboro, "why, even in Vacationland," she'd say, with goofy self-deprecation, "as it says on the license plates in Ogunquit, Maine."

For all her dismissiveness, she hadn't failed to draw notice. She must have had some roles substantial enough to sink her teeth into. Hale Rubin himself had caught her performance in a play the previous summer, and had been impressed enough that he remembered her a year later, when casting the current project.

"So he came to you?" I asked.

"Mm."

"How? Did he just call you up out of the blue?"

"Yes, and my voice got all high and breathy, it was terrible. I was so embarrassed. I lied! I told him I'd just run up a flight of stairs." She laughed at the memory, and it was her signature laugh, which had a way of bubbling out as if in spite of her, and lent her a look of surprise even as she submitted to the cascades of mirth. As I laughed along I couldn't help marveling at her lively face, freckled and heart-shaped. I had to admit she'd been well cast as the "surpassingly beautiful" Psyche. It gave me a little pang to think this was not lost on Hale.

We were asked to assemble in the barn after breakfast on Monday. Already the sun was drying the dew on the long grass outside, but the barn's interior remained chilly at that hour, and the dim of it was lovely and airy and bluish white; it made me think of sailing ships, even though I had never sailed. Something about being in the Berkshires, at Jacob Freundlich's Farm, had made me susceptible to associations I wouldn't have made back in Cambridge. Even after only my first weekend at the place, some kind of change seemed to be at work. I don't know whether it had to do with the mountains, the firs, the color and shape of the clouds, the cry of loons at night, and of owls—or whether it was occasioned more by a shift in my internal landscape. I only know that I felt, pleasurably, and at the same time with some agitation, that I was milling about in a great untried broth of possibility and play. Uprooted and aloft. Everything was different out here. The quality of light . . . the smell of damp wood and earth in the stable . . . the sound of the grasses as you walked wetly through them on your way to the farmhouse kitchen . . . the drowsy morning interactions once you got there . . . the banged-up enameled mugs from which we drank strong coffee.

I had my hands cupped around one of these mugs that first Monday morning when we gathered in the barn, in the first few rows of the old pews that had been salvaged from a country church, and now served as audience seating. Surveying the group curiously, I spotted two unfamiliar men. Hale introduced them as Kaliq and Phil, the late additions to the cast. They'd taken the train up from Grand Central the night before; Hendrik had met them at the station, close to an hour's drive across the state line on county roads; they'd gotten in well past midnight and were valiant in joining us so early this morning, Hale announced. I of course had a vested interest in Kaliq, my Pyramus, and checked him out as discreetly as I could. He looked thirtyish and aloof.

We got down to business. The stage manager, a wiry gray-haired woman named Barb, made lots of announcements. A weekly rehearsal schedule would get posted on the door of the barn, and a duplicate copy in the farmhouse kitchen, where we should look also for a k.p. schedule, as everyone would be required to take turns shopping, cooking, and cleaning up after meals. Daily updates to the rehearsal schedule would be posted by nine each morning, and we were asked not to make other plans or leave the Farm until we had consulted this and made sure we weren't needed.

The absence of a single complaint throughout any of this, even of a nonverbal, atmospheric complaint, was notable. It seemed a powerful indication of how much everyone had come here out of the deepest and most selfless desire to *participate*. As I had been back in Cambridge, at our first read-through in the mini-lecture hall, I was quite struck by it, and by what I assumed to be its rarity. But while the previous time my feeling on the matter was chiefly disappointment—the general air of compliance, of being willing to forgo any promise of glamour, had seemed to me a mark of this production's inauthenticity—now I felt lifted by it, in solidarity with it. Barb sat there on the back of the pew like a wizened old drill sergeant, her hands folded on her clipboard, warming to her subject as she detailed the nitty gritty of our k.p. duties (". . . the disposal *will* back up if you try to put anything hard, like watermelon rind, or a stub of raw carrot, down it . . ."), and all around me, the actors and singers and crew sat and drank it in with sanguine, even rapt, expressions—really, there was a *happy* feeling in the barn. It was as though our purpose in being here was enhanced by—even dovetailed with—the menial labors Barb was detailing.

And then I had a clear inkling—it was the first time such a concept had ever occurred to me—of how making theater could be a form of doing service. How acting might be considered serving. And I thought back to my grandmother's and my March meeting in the tea shop, when I'd sat with my wet cold toes curled up inside my pumps and proudly delivered my line about being "an instrument of beauty," and it was apparent to me now how absurdly, utterly self-serving had been my use of that phrase. A glittering rush of Maeve-ish laughter at my own foolhardiness rose in my throat, and I had to cough several times, rather loudly, in order to avoid unleashing inappropriate giggles.

Around me in the barn, I could feel people taking notice. Barb stopped talking.

"Could be the hay," speculated someone, which made the laughter swell more dangerously.

"You okay?" whispered Maeve, beside me.

I nodded and managed to look up with a sober expression, only to find Barb eyeing me with a mixture of ennui and suspicion, as though she had pegged me for an attention-grabber. "Sorry." I smothered a new smile.

She went on at some length, and I relaxed against the back of the pew, smelling the cool of the barn, registering the minute sounds of the birds outside, letting myself feel the whole, luxurious weight of being one among this number.

WHATEVER NASCENT ROMANTIC pairings might have been developing (and given so many people, of a theatrical bent, thrust into close quarters with one another, it would seem only logical to expect a few), they remained, so far, in the wings, peripheral to the general conviviality of life on the Farm. Privately, Maeve had confessed an interest in Kaliq, which I found odd, since he was the person with whom I felt least at ease. Of course, as Thisbe, I had special reason to be shy of him. And he was not actually aloof, as I'd first thought, only self-possessed, a little reserved in a way that made me wonder if he was somewhat skeptical about the whole scene out at the Farm.

If I hadn't know about Lawton Shumway, I might have sworn something more than friendship was kindling between Ida and Randy, but if this was so, they conducted themselves with enough discretion to keep everyone guessing. Javier came out to spend some weekends with John, but as he was teaching a summer playwriting seminar in Cambridge, could not stay longer. Besides, they were already a couple, and so didn't count as intrigue. The same held true for Hendrik and Jean. So there was very little coupleness in the mix; it was really a familial feeling more than anything else that characterized our interactions and proceedings.

My feelings about Hale I had told no one but Hale. I was unambivalent about this. Oh, well, that one time, when Maeve had whispered to me about Kaliq as she and I lay in our cots side by side, well past midnight, in our former horse's stall, the tremulous excitement in her voice heightened by the knowledge that Kaliq himself might be lying at that moment in his own cot just down the other end of the stable—fleetingly then, I might have been tempted to reciprocate. But for the most part, I had no urge to spread word of my passions. Generally, people confess the object of their love when they suppose doing so might bring them closer to attaining that object, whether closer in practical terms or closer spiritually, simply through the act of sharing the information, of doubling the idea's potency by having another, sympathetic, person entertain the fantasy simultaneously.

But I think in my case I knew that I could only endanger the fantasy by revealing it. I couldn't expect anyone, not even Maeve, compassionate as she was, to endorse the idea of Hale and me as a couple, with him forty-eight and me twenty, him so accomplished and important and sought after and me so green and unproven and lacking in any virtue except the ubiquitously cited, yet utterly dubious, virtue of youth. If Silke had been alive, she might have been the one person I would have told. Anyway, when I was with Hale, I didn't feel anguish over the impossibility of our coming together. I felt improbably peaceful, unhurried, and content.

The problem was that I was rarely with him except when we were rehearsing. He and Barb naturally had the busiest rehearsal schedules of anyone, and were therefore less a part of the burgeoning family dynamics than the rest of us. They were sort of the mom and pop, home for supper with the children every evening, while the rest of us were the wild and plentiful siblings, weaving our own capers and dramas together throughout the day. But even this limitation—the fact that we spent so little time together that wasn't work time—might not have been a problem if rehearsals of Kaliq's and my scenes had not been going so badly.

As it was, they were dismal. I knew this to be true not only by my own estimation, but Kaliq's and Hale's as well, based on the former's brewing frustration and the latter's air of polite, perplexed concern. And while neither of them seemed to hold me responsible for what was going wrong, it seemed more than obvious that if there was a weak link, I was it, and I grew increasingly anxious about being sacked from the production, or if not from the entire production, then from that role. This was something I did confide to Maeve.

It made me a bit sick to say it out loud, because for days I'd been adopting the strategy of trying to pretend away the problem. I'd show up for rehearsals with a concertedly cheerful air, go through all the motions with as much confidence as I could muster, listen earnestly to Hale's notes, remember and reproduce everything—blocking, inflection, timing—to perfection. I was strenuous in my effort not to betray doubt, in hopes that he would be persuaded that the scene would come, that it would blossom accordingly, in time, with more practice. But the pretense was taking its toll. The more I fell in love with being at the Farm—sharing meals, chores, strolls, night frolics in the Pond, staying up late on the porch, wrapped in sweaters as the night brought its chill, everyone's faces flickering in candlelight, Hendrik and Kaliq strumming their guitars, the older folk reminiscing, the younger ones trading flirtations, Hale never saying much but providing a constant, somewhat inscrutable, but emphatically appealing center of gravity—the more all of this grew to mean to me, the more I dreaded exile. Until one night, on the verge of tears, I confessed my fears to Maeve.

"Hale wouldn't have cast you if he didn't think you were able to do the part," she consoled me. We were lying on our cots, whispering. I could see her fairly well, even though we'd turned out the light. There was a window between our cots, curtainless, with a tall lilac bush outside, which lent privacy yet allowed moonlight through its branches. Maeve lay on her side, head propped on palm, and her bare arm, softly voluptuous, gleamed alabaster. It was as if one of the missing arms from the Venus de Milo had suddenly shown up in a stable in the Berkshires.

"I didn't even audition, though."

"Neither did I."

"But at least he had seen you perform; he had some evidence of what you could do."

"He'd been in the salon with you for months."

"But that's not acting."

No answer.

"It's not the same as acting," I insisted.

"He's been around the block. He wouldn't have cast you if he didn't have faith you could do it."

"Well he doesn't have faith now. You should see the look on his face when we play our scenes. All sort of wincing and genteel. And Kaliq is outright fed up with me."

"He is not," said Maeve. "He likes you."

"He said that?"

"He says it's fun working with you."

"Well, he's being nice. He's being polite."

Maeve emitted a breath that was the aural equivalent of rolling her eyes. Despite her sympathetic nature, she was annoyingly steadfast in her refusal to help me pity myself.

"He's probably going to call Keeley to come take over the role." I had told Maeve about Keeley, and been somewhat comforted to learn that she'd never heard of Keeley, or of Hale's brief, early marriage, either.

"I'm sure she's already on her way," said Maeve.

"He's probably getting ready to give *you* the part. Having noticed all your natural chemistry with Kaliq."

"He already offered it to me," she came back—so quickly I thought she was serious, and my heart sunk. Then I realized she was joking, and chided myself for being gullible. "I turned him down. Told him *he* should play Pyramus."

There was a beat while I digested her last words. "What did you say?"

"Hale should be your Pyramus."

I could feel my face go red in the darkness. "How come you said that?"

"I didn't—I'm just teasing."

"No, but right now, to me, why did you say it?"

"Oh. Well. I'm not—you know, blind. I'm not actually *insensate.*"

The way she said it, in a cracked whisper, for some reason made us both dissolve into giggles, which we had to muffle hurriedly against our respective pillows.

I had never laughed so much in my life as with Maeve. Not even when I'd been with Ezra, whom I might describe as the greater wit, and with whom I would have said I had brilliant fun. But Ezra's humor, I had now begun to see, was premised on maintaining a level of tension that never led to release. It was stimulating, and pleasurable in its own way; it carried the crackle and whiff of brimstone, but never *arrived*, never *delivered* us anywhere, and so eventually wore thin, like a promise unfulfilled, an endlessly stretched-out ellipsis.

With Maeve, it wasn't her wit or cleverness that unleashed such rolling waves of mirth. It was her knack for speaking truly, for pointing out—or blurting out—some truth I might have expected her to keep discreetly under wraps. Partly I laughed because her habit of forthrightness was shocking. But there was a component of something else, too, not just shock but gladness, lightness. She taught me, through these rounds of laughter we shared that summer, how candor could be fundamentally liberating.

Her insight that night caught me radically off guard. I hadn't thought my feelings for Hale showed, and the fact that she'd seen right through me was unnerving. Or ought to have been; the funny thing was that after my initial shock, I sort of prodded myself for signs of distress—and found none. I'd been so wrapped up in the assumption that the thing was perverse, or would at any rate appear that way to others, that I'd never paused to consider the alternative. But Maeve didn't seem scandalized, or worried for me, or even particularly surprised.

"Do you think it's messed up?" I asked.

"What?"

"That I—have feelings for him?"

"No."

"Even though he's old enough to . . . Even though he's older?"

She yawned and said something garbled.

"What?"

"I said"—her voice drowsy now—"that it isn't unheard of."

She was a great sleeper, that Maeve: could go from raucous laughter to near-comatose in a matter of minutes. She was like a little kid that way. It was another thing to envy.

As for me, I lay on my back and stared at the shadows above, which deepened at angles as the pitched roof receded up and away. The stable had been built in such a way that there were spaces between the roof and the wall where moonlight got through, clean silvery knives of it—not worrisome chinks, the odd slit here and there, like in the attic of our house back in Cambridge, hinting at greater disjointedness behind superficial drywall and plaster. These were frank gaps where a spider might weave its web, or a bird build its nest, or a mouse scurry through.

Old enough to be my father.

Those were the words I'd stopped myself from speaking, and they reverberated above me, unvoiced, in the hollow of the moonlit rafters.

My father. I'd been so successful at not thinking about him since I'd come out here. Since before that, really. This was only an extension of the success I'd had not thinking about him very much all spring. Ever since that night at the Pudding, I'd not only minimized my interactions with the man, but trained my thoughts pretty well away from the idea of him, too.

Now I lay as awake as I'd ever been, in the unrelieved stillness of the stable. I listened hard, and could hear no one stirring, not even a cough or the creak of a cot from one of the other converted stalls.

No owl or loon cry. No passing automobile on the county road. Only soundless moonlight playing through the branches. "Maeve," I whispered, after a while, futilely. Of course she was asleep. I got out of bed and pulled on my heaviest sweater.

What if my fixation on Hale was just some sort of warped response to my having learned of my father's transgressions? All the good feeling I experienced in his presence—or not *good*, not that too-bland word—but all the effervescent joy, the saturated-with-delight feeling—could it be that this was merely some kind of twisted reaction formation, in the parlance of my parents' profession? A subconscious attempt to convert an unacceptable desire into an acceptable one? And if this were the case, if horror over my father's betrayal was in fact the genesis of what I had taken to be real feelings of love for a man about his age, then where did it leave me? What ought I to do with those feelings?

Trust them, abolish them?

Either would be easier said than done.

I went outside, and saw a light in the farmhouse. It must have been around two in the morning. The light was on the first floor, muted enough so that I could tell it was coming from the back of the house: the kitchen. I headed over.

Gentle with the screen door, gentle going over the old wooden floorboards, I made little sound until I reached the kitchen doorway. At the stove stood my grandmother, with an old red corduroy jacket of Maynard's over her nightgown and shearling slippers on her feet, lighting the ring under a saucepan. In the rocking chair sat Teej, a pink blanket wrapped around his bony little-boy shoulders.

"Hi," I said quietly.

My grandmother turned from her task and her eyebrows went way up. "Always turning up in the most unexpected places," she remarked. It was clear that it was a kind of welcome.

Teej asked, rather brightly, "Did you have a bad dream, too?" as though inquiring whether I'd received an invitation to the same party he had. He was wearing his praying mantis pajamas.

I smiled—"No . . . just wakeful"—and took a seat on one of the long benches, at the end nearer the stove. My grandmother used a wooden spoon to stir what was in the pot, milk, and settled onto the bench beside me. And then she did something both ordinary and entirely surprising: she began to rub my back in slow circles. It was such an easy motion, so casually undertaken, but this lay at odds with the fact that she had never touched me before. I lapped it up, but at the same time held myself alert to its possible meaning. I couldn't help but think that her rubbing my back was meant to convey something, a message, which it was my duty to interpret correctly.

We Fisher-Harts had never been particularly physical with one another. When we did touch, it often held a faintly utilitarian quality. Not so much touch for the sake of contact, but touch as encoded memorandum. So that when my mother had swept her fingers along my chin, that night she'd first told me about the complaint against my father, the gesture had contained a message: a promise of approval contingent on my compliance. And when I had found her weeping in the pantry after Maynard's funeral and gone on tiptoe to smooth her stray wisps of hair back in place, this, too, had carried an implicit binding agreement: a pledge of allegiance contingent on her self-control. Touch could seal a pact, or substitute for words; it could communicate reminders of responsibility, duty, and one's correct role, whether submissive or dominant. These were the functions of touch in the Fisher-Hart household. Even when, as a child, I had scraped my knee, the ensuing hug or time allowed on a parent's lap was somehow understood to be not the thing *itself* (I was never in my life clasped spontaneously to a parent's bosom, never encouraged to climb upon or loll against a seated parent at any length), but rather a symbol, a physical representation of comfort, the gestural equivalent of the words, *There, there.*

My grandmother rose to check the milk, stirred it once, turned off the flame, and decanted it from the pan into one of the enameled mugs. I was put in mind of my mother, preparing warm milk with liqueur on a different night in a different kitchen. I hated it that my mother had spiked the milk that night, even though I had felt, admittedly, a little elevated to partake in such an adult ritual. I hated to think that my mother might have calculated this likelihood, and added the liqueur as part bribe. And I hated it that my mother had signaled the severity of the situation indirectly, with alcohol, instead of directly, with language. Worst of all was the implied directive that we encounter this travail obliquely, with the aid of a muffling agent.

My grandmother handed Teej his mug, left the dirty pan where it was, and settled back beside me, hands in her lap. "Now drink that up, honey. We all need to get back to bed."

He drank. We watched him begin to fade.

I spoke softly. "I was thinking about my father. And, you know, mother."

"Have you been in touch with them since you've been here?"

"No." And, "Have you?"

"No."

"My mother was telling me—before I left—about her earliest memory, of Silke playing with her on a blanket on the floor of your dressing room. She remembered the soldiers, but not that they had belonged to her father. Maybe no one ever told her that." My grandmother didn't respond, so I went on. The sound of my own voice issuing from my body, so low, was calming. I didn't want it to stop. I followed it like a thread, unspooling as if of its own accord. "She told me that at your wedding dinner, when you got married to Maynard, Silke pulled her aside and told her that you had been going to leave Neil Fisher, and that's why he killed himself, and not because of being blacklisted.

"I used to drive cars on her when she had a headache.

"I thought you were kind of bad because you'd given up my mother. Not given her up, but in a way. And I thought she was kind of bad because she'd been given up by you. I know that doesn't make any sense.

"I thought my father was a god. The way I loved him."

It was like dream-speech. Coming from who knew where. Abiding by no nicety. My grandmother stood up, disturbing the stillness, and I watched as she pried the mug gently from Teej's hand. He was asleep for real now, held up only by the pink wooly cocoon wrapped snugly around him. My grandmother placed his mug in the sink and returned once more to the bench beside me. I didn't worry that I'd overstepped.

"Borges says being in love is like creating a religion with a fallible god," she said almost conversationally. "All human gods are fallible. Your mother's childhood was far from ideal. Far from ideal," she repeated. "It was what I could manage. Which is not a defense. It's merely true."

"I don't blame you about it."

"That may be," she allowed. "*I* blame me."

We sat in some good silence. Teej's breathing, fetchingly adenoidal, was the only sound.

"What about what Silke said? About why Neil Fisher killed himself?" I asked.

"What about it?"

"Is it true?"

"It is. I couldn't stay in that marriage. I didn't wish him ill, but it is a terrible, true thing that when he killed himself, I was freed. Free from the marriage and free from the burden of having to divorce him. And free from the stigma a divorce would have carried at that time, not only in the larger society but among all our friends, everyone in theater who loved and respected him." She turned to me. "I don't blame myself for that, though, his death." And she studied me, her eyes flitting back and forth across my face, as if searching out something specific.

"Did Silke?"

She shook her head. "No. She never did."

"Then what did she have to forgive you for?"

"Sorry?"

"You said it in Boston, after the memorial service, when you lay down on the bed in the study . . ."

"I said she had to forgive me for something?"

"You said, 'Silke forgave me.' "

My grandmother looked at her hands, folded on her night-gowned lap. The red corduroy jacket she wore was so big on her that the cuffs came to her knuckles, making her look childlike, despite the blue veins and raised tendons that showed through her rather translucent skin.

"For your mother, I meant. For not keeping Sarah with me."

"Oh."

The feeling of sorrow coming off her, in almost palpable waves—sorrow not for what she'd done or might have done to Neil Fisher but for what she'd done to her daughter, my mother—gave me a clearer sense of the magnitude, the relative grievousness, of what she'd done in sending my mother away. Even as my grandmother's confession of guilt allowed me to stop holding her responsible, it also, in a sense, absolved my mother. I had long assumed that my mother was overly sensitive about this matter, that she nursed too protectively her resentment and hurt. I'd thought of it as my mother's weakness, her childish insistence that she'd been unforgivably wronged. It lent her a brittle carapace that was unattractive. And although my father and I had never discussed it openly, I thought he and I were in agreement on this; that while we were both charitable in offering her our sympathies, we were privately bored by her sense of injury, and the way she hauled it along everywhere she went, as if on a stubborn, wordless quest for reparations.

But sitting beside my grandmother on the bench, I soaked up the heaviness of her unresolved sorrow, and it seemed to validate my mother's claim: I had to consider that her sense of injury might be just. Then I remembered the words she'd spoken long ago, on the night of my cello recital, about the impact of a parent's suicide on a child.

"But," I said, "at least there's the possibility of resolution."

"What?"

"It isn't as if you killed yourself. If you had abandoned her by committing suicide, there'd be no hope of resolution. But you're still here. She can . . . talk with you, work it out."

"If she wished."

"But she *could,* I mean. I just mean that she could."

"Ah. Well."

"Grandmother?"

"Yes?"

"You're the one who asked Hale to give me the part of Thisbe?"

"I asked him what he thought of the idea. It was his decision to make the offer."

"Why did you suggest it?"

She didn't respond right away.

"Why did you think of me for the part? Was—was it charity?" I voiced my fear. "It was charity—a debt? Because of my mother?"

"Well. Oh, my dear. It wasn't *one* reason. Part of it was, I would say, yes, activating a wish. Several wishes. To give something to you.

To . . . *connect* with your mother in some way, through you, yes. To make amends? I don't know whether I'd go that far. But Beatrice." She looked at me squarely. Her eyes glinting like brilliants, her Roman senator nose prominent, her chin lifted. "Not charity. No. If I hadn't seen some possibility in you, I would not have suggested it."

"What possibility did you see?" *And do you still see it?* I wanted to add.

"Brightness. Hunger. An ability to grow."

With each pronouncement I felt raised, and bathed in silvery promise, for I'd never heard myself described in any of these terms, nor had I even thought of these as specific attributes to which I ought to aspire. My parents' words of praise for me had run along the lines of: clever, undemanding, empathetic. The mirror my grandmother held up was novel, and I wanted to peer into it more deeply, and at greater length.

But Teej rumbled out a little snore then that made us look at him, slumped in the chair, and my grandmother said, "Golly, it's late." She pressed her hands against her thighs to help her stand up. "I wonder if you would carry him back to bed, Bea, with your young muscles."

"Sure."

When I scooped him up my cousin nestled against me. Upstairs, after I'd tucked him in, I saw that my grandmother had waited in the hall.

"Good night, Thisbe," she whispered, embracing me.

This was unprecedented. As my arms went around her in turn, I could feel under Maynard's corduroy jacket the framework of her bones, less robust than I would have imagined. They felt disconcertingly delicately assembled, and recalled to me again that quote of Hale's: "It isn't bravery. That she makes you *think* it is, that's the marvel of her."

———

JUST ABOUT EVERYONE in the company had gone to the Pond for the afternoon. I knew because they'd all made noisy plans to go at lunchtime. I, however, was not at liberty to join them, as I had been scheduled to rehearse, Kaliq and me both. The two of us were scheduled, exclusively, for the rest of the day. Everyone else had been given a free afternoon. This kind of thing had not happened before, but I'm sure no one was wondering why. It was obvious I needed the extra work. My acting was simply not up to speed with the others. I knew it, but not what to do about it.

After lunch I got down to the barn a bit early, and rather than go right in I hid out around the side of the building, delaying the moment when Hale would inform me (as I had convinced myself would happen) that I was dismissed from the cast. Surely it was inevitable. Hale would be very nice about it; he'd feel the more sorry since he'd had misgivings about giving me the part in the first place. He'd feel that he'd set me up, against his better judgment, for failure. So heavily did this conviction of failure weigh upon me that I didn't even hear him approach.

"Kicking up a tempest," came his voice from behind me. He was peering around the side of the barn, cocking his head in amusement at the ochre dust clouds I had scuffed in the air with my toe.

"Oh, am I late? I thought I was early—"

"You're right about on time. Barb's inside already, and Kaliq. We're still waiting for Margaret. I've asked her to sit in on rehearsal."

"You have? Oh." I was flustered. Could he actually be thinking about asking *her* to take over the part? "I'm sorry. About how it's been going, I don't . . ."

"We'll get it," he said lightly. He smiled that minute smile of his.

We stood in silence. His eyes warmed and then burned. There

began to be such potency in the gaze passing between us that we simultaneously broke off looking at each other, and our gazes mutually fell, then, to the ground, where some old flowerpots had been stacked by the wall of the barn, and a metal watering can left beneath a spigot. The can was full of water, and when every so often a drop fell from the leaky spigot, it made a cool *plip*. Beside the watering can grew a patch of cowslip, some of the pale yellow petals lolling against the rim as though helping themselves to a drink. As we watched, one of the blossoms shifted, even in the windless air, and then, metamorphosing, lifted and flitted softly across the tangle of meadow between the barn and farmhouse.

I looked at Hale; his eyes shot mild exclamation points; he had seen it just as I had. We both turned again toward the meadow and watched the butterfly, for that is in fact what it was, travel in all its choppy grace.

"There's a poem about that," remarked Hale. Though when I looked back at him, squinting across the haze, smiling in that way that made it look as though he were manipulating a tiny seed between his teeth, I could not tell whether he meant he knew of an actual poem that captured such a moment, or whether he meant there *ought* to exist, in the ether of as-yet-unwritten poetry, lines to enunciate a moment like the one we'd just dually experienced.

"Yonder comes Miss Maggie." Hale pointed with his chin. When I looked in that direction again, the butterfly had vanished, and there was my grandmother instead, striding toward us in a long white dress.

She picked her way across the field, stopping before she reached us and standing there, stock-still, her dress billowing around her ankles. Gone was any spark of special warmth or recognition I might have expected to linger from our kitchen conversation the night before. She was very much the Margaret Fourcey of the tea shop in March: imposing, imperious, grand. Any calming effect I'd enjoyed from the shared moment with Hale fled. My nervousness came back in droves. It wasn't only a sense of doom I felt now, the cold certainty of my small imminent failure; it was the wretchedness of having to parade that failure once and for all before my grandmother's appraising eye. She would know I had in some sense lied to her the previous March, or misled her, or had at the very least been dishonest with myself, kidding myself that I could be any kind of useful instrument on stage.

"Hello," she said.

"Let's go in," suggested Hale.

Kaliq and Barb were waiting for us.

"From your first entrance, Pyramus," was all Hale said, and we began.

We put our scenes through their paces. We did not receive direction. In between scenes, when Kaliq and I would sort of gaze out into the house for some sign of life, Hale rarely even looked up. "Go on," he might say, gesturing with one hand. We delivered our lines and followed our blocking, and the whole thing juddered mechanically along, failing utterly to come to life.

I could feel the impatience growing in Kaliq.

"Let's just take the opening lines," said Hale at some point in the afternoon. I had no watch but it must have been nearly four. My stomach had been growling softly, from time to time, and I had a headache gathering focus behind my left eye.

"From where she sees him dying?" I asked, because that was the scene he'd just interrupted.

"No, the opening of the play. At the wall."

Kaliq entered first, sidled to the wall, and hissed for me through the imagined chink. As directed, I came dashing in halfway across the stage, caught myself up short, then made myself cover the rest of the distance in measured steps. We went through our first few lines. Hale stopped us.

"No, just the opening."

We looked at him in confusion.

"Again."

"With—do you want the blocking?" I asked.

"Yes. Bea, I like what you're doing with your cross, but it's a little broad. Just take it down a notch."

I nodded. We moved back to the wings and took it from the top, but before we'd gotten out two lines apiece he stopped us once more.

"Just your opening lines, please."

"But that—?"

"Just your opening lines. *Your* opening line, Pyramus, and *your* opening line, Thisbe. Then stop." It was the first time I'd ever heard him take that tone.

We delivered what he asked—

PYRAMUS: You tarry.
THISBE: I hurry.

—then stopped and turned to face the house.

It was the lines' meagerness that confused me—what was the value in having us speak so slim an exchange?—but apparently this was what he had wanted.

"Are you really angry at her?" Hale asked Kaliq.

"Yes."

"Do you believe he's angry with you?" Hale asked me.

"I don't know," I said. "I know if he is, it's just because he can't wait to see me, just that he's impatient."

Hale turned back to Kaliq. "Is there anything playful in your accusation?"

"Playful, yes," said Kaliq. "But his impatience, his desire for her and his impatience with the whole situation, really comes through and informs the way he says it. He's pissed."

To me: "Does Thisbe feel his annoyance as frustrated lust?"

"I—I don't know."

"Does Thisbe feel frustrated lust for him?"

Again, I shrugged, rounding my eyes and trying to make light of my cluelessness.

Hale said, "When Thisbe protests, 'I hurry,' is she telling the truth, or just placating him?"

I put my head on one side.

Hale sighed. "Look, what do you want more than anything?"

"Uh . . ."

Hale turned to Kaliq. "What do you want more than anything?"

"I want to break down this fucking wall." Kaliq mimed kicking his leg through the wall. I envied his clarity.

Hale, back to me, again, same question: "What do you want more than anything?"

"To . . . ?"

"Whose idea is it, in the script, whose idea is it first, to disrespect the rule of the parents, to leave the safety and limitations of the wall and rendezvous in the wide world? Whose idea is it first, to transgress?"

". . . Mine?"

"Thisbe's," he agreed. He pushed his glasses on top of his head and they caught a shaft of light leaking in from the roof of the barn and glinted like a couple of coins. He repeated, almost apologetically, "What do you want more than anything?"

"To be with Pyramus?"

"Is it to be with Pyramus? How well do you know him?"

"Well, if you're saying it's not to be with Pyramus, then—I don't know what she's supposed to want."

"Whose wall is it?"

". . . the parents'?"

"Who has she known her whole life?"

"Her parents."

"Whose law has she lived under her whole life?"

"Her parents.' "

"What does she want more than anything?"

"To leave them?"

He nodded, offered it another way: "To transgress."

We took it again from the top. Almost immediately he stopped us.

"You're being careful, Beatrice." It was an accusation, the way Hale said it.

"I know. Sorry." I slapped a hand to my forehead. "I don't know how to get rid of it!"

"What is 'it'?"

"Nothing." I shrugged. "Sorry. Let me try again."

But, "Don't you know?" he persisted.

Miserable, tongue-tied, I said nothing.

Hale sounded almost pleased all of a sudden, energized. "Thisbe has to be able to transgress. It's the most literal of transgressions. She's got to breach the wall, the material as well as the figurative wall the parents have placed between them. And you're shackling her with your own integrity. Not Thisbe's integrity, Beatrice's."

Hale turned to Kaliq. "Thank you. Sorry to have kept you so long today." He walked Kaliq to the door of the barn, where they talked with their heads together a minute, silhouetted against the bright rectangle of daylight. Then Hale came back and spoke with Barb and my grandmother, and after a few minutes he raised his head and said,

"That's all for today, Beatrice. But starting tomorrow I'm going to shake things up a bit and have you work on the role with Margaret."

I was confused. The role with Margaret—my grandmother's role? It was a much smaller part, with hardly any lines; it made sense he was having us switch. At least I wasn't out of the production altogether. At least I didn't have to pack my bag and leave the Farm. "You mean Eurydice?" I asked.

"What?"

"I'm going to be playing Eurydice now?"

"No." He looked confused. "No, you're Thisbe. I'm just saying in addition to regular rehearsals, I want you to work on the part with Maggie. I'm asking her to be your acting coach. I think it will be a fruitful pairing."

I looked from one to the other. "Oh—you don't have to . . . I . . . I don't want special treatment. If you'd rather just cast someone else in the role."

"But I wouldn't," said Hale.

"No one is suggesting it," said my grandmother.

"Look, Bea, parts of it are working beautifully." Hale pushed up his glasses again, regarded me unobstructedly with his clear gray eyes. "I just want to push it as far as it can go. I want to see if we can bring it along, tease out Thisbe's motives, make her more fully realized." He looked at me as though I was a bit daft. "You're doing well in the part, you know. I just think . . ." He studied my face. "It's just that I suspect—and now Maggie tells me she agrees—we just suspect you're giving us about half of what you could do."

ONCE DISMISSED, I raced to the stable, where I struggled sweatily into my bathing suit. My head was teeming with confusion and relief and excitement, but my body was calling out for the cold water of the Pond. I crossed the meadow, cutting right through the area where people parked their cars, but not being one to notice make or model or license plate, I might honestly have walked past without noticing the 1993 maroon Saab at the end of the row if its engine fan hadn't been running. As it was, the sound made me stop to glance whether someone was inside, and only when I spotted the familiar Lilly Pulitzer handbag in the passenger seat of the other-wise vacant vehicle did I do a double take and register that it was our family car. And the engine still warm.

Immediately I guessed something bad had happened. Something even worse than the accusations that had already forced my father to leave the university and my parents to sell their house. What could have made them drive all the way out here without warning? Thoughts of my father—bent oddly over the pork chop in his lap, shaking out his left arm before the toaster—gave credence to my dread. These moments had been foreshadowing a real heart attack; my mother had driven out here with the news of his death. Even Silke's sudden heart failure now struck a chord as a kind of clue. Everything had been pointing toward this calamity, yet my last inter-action with my father had been hurtful, harmful. I had threatened him. Of course I never really would have sought out his accuser, never would have knowingly jeopardized his settlement. But I had made the threat, and I had been hateful, and he had—what? Smiled at me. Offered me that single pale smile before removing himself from sight. At the time I had felt abandoned, but now, standing frozen on this extravagantly hot day with the tall grass brushing the backs of my legs, I saw it another way: in leaving the room, he might have been offering me the one thing he thought I wanted and that still remained in his power to give. The depths of disgrace communicated in his act, the sad eloquence of his self-abnegation, touched me seismically.

With a terrible feeling, I headed into the house.

My mother stood in the kitchen with her hands clasped behind her back, reading the rehearsal schedule taped to the fridge. She turned when I came into the room. Her hair was not clipped back but down, falling loose over her shoulders. She wore a pink T-shirt and a long denim skirt, a faded work shirt tied around her waist. She looked rested, soft.

"Bebe, love."

"What's wrong? Why are you here?"

"Nothing's wrong."

"Where's Dad?"

"Back in Cambridge. Packing boxes. How are you, Bea?"

"Is he okay?"

"He's fine."

"Are you leaving him?"

"What? No. No. He's actually doing okay. We're okay. How are you?"

"Fine. What?" I sighed. I was muddled. "Why did you come?"

"I drove out to see you. We sold the house."

"That was fast."

"Well, we've accepted an offer. And we've found a place, in southern Maine. That's why I wanted—I guess that's why I drove out. It seemed like a lot for a phone call."

"I see."

"Let's—are you free to take a walk?"

"I need to put something on."

"Want this?" She untied the work shirt from her waist. I put it on over my bathing suit.

We walked more than a mile along the county road. By the time we turned back, the shadows stretched halfway across the road, and an early evening breeze pushed aside the scrim of haze so the air grew more pleasant.

My mother talked about my father. She explained that he had such an excess of personal integrity, that he really could not see why his remarks were sometimes misinterpreted. In his mind, my mother said, he was fully honorable. He never saw his remarks as sexual advances because the idea of making sexual advances toward his patients or students was so utterly beyond him. His remarks were rather a function of an unfettered mind, a mind capable of all manner of associations and intimacies, a mind that didn't bother to censor or stifle.

"'An unfettered mind,'" I repeated. Something about her logic didn't hold. I tried teasing it apart. "You mean he's so sure of himself, he's not bothered by doubts."

"Yes, in a way, I guess that's what I'm saying."

"But"—I turned to her; it was as though I'd experienced a sudden arrival of good sense—"we *need* our doubts. It's dangerous to have no doubts. It's just a different kind of fetter, Mom, having no doubts. It keeps people from questioning themselves, from being able to question, and, and, change, and—break free."

But no, she insisted, that wasn't what she meant. It was simply that my father was so pure. He was a true believer in the unimpeachable nature of words; speech, to him, could be only a beneficent device, useful even when misapplied, for even in error words held the potential for paving the way toward illumination.

We walked a little way accompanied by the sound only of our sandals on the side of the road. I thought in earnest about what she proposed.

"That's naïve," I said finally. I was surprised by the firmness in my voice. "And you're not a naïve person."

"Bebe, love," my mother said. "No one—no one has ever understood him like I do." It didn't come off as a boast, but as a lament. "It's what *he* believes, and he really believes it." She stopped walking and turned to me. "His innocence is real."

"How can you make that argument?" I said. "How can you

expect me to go along with it? How *dare* you expect me to go along with it?" But I said this last bit gently; almost in spite of myself I felt less enraged than desperate to edify her, to make her see once and for all that this was their grave error, this was what they had always done: expect me to endorse their version of things, comply with the picture they wanted to present. I had aided and abetted in the construction of the image we Fisher-Harts put forth all my life. The very construction of myself, or rather more specifically of Bebe, had been a kind of favor to my parents, an obliging gesture. Was it always this way? Were children always pressed into the service of their parents' version of reality? I thought of Pyramus and Thisbe, at last refusing the impediment of their parents' houses, absconding into the open in hopes of meeting truly face to face.

I cast about for a way to put all this before my mother, but the words swam wildly and refused to string together in any coherent fashion.

My mother, similarly, seemed to grope for speech. At last, shaking her head, she said, "He's so worried he's lost you."

"Well, he should be."

But the memory of that last night at home, when he had made his final, terrible exit, returned to me. I did not want to inflict that kind of pain, not with bluster, not in retribution. As if from a need to prevent myself from traveling further down that path, I sat. I sat right down where I was, in the grass on the side of the road. My mother lowered herself beside me. At once, without warning, I was ready to do what scared me most: question her.

"How many were there, Mom?" I asked. "In all."

She looked at me awhile before answering. "Upwards of ten."

As if by tacit agreement we looked away from each other then, turning our faces toward the towering pines, the endless repetition of their trunks spaced out in the shaded woods.

"How many were patients?" I asked.

"Three. Two before you were born. And the one you knew about."

"The rest were students?"

"There was one colleague."

Our voices were supremely calm. I understood that I held the majority of power in this conversation, which in itself was dizzying. I had to steel myself to keep on asking.

"What did he say? The things he got in trouble for."

"He—crossed boundaries. He scorned the idea of rigid boundaries, rules about what you can and cannot say, irrespective of the particulars of a given patient's—or supervisee's—circumstance. He refused to hew to this line, what he would call the fascistic guidelines of our profession. And in many respects, he's right; I agree with him. There is a fundamentalist mentality that can inhibit the therapeutic process."

"But what things did he say that he got in trouble for?"

"He would share his thoughts. He would be playful with his speech, with double entendres. Occasionally, he might tell about a particular fantasy he had about a woman. Sometimes this was a means of creating a space for the woman to inventory her own fantasies. Or for the two of them to explore together whether such a fantasy might mean something to her, whether it might be something she was projecting onto the screen of his psyche."

"But Mom." My throat felt stiff. "You're dancing around the question. I'm not asking for the therapeutic rationale. I'm asking you *what did he say* that got him into trouble?"

When next she spoke, her voice was so low I had to strain to hear, and it grew lower as she went on. "Well . . . well . . . he told this last one, this supervisee, that she reminded him of a horse. A wild horse. That he imagined himself putting a bit in her mouth and—

mounting her. That he would ride her until she was tamed. And that he would groom her, feed her. He would have sugar for her and she would eat it."

My heart raced. I tried to think: could there be a way, any way, to understand his words as not invasive, not erotic?

As if anticipating my shock and trying to stem a barrage of horrified questions, my mother pushed on, her words stabbing and fierce. "He didn't say it during supervision. That part isn't on tape. He told me because he is honest with me, because he is honorable. Because he lets me in on the kind of risk-taking he is willing to do with his students. When he trusts them. They explore things—verbally. He believes in it, he believes it is not untoward."

I asked, looking only at the trees: "Did he have sex with any of them?"

"No. There was never physical contact."

"How do you know?"

"Because he told me. In the end. He tells me everything. We have this—this crazy trust."

"Did you know them?"

"I . . . knew them."

"And it was okay with you?"

"No! Bebe. It's not like I gave my *consent*."

"I can never see him again."

"Bebe."

"I'm going to be sick."

"Love?"

I closed my eyes. The sun made patterns inside my eyelids; insects droned; a distant motor started and stopped, a lawn mower perhaps, or a chain saw.

"What do you want to ask? I'll answer," promised my mother, and from this I realized she, too, was scared about losing me.

"The girl from back when I was thirteen. The one with the violin. Did he ask her to masturbate in his office?"

If she was surprised that I knew this much, she didn't betray it.
"That's not exactly what happened, Bebe. They were talking about
the subject; he wanted her to understand that it isn't a *wrong* thing,
and she misunderstood him to mean that it was all right to try it
during their session—"

"Stop." I covered my ears. I wanted-and-did-not-want-to-know
their names, what they looked like, their ages, what he'd said to each
of them, how long it went on before they'd objected. But my only
real question now was for her alone: "Why did you—why *do* you—
stay with him?"

My mother's answer flowed readily, as though she was relieved to
have been asked, relieved to have been invited to explain. "Because
he is magnificent. He has faults. Serious faults. I do, too, I know. But
we—it doesn't matter if you—I can't make you believe—but I love
him, and he loves me, after all these years. We see each other best.
He does things for me no one else could, and I do the same for him.
It's a kind of passion. It is—" She was fighting against crying now,
her voice at once broken and strident. "It is no less a thing than
what my mother and Maynard had."

The pathetic transparency of her need to draw that comparison
went further toward helping me understand than anything else
could have.

It was still not enough.

"I switched *schools*. I gave up *cello*."

"You were happy at Bowers Academy. You were glad to give up
practicing."

"You don't know how I felt. *I* don't even know how I felt. I
didn't have a chance. I didn't have a choice. That I was 'ready to quit
cello anyway'—that was just the story—the way *you* told it was the

story. You chose to protect him, to keep his secrets, stay with him. For me it just—I never got presented with a choice."

"Bebe, listen to me." She turned and looked me in the eye. "I know how it is not to know something about your childhood, about your own father. That's why I'm telling you now. Yes, he transgressed. I forgive him."

"That's insane."

"No it's not."

"How—how can it not be?"

"You don't know what it's taken me, to forgive him. And you have *no* idea what it would cost me not to. I'm not saying I don't feel angry. And I'm not telling you that you have to forgive him. You're right, you didn't have a choice when you were younger. But now I'm telling you the facts. Don't judge me for what I choose. And you can choose for yourself." Eyes welling, she looked away again. "You just don't have to choose *yet*," she begged just above a whisper. "If I could ask one thing of you, it would be to hold off on making a permanent decision about him."

"If you could ask one thing of me!" I gave a dry laugh. "Well, you can't. And you're a hypocrite, anyway, to ask that."

She looked at me, helpless anger and grief and confusion all seeming to compete for her expression.

"*You* seem to have made a pretty permanent decision about your mother."

The sun, on its downward course, shot suddenly through the trees, cutting almost horizontally through the woods to inflame half her face.

"It's brought me no happiness," she said.

There was nothing I could do then but let my head fall forward. After a minute, her fingers lit on the back of my neck and hesitantly stroked my nape.

When at last we stood, we headed along the road in the direction from which we'd come. We were in the long shadow of pines.
Bees flew among the wildflowers along the side of the road. Every
so often a car passed; mostly the road was quiet.

My mother, steady-voiced, began to volunteer practical kinds of
information. She'd been offered a job at a community hospital in
Maine. My father would try to start a private practice there. He
wasn't losing his license, and anyway, even if he were, anyone was
allowed to hang out a plaque. They'd found an apartment already,
near the hospital's campus. They might look to buy a cape or a bun-
galow in a year or so, when they'd gotten more of a feel for the area.
She said she wasn't sorry to be leaving Cambridge.

I expressed skepticism.

It was true, she maintained. The pressure in Cambridge always to
project a certain aura, the anxiety around maintaining status in the
eyes of the university, all their colleagues and friends, had been
exhausting. It had taken a toll on them both, and on their marriage,
in a way they were only coming to realize now that it was being
stripped away. They felt strangely liberated, she said. Even giving up
the house—she laughed—it was like being released from an incredible weight to which they'd been yoked all these years. "The
upkeep, the expenses, the old windows that never shut properly, the
oil bill alone . . . good riddance!"

I looked at her sideways. My mother looked both older and
younger than I remembered. I could see fine lines around her eyes
and mouth, and the skin of her neck where it met her pink shirt
was more heavily freckled, less white and smooth, than in my memory. But her smile was more relaxed, and broad enough that I could
see her eyeteeth, shiny and white. Her gait seemed easier, too, something about the way she let her arms swing naturally at her sides as
we walked. Could it be that my parents had been actors all these

years, trapped in roles they hadn't really liked? And something else: the extreme, practically sanctifying love my mother had vouched earlier for my father—such an improbable love seemed in plain evidence now, in her prosaic memoranda about the imminent changes they were facing.

"We'll put your things in storage for you, Bebe. We won't have as much room in Maine, and you might want easier access to them anyway. Do you know your plans for the end of summer?"

I shook my head dumbly.

"You know you can come and stay with us anytime you like. Just because we're selling the house—just because of, well, everything—we don't want you to feel your home is gone."

We were walking past a field with a shed in it, a glimpse of house tucked away in the trees beyond. An oldish man stood splitting wood. A couple of swallows dove and soared after each other.

"You sound happy," I admitted, mystified.

"Daddy and I are the closest we've ever been. I think this move, this change, is, you know, ironically—and not to make light of it at all—but on the contrary, to speak of it in serious terms: the best thing that could have happened to us."

A small laugh escaped me.

"No, really. The disaster has already happened. In my heart, I must believe that the suffering is in its own way a gift. That it must contain some lesson. Some opportunity for growth. It's like the shell of our lives has been cracked open; we've been brought low, but now we're also in a way free to grow differently."

She was either very brave or very deluded. It was painful in me, the not knowing which.

"I'm only . . . " she began, and broke off. "We're both just so sorry that it's caused a rift with you."

"But the rift has been there always."

We were nearing the dirt road that led up to the Farm. "Maybe there's always a rift," she conceded, "between parent and child. But this feels like a more malignant one. That's what I mean, that's what we are, Bebe"—her eyes searched back and forth between my own—"so deeply sorry for."

WHEN WE GOT BACK to the Farm, Jean was standing out on the porch ringing the bell.

"That's dinner," I explained. It occurred to me I was quite hungry.

"I'll say goodbye, then."

"Okay."

I walked her to the car. It was a long drive to make twice in one day. I took off her work shirt to give back. She glanced at my bathing suit. "You can hold on to it," she offered.

"That's all right, I'll go back to my room and change."

"You won't be late for dinner?"

"It's not like that."

Reluctance to part hovered thinly in the air between us. She opened the door of the car.

"Sarah?" called my grandmother, her voice great with surprise. She was striding across the grass from the house, looking very much the legendary stage actress, still in her gauzy white dress with the setting sun behind her.

"Hi, Mom," said my mother.

"Sarah!"

"Hi."

For a moment we stood in extreme awkwardness and without talking. I, who was so used to considering myself a Fisher-Hart first and last, realized we were a trio of Fourceys here, the shared blood evident in our height and noses and chins. Then my grandmother urged my mother to come inside for dinner; my mother demurred, but somehow, not really surprisingly, my grandmother prevailed, and next thing the two of them were heading for the house, and I was running back to my room to change out of my bathing suit.

When I got to the stable I could tell from the quality of the silence that the entire building was deserted; everyone must be at dinner by now. Despite my hunger, when I went into Maeve's and my stall I did not put on clothes right away, but sank onto my cot, reeling from the interaction my mother and I had just had. The stable air smelled sweet and fermented. Amber light came in the window. A fly buzzed somewhere, mutedly, and bumped against glass. I thought of our house, now sold; I would never again go in it. I thought of my mother and all she was giving up, and how strange it was that she seemed—she *did* seem—happy. Last, I thought of my father: the head-hurting puzzle of how one person could be so good and so bad.

Always the story of him and me began with an image of Memorial Drive, the two of us walking past the mottled trunks of sycamores, the sunlight on the Charles. His big hands. His browny bronze hair curling back from his high, rounded brow. His voice so deep in his barrel chest, so full of authority, of truth, in everything he said: from once upon a time to the last word on everything.

I thought again of the house, my house, my attic room. What had prompted me at thirteen to request the move to the attic? Had I sensed something hidden and appalling behind the perfection of his form? Or had I been moved by a garden-variety assertion of independence, a routine adolescent desire for greater privacy and distance? I could remember the project of moving upstairs. My mother and me painting the walls buttermilk. Shopping for a new bedspread, picking out curtains to match. But no, no memory of anything unpleasant around my father. We had long ago stopped our Sunday morning walks. Nor had he read aloud to me in years, nor had I sat beneath the table, at his feet, crayoning or driving my toy cars and absorbing, exalting in, the wonderful timbre of his voice holding forth in the commensurate, attentive hush of all others in the room. By the time I finished junior high we had already begun treating each other differently. Our familiarity with each other had been replaced by something like modesty, our closeness by a certain distance. Still, delve as I might into the most shadowy recesses of memory, I was relieved to find no cause for these changes other than the fact of my growing up.

But I was equally confused and upset to find that thinking about him had made me miss him.

No longer caring about dinner, or about changing out of my bathing suit, I let myself fall back on my cot, beyond exhaustion. When my head touched the pillow something rustled. Reaching back, I felt paper. I sat up and held in my hand a sheet torn from a legal pad, folded in half, *Beatrice* written in compressed, squarish letters across the back, the letters formed in a mature, almost old-fashioned hand, so that my initial thought was that my grandmother had written me a note. Curious, I opened the sheet of paper, smoothed it on my knees, and read:

On Having Mis-identified a Wild Flower

A thrush, because I'd been wrong,
Burst rightly into song
In a world not strange, not lonely,
Not governed by me only.

—Richard Wilbur

The first thing I felt, even before wondering how the poem had gotten there, was enormous, bright peace, as though the dome of the world had cracked open and beyond it lay sweet, complicated order, nothing I was responsible for understanding, just order all around and far away.

Then I did, of course, immediately try to figure out who had put the scrap of paper on my pillow. Could my grandmother have left it: was it meant to help me with Thisbe? It couldn't possibly have been my mother; no, it wasn't even her handwriting. Not Maeve, I didn't think, but who else would come into our stall? Then a prickling heat came over me. Hale. It was the poem he had alluded to earlier. At some point in the day, after our butterfly sighting by the watering can, he must have made time to copy it out, come down to the stable, determine which was my stall, which my cot, and place it on my pillow. Each successive thought a cause for further warmth.

I read the poem over many times.

It was a love token, I could see that. A sign that the feeling between us was real, and would be attended to with infinite care.

I lay back again on top of the covers, neither hungry nor tired anymore. I did not stir for some time.

MY MOTHER LEFT early the next morning, before breakfast, having spent the night on a spare cot in Barb's room. She came down to the stable to say goodbye to me. Maeve, who'd been out late with Kaliq, was still sleeping. I walked out in my nightgown with my mother across the dewy grass and stood with her at the car. She didn't reveal much about how things had gone with my grandmother. I knew they had spent a good part of the evening alone together in the farmhouse's small and rarely used living room, with the door closed.

"She's a hard woman," was all that my mother had to report.

It seemed a terrible characterization. I felt defensive, wanted to tell her she was mistaken, but I did not. We faced each other in the small chill of postdawn, with mist hovering above the grass and sun streaking through the pines. We were very nearly in the same positions as the evening before, my mother's fingers already resting on the door handle, my arms wrapped around my middle, both of us not quite saying goodbye, when once again my grandmother came toward us from the house. The repetition of event was almost comical. At the sight of her own mother marching our way, my mother sucked air in through her teeth. Like a teenager, I thought.

My grandmother was slightly out of breath by the time she reached us. "I wanted to thank you for coming, Sarah."

"Really?"

There was a pause.

"Sarah—" My grandmother had to squint against the sun. She looked older in the stark light, the wrinkles on her face and neck more apparent. But this served to underscore the grand symmetry of her features, the unrepentant jut of her profile. "I can't accept your forgiveness on the terms you offer it. But that doesn't change my appreciation of the fact that—oh, Sarah, I do thank you, for coming, for trying."

Silence.

My grandmother dove in again. "I can't accept the blame for everything you want me to. I won't pretend something different simply in order to win you over. But—I've *missed* you."

"You don't know me to miss me."

Now my mother was the one met by silence. My sympathies were with my grandmother. *A hard woman*. If anyone was hard, it was my mother.

And yet, when next she spoke, it was in a voice so tiny and uncertain that I felt pity. "Well," she said. "I did try."

"And I," returned my grandmother, slowly, cautiously, as though picking her way across a field of ice, "would like to continue—trying."

My mother nodded. Then, apparently at a loss for language, she turned to embrace first me, and then, more stiffly, my grandmother. I surprised myself greatly by reaching out to her as she opened the car door. The Fisher-Hart lexicon did not include the request for a second hug. But she understood what I wanted and put her arms around me again, and I drank in the sheer strength of her body, the inimitable and undyingly good smell of her. I let myself miss and love my mother not despite, but along with, all the anger I also felt.

MY GRANDMOTHER TOOK Hale at his word. After that weekend she became my own personal acting coach, working me hard and with relish. I loved it. It was unlike anything I'd experienced. It was exactly what I had been rooting around for, in an ineffectual, abstract way, since March—since February, really, when I'd sat at my attic desk, beneath the frost flowers blooming across the windowpanes, and written her the letter in sepia ink.

My dream is to act.

She stripped me of acting, first thing. Stripped me of artifice, intention, thought. Stripped me of my very breath—literally, for the first thing she had me do was take Thisbe's monologue and break it down into three- or four-word fragments, which I then had to deliver in between sprints. We practiced late in the day, after regular rehearsals were finished, under the copper beech tree in the far meadow between stable and woods. The first thing she did, after sitting on a folding chair she had me carry out for her, was take off her wide-brimmed straw hat and toss it into the meadow. An impressive throw: it landed some twenty feet away.

"Now then, Beatrice," she said, and I was struck by how officious she sounded; Hale's assignment seemed to have brought out a whole other side of her. "You are to run to the hat, turn around and come back to me, deliver a line fragment, run out again and back, deliver the next line fragment, and so on."

I regarded her with frank skepticism.

"Well?"

"Just run there and back?"

"As fast as you can."

I jogged through the tall grass into the dazzling sun as far as the hat, turned and jogged back, uttered my first few words ("Here is the tree"), and gave her a look.

"Go on, quickly," she prompted. "Without stops."

Rolling my eyes, I complied, humoring her.

She didn't seem to notice. "Faster," she said, fanning herself. "Don't think about what the words mean."

We kept this up for close to an hour. I soon gave up delivering my line fragments with sarcasm—a hard tone to maintain when you are panting—but I continued to feel ridiculous until heat and fatigue overtook me, and then I grew annoyed. But then something funny happened: real exhaustion set in, and the sweat ran freely down my face and neck. And I felt nothing but the task at hand, which became my whole, my single, almost ceremonial purpose. Everything was gone but physical endurance and the need to speak Thisbe's lines, but in such small bits that meaning could not cling to the words. The words became little parcels of sound. There was no wall between me and them, no barrier of thought, of will or intellect, between me and the girl Thisbe.

When at last my grandmother said, "That's enough for today," I sank to the ground in a kind of ragged, transcendent delirium, my face hot and tight-feeling from all the evaporated sweat.

"Grandmother," I said. The ground cradled my head; the sky, chopped up by the branches and leaves of the copper birch, shone in slivers and slices as fine as the fragments of Thisbe's speech. My voice was hoarse. "Thank you."

We worked together every day after that, for an hour or so before supper. The tasks my grandmother set me were often strange, but I threw myself into them with ardor. One day we didn't "rehearse" at all; instead, she handed me stationery and a pen, and had me spend our time writing letters, as Thisbe: one for Pyramus, to tell him I'd changed my mind and wasn't meeting him after all; another for my parents to find after I had gone, as planned, to meet him.

Writing the letter to Pyramus was difficult but doable; I got so into it I even wept a few real tears. It was the letter to Thisbe's parents that I could not bring myself to write.

"What stops you?" my grandmother asked. "What happens when you try? What are you feeling?"

"Sad. And scared."

"Why sad?"

"Because it'll hurt them to read that she's left. So, sad for them—she doesn't want them to be hurt. And because I know she dies, which I realize *she* doesn't know when she's writing the letter, but it makes it all the sadder, knowing she'll never be able to come home to them. Who knows? Maybe she even does have some premonition of this."

"Mm." My grandmother fanned herself. I sprawled on the grass at her feet under the copper beech. "And why scared?"

"Because it's dangerous, what she's doing. It'll make them mad, and they might never *let* her back. Plus the world she's going into, beyond their walls, *is* dangerous. As evidenced."

"So why write the letter? Why go through with it?"

"Well, because she loves Pyramus." I let a shrug slip by.

She narrowed her eyes. "Not persuasive."

"Well, then because she wants to find things out, for herself, away from the house she grew up in."

"If she writes that, will her parents understand?"

"I don't know. She can tell them what she feels. It's not really her job to make them understand it."

"Amen to that."

I WAS IMPRESSED by the immediacy with which the work I did with my grandmother made its way into my scenes with Kaliq. He commented favorably on it, as did Hale, and even Barb said, "Nice work, kiddo," to me one afternoon when I was leaving rehearsal, which, coming from her, was almost the greatest compliment of all. By the end of the first week of August, the daily schedule had begun to call for the entire cast at every rehearsal, and I garnered more appreciative comments from other actors, several of them witnessing my work as Thisbe for the first time. While the accolades made me feel wonderful, they didn't actually surprise me; I could feel the transformation.

About a week before we were due to give our (extremely limited) public performances—there would be only two—Maeve slid into the pew beside me during rehearsal and whispered, "You're a big liar." She had just finished her penultimate scene, in which Psyche discovers Cupid's true identity and he abandons her. Alone on stage, she delivers a soliloquy in which she breaks down, then gets righteously indignant, then musters the resolve to find him and make him hear her out. It was a difficult speech, and she had crackled and shone, nailing the mercurial transitions and carrying the audience with her at every moment. Watching, I'd felt proud to know her.

"Why am I a big liar?" I whispered back.

"You glow on stage."

"Get out. *You* glow."

"You."

Barb called out sharply, "Quiet in the house, please."

"How much time do you have before your next scene?" Maeve whispered. "Want to go outside?"

We tiptoed toward the door and slipped into the sunshine behind the barn.

"So when are you going to speak to Hale?" she asked immediately.

"What can I say? He already knows how I feel."

"I don't know. Summer's almost over. You should ask him out."

"Out?"

"Ask him to dinner."

"I can't do that. I'll still see him when we're back in Boston. At the salon, if nothing else."

She shook her head. "That's what I wanted to tell you. I don't think he's going back. I think he's going to be directing something in New York."

"What!"

"I know. Right before lunch today, I was cleaning the third-floor bathroom in the farmhouse, and I overheard him talking about it on the phone."

"Are you sure?"

"Pretty sure. He was telling someone about previews starting in November."

"Oh . . ." Disappointment spread like a quick-dissolving pill.

"You should ask him out," said Maeve again.

"I can't. He wouldn't be interested."

"Right."

I looked down and toed the yellow dirt. Not only hadn't I ever told Maeve about my father, I hadn't even told her about the night I'd spent at Hale's before coming out to western Mass. I couldn't get over how strange it was that she wasn't scandalized by the whole idea of my liking him. Now it occurred to me that I was the one who was scandalized.

My worst fear was that I might be like my father. If he, with all his rare and subtle intelligence—in which I still believed—could fail to see the error in committing his fantasies to speech, how then could I possibly trust my own thoughts and feelings to expression?

And yet, I had already revealed myself in words. First on that night in my grandmother's kitchen, then again a week later on Marlborough Street. And what had resulted had not been harmful or distressing. My words hadn't appeared to disturb Hale any more than his responses had put me off. On the contrary. I recalled in a molten rush our playing chess; his trying to teach me the queen's gambit; my flip-flops pushed under his coffee table; the Thai food; my hands on his forks and dishes; the thick length of driftwood on his fridge; the way he had looked through the cutout window, pulling an album from its paper sleeve; the way he had looked when he said he didn't think he could kiss me.

"I'm not really even sure I like him," I mumbled.

"Oh, please." She flopped onto the ground.

I sat beside her. "Do you think," I said.

"Do I think what?"

"Do you think there's such a thing as too much integrity?"

"Yes." She was so matter-of-fact, and so fast with her response, that I could not help bursting into laughter.

"What do you *mean*?"

"What do *you* mean?"

"I don't know . . . Do you think I—"

"Yes, I think you should ask Hale out."

"But do you—"

"Or not," she snapped, so that I looked to see whether she was really exasperated. A breeze whisked around the side of the barn and pushed at the grass-smelling air. Maeve tucked away the hair that had blown across her face. She did look irritated, but whether at the tickling hair or at me I wasn't sure.

"You should just—" She sighed.

"Do one or the other?"

"No, you should just—"

"Stop bugging you about it?"

"Stop asking permission."

AFTER OUR FINAL dress rehearsal, a bunch of people rallied around the idea of a group midnight swim. The older generation, my grandmother and Barb, Gracie and Hendrik and Jean, begged off, but Hale, somewhat surprisingly, came along. As far as I knew, he hadn't been to the Pond all summer, but this night he relented before the pleading and badgering of the cast. We all went noisily down the narrow, moonlit path, and on the sandy beach shucked various articles of clothing and splashed in. Hale rolled up his pant legs and waded.

"Come on, Hale, get wet!" people coaxed, just their sleek heads showing above the water.

"I don't have a suit."

"We don't care!"

But he wouldn't go in past his knees, and after a short time I saw him get back out and sit on the beach. All I could make out was his silhouette, but even from that I could tell he wasn't forlorn, as I might have been if it were me sitting alone on the sand while everyone else went swimming. He gave off an air of being unimpatient, content. That is a quality I have always loved about him.

I wondered why he had come to the Pond this night. After a while I decided to go and sit beside him.

"Hey, Hale."

"Water nice?"

"Yeah. You don't swim?"

"Sometimes."

"When?"

"It's really *where*."

"Where?"

"The ocean, mainly."

An abrupt silence fell between us. We were sitting three inches apart, looking straight out at the Pond. A loon cried. The sand was cool on my skin. Suddenly we both spoke at once.

I said, "Is there a poem about *this*?"

At the same instant Hale said, "Someday I'd like to go swimming with you."

I looked at him. His tone had been so mild I thought I might not have heard him right. "Why?"

He raised his eyebrows and the moonlight bounced off his glasses, but he wasn't looking at me; he was looking out at the inky pond, and his reply sounded almost curt. "I just think it would be a nice thing to do."

"Oh." I thought about touching his hand. I willed myself to do it. My heart was knocking about.

He sighed.

"What?"

"I don't know. Or a dangerous thing, I was thinking." He sort of mumbled this and cleared his throat and then he stood up and brushed sand off his pants. I scrambled up, too, and saw that others were just then strolling drippingly up onto the beach and coming toward us—Ida shook her wet curls, spraying water like a dog; Randy grabbed her around the waist; she shrieked; Maeve said she was starved; Kaliq said he had something she could snack on; Phil said let's go see if there's any brownies left—and the quiet intensity was all shifted and broken up.

"Yes, let's," I said, meaning the brownies and turning toward Hale to include him, but he'd used the arrival of the others to distance himself. He was already standing at the edge of the path, and with a genial wave to us all, announced he was going to bed.

Later in the kitchen Maeve drew me aside. "I saw you sitting with him. Did you ask him out?"

I shook my head, regretting that I hadn't been quicker to touch his hand when the impulse had struck, regretting even more the awful doubt that had stopped me.

THE PERFORMANCES TOOK PLACE on two successive evenings. The first night's audience was a gentle, good-natured crowd, consisting mostly of family members of the cast and crew and of locals with whom we were friendly. Closing night of our short run, however, was attended by a surreal mishmash of people, many of whom I glimpsed while stealing a surreptitious look at the house a half hour before curtain. I'd found that by positioning myself stage left, I could see through a slender gap between the front curtain and one of the blacks hung diagonally in the wings, and from here I leisurely scanned the house, looking for recognizable faces among the people milling about and choosing seats in the rows of pews.

There was a smattering of ridiculously famous people in attendance: actors whose faces I recognized not only from the large and
small screens, but also from the glossy pages of magazines and
checkout-counter tabloids. It was good sport, kind of like an Easter
egg hunt, spotting them among the rest of the audience members.
The more my gaze roved, the more celebrities seemed to materialize, all sprinkled oh-so-casually around the house. I lingered on at
the chink between the drapes like Thisbe at her wall, unable to tear
my eyes from the specter of all those who had gathered to see our
performance.

Then I saw my parents. I was the one who had mailed them the
invitation, so I should not have been shocked to see them. But I had
not been able to bring myself to picture them actually coming.
Such an act would require what seemed an impossible bridging of
worlds. Nevertheless, here they were, in the seventh row. I suppose
they would not have struck anyone else as being out of place, but
to me they seemed conspicuous, with their conservative garb and
somber air, amid the greater sartorial flamboyance and gaiety of the
people congregating around them.

I stared through the curtains' slit. How funny to think that years
ago I'd been sitting out there with them on that side of the curtain,
and now I had crossed over. How did they look from this vantage
point? My mother, of course, I'd seen less than a month earlier, but
it seemed an age since I'd laid eyes on my father. How long had it
been really? I counted. Almost ten weeks. I studied him intently. It
was like slaking a long thirst.

In his blue polo shirt and gold-rimmed glasses, he looked his
quintessential self: still striking, with his golden brown curls crisp-
ing back from his brow, his features that were at once chiseled and
craggy. But he also appeared vulnerable, ill at ease here in this barn
way out in the country, surrounded by theater types—or more to

the point, surrounded by people who did not know who he was and had nothing to offer in the way of confirming or enhancing his status. I saw him glancing around the barn as if impatient or anxious. Really, he was almost fidgety. He kept looking here and there, consulting his program, craning his neck around to see into the back of the barn, or up into the rafters, as though awaiting a sign or signal of some sort, something by which he might orient himself.

Beside him, in a taupe shell, my mother looked *her* quintessential self: the very picture of serenity, dark hair sleekly knotted, eyes and mouth steadily composed, nose and chin pointing straight, almost determinedly ahead—I'd never before noticed how she seemed actively to will her serenity. Diamond studs, tastefully small, glinted in her earlobes. As I watched from backstage—only a narrow band of them was visible to me, framed between the main curtain and the black, and it created a reversal effect, as though they were the ones on stage and I an observer from the audience—my mother turned, placed a kiss on his temple—a prolonged and what could only be described as tender kiss—and then directed her gaze back toward the front of the house. He seemed to relax, as if her kiss had injected him with a centering dose of peace; his glancing about ceased, and although the people sitting directly in front blocked my view of them below the chest, movements of his shoulder suggested he'd taken her hand and brought it into his lap.

And there you had it, I thought: the whole of their story reproduced in an economy of gesture. But no—factor *me* in, too, peering so voraciously at them through the curtain slit, bearing essential witness to their balancing act, which they were in fact performing for a wider public at the same time as for each other, and there you had it: the whole of *our* story.

A few hours earlier, just after supper, my grandmother had asked me, rather mysteriously, to accompany her upstairs. In her bedroom, she had opened a little porcelain box on her dresser and presented me with a closing-night gift: a pair of hoop earrings so delicate they looked like golden threads. They had been, she explained, a gift from Maynard on their opening night in *Pyramus and Thisbe* some thirty-seven years earlier.

"Grandmother," I'd breathed, as she set them in my palm. I'd been sitting on the edge of her bed, which was neatly made and spread with a faded red counterpane. She stood facing me. "I don't know how to thank you. I don't even really mean the earrings," I'd said. "I mean, not only them—but more, the salon, the—the asking Hale to let me try Thisbe, the rehearsing with me under the tree, the—the, my mother."

"Your mother?"

I nodded.

"I don't know what that means."

Nor did I. I frowned, trying to think, and distracted by the familiar sound of her words. I had the distinct, fleeting impression that all utterances might really be lines that have been spoken before. It hit me what her last remark conjured: the memory of our meeting in the tea shop in late winter, when, to my prepared statement about being an instrument of beauty, she'd retorted with those exact words: *I don't know what that means.*

At the time I had received her statement as an indictment and a blow. Now I could see that those words had been her first gift to me, a gift as great and lasting as the heirloom earrings I was cupping in my palm. For with that statement, she had told me that words which only *sounded* meaningful would have no currency with her. Words, with her, would have to count, might well be called *into* account, and would have to stand for something—something more than simply the way they sounded. This seemed an almost unreasonable challenge—yet I liked it, gravitated as if hungrily toward it and what it implied.

I tried now to put that into words for her, and when I had done fumbling out an explanation, she said, "You're welcome, Beatrice."

My grandmother had a remarkable capacity, I thought, to accept gratitude. Perhaps it came from her long experience accepting accolades; in any case, there was uncommon grace in the way she did not deflect or diminish but simply said "Thank you," to a compliment, and "You're welcome," to an expression of thanks. She bowed her head slightly toward me. "But I thank you for her, too, you know."

"You do? In what way?"

"The most obvious. Her coming out here last month, the time we spent, would never have happened if not for you."

From this I learned that my grandmother looked upon that difficult visit as a beginning.

THE DRESSING ROOM, a long narrow space at the back of the barn, was crowded but calm, as all the other actors seemed to be occupying private isles of concentration. So many bare bulbs, fixed around the makeup mirrors, made the room stifling. There had been much exchanging of flowers the previous evening, and various bunches and bouquets now filled the small space, the smell of their natural perfume mingling in the heated air with the chemical sweetness of pancake base and hair spray.

This was the last night we would spend at the Farm. Tomorrow we would strike the set, pack up our things, and return to all the different places from which we'd come. Or not, in my case. My home wasn't even there for me anymore. Maeve had said I could crash with her in Somerville while I looked for a job and planned what to do next. But she herself was thinking about pulling up roots, and going to live with Kaliq in Brooklyn. Come Monday morning I wouldn't even know where to reach half these people with whom I'd made a life this summer. Hale wouldn't be going back to his home in Boston either, if Maeve was right, but to another project in another city, another state.

Barb came in and called five minutes to places.

Five minutes. Butterflies kicked up in my stomach, struggling past my sadness at the summer's ending. I sat at my "station" at the long wall of mirrors and took a good look at my reflection, making sure nothing had smudged or smeared since Maeve had applied my makeup. There I noticed, tucked into the bottom of the mirror, a small white envelope with my name on it. Along with the previous night's flower-giving, cards had been distributed by many of the ensemble, but I didn't remember having seen this one. I was quite sure, in fact, that it had not been there until now. I plucked it from the frame, broke the seal, and slipped out a card, which showed a woman with voluminously piled dark hair, barefoot and bare-shouldered, one ear pressed against a wall through which ran a long, meandering crack. I flipped it over: it had been painted by John William Waterhouse and was called *Thisbe*. I opened the card and read:

> To This-Bea,
> Who has made the role her own.
>
> —
>
> (at a loss for words),
>
>   Hale

So he was at a loss for words and I was unable to act.

And yet, here *were* words. It was up to me now.

"Places," called Barb. Fingers shaking, I slipped the card back in its envelope and filed with all the other actors into the wings.

AFTERWARD THERE WAS wine and cake. Everyone was invited back to the farmhouse for the cast party. The night, when I try to remember it, filters back kaleidoscopically, a fast-changing array of snapshots, one melting into the next: charades in the kitchen, dancing in the living room, people sprawled all over the staircase, lines outside both bathroom doors, half-filled paper plates and plastic cups left on every surface, live music and dozens of paper lanterns out on the porch.

I enjoyed myself, eating and drinking, dancing and socializing. I was wearing a brown silk halter dress Maeve had lent me, feeling very much the just-discovered ingénue. But I was jittery, too, all this while, because part of my attention was given over to keeping a lookout for my parents. Initially, I told myself I was seeking them in order to avoid them—not avoid them absolutely, or indefinitely, but at least until I was ready to approach them; I wanted to be the one in control. But as I wove in and out of the rooms of the house without spotting them, the search took on a desperate feel. The cool desire to maintain the upper hand gave way to the helpless desire to *find* them, period. It seemed unthinkable they would have left right after the play, without speaking to me, even if only to say hello and goodbye. But I saw that this is what must have occurred.

Trying to ignore the feeling that I'd been abandoned, I concentrated instead on what I would say later to Hale. I knew it would have to be later, for he was too much in demand while the party was in full swing. At some point between giving up on my parents and waiting for time alone with Hale, I grew so hot from dancing, and so tired of the noise and being jostled, that I stepped outside for some air. I saw that a few people were already beginning to leave, and thinking I might have glimpsed Hale among a cluster of five, I trailed the group, following them to a row of parked cars. If he had gone to bid them farewell, it would work perfectly to catch him on his way back. That way we could have our moment of speech and action in the private darkness of the meadow.

But he was not among them. I watched all five people climb into the car, which drove off down the dirt lane, in a roar of broken muffler, the headlights careening wildly as the car jounced over the bumps. I turned and headed back toward the farmhouse, which shone like a lighthouse at the edge of a dark, grassy sea. As I reached the end of the row I came, incredulously, upon our family car: the unmistakable old Saab. It was positioned somewhat away from the rest of the row, closer to the woods. The engine was off. As I drew closer I heard issuing from the open windows a sound I knew better than perhaps any other in the world: my parents' voices intertwined in soft, pressing speech.

I came around toward the driver's side, but remained several yards back. "You guys?" My voice sounded tentative.

A pause. "Bebe?" My mother, from the passenger seat.

"What are you doing out here?"

"Just talking." Her voice was smooth and bright.

". . . Okay. You've been here all night?"

"For a little while."

"Hours." I couldn't quite believe it.

No response.

"Well, are you . . . planning to come up to the party? It'll be ending soon."

Another pause. My mother's voice again, too light and smooth for the absurdity of the moment: "That's what we're discussing."

"Oh."

I remained where I was.

Silence from the car.

My father had said nothing, had not moved, nor given any indication of his presence; he might almost have been pretending not to be there. I had the queer impression that he actually hoped that by sitting completely still, he might prevent me from noticing him. I peered at the shadowy outline in the driver's seat, the murky profile, the slightly slouched posture; of course it was he.

"Dad?"

No answer.

"Dad?"

He cleared his throat. Then nothing.

"You're not even going to talk to me?" I said. There was a cracking note in my own voice that threatened to undo me. I came several paces toward the car. I could just make out his face, very dimly. He was studying the steering wheel. "Dad?" My voice began to break. I took another step toward the car. "Don't you even want to look at me? Did you see me in the play? Dad? Daddy, what did I do?"—I had to concentrate very hard on forming the words and pushing them past the constriction of my throat, while I came closer and still he kept his gaze doggedly on the steering wheel—"What did I do—that's so *bad*—you can't even look at me?"

The sound that came out of his mouth was the worst thing I'd ever heard. His face crumpled and he emitted dry, awful, rusty-sounding sobs, collapsing in slow motion forward until his brow came to rest on the steering wheel, the sound continuing in ragged heaves from his slack jaw. My mother, I think, was crying then, too. All of us knowing it wasn't anything bad I had done.

I put back my head and looked at the sky. Drank in the pitch-black dome, its furious stillness, its fixed distance, its endless auspicious stars. Felt my breath grow calm, my lungs admit and expel the steady night air.

"I'm so sorry, I'm so sorry, I'm so sorry," my father, as if incapacitated, was gasping, almost unintelligibly.

I began to back away.

"Bebe," came my mother's voice. "Wait, please wait, love."

I backed farther away.

This is what they had been doing the entire time. Sitting in the car. So immobilized by their own brokenness that they could not cover the hundred yards between car and house, could not manage to seek me out, respond to my performance.

I heard the door open, but I'd already turned and was running from them both, from their stasis, his tattered voice, her entreaties that I return. When I crossed the border into the light cast by a string of paper lanterns on the porch, I slowed, trying to regain my breath and a semblance of normalcy in preparation for reentering the party. I heard the sound of running behind me, and labored breath, and then a hand grasped my arm, and it was my father. I was surprised he could run that fast, disturbed that he had. Fisher-Harts did not make scenes; we didn't chase one another over dark fields at night; we didn't lose control in public, and if one of us did, we feigned illness and closed ranks and beat a hasty retreat, salvaging what dignity we could.

He was panting and sweating. He looked both angry and infirm. There was a fringe of people nearby, a few on the porch, a few on the lawn.

"Get off," I hissed, pulling my arm from his grasp.

He seized it again, higher up. This was in itself strange. For him to hold me there, his thumb against the pulse on the underside of my arm, was an infraction of the Fisher-Hart prohibition against touching, against any but the most highly formalized touch. I tried to yank free again but it was harder to pull away with his hand in this position. And yet I was aware, oddly, that I held the greater power in this situation.

"I said get off."

"Wait," he breathed.

"Get off." I could feel the people in closest proximity pause in their conversations. I had the sense of them cocking their ears toward my father and me, as if poised for possible intervention.

He dropped his hand.

We were both still working to catch our breath.

"You were wonderful, Bebe," he said quietly, hopelessly. Sweat gleamed on his neck, on his Adam's apple. The collar of his polo shirt was dark with it. "I was immensely proud. Proud of my beautiful, talented daughter."

A laugh cracked in my throat. I struggled to keep my voice low, and it came out clotted with disgust. "We're not having this conversation. As if you were a regular father."

He winced. "I want to do what'll make things better."

"You wouldn't know how." I started away.

"Don't," he pleaded, his hand finding my wrist.

I spun on him. "Get *off*!"

"Everything all right, Bea?" John's voice projected from the porch steps with forced pleasance.

I hadn't realized he and Javier were among those who had stopped talking and were paying attention to my father and me. The two of them came down the steps now, not slowly, and approached me and my father, who dropped my wrist. I saw in their faces how serious they looked, how alert and ready for action. John's chest puffed out as if instinctively, and he came around to position himself between my father and me. "Is this person bothering you?"

The quality of his address—chivalrous, gallant—and the look in his eye as he regarded my father—cold, forbidding—made me go light-headed with shame. John had no idea who "this person" was. He assumed my father was just some man, some audience member who'd seen me in the play and was pursuing me now, making an unwelcome pass. Or worse, he assumed this man *did* know me, with impropriety.

"No," I mumbled. "Just leave him alone."

"She wants to be left alone," John told my father.

"You can leave *us* alone," my father retorted.

Javier said, "Come, let's be gentlemen."

"You don't understand," I tried to explain, but ineffectually; it was like those dreams in which you want to speak but no sound comes out. My father moved closer to me. Javier put a hand on his shoulder, an almost friendly-looking gesture. My father shook him off. John stepped in and took him by the arm. I pressed my hands against my forehead, cried, "Stop it, stop—he's my father!"

Then everything sort of suspended and went into slow reverse: John released his hold; Javier withdrew, bowing his head; my father, his shirt twisted at the collar, turned toward me, his face a cipher. Once more, needlessly, I said, "Just *stop*."

I swiveled toward the house and saw that several more people had come out to the porch and were gathered by the railing, their gazes full of curiosity and concern. Everyone had seen; everyone had heard. Now, as if they were the ones who had anything to be ashamed of, they began to shuffle off, avert their eyes, clear the steps. For a brief, horrible moment, my eyes met Hale's among the crowd. He did not move or look away. I felt something inside me shudder and collapse. Then I ducked my head and ran past everyone, the blood pounding in my ears, my feet pounding across the porch and into the farmhouse and up three flights of stairs.

———

"BEA?"

Hale.

"Bea?"

The second time he said my name he switched on the light, and I propped myself on an elbow, blinking against the sudden brightness. I'd fallen asleep on top of his bed on the third floor of the farmhouse, where the ceiling sloped down like the ceiling in my attic bedroom at home in Cambridge, which for an instant after I woke up was where I thought I was. Except that it had been sold.

"Are you all right?"

I sat up and put a hand to my forehead, shielding my eyes. I was still wearing Maeve's halter dress. I could hear remnant sounds of enjoyment from downstairs.

"Do you mind turning the light back off?"

He restored the room to darkness and closed the door, then came to sit beside me on the bed. This should have registered as surprising, yet it did not. The words we spoke next should also have registered as surprising, yet they felt close to inevitable: again I had the peculiar impression that we were speaking lines which had existed long before either of us was born. Not that our words felt scripted or stilted. It was all happening in the moment, each thing newly and truly felt and voiced—yet there was nevertheless a sense that it was timeless and ineluctable.

I said, "Do you think it's bad that I like you?"

"I don't know."

"Is it true you're going to New York after this?"

"Yes."

"Can I come?"

He laughed very softly. "Maybe."

"Do you want to go to sleep?"

"Yes."

"Can I stay?"

A long sigh. Silence.

"Okay." I rose to go.

With startling speed he reached out and took my hand. "No."

There was a very bad feeling to this. It reminded me of something I didn't want to have to think about. Oh.

"You were on the porch. You saw me with my father."

He slid his hand from mine. "Yes."

"That's the problem."

"Is it?"

"I don't know."

"You ran away."

"This is where I was going."

"I didn't know. I looked for you later. I mean I kept looking to see when you'd come down again, but I never saw you, and then I assumed you'd gone off to bed and I'd somehow missed you."

"I wanted to be here. I wanted to sleep in your bed."

I thought this statement contained a question, but he didn't say anything.

"Do you think it's bad?" I whispered.

"Do I think what's bad?"

"Me."

"Why would I think that?"

"You think I could be—afflicted? My father, his—predilections. You think I'm like that? In reverse?"

"No. Beatrice." I felt him turn toward me, felt him waiting.

I made myself face him. There were his glasses, and behind them, his eyes, and there was the line of his nose and mouth and chin, all of these lines interesting and beautiful to me, with the thin light gracing the side of his face from the two small windows set in the wall behind his bed.

"Don't confuse yourself with him," Hale said simply. "You aren't. You're you."

The words poured into me slowly, filling me with sad happiness. It was as though I'd lost everything and gained everything. It was nothing, no great wisdom, but it seemed the world, to hear him say that.

"There ought," I said, "to be a word for happy and sad."

"Bittersweet?"

"A better word."

"Life?"

"Oh—yeah." A minute went by. I said, "I'm just going to go to the bathroom."

I went to the little bathroom down the hall and peed and washed my face. I listened. The house was all quiet now. I regarded the person in the mirror with curiosity and equanimity, but it didn't solve any great riddles, so eventually I gave up looking and returned to Hale's room. I felt sober and unafraid.

The windows over his bed were admitting bluish starlight from above and the warmer glow of paper lanterns from below, which together bathed the room in enough light for me to be able to see him sitting exactly where I'd left him, fully clothed, on the edge of his bed. I sat beside him again.

"Are you tired?" I asked.

"I thought I was."

"You're not anymore?"

"I'm . . . at a loss."

"Please don't be. I don't want you to feel lost."

"I didn't say I felt lost."

"Oh." That I could yawn in the midst of this seemed an absurdity.

"Are you tired?"

"Yes."

"You lie down, then."

I got under the covers and moved over to lie up against the wall, leaving room.

He sat still another minute and then I listened to the slow sounds of him taking off his shoes, the muted clunk as they hit the floor, the creak of the bedsprings as he bent forward to strip off his socks, the sound of his voice as he began to talk, softly and musingly, almost as if to himself. "The thing is, there would be a part for you, if you wanted it, in this play I'm directing. Rehearsals start in just over two weeks. It's quite a small part. I've been ambivalent about whether or not even to mention it. You'd only be in one scene. You'd have to relocate again, and this time the production doesn't provide lodging. I should have said something earlier, but . . . I . . . I've been hesitant about whether to mention it at all."

"Hesitant why?" It seemed at once astonishing and completely natural to find myself lying in bed in the dark, arms crossed under my head, listening to Hale talk as he unbuttoned his shirt, removed it, and draped it over the footboard of the metal-frame single bed.

"Not about your abilities." He took off his glasses with one hand and laid them on the bedside table. Then he stood, turning as he did, so that he was facing me. "About my motives." The window over the bed allowed enough scarce light to illuminate his features. As he stood there, though, it suddenly dimmed; someone had put out the string of paper lanterns below, leaving only starlight, rare and constant. "Do you mind if I take off my pants?"

I was embarrassed and touched by such formality. A nervous laugh trembled in my throat; I coughed. "No."

He undid his belt, his fly, stepped out of his pants. His movements were unhurried and graceful, and although we both knew they belied trepidation, they seemed less a mask or charade than an expression of courtliness.

In his shorts, he climbed into bed.

We lay on our backs. I waited quite a long time, until my heart wasn't pounding so violently, before I touched him. He lay perfectly still, admirably still, it seemed to me, except for the rise and fall of his chest. As slowly as though I had days to do nothing else, I touched his chest and arms and stomach and face. After a great while, an age, he said, "Can I lie on top of you?"—another formal request, but this time no laugh threatened to loose itself from my throat; with damp eyes I whispered yes and he lay on top of me, very still, all of him weighing on all of me, and in the stillness of it, I was able eventually to bring my eyes up to meet his, and we stayed like that, motionless, for a long time, me in my dress and him in his shorts.

At some point I noticed a certain pearliness around the sky's rim, and I said, "It's getting light out," and Hale said, "Now let's get some sleep."

FOUR

The Round Trip

HAVE BEEN REPLAYING the events that transpired between March and August of the year I turned twenty, half my life ago, ever since I woke up this morning, which happened around three, to the sound of Hale's coughing. He's been coughing for a week. Yesterday he finally gave in to my badgering and went to see Doris Liu, our general practitioner and a good friend. She diagnosed bronchitis and wrote a prescription for a nighttime suppressant. When his coughing woke us both this morning, I rose and poured him a dose, then sat up beside him while he fell back asleep, only to find myself unable to do the same.

Hale is in good general health. Doris reminded me of this yesterday.

"You look far too upset," she observed as we waited in her office for Hale, who was dressing in the next room. I sat on the love seat; she leaned against the front of her desk. Her Gramercy office was tiny and cluttered. "Look, nine times out of ten it's viral, but if you want I can write a script for antibiotics."

"No, I know," I said. "It's not that."

"For seventy he's in remarkable health."

"He's not seventy."

She glanced at the chart. "Sixty-nine. We should all be so healthy." She rapped her knuckles on the wooden desk.

Though Chinese-born, Doris speaks English with virtually no accent and has even picked up a New Yorker's Jewish inflections, something we have joked about in the past and which ordinarily might have caused me to smile.

"His heart's strong, his cholesterol's good, his mind's clearer than mine," she went on telling me in her fortifying way. Hale came in during this and smiled at the last bit. It was his trademark conservative smile, the edges of his front teeth lining up behind compressed lips.

"I know," I repeated, squeezing his hand back as he sat beside me and took mine.

"You've got to take care of this lady," Doris told him. "She's worrying too much."

"She's not worried about me, Doris," Hale told her gently. "Bea's mother just passed away."

Doris turned back to me. Her hair, slate gray, was as always parted in the middle and drawn into a twist. She wore a black turtleneck sweater and a sable wool skirt, no lab coat. Although her eyes were darker and almond-shaped, there was, in the serene symmetry of her features, her stylish but subdued wardrobe, and her upright posture, an echo of my mother; I had had this thought on several occasions previously, but never so strongly as now. "I'm very sorry to hear that. Had she been sick?"

"Hit by a car."

"Oh. Oh, I'm sorry."

"Thanks, Doris."

That exchange, also, was among my thoughts during the early hours this morning. Hale had been wrong when he said I wasn't worried about him. I suppose my worry has been amplified by the news of my mother's death, but the truth is I worry about his health, generally speaking, more than I let on. It's something of an occupational hazard, I've found, having married a man twenty-eight years my senior. Of course, we joke that I'm catching up. At our wedding the difference between our ages (then twenty-four and fifty-two) seemed colossal. But on my last birthday I was forty-one, and he had only just turned sixty-nine. One feels the gap is closing. At any rate, we raise fewer eyebrows.

I don't usually dwell on the difference in our ages. I think it's just that he has had this cough, and now my mother is dead at seventy. She had been walking home from the library, my father told Hale after I refused to take the phone. The roads had not been icy, the driver not drunk. The car had just slipped out of control. She had died instantly, I was told, but I have no idea what this really means, how they can know for certain. It sounds like something they might say out of kindness, or simple tact. It happened on Sunday afternoon, around four-twenty, almost precisely at sunset, and it happened at a bend in the road. She had gone to the library to return a cookbook, and had been coming home with a CD, Henryk Górecki's Symphony No. 3, which was found, still in its case, in a pile of snow some thirty feet from her body. One of her mittens was found a couple of feet from the CD.

I know the library. My mother volunteered there once a week, processing donated books. I have been there with her a handful of times over the past twenty years, which is nearly as often as I have visited my parents in Maine. It is called Bovine Free Library, as though promising to be devoid of cows. In fact, Bovine is the name of the town, thirty-five miles northwest of Portland, where my parents live. Lived. Where my father lives and my mother lived. In a split-level ranch. Later this morning Hale and I will take a cab to LaGuardia, fly to Portland International, pick up a rental car, and make the drive to Bovine. The service is being held at two, latish because of me, since I said I would on no account fly up the night before.

I tried to dissuade my grandmother from attending. She is ninety-two now, still living in Boston, in an assisted-living facility. Her mind is not quite the same; she's not diagnosable, but there is a definite fading in and out that I, and others who are close to her, have recently begun to perceive. Nevertheless, besides her declining eyesight and hearing, and her troublesome feet, on which she has had several surgeries over the years, there is, as she likes to point out, nothing fundamentally the matter with her. Still, it will be a long day for her.

"Don't try to boss me," she'd said over the phone, after I tried to talk her out of her plans to attend.

"But I think I should."

"Beatrice: I will go to my daughter's funeral." She delivered that like an actress, in a tremolo brave and stirring. I could picture exactly how she must have lifted her chin to say it, and couldn't help smiling at the tenacity of her craft. At the same time I was shot through with a perverse jealousy: *my* mother would never have the chance to speak up so staunchly on the event of my death.

"I just mean, you should take care of yourself. Conserve your energy." I tried to sound reasonable.

"Don't you see, my dear, at my age, there is very little to conserve my energy *for*." She made this observation lightly, without rue. She has softened with age; her humor remains indefatigable, but her imperiousness has abated. If once she seemed the embodiment of that old needlepoint at the Homestead—I WILL BE AS HARSH AS

TRUTH AND AS UNCOMPROMISING AS JUSTICE—now she is more the Richard Wilbur poem Hale left on my pillow long ago: open to, indeed delighted by, her fallibility and relative inconsequentiality in the face of things.

"Oh Grandmother," I'd sighed.

She went on to relate her itinerary. One of the aides at her facility, a favorite of hers who happens to be off that day, would serve as her traveling companion. My grandmother had cleared it with the wellness director. They would rent a Lincoln Town Car at the airport—she'd already made the reservation, and seemed pleased with herself for having specified this make and model—and the aide would chauffeur her to the service and back. When I suggested Hale and I share her rental car, so we could at least make the drive together, she declined on the grounds that her flight was getting in earlier, so that she and her aide, whose name was Alvarez, and who was "a peach," would have time to stop for "a nice lunch." When I said Hale and I would pay for the extra plane ticket and whatever per diem the aide was charging, she said, "Pish-posh, Bea. You will not."

Her imperiousness has not expired altogether.

We ended the phone call as we always do, each of us saying, "I love you." Neither of us had cried at any point during it. Nor had we, for that matter, talked about my mother.

THE SKY OUTSIDE our bedroom window is whitening, the skyline going from majestic to wan. There is a welcome aspect to the sight, for as the buildings themselves come into view, their lumbering grays homely against the low-slung cotton-batting of the sky, their lights come to represent not starry jewels, but people: all the men and women and children rousing themselves to cereal and coffee in countless kitchens, pocketing subway passes and cab fare, inclining themselves toward a million different destinations, a million different intentions, within this city.

I have lived in New York ever since that September after the Farm, first in a Washington Heights studio sublet Javier helped me get, then in a Hell's Kitchen flat I shared with Maeve after she and Kaliq broke up, then briefly in Hale's University Place pied-à-terre, and for the past seventeen years here, in our own two-bedroom on West Twelfth. I have come to love it as only an adoptive New Yorker can: with an edge of defiance and an admitted tendency to overcompensate for not being a native. I have gone on the walking tours, read the histories, visited the out-of-way landmarks. I take advantage of its cultural and culinary offerings, often to Hale's professed amusement, although he has never complained when I have "dragged" him off to hear someone speak at the 92nd Street Y, say, or to sample some Argentinean food in Jackson Heights.

I go to Boston infrequently, in order only to see my grandmother, for I have lost touch with any friends I once had in the area. I generally stay east of the Charles when I go, although once, some years back, and against my better judgment, I gave in to the desire to drive past our old house in Cambridge. I was surprised at how little I was affected by the considerable changes that had been wrought. The blue oval plaque with the date *1818*, which my mother had labored to procure from the historical society, was no longer in evidence. The house had been painted a kind of beige-ochre. The old peastone path had been paved. And oddly, improbably, almost as though it were being staged for my benefit, roofers were there reshingling at the very time I drove by, slowing to something like two miles an hour without ever actually braking.

The last contact I had with Ezra was a postcard he sent me two years after the summer at the Farm. It was postmarked Barcelona; he wrote that he was traveling around Europe with his fiancée, and in the remaining space mentioned that the Jimerson Homestead had been closed due to the surfacing of new documents which cast serious doubt on whether it had ever served as a station stop on the Underground Railroad. I'd assumed of course that he was being funny, and thought nothing more about it until the next time I was in Boston, and on a whim drove by the site in Watertown. The old house was almost unrecognizable, so drastically had it been remodeled. The outbuildings had been torn down, and what looked like condos were going up in their place. A sign in front of the whole property announced "six new luxury townhouses on a grand historic site" above the telephone number of the developer.

So Ezra hadn't been kidding. I thought it darkly funny—and how *fitting!*—all that history turning out to be myth, after all.

I work more or less steadily. Every now and then I perform in something that receives a lot of attention. More often I work in smallish venues, off- or off-off-Broadway and regional theater, the occasional guest spot on a television series. It isn't my grandmother's gorgeous career, but I am not complaining. I don't as a rule get recognized walking down the street, although twice in the same restaurant I have been asked for my autograph. I realize I have been lucky to work in several projects I have really loved. The fact is that my ambition changed. What I wanted at nineteen was a dream of acting, and that dream was like a place marker for things I couldn't yet comprehend.

Beside me Hale is in a deep sleep, and his mouth-breathing reminds me of a child's, surprisingly gentle, unimpeded. I put my face close to his and feel the warmth of his breath. He smells like wool in the rain. He doesn't have so much hair on his head. I think it is a fine head, round and spotted here and there with age. The curls at the back are still quite dense, and white as candles. Ginger and white stubble covers the lower part of his face, his great firm chin. In the morning before he has shaved, he makes me think of a dog that has rubbed its wet muzzle in the sand.

I am just gathering the will to get out of bed and shower when the phone rings. I take it into the bathroom with me and shut the door so as not to wake Hale.

"I'm taking you to the airport," says Maeve. "What time is your flight?"

"Sweet pea." I sit on the edge of the tub. "We'll get a cab."

"Just tell me the time."

"It'll be easier to call a cab."

"You don't have to tell me, but in that case I'll have to idle outside your building starting now."

"Your looks are deeply deceptive. No one would ever peg you for the hard ass you are."

"How are you?"

"Okay."

"How's Hale feeling?"

"Better, it seems. He's still sleeping."

"Have you cried yet?"

"No."

She's asked me that at least three times since I called her with the news Sunday night. I tell her she can come at a quarter to ten, knowing she'll be curbside by nine-thirty. She's one of the few people we know who keeps a car in Manhattan. She had offered to come to the funeral, but I told her no. It would have meant her missing two performances, as this is Wednesday, matinee day. "It doesn't matter," Maeve had said. "Try telling that to the ticket holders," I returned. "Try telling that to the ticket holders flying in from Boise." Her show is sold out through April, and nobody who has been waiting months to see it wants to see the understudy, nor does Maeve, for that matter, want to disappoint.

Nor, in truth, do I want her at the funeral.

Maeve has met my mother a handful of times, on her biannual visits to the city. She has never met my father. And although I have, over the years, filled her in on the basic details of his checkered career, the reason behind both my parents' move the summer I met her, as well as why I have only brief and sporadic contact with him now, I'm not about to let them meet, my best friend and my prodigal father, certainly not today, under circumstances such as these. It'll be fraught enough, having my father and Hale in the same room. Thus my insistence on flying there and back in one day, and spending as little time as possible at my parents' house, which is where the postfuneral gathering is to occur.

A very long, hot shower. When I come out Hale is awake. "Hello, Beauty," he says.

I sit on the edge of the bed and we hold hands. "How are you feeling?"

"Middling."

"Do you want to not go?"

"No."

I touch his forehead. He isn't feverish. I stroke his pate, finger the short curls at the back of his head.

"Do *you*?" he asks. "Want to not go?"

"Yeah." Thus he gets a grin from me.

Hale goes into the bathroom. He has developed in his dotage a compensatory gait, a way of favoring his arthritic back and knees that gives him a paradoxically spry look, a walk that, although uneven, is almost lilting. I feel a torque in my heart to see him make his way across a room.

I switch on the floor lamp and dress in front of the window. It's still dark enough outside for the glass to retain some properties of a mirror, even as it gives a view of the dim, milky morning city. I put on ribbed tights, a black pencil skirt, the moss-colored sweater my mother mailed me last Christmas. I put on the golden thread earrings Maynard once gave my grandmother. I put my hair in a ponytail. It's been a long time since I had it cropped short and dyed platinum. I have let that faux pixie look go. My hair's natural color is not unlike my mother's. My whole look today, I realize, as I zip up my boots, is not unlike my mother's. On the other side of the glass, snowflakes small as sparks begin to appear.

In the kitchen, orange juice for me, tomato juice for Hale, in little juice glasses. And eggs. And bread, the end of a loaf of sourdough, which I find and slice and begin to soak in the eggs, which I have beaten and poured onto a plate. And butter set heating in the pan. And an avocado in the fruit bowl, I begin to slice that, too, and then cheese, an aged provolone, slices of which I arrange on plates between the slices of avocado. We have no syrup, but I set out confectioners' sugar and apricot preserves. The French toast is hissing in the pan, and the teakettle warbling, and Hale comes into the kitchen and says, "What's all this?"

"I don't know." It comes out defensively. I feel irritated by his question. The truth is, when I came into the kitchen I had no idea I was going to make a big breakfast, and am a little surprised to find myself in the middle of it.

Hale gives me a look and makes the tea.

We eat. I tell him Maeve is coming at nine forty-five. He says of the minuscule pricks of snow falling past the window, "This shouldn't affect us." He says, "This is good," meaning the food. I am starting to go chilly inside myself.

After we wash the dishes together, Hale makes us sandwiches for the plane and I go make the bed. After this there is still too much time. I double-check to make sure Hale has packed what he needs: the prescription cough medicine, ibuprofen, antacid, herbal tea bags, tissues, throat lozenges, water bottle, book. He is reading the latest Shakespeare biography. I check to make sure I have packed what I need: lipstick, hand cream, book. I will bring my mother's copy of *How to Cook a Wolf*. She had lent it to me on her most recent visit, over the summer, and without beginning it, I had placed it in a pile of things to give or return to her on her next visit. We had spoken of the possibility that she might come for a week in the spring.

Now I pack the book inside our carry-on bag with everything else, and stand in the living room listening to the clock tick on the mantelpiece, waiting for it to be time to go downstairs. We will be back tonight. We will be back in—I count on my fingers—eleven hours. The clock's tick seems to be the soft sound of the snow descending outside. In the bedroom, Hale is coughing; I check my urge to go to him. I know I do fuss too much over his health. I look at the clock, watch the second hand make a full revolution. The coughing in the other room subsides. I lift my eyes to the wall above the clock.

Mounted over the mantelpiece is the piece of driftwood I first saw on Hale's refrigerator in his Marlborough Street apartment. Some seventeen years ago, when we first moved into this place, I had come across it in a box of things he'd put into storage. Secretly, I'd set it aside, and a week later, when Hale was out, I'd spent an afternoon rubbing it with tung oil, using an old undershirt of Hale's as a rag. Then I'd screwed a couple of eyehooks into the back, strung a wire between these, fastened it above the mantelpiece, and waited for Hale to notice it. When he did, that evening, he'd said, "Oho!" and smiled in a blushing sort of way, and then spent several minutes kissing me on various parts of my face and ears and neck.

But just now I have a knot in my stomach, looking at the piece of driftwood. I love it for reasons I don't entirely understand, but which relate to my occasional misgivings about having turned it so deliberately into a piece of art. In some ways, it seemed better back when it was on top of Hale's fridge—just as my delight in it, back then, had to do with its embodying the antithesis of my parents' aesthetic. I wonder whether my ministrations, the strategic polishing and mounting of it, constituted a breach, a perversion of Hale's easy, unprepossessing fondness for the thing. On impulse I go to the fireplace and stand on a log and lift it from the wall.

Hale comes in, sees me perched there with the driftwood in my hands, and holds his tongue.

"I-I'm not sure I like it—there," I stammer, snappishly.

He has the glimmerings of a twinkle in his eye, but I see him decide not to make a joke about it. He is wary of me this morning, and I hate that, I hate it.

I step off the log and set the driftwood on the coffee table. The phone rings. Hale gets it. It's my father, calling to see what flight we are taking, making sure we will get in on time. All this I gather by listening to Hale's end of the brief conversation.

My father has not visited Hale and me once during our entire marriage. If I never extended him a welcome, it is equally true that I have no memory of his ever inquiring after one. There may have been a few years in the beginning when, if he had asked, I would have refused and relished doing so. But for many more years than that I wished he would ask, or would at least express an interest in visiting us, me, here. "Do you think Dad might come, one of these times?" I would ask my mother every so often. It would cost me something even to mention it casually, and then, in the interval before she replied, I would half regret it. But always she'd say, "Oh I don't know, Bebe, love. His hip's been bothering him," or "He would find the pace overwhelming." Two years ago, I stopped asking altogether.

Now Hale hangs up, and we turn our heads in unison to the clock: nine thirty-five. Without speaking, we help each other on with our coats and hats, something I suppose a spectator could find too precious, but we have long performed this mutual intimacy, and it isn't put-on. I mean it is heartfelt, and I take comfort in it this morning. We ride the elevator to the lobby. I am right; through the doors I see Maeve is already idling in her black Jetta.

Eqbal, the doorman, says, "Another for you, Ms. Fisher-Hart. They came this morning." He gestures to a large flower arrangement in a glass vase: yellow, red, pink, white, and orange roses. The card says, "With our love and sympathy, Javier and John." They live in London now.

"Thank you, Eqbal. You keep them, will you?"

He inclines his head decorously. "I'll keep them at the desk."

It is very cold. The soles of my feet, even through my boots, feel it almost at once. The exhaust lingers torpidly in the air behind the car; it can't get altitude. Eqbal insists on supporting Hale's elbow all the way to the curb. Ordinarily I am happy to defer to Eqbal's judgment on such matters; he has an unobtrusive bearing and I have great regard for what can at times seem like his telepathic ability to sense the needs of his clients. But today I think he has made a mistake, and I find myself infuriated to see him relating to Hale as infirm.

In the car, Maeve turns around and hands us a brown paper bag of clementines. "Is it warm enough back there?" she asks. It is, deliciously warm, and the car smells of the fruit. The traffic isn't heavy. She and Hale chat about her show; there have been some changes, both to the script and the way she is now playing a pivotal scene; she asks whether he'd be willing to come see it again and tell her what he thinks. Their conversation progresses as a soothing sound, a brook, punctuated every so often by Hale's coughs. I look out the window. There is the East River, with pinprick snow falling against it, and there, a barge moving so slowly I would like to be on it, a crew member, with a life far removed. We enter the Midtown Tunnel: fumes, brake lights, the absence of sky. I am grateful for the luxury of easy silence. I know that these two people, who know me better than anyone, have no need for me to talk.

Nor do I think. Not beyond the most basic points of orientation, like those I imagine one might have after a stroke: car heater, clementine, coughing fit, exit ramp.

At LaGuardia, Maeve gets out of the car to hug us each in turn. She holds on to me until I push her gently away. "Get back in," I chide her. "You're freezing." She's shivering in a pink crocheted sweater.

"I should be going with you."

I tell her in all honesty, "I really wouldn't want you there."

"You're such a peculiar friend," she says contemplatively, hugging herself around the middle. She's so cold she's bent at the knees.

"Get in the *car*," I repeat. I realize I'm playing it up a little in hopes of getting her to say something funny. Something that might get us both to dissolve in gales of laughter. A Maeve-ish laugh right now would be a release almost on a par with crying.

She gets in the car, lowers the passenger-side window, leans over, and pipes out, "This is snow-globe snow!" before pulling away from the curb and veering into the far left lane, for the airport exit.

It *is* snow-globe snow, tiny and whirling in slow motion, more glitter than flake. As though the props master has released it from machines mounted high above the stage, as though the stage crew will have to clean it up later, sweep it all into barrels to be used at a repeat performance.

Hale and I go through the revolving door and come out into the warmth and bustle of the terminal. We read the monitors for information about boarding time and gate. Hale and I have been to this airport so many times, traveled so many places, but we have never been to Maine together.

It has been a little under two years since the last time I was in Bovine, which was also the last time I saw my father. Despite my mother's protestations, as far as I know he is well, in good general health and fitness. He is seventy-four. Up until two days ago, both parents had continued to work, seeing private patients in an office suite they rented together with another therapist in Portland, although my mother retired from her job at the hospital a few years back.

Both parents had still enjoyed fine cuisine. In their new life they'd eaten out only rarely, however; cooking together had become a more central activity for them over the years. They'd joined a local agrarian cooperative and taken an interest in eating seasonal, regional foods. They'd also taken up walking, which they did daily and with the zeal of converts. They were expert at layering breathable fabrics, and would speak with pride of their adherence to the routine regardless of the time of year or the weather. I'd heard them hold forth more than once on their new creed of silk long underwear, of down vests, of wool and Gore-Tex. When they went out, they carried organic nut and fruit bars in their pockets, and key chains with photon LED lights.

For the past several years, they had also both volunteered once a week: my mother at the library, my father at a nonprofit organization that recorded people reading aloud for the blind. They attended the regular series of concerts at the local Unitarian church. My father had joined a group of amateur ornithologists, and on my last visit, was excited about a new pair of Audubon binoculars my mother had just given him, along with an Audubon lens cleaning kit. Also on that visit my mother had recently begun taking yoga, and proudly showed me the Ashtanga yoga rug my father had bought for her online, imported directly from Mysore. Since they used sticky mats in her class, she explained to me, she'd decided to use it as a wall hanging; it decorated the little upstairs hallway, between the bathroom and the closet.

In other words, the trappings of their new lives were, in their own way, as immaculately self-congratulatory as those of the old. For my part, I have alternated between impatience with what seems essentially their painstaking replication of the old traps they'd set for themselves in Cambridge, and compassion for their inability to see, let alone extend themselves, beyond such a life.

That was not a good visit, my last. It occurred during the week between Christmas and New Year's. I had just had a miscarriage, my sixth in eight years, information I withheld from my parents on this as on each of the other occasions. By the time my mother picked me up at Portland International, I'd felt fine physically—which only made it harder. The end of cramping robbed me of the final vestiges of that which I was mourning.

Each of the previous times I'd miscarried at around eight or nine weeks; this time I'd made it to fifteen, and had just started to let myself believe I might really have a baby. Worse, Hale, who'd been conflicted about fathering a child in his sixties and had agreed to try only because he saw how much I wanted it, had just begun to slip into a state of unguardedly joyful anticipation.

(We had joked about it, he and I, in those early days after the miscarriage when I was still bleeding, still crying so much of the time that I'd more or less ceased to notice whether or not tears were running down my face. It was then, late at night, the two of us huddled under the covers, that Hale would perform a tasteless and macabre routine, "doing" the voices of our six dead fetuses counseling us from beyond the grave. He gave them perky, falsetto Freudian accents, and had them saying things like, "What you're feeling right now is well within the range of normal," and, "Just so you know, if I'd gone full-term, I would've had ears on my knees. And been allergic to water." Even though the humor was unabashedly dumb, he and I would laugh so hard I could feel us *physically* soaring almost beyond the grief, right to its outer limits, even as we pulled the covers over our heads in a sadly superfluous effort to muffle our laughter.)

But the following week I had gone to Maine, on a trip planned months earlier, and there, absent Hale's tender irreverence, I lost my sense that everything would be all right. I should have known better than to go. On the planet Fisher-Hart the truth did not exist, the atmosphere being too thin to support it. My parents and I spent the week as we always did: going through choreographed motions, like the mechanical holiday displays still up in Bovine Center's shop-windows—an endlessly circulating train, stiff celluloid carolers, a "yipping" terrier in a tartan dog sweater. Undoubtedly, I had been more distant that week than usual, which caused my mother to be more managerially ingratiating, which caused my father to be more responsively chipper, which caused me to be more distant . . . and so on.

On the morning of the last day of my visit my father's knees were troubling him; he has osteoarthritis, as does Hale. Feeling somewhat contrite over the fact that I had been dour the whole visit, I did something I normally do not, which was to share information relating to my husband: I told my father about a new drug, not yet FDA-approved. Doris Liu had offered to get Hale in a trial of it, and now I offered to get my father the information.

"Ah then," my father said, "he is a sufferer, too?"

Something about the pomposity of locution provoked me. "Not that he'd phrase it like that."

"No, no of course not—well, he has you to keep him nimble."

My father might have said this in all innocence, I don't know. It seemed to me he said it with the exaggerated diction of a double entendre. I heard it as a jibe about sex.

My mother was not in the house just then. I don't know where she was, returning Christmas presents, probably, exchanging something that was not precisely the right dimensions, the right color, the right scent. My father was sitting on the sofa in their little front room, what they referred to as the den. His feet, in wool socks, were up on a pillow on the coffee table, an afghan and a heating pad across his knees. The morning light was flashing white-gold into the room through the bay windows with their raised Roman shades, reflecting off the snow and the dripping icicles.

"Please," I spat. "You know nothing about us."

My father breathed, audibly and at length, through his nose. He said, "Well," and stopped. He said, "Well, I know you picked someone about the same age as me. I know that."

The den was crazily still. My mother had done it in the colors of lemons and pears. My father's book, beside him on the sofa, looked exactly like a prop.

"I don't want to hear anything you have to say about this."

"It's a bit of an elephant in the room, though, isn't it, Bebe?"

"I can't believe you would speak to me of an elephant in the room! All you are . . . all—you—*are* . . . is willed blindness!"

He sucked his teeth. "You know what?" Maybe it was the pain in his knees; something made him cast off the decades-long deference he'd been clutching about him like a sick man a blanket. "It doesn't play anymore, your righteous indignation. Twenty years on. You've been nursing it a bit long, sweetheart. It's time to get over it."

Such was the voltage of my shocked rage that I could not find speech.

The quality of his voice, when next he spoke, was changed. It was the voice I'd listened to from beneath the table so many times in my childhood, the one he reserved for dénouement, when all his colleagues and acolytes would grow still, as would I, playing at their feet, hidden by the tablecloth, in delicious anticipation of his delivering the final blow. Slowly then: "Don't you think it's punishment enough to see your only child marry a surrogate father and repudiate the act of growing up?"

"*What?*"

"You're completely arrested, Bea." The tone of dispassionate authority made what followed that much more bilious. If he'd said it in a flood of anger, with loss of control, I might ultimately have found it forgivable. But in a clinical manner he went on, "You've got your 'good daddy' to take care of you, your 'job' is playacting, and you've steadfastly avoided the complicated responsibility of parenting. Perhaps this last choice is really your way of punishing me."

I remember how hateful the light in the room seemed then, strippingly bright and cold. How hateful the colors, the stillness, the afghan and heating pad on his knees, the minute, cloying sound of icicles dripping, like a cat lapping milk.

"Maybe it wouldn't have turned out this way if you hadn't been asking little girls to touch themselves in your office."

He went gray. This is actually true, I don't know the physiology, but his face turned gray. He said, "I didn't do that." He took his feet off the coffee table, bending his sore knees with a grimace, and leaned forward, looking me in the eye. "That—is—not—what—happened."

The absurd thing is that I believed him. Though it made the room tip, the house tilt, I believed him—there was no alternative; his center, his sway, were too powerful to brook disagreement. I knew, I actually *knew,* that he had invited the violin girl to experiment with touching herself sexually during their session, yet also, somehow, impossibly, I believed he had not. It was his face, his eyes, the strength and steadiness of his voice. I believed that whatever had occurred between them, whatever had occurred between him and all the women and girls who'd accused him of misconduct, he had not intended anything untoward or harmful. Perhaps it was his own dis-astrously outsized ego that let him believe he had acted within the bounds of propriety, but he did believe it. I saw for myself how it was that my mother could believe him, and stay with him. For now I could feel myself believing him, too—and despising myself for it.

I put my hands over my stomach, took a step back. "Is that how you do it? Is that how it works?" Shaking my head, nearly whisper-ing in incredulity. "You get everyone on your side."

I do not remember leaving the room, packing, or calling the taxi, but I do remember staring out the window during the long, expen-sive ride from Bovine to Portland, where I got a room at the airport Hilton and spent a fairly sleepless night before flying home to Hale in the morning. I remember that I said nothing to my father before leaving the house, and that I told myself I would never spend another night in it: a silence and a promise I have not broken to this day.

"WHAT ARE YOU thinking about?"

Hale gives his enigmatic smile. "Silke."

We're on the plane. Our books are closed on our laps. Hale has finished his sandwich and two clementines; I'm not hungry.

"What about her?"

"I was kind of"—he breaks off, looking bashful—"fantasizing about her meeting up with your mother. In, not heaven, but some-thing."

"Oh." I study him. Twenty-one years I've known him, and he says the last thing I would expect. "That's so nice." I slide my hand around his arm, turn and look out the ovoid window, speckled with precipitation. Beyond is white.

Hale's cough is not too bad on the plane. I keep pressing bottled water on him, which he sips obligingly. I think about what he said about Silke and my mother meeting up. I don't think he really believes in an afterlife, but that he would entertain this notion, even as fantasy, is something I find oddly comforting. We do speak, on occasion, of the probability that I will live a long time after he has died. It's always Hale who brings it up, always gently but stubbornly insisting that we acknowledge this likelihood. Sometimes he issues specific wishes for me; other times he simply observes the fact that I will most likely have a whole other life without him. I used to feel distraught when he would say such things. But now I take it as a difficult kindness on his part, as though by making regular reference to the years I'll be here without him, he is blessing me in that time.

During the last twenty minutes of the flight, I experience nausea and wind up vomiting twice into the airsick bag—strange because otherwise I feel fine, and I have never gotten airsick before in my life. I don't even get seasick. Of course, as Hale observes, wetting a paper napkin with some of the bottled water and handing it to me, it is an emotionally laden day. I wash my face, lean my head against the back of the seat.

I feel better almost the moment we land, and better still when we cross the tarmac and the harsh air, stippled with Lilliputian flakes, hits my face.

At the same time I feel worse, because with my first inhalation there is that familiar sense of provincialism, as if it were actually conveyed by microscopic particles in the very atmosphere: the overriding smallness of Maine, which evokes for me the smallness of my parents' lives, which evokes for me the smallness of my own heart.

I have no illusions about what made my father's and my last exchange singularly agonizing: it's knowing the role I played in creating the situation that led to his contemptible speech (which he made, I must remind myself, having no idea that I had spent almost a decade trying to carry a baby to term). In a way I take responsibility, not for the things he said, but for his anger, for the sense of helplessness that must have lain behind it. I know that I have continued to fault him without compassion for mistakes he made long ago. I know that this is unfair—even I feel it is excessive—and that it torments him, that he has long felt frustrated by me at every step. I know this and still I can't help it.

Maybe it's the old problem of the fallible god. Maybe my love for him was too worshipful in nature to survive such a fall. My mother's love survived it, how? It was of a tougher, scrappier variety. Or else more elastic, more creatively accommodating. Or else phoenix-like, it did die, only to resurrect itself from its own ashes. Suddenly, right now, I wish I could ask her the secret. Because try as I might, I cannot make myself love my father again.

I try to think back to what it felt like when I did love him, in early childhood, only to run smack into the brick wall of idolatry. Which is not love, which disqualifies love. Which is predicated on colluding in a fantasy, performing in a play, about power and powerlessness, about favor and regard.

So then I try to think back to what it felt like when *he* loved *me*. But whether it be memory's dirty trick of distortion, or maturity's gift of clarity, all I can see is his vanity, his pleasure in me as an object to confirm his exemplary status, to satisfy his sense of well-being and accomplishment. The old apocryphal image of the racing shells skimming across the Charles, and the members of the crew team being diverted, captivated, by the sight of him on the grassy bank, a

striking figure made all the more impressive by the gaze of the supporting character, in this case the admiring daughter.

Hale catches his foot on a bit of uneven ground as we make our
way across the bright, frozen tarmac. He stumbles slightly, and I
catch his arm. But he is the one who turns to me and says, "You all
right?"

"Fine," I return. I hear that I sound defensive.

I hate being horrible to Hale. I'm hardly doing anything overt,
but he can read me, and I hate it, hate the look of wary sympathy
in his eye. I can't explain what's in my thoughts and my gut as we
draw closer to Bovine. That I feel myself becoming an uglier person, that I blame my father for it. Keeping it to myself only makes
me more alien, more awful. But I can't share it with Hale. My feelings about my father are off-limits to my husband. It's one of the
only subjects, maybe *the* only subject, I would on no condition dis-
cuss with him.

I'm too afraid. What if it were once and for all to illuminate a
causal connection between my relationships with the two of them?
My absolute worst fear is that my soured relationship with my
father might have catalyzed, have *brought about,* my love for Hale.

INSIDE THE TERMINAL, a wonderful surprise: Pax. He calls out
my full name, which is unchanged: "Beatrice Fisher-Hart!" and I
turn around and there he is, over six feet, in dreadlocks and a navy
peacoat.

We hug and I am shot through with longing—how good it
feels to be held by a man so tall and strapping!—followed quickly
by embarrassment at such a thought. I last saw my little cousin
about four years ago, very briefly, near the Port Authority on
Forty-second Street. Pax had deferred his college admission and

was riding Greyhound buses around the country. He'd had a giant, filthy duffel bag, a Kronos Quartet T-shirt, and a careless, beguiling smile. We'd had an Orange Julius together before he had to get on his next bus. Now in the terminal I disentangle myself from his powerful arms and reach toward Hale, and he and Pax hug, too.

"I tried e-mailing you, but it bounced back," says Pax. "Sorry about your mom passing."

"Thanks. What are you doing here?" I know he's based in Maine, now. Unlike mine, Pax's college deferment did eventually lead to enrollment; he's a music major at Bowdoin, in his last year. I knew from my grandmother that he was planning to drive down from Brunswick for the funeral. What I don't understand is why he's here at the airport. "Is your mother flying in?"

"Nah, she couldn't. She's got a thing now, Wednesday nights, a standard gig."

Ida lives in San Diego, still singing. She and my mother had virtually no relationship with each other, though; I certainly hadn't expected to see her today.

"Then what are you doing here, sweetie?" I squint at him, wonder fleetingly if he could be here to pick up Hale and me, but that wouldn't make sense; how would he have known what time our flight was getting in? Unless our grandmother told him, but—

"Picking up Thomas James."

Tears spring to my eyes. "Really?"

I haven't seen Teej since his wedding. He has two children now, a boy and a girl, Tom and Zahra, four and two. I've seen pictures. They live outside Philadelphia. He works in finance. His wife's a pediatrician.

I shake my head. "I didn't know he would come."

"Family," Pax says simply, which makes my eyes well over.

When Teej's plane gets in soon after, he's one of the first people through the door. He's not as tall as Pax, but the change in him is almost more dramatic. At twenty-four, Pax still has a boyish air. At twenty-seven, in his dark suit, his elegant overcoat, and fawn-colored cashmere scarf, Teej is all man. His face has grown quite chiseled and he's sporting a thin black mustache. But when he spots me he calls out "Cuz!" and his grin is exactly the same as when he was six.

We cancel the rental car. I have misgivings about this, about forgoing the quick getaway, but Pax promises to bring us back to the airport the moment we say the word, and it does seem silly to drive two cars when he has plenty of room in his, which turns out to be a roomy if rusty Kia, decorated with bumper stickers that say LEGALIZE FREEDOM and DON'T BELIEVE EVERYTHING YOU THINK. "Don't worry about stepping on any of it," advises Pax, unlocking the doors. Hale and I push away papers and books and old coffee cups and soda cans and a pair of sneakers and a broken umbrella and an empty instrument case—oboe? bassoon?—and take seats in the back. Teej slides into the passenger seat beside his younger brother, Pax cranks the heat, and the sun comes out and dazzles the cavalcade of flakes skittering past the windows. They're like trick flakes, the way they've followed us up from New York, the way they persist without amounting to anything, just catching the light like crumbs of mica, revolving, being blown about, winking and vanishing. Vaudeville flakes.

This time it comes on so fast I barely have time to ask Pax to pull over. One moment I'm admiring wallet-sized photos of Teej's children—Tom posed in a pumpkin patch, a paper pumpkin reading PRESCHOOL 3 on yarn around his neck; Zahra in a purple velvet dress and a silver tiara, feet planted wide, hands on hips, looking balefully up at the lens—and the next I'm standing by the side of the road, throwing up into a frosty ditch while eighteen-wheelers behind my back make the whole ground tremble. Hale comes out to hold my forehead, but by the time he gets to me I am already finished.

"At least I didn't get any on my coat," I observe, inspecting my front and waving off his help. "Get back in the car, Hale. *Oh,* it's cold. Get in, sweetheart. Don't look at me like that, it's just—anxiety." Because he is looking at me with an inscrutable expression on his face, part concerned, part something else.

Back in the car, Teej turns around to offer a wad of Tim Hortons napkins he's dug out of the glove box. His brow is all wrinkled. "You sick, Bea?"

"I'm fine. Just having a little psychosomatic whatever. Hale's sick," I announce brightly. "He has bronchitis."

As if on cue, he coughs.

I thrust the napkins at him. "Here. These are for you." All three men in the car seem to be regarding me with some apprehension. "We can go," I say. I make a little Queen Mother gesture. As Pax merges back onto the highway, it occurs to me I was dead wrong in asking Maeve not to come. She is who I need here now. Someone to be madcap and absurdist with. I chew my lip, squelching the odd lump of laughter that is threatening to discharge from my throat. In spite of me, in spite of all reason, my mood has leapt forward into something like precarious excitement. I wonder if Hale is thinking the same thing I am, if that's what accounted for his curious look by the ditch. I turn from everyone and gaze out the window, both in order to regain some composure and to do some math.

BOVINE UNITARIAN UNIVERSALIST CHURCH is a perfect postcard: white clapboard perched on white snow; white spire rising into a blue and white sky; the minnowish snowflakes whisking and darting around before it like schools of impertinent fish. Pax parks opposite the graceful slope on which it is built, and we all extricate ourselves rather slowly from the car, only to stand there looking at the structure, as though that is our purpose in coming: to observe the architecture and landscape, make mental note of it, and move on. I imagine saying, *All right, then*, slapping the roof of the car once, and the four of us without further ado getting back in and returning promptly from whence we came.

According to the clock on the church spire it is ten past two. In the frigid air the sound of car doors closing carries brusquely. Other latecomers, in twos and threes, are hustling from various directions toward the church, entering through the arched doorway. I notice, to the side of the steps, a wheelchair ramp, and imagine my intrepid grandmother having been wheeled in by her peach of an aide. Now she'll be sitting snugly indoors, having had a nice lunch and a nice ride in her Lincoln Town Car. A swell of affection: I am eager to see her. She is the sole force impelling me toward the church instead of away. Is that why she insisted on coming? For my sake? To balance out the terrible repelling force of my father, who must also be already snug inside?

I chide myself for such self-centeredness. *Silly.* As if she has no reason of her own for wanting to be here.

Hale comes around to my side. I glance at him. The lines around his eyes and mouth are etched deep; he is squinting against the sun, whose grand reappearance now, over behind the church spire, seems shamelessly theatrical. He has left his hat in the car and already the tops of his ears are brightening in the wind, the tip of his nose collecting a drop. He sniffs and coughs rackingly. "Your hat, sweetheart." I go into the backseat to retrieve it. It is a sensible, knitted hat. I fit it over his sparse curls, his naked scalp, and then I bring my face close to his, press my cheek against his temple. The earpiece of his eyeglasses is cold on my skin.

I am lying a little bit when I say that I love the way we always help each other on with our coats. I recognize that the feeling behind it is genuine, but the act itself I find cloying. When he holds my coat for me, it carries shades of paternalism I would rather not think about; when I hold his for him, especially now that he is older, it carries too strong a reminder of human frailty—and the prospect that I may at some point have to "parent" him. I love him so much and yet—how can this be?—I am angry with him for being old and sick—what is wrong with me?—on this day of all days, when I am bringing him home to my parents for the first time, or rather I mean only to my father. I wish, for just a moment, that I were returning to my father with someone as tall and imposing as Pax, as handsome and chiseled as Teej, and then the guilt that correctly follows such a wish comes flooding in so that I want to drop to my knees and beg Hale for forgiveness. I kiss his ear, warm it with my breath. "My Beatrice," he whispers, innocent of my thoughts, and pats me.

Teej comes around the car. Dear Teej: he is a family man, now, and seems to have incorporated this into his bearing, for as he steps close I feel emanating from him both a patriarchal protectiveness and a resolve: he is here to support me as I cross the street as well as to ensure that I get there. I contemplate the ramifications of stuffing snow down the back of his shirt. Then I pull sunglasses from my coat pocket, put them on, take Hale's arm with one hand, Teej's with the other, and we start off, Pax loping alongside. I like to think we four are obvious out-of-towners—my cousins certainly are, being the only two people of color probably within a fifteen-mile radius—but Hale and I too must surely be giving off some kind of urbane air that the locals can sense. I wonder whether the locals will be surprised at how utterly different I am from my parents. That's *Sarah's daughter?* I imagine them whispering to one another. *I never would have guessed.* But then I castigate myself. Who am I to make shallow suppositions about the people with whom my parents found welcome in their disgrace?

I hold Hale's arm tightly as we ascend the church steps.

Just inside the vestibule there is a little traffic jam, whose cause becomes apparent as we make our way inside. People are not proceeding straight through into the sanctuary, but rather slowing down to examine two easels, both of which have been plastered with photographs of my mother. Bizarrely, it is this sight, the image of her over and over, captured at so many different ages, that ultimately drives home for me the reason we are here: because she is not. With a murmur of "Sorry," and "Excuse me," I press in close to the easels.

A baby picture, hand-colored: the palest rose on her round cheeks and bow lips, a dandelion yellow on her crocheted booties. A school photograph in black and white: my mother at the end of the second row standing next to the teacher, who manages to hijack the picture with her beehive, cat-eye glasses and gigantic bosom. A college graduation photo, airbrushed, in which the contours of her face glow creamily. A recent shot of her at the library, grown slightly plump and rather gray, smiling easily beside a cart of books. Here is one I recognize: my mother, brand-new, looking like nothing so much as a sack of sugar, cradled in the arms of her rumple-haired, undershirt-wearing father, who is transfixed with adoration.

"Hey, here's Grammy," says Pax, examining another. "Look how fine she looks."

"Is that one—of Silke?" wonders Teej, scrutinizing the one above it.

Hale confirms that it is. They are all whispering, as though we were in a museum.

"There's Aunt Sarah with you and Bea," Teej points out to Hale. "What is that, the Empire State Building?"

"Yes."

The picture had been taken shortly after our City Hall wedding, to which no one had been invited. My mother had come to visit a month later, bringing a green-glazed ceramic bowl as a wedding present, and nursing her wounded feelings with admirable reserve. I had failed, inexcusably really, to consider that it was the second time in her life she'd been invited to Manhattan to celebrate a wedding *after* the fact: first Maynard and her mother, then Hale and me. It dawned on me only when I was meeting her train at Grand Central, as Silke had done close to a lifetime ago, and I'd been mortified to realize how closely I was replicating that experience. But she had borne no grudge.

Looking at the picture of her flanked by Hale and me on the deck of the Empire State Building, I see only willingness in her expression, a kind of availability to surrender to anything we might offer. One hand holds her hat on her head; the other is linked through my arm. She looks a bit unsteady in the wind, but game.

"Check Bea out in this one." Pax lets out a soft laugh. "Look at those *thighs*."

I am maybe a year old in the picture, not even. Dressed only in a diaper, both of my feet clutched in my father's right hand; my thighs, yes, sausage-fat; my knees locked so that I am "standing" as he balances my weight; and beside him, my mother in a high ponytail, laughing with her head tipped back, her mouth so wide you can see the dark fillings in her molars. In the picture I look dazed; my father, omnipotent.

"Bebe." There is only one person left in the world to call me by the old detested nickname.

I turn around. "Hi Dad." No emotion. I introduce him to Hale, Teej, and Pax, none of whom he has ever officially met. He shakes each of their hands. His hair is more severely cut than I remember, almost militaristic. His frame is leaner, and wiry from daily walks. His cheeks seem slightly sunken, and there's a gray cast to his skin that appears to be more than a matter of needing a shave, which he does, but I have no way of knowing whether this aspect of his look emerged only since my mother's death, is only the masque of grief, or something more permanent that has come upon him since the last time I was here.

I realize that my father must be the one who selected all these pictures, is responsible for their display.

"We should sit," he says, stiffly. We follow him down the center aisle toward the front pew. I'm surprised by the number of people in attendance. There must be sixty or seventy, far more than I'd expected. I am so accustomed to thinking of my parents' life in Maine as smaller than their life in Cambridge. I feel humbled and also uplifted by these numbers.

In the front pew, positioned right on the aisle and dwarfed by her caregiver, who looks about my age, sits my grandmother. Parked off to the side is her wheelchair. When I first glimpse her, the top of her head rising not so high above the back of the pew, the short white hair on which has grown less dense, so that the light shines through it like spun sugar, relief and disappointment tears through me. I always have to remind myself now when I see her that she is at once the same and not the same Margaret Fourcey. Today of all days I want so badly for her to be a *force*. I want to siphon off some of her lacerating strength and clarity for myself. Like a fool I have managed to forget she is ninety-two, a faithful but fainter version of her former self.

I am not really sure how acutely my mother's death affects her. They did eventually reconcile, if this is the right word. Or no, since neither ever truly relinquished her sense of bearing a grievance. But they did each allow themselves reentry into one another's life.

Maybe that is reconciliation. My grandmother made a few trips to Maine over the years; my mother made more to Boston; they both visited Hale and me regularly in New York, sometimes overlapping on purpose. Once—I do not know what possessed them—they took a cruise together, the two of them in a single cabin, in the Caribbean. I heard minor complaints from each about the other for months afterward.

The truth is I secretly cherished that luxury—the supreme *normalcy* of hearing a certain kind of petty complaint from one's mother and grandmother, and the overarching intimacy between them—among all three of us—it implied.

I wonder if the intimacy my grandmother had won back makes this death harder or easier for her to bear. Or both. As with that old riddle we used to bandy about the salon: Which is an actor's greater asset, skill at lying or skill at truth-telling?

"Grandmother," I say, quickening my step so that I pass my father and reach her first. I bend and kiss her, her cheek crinkled and soft, and kneel and hold her hand.

"You're late," she says, "darling."

Then Teej and Pax and Hale bend to greet her, and she receives their kisses in turn, and introduces us all to Alvarez, a husky man with a big mustache. He shakes our hands and offers formal, identical expressions of condolence to every one of us, including my father, who takes his seat on the far end of the pew, by the wall. Then come Teej and Pax, and Hale sits next to Alvarez. My grandmother's eyes are limpid, glistening as she follows the men's progress to their seats, but I am not sure whether they are moist with emotion or age; their gray-blue is blurrier now than it once was. I can't resist touching my face to hers again, on my knees, and whispering, "I'm so glad you're here." She gives me a tiny punch on the arm. I squeeze in between Hale and Pax.

Someone who seems to be a minister speaks. My mother, never religious during my childhood, had begun attending services regularly these past few years. It is a part of her that, being foreign to me, seems suspect. I tune him out. My mother wanted cremation, and I am glad not to have to look at a coffin. Instead I focus on the flowers, lilies, and on the stained glass window—there is only one, which seems to me the right number, and it is high and round and letting in direct light at this hour. I think about the clear plastic cup somebody has left on a chair up on the dais, and I think about the vaulted ceiling of the church, which is plain and timbered and seems cousin to a barn, and I think about my grandmother, whom I miss although she sits two people away from me. It is a kind of missing that feels like practice for the real thing, for the missing that will come once she has died.

She'd been incensed when first she found out about Hale's and my involvement. I told her before I told my parents. I told her in that same tea shop off Charles Street where she'd gotten angry with me once before. It was the summer after I'd moved to New York. I'd gone to visit her, as well as Ida and the boys, who were living in their own place by then in Jamaica Plain. On this day my grandmother and I had been sitting at a little round linen-covered table, waiting for our drinks, Italian sodas, and I delivered the news only after a lengthy preamble about how apprehensive I was, how worried that she would disapprove. I figured this ought to preempt such a reaction on her part, but instead she slammed her fist on the tablecloth and roared, "No!" and then added quietly and definitively, "The bastard."

She is *a hard woman,* I'd thought, stung, even as a voice in the back of my mind lectured me patiently, *It isn't hardness; she simply won't be manipulated out of feeling what she's feeling.*

However, it turned out she was mostly angry with Hale, and not for the reason I'd feared—that our age difference made our involvement objectionable, that he was somehow taking advantage of me—but because she had actually sensed something between us the previous summer, and queried him about it, only to be told (rather curtly, according to her) that she was not only mistaken but depraved.

"Grandmother. He said no such thing."

"It was im*plied*."

By then Hale's play, in which I'd had a tiny part, had closed; its limited run had not been extended—to be honest, it hadn't been very favorably reviewed—but I'd gotten a nice one-line write-up in the *Village Voice,* and I'd gotten my Equity card, and I'd been on lots of auditions, with two call-backs, and some real encouragement from casting directors, so in all sorts of ways I felt a different person from the girl who'd first sought out Margaret Fourcey a year and a half earlier. For example, I felt bold enough to ask, "What was it that made you guess there was something between us?"

She peered down her long nose at me. I stared straight back. She said, "It was his asking me to coach you in the part of Thisbe. It's so unlike Hale, to want someone else directing his actors. I felt very much he wanted to hand you off to me. And then, when you and I did rehearse one-on-one like that—remember all those afternoons?"

"Do I *remember* them? I was the one doing all the sweating, hello?"

"And there was an intensity, an intimacy, and . . . I remember us growing quite close during those rehearsals . . . and then I thought again about why Hale didn't want to rehearse you himself. And it seemed there were two possibilities. One: he was being generous with me, wanting to give me this opportunity for closeness with a granddaughter who had been trained her whole life to despise me."

"Grandmoth—!"

"Or *two*: that he was trying to protect himself from feeling more strongly about you than he already did."

"Or three," I put in, "that he knew you to be a brilliant actress who understood the part of Thisbe better than anyone, and might therefore be uniquely qualified to help me grow into the role."

She'd sniffed. "Well, it's moot, isn't it? Now we know I was right. He was in love."

Sitting in the church, I smile at the memory, at her toughness, her shrewdness, her honesty. What a shame, I think, that my mother hadn't known her until so late in life. What a shame: my grandmother's shame, the magnitude of which I have come to understand more the longer I've known her. It never goes away for her, the fact of that shame, not even after she and my mother became friends of sorts. She just lives with it, a constant burden she shifts around without taking any particular pains to hide. Now I think about the fortitude with which she has carried this burden, the forbearance, and I believe it is what has lent her that peculiar grace that is unlike any I have encountered. And I wonder: did she have this quality at my age, at forty-one, or did it come later? And if so, *how* did it come about, how does shame transform from a stultifying burden to an ennobling one?

There she sits, two people away to the right. Two people away to the left sits my father. And sitting nowhere at all, but uniting us in purpose today: my mother. The whole arrangement suddenly appears to me an improbable sculpture, kinetic, precarious, a thing made of steel and wire that will come into balance once and never again. So there is some urgency, an imperative not to squander the occasion, the alignment. A need to make excellent use of it.

In the meantime, I don't know what to think about my nausea, which has eased but not lifted completely. Even as I try to take in

and process the magnitude of everything—death, betrayal, forgiveness—I keep trying to tally weeks, but I forget the date of my last
period. I've never been very regular, and as Hale and I haven't been
trying, I haven't been paying particular attention to the calendar. I
am ravenous, though. Is that a sign? My mind wanders off in the
direction of guessing what the citizens of Bovine customarily
bring, in the way of gastronomic offerings, to a postfuneral gathering. Maeve would fall out laughing at this: my thinking of food
during my mother's funeral. But after all I never did eat my sandwich on the plane, and I more or less threw up breakfast. Come to
think of it, my hunger might well signify nothing else than an
empty stomach.

After the minister speaks, and a woman from the library, and a
man from the hospital, none of whose words I am really able to take
in, and during whose speeches Hale breaks into small coughing fits,
my father goes to the podium. I didn't anticipate this, and feel a flut-
ter of nerves, for which of us I do not know.

He stands a little round-shouldered, which he never used to be.
His tweed sports coat seems roomy on him. He looks around the
church vaguely, as though not seeing the people in it. And he
doesn't speak. The congregation, already quiet, grows quieter. For a
moment it has a familiar feel; it is like the silence he used to let swell
before speaking at the table at our house in Cambridge, the silence
that underscored his centrality, his command. But this silence pro-
longs. His face is tilted toward the ceiling. He has the look of an
actor who's lost his lines.

I remember—powerfully, in a rush—standing with my head
tilted just like that in order to gaze at *him*. I remember when he
loomed tall and strapping, the autumn sunlight spangling the
Charles River behind him, and rimming his head, so finely adorned
with gilded locks, so kinglike, so godlike, rising up above me, up

against the towering sycamores, their pied trunks and their great, muscular limbs. We are on Memorial Drive; I am six, on new roller skates. Flailing, I grab at him; his fingers, long and cold and strong, are my anchor. I look up at him, and he is telling me the story of Jason and Medea, or Perseus and Medusa, Theseus and Ariadne, some story that is older and darker and more complicated than the stories most parents tell their children, some story in which the very names of the characters are harder to pronounce and remember, and we both know this is my privilege and my test. He will offer me the finest he knows and I will prove my worth by preferring it to anything else.

I look at him now, floundering on the dais, and see what it is that happened to us. He broke our trust by falling from iconic status. I broke our trust by seeing him plainly. For the first time it occurs to me that this might not be all bad. For the very first time it dawns: this might actually place us at an advantage.

He opens his mouth and shuts it. He is still peering at the ceiling in a way that suggests something is there. He half turns toward the minister, who is sitting behind him, then faces the congregation again. "I . . ." He clears his throat. "There was something I wanted to say . . ." From the way his eyes are traveling, however, he seems to have lost any thread of it.

The mourners are patient.

"Ahh . . ." he says, and frowns.

In the silence I hear fresh weeping from multiple sources, all the more wrenching for its restraint. It seems to me people are weeping not for my mother in this moment, but for my father, for his grief as evidenced by this public loss of composure. Any second now, I think, someone will go up there and take his arm, whisper something consoling, lead him back to his seat at the end of our pew, next to Pax. Surely the minister is going to step in, to rise from his seat and put an arm around my father. Someone will rescue him. *Where is she?* I catch myself thinking, and who I mean is the person who has always up until now been there to rescue my father.

"There was . . . ah . . . something . . ." My father strokes his grizzled jaw, looks at the floor, as if pensive. "The way that I loved her," he begins.

A long pause.

He clears his throat.

Silence.

Then his head bows forward and his shoulders shake, like that night at the Pudding. His sobs are soundless, and this time there is no one to help him. No one to ask for our check, no one to make our excuses, to lie to the waiter, to usher him safely past the curious gaze of all the other diners. Until out of terrible need I rise and go to him, put my arm around him, whisper "Dad?" whisper, "Come on," walk him down the two carpeted steps, walk him to the pew, pressing the dark wool of his tweed coat, feeling the lean, wiry arm within, supporting him while he lowers himself, and then I return to my place beside Hale, shaken—by the enormity of my mother's absence, and the realization of how radically my father is *without.* But mostly by the astonishing discovery that all love for him is not dead in me.

MY PARENTS' HOUSE—my father's house, I will have to learn to call it—is warm and crowded and smells of meat and onions and cigarettes, not that anyone is smoking inside the house, but some of these older men's and women's clothes reek. I stand with Teej and Pax and Hale in the little front room, the den, listening to them converse and keeping an eye out for the Lincoln Town Car. When it pulls up I go to the door and watch Alvarez set up the wheelchair,

help my grandmother into it, and maneuver it from the street over
the long cement walk that leads to the house. He is built like a foot-
ball player, and the three-piece suit looks accordingly out of place
on him. She sits erect in the wheelchair, looking regal, papal. I smile
to watch them. They go slowly. The wind stirs her sparse hair, makes
it catch the light like milkweed.

Alvarez parks the chair at the bottom of the steps, and supports
my grandmother going up them. I hold the door, then help Alvarez
get her settled in the living room by the fireplace, although he
hardly needs my help. He seems to know just where an extra throw
pillow is, and precisely how to position it in the chair for my grandmother's maximum comfort. He's chosen the Queen Anne chair
that used to sit in a corner of the kitchen in Cambridge. The eggnog
brocade has worn to a glossy sheen, the blue hydrangeas faded to
the color almost of dust. A fire is burning mightily in the hearth
beside her. "Too warm for you, Maggie?" asks Alvarez.

"No: delicious. But you're too warm, I see. Take off the jacket at
least, if not the vest."

"No, I'm good."

"If you say so. But don't stand on ceremony, my dear."

"Okay, Maggie. I'm going to put the chair in the basement and
then I'll get us some food."

He doesn't ask where the basement door is or anything. I sit on
the ottoman at her feet and we watch Alvarez expertly navigate the
house.

"He's like a Navy Seal," I observe.

"What?"

I speak louder. "He's like a Secret Service agent."

She smiles, her eyes crinkling at the corners. "He's a peach," she
declares. And with no transition: "Have you connected with your
father?"

"What?" I'm not sure I understand her meaning. ". . . You mean, since we got to the house?"

She merely repeats, slightly louder, "Have you connected with your father?"

"Have I spoken with him?"

She gives me a look, but I don't always know how to interpret her looks these days, her face having altered with age. Sometimes I can't tell whether she is shaking her head on purpose, for meaning, or whether it's the result of a slight involuntary tremor. Her nose and chin jut forth more sharply than ever, and her eyes are at once bright and glassy. There is a birdlike quality to her that there never was before, although not birdlike in the sense of diminished or fragile. It is a pared, nearly raptorish quality. The firelight glazes her hair; I can see the pinkness of her scalp through it.

"I'm sorry, Grandmother, I don't—"

"He is the only one you have left now."

This is crushing to me, not the news itself, but the inanity of her pronouncement. I want her to be shrewd and powerful. But she is out of touch, my grandmother. I think I have waited too long to ask her some important questions, questions about shame and grace, blame and forgiveness. She is still here but she is not all the way herself.

"I have you," I counter tentatively. "And Hale. And—Maeve, the boys . . . other people."

"Yes, of course you do." She makes a little fist and stabs the air in victory. "*Good* for you."

I feel bereft, so lonely.

"Grandmother? Are you saying you think I should talk with my father?"

"Should, shmould." She sounds more like Silke the older she gets. " 'Speak what we feel, not what we ought to say.' "

I don't understand. Is she intending to reference the play, or simply deliver the imperative of the line? "He's no Lear," I say rather softly and mostly to myself.

"You're no Cordelia."

I turn to look at her so quickly I hurt my neck. This sounds like the grandmother I know. Her eyes, reflecting firelight, search my face with equal interest. Now I want the conversation to go on, but at this moment Alvarez returns with a plate of cheese and grapes, and Teej comes over a few seconds later, saying, "Grammy, how are you doing?" I give him my seat on the ottoman and drift off to find Hale or food or Pax or wine.

Hale, still in the den, is giving his attention to a conversation with the minister and the head librarian, who, through no fault of theirs, are people with whom I have no interest in socializing. I am frustrated with Hale, who, through no fault of *his,* is letting me down just now: *I* want him; why must he be so gracious and charming with strangers? From the doorway, I mouth and mime to Hale that it is past time for his next dose of medicine; has he taken it yet? No, he shakes his head. I signal, with slightly fierce, poking gestures, that I will fetch it. Then I head to the kitchen in pursuit of a glass of skim, which he needs to drink in advance or else his stomach will be upset.

The kitchen, not large, contains seven or eight women, all of them busy with food prep, and engaging one another with almost magical familiarity. They are fun, these women, I can tell, which is a little revelation: my parents had no "fun" friends in Cambridge. One of them, wearing an apron of my mother's decorated with an eggplant and the legend *"une aubergine,"* pulls a casserole from the oven. Another removes plastic wrap from a Jell-O salad; another opens a bottle of wine; another cracks ice cubes into a bowl. They greet me with hands laid on my back and arms, tell me how sorry they are, introduce themselves as fellow volunteers at the library, fellow yoga students, or fellow members of a book club I never knew my mother belonged to. They shower me with their names: there is a Jan, and a Patty, and I think a Marge. They know me as "the actress." Some of them have hair and sweaters that smell of cigarettes; some have popped breath mints; one has been drinking. These smells, and that of the food coming out of the oven, and the lemon-scented dish detergent, mingle chaotically. One woman, the one wearing my mother's apron, pours Hale's milk for me. As she hands it over I gag.

I wheel toward the sink, grip the edge of the basin and bend over, salivating profusely. Sweat breaks out on my brow. The nausea passes. The women fuss, seat me, give me a glass of water. "Hand me some of those crackers, Betty," says one of them, and a few seconds later a short stack of saltines nestled in a paper towel arrives on my lap. "Try a few of those."

I look up into her face, this woman in the eggplant apron who was a friend of my mother's. I try to fathom their friendship, to picture them together—would they be funny, would they laugh? As uproariously as Maeve and me, even?

She inquires kindly, "How far along are you?"

I stare.

Her face goes red. She says, "Oh!" She says, "That's not," and, "I didn't mean," and then she turns away and says loudly, "Mary, what time did that lasagna go in?"

I look at my lap, busy myself with the crackers and water.

So I am pregnant. I must be. Today of all days, to have it made known. The hope, the joy, rockets through me before I can remind myself of my body's history, lecture myself about all the disastrous attempts, all the fetuses I've lost, their desertings heralded either by wrenching waves or by silent spots of blood but in any case final and emphatic, every last one. And yet. This time could be different. This one could be the one. If there really is a one.

I drain the glass of water, take Hale's milk, leave the kitchen without making eye contact, go back to the den.

Lots of amateur ornithologists in here, to judge by the snippets of conversation. My father is ensconced in a corner of the couch. The man beside him is saying, "It's wireless. You actually position it inside the feeder . . ." My father listens gravely. He either does not or is pretending not to notice me looking at him.

Good: I couldn't talk with him now anyway. I'm in a confused state, a mini-delirium. Here we are marking my mother's death; my grandmother, though unreliably herself these days, may yet have important wisdom to impart; my husband, whom I love, is old and sometimes I hate him for it; and now I am learning that he may have made me pregnant a seventh time, and although, if true, it may end in early loss, I cannot deny being overridden at this moment by joy. My brain, having become through experience a confirmed pessimist, harangues my unruly heart, but to no avail; I cannot make it stop dancing.

My best estimate is that if I am anything, I'm around eight weeks.

I go to Hale, hand him the glass. He puts his arm around my waist. The minister is telling about a play he saw last summer in Toronto. Hale is listening attentively. I know his courteousness is a kindness to *me*, really; he is playing ambassador for me so that I don't need to behave so graciously with all the guests. But like a child, I feel petulant about having to wait for his attention.

What will he say to the news? In the past he has reacted variously with happiness, disbelief, trepidation. Once he reacted with coolness. It had been my fourth pregnancy. I'd made the announcement and burst immediately into tears. Without getting up from his chair, Hale had inquired, "What are you crying about?"

We had a rare, rip-roaring fight then, in which I accused him of being shut down and he accused me of being selfish. Later, we had a good talk about it. He observed that if he was acting shut down, perhaps it was a way of dealing with the fact that his body would literally be shutting down before this child was grown. And he said he was afraid of a baby stealing my attentions right at the time when he would be wanting and needing them more. His honesty awed me. It made it possible for me to admit some of my desire for a baby might be connected to protecting myself from losing him. We were closer after that good fight. It left us clearer about our motives and, surprisingly, strengthened our resolve to become parents. I'd been certain I'd carry that baby to term.

Now I spot Pax, standing alone by the bookshelf, and as Hale is still in conversation, I slide out from his fingers upon my hip.

"Hey, Pax."

"Look," he says, gesturing with his chin. The wooden box on the shelf beside him.

I nod. "Did you look inside?"

He lifts the lid; the lead soldiers are all there, every last one, tucked into their slots in the velvet-lined case.

"Teej should take them," I say, "for the kids."

"Grammy gave them to your mother?" Pax sounds puzzled.

I turn the box over, show him the markings burned into the wood. N. FISHER, BERLIN, 1929.

"They were—who's that?—your granddad?"

I nod.

"No kidding, I didn't know that. They're like an heirloom. I totally remember playing with them."

"Hey Pax," I say, deciding suddenly, "you mind taking me somewhere?"

"Sure. Right now, you mean?"

"I just need a lift to the drugstore and back."

"I'll go. What do you need?"

I consider telling him. "No, that's all right. I wouldn't mind getting out of here for a minute."

He goes to find our coats.

I go back and murmur to Hale, "Pax and I are going on a quick errand."

Hale looks at me, his beautiful wise eyes reckoning behind the lenses of his glasses. He bends toward my ear and whispers, "You really think you can score drugs out here in the middle of the day?"

"I know a guy," I whisper back.

He doesn't ask where I'm really going. I wonder if he knows.

I nod, as if to reassure him, and after a moment he does the same. And I feel—walking away from him, putting my arms into the sleeves of my coat which Pax holds for me in the hall, striding down the steps and across the snowy lawn toward my cousin's rusty Kia— I feel bound to Hale, and light because of it.

At the drugstore, I tell Pax he can wait in the car, but he says nah, he'll come in, and then proceeds, companionably, to accompany me right down the aisle, continuing a story he was telling me in the car about a twelve-tone band he's helping get started at college, and I figure, oh well, and bend down to read the boxes of the different brands, and after a moment Pax goes quiet mid-sentence. Then he says, "Whoa. Are you pregnant?"

I look up sweetly over my shoulder. He's standing with his hands in the pockets of his peacoat, and he thinks about what he's just said and blushes.

"Oh . . . I guess you don't know."

I choose one of the boxes and we head toward the front, Pax still trying to work it out. "Is that, I mean, is it for you?"

I laugh.

"Well, good luck." Then he adds thoughtfully, "Whichever way you want it to turn out."

"Thanks, Paxton," I say, squeezing his hand. "You won't go spreading this around?"

"Definite," he agrees.

We ride back in silence. The sun has just slipped below the line of bristly firs. I am remembering when Teej and Pax, ages six and three, would go around so proudly pronouncing trees either deciduous or coniferous. I am remembering evenings of eating ice cream with the whole ensemble down the road from the Farm. The walk my mother and I took along that same road one evening, the way the light broke through the trees as she told me hard facts about my father. The light filtering down through the branches of the sycamores on Memorial Drive, when my father and I would go out walking on Sunday mornings and he would spin me myths. I lean my head back in Pax's car and the January sun cuts and slashes through the trees, patterning my closed eyelids.

At the house I go directly to the upstairs bathroom, take out the kit, unwrap the stick, and pee on it. I skim the directions: results will appear in five minutes.

The upstairs bathroom is long and narrow, with a little blue-curtained window at the end and a stall-type shower. Someone, one of the women from down in the kitchen no doubt, has been in here to clean; it looks hotelish, almost completely devoid of personal effects. The sink and countertop are spotless, with only a soap dish filled with small guest soaps, and a neatly folded hand towel. I peek inside the shower, half desiring, half afraid to see something specifically my mother's—a woman's disposable razor, a shower cap, some scented body wash—but there's only a single bottle of organic, gender-neutral shampoo and a bar of plain white soap. Similarly, behind the sliding door of the closet I find nothing but neatly folded linens. The contents of a medicine cabinet ought naturally to be more personal, but even they include nothing enormously indicative of my mother's existence: no cosmetics, no prescription bottles bearing her name. The removal of her personal effects is so thorough that I begin to doubt my first assumption, that one of her woman friends was responsible for it. In fact I think it has to have been my father.

Why? Why would he have felt such an imperative to clean up after her this meticulously, this obsessively, within the first seventy-two hours after her death? Almost as though he were covering tracks. Is that how he plans to manage his mourning? By adhering to the old Fisher-Hart ethic? Spit and polish, pretend nothing's wrong, nothing happened. How could he of all people, doctor of the human psyche, misstep so badly? I am torn between pity and fury.

I lift the lid of the wicker clothes hamper, and find the one place that whoever tidied so scrupulously missed. Oh, this is hard. At the bottom, beneath a few of my father's things, I discover a pair of her socks, underwear, black yoga pants, and a peach-colored long-sleeved T-shirt. These must have been the last clothes she wore before those she died in; she would have put them in the hamper Saturday night. I bring the cotton shirt to my face. It's so soft. I fold it into eighths and press it deep inside my coat pocket.

After my father's and my final disastrous encounter two years earlier, I did wind up telling my mother about all the pregnancies, all the miscarriages. The irrational but unshakable conviction that they were a sign, had meaning. That I was not supposed to have children, that a line of bad genes was being extinguished—all of which I had already confided in Hale. But I also confided in her something I had never told Hale, or Maeve or anybody: my fear that I had proven myself marked by a version of my father's sickness, a sickness of discernment. My fear that in his vile speech to me he had hit upon a truth. Because as much as I loved Hale, I couldn't—how could I?—verify that my love for him wasn't unconsciously a reaction to my father's misdeeds. And if that were so, it seemed to follow by nightmarish logic that the failed pregnancies were in some way the result. Just as my father believed I remained childless in order to punish him, to exact a price, I feared the miscarriages might be the price of my own misconduct.

"What a terrible fear to hold in secret," my mother had said over the phone.

I had called her in tears on a Saturday morning, when Hale was at a production meeting and I knew my father would be out of the house with his birding group.

"It's helpful that you know Dad's theory is wrong, because you can extrapolate from that to your own. A miscarriage is never a punishment for anything." Her tone was professional, but for once I didn't mind.

"I know, I know intellectually it's bullshit, but it *feels* true," I had cried.

She spoke slowly, with great authority and conviction. I let myself fall against her voice and be held up by it. "The people we wind up with, whoever our partners turn out to be, it's always for a plethora of reasons. It's always complicated. Some of the reasons are transparent, some are obscure. But the knottiness of the reasons—listen to this part, Bebe—the knottiness of the reasons doesn't render the love less real."

I'd snuffled and hiccuped.

"Look," she'd said then, differently, "all shrinkiness aside. I should tell you I had five miscarriages before you. And two after."

"You did?"

"Although," she mused wryly, "it's entirely possible *I* was being punished for something. Probably for not talking to my mother."

It was the only time I ever heard her crack a joke about their long estrangement, and I laughed in surprise. She seemed pleased with herself, on the other end of the line, for having come out with such a bold witticism.

Then without segue I'd asked, "Why has Dad never visited us?"
She was silent for a while before she said, "I don't know."

I so wanted her to say, *Because he's a horrible person. Because he's stunted, completely arrested. Because he's punishing you for his shame at misdeeds he committed.*

"Yes you do."
"You should ask him."
"I don't talk to him," I said coldly.
"I know."

And so the conversation that had begun in tears and progressed to laughter ended in clipped anger.

Now in the bathroom that has been almost spookily cleansed of my mother's earthly artifacts, I look into the mirror at the face that is becoming more and more over time like hers and think about what she said—about the complicated reasons we might love someone not canceling out the truth of that love—only I think about it this time as applied not to my love for Hale, but to her love for my father. I don't like it that she stayed with him, but I can accept it, even respect it. I wish I had been kinder to her around that choice, wish I hadn't so often brought my resentment toward him to bear on her. At times I treated her as though I believed she stayed with him because she feared change or loved convention. But do I really believe that?

I am gazing sternly into my own eyes, thinking in grave sentences inside my head. I think she made a difficult commitment *to her commitment*, and chose to see it through. Maybe this choice was of particular importance to her because it broke from the model of her parents. Her mother and father had not only failed the commitments they'd made to each other, they had both of them failed their commitments to her. And when I think how she came forward after years of silence toward her mother and relented, and when I think how, although their relationship continued to be rocky and fraught, she stayed with it; they both did; they persevered—I am awed.

I don't know if my mother died a happy person, but I do think she died a growing person. That is something she modeled for me. I am left with it now, that model, like an inheritance, and it strikes me, as I stare at my reflection in her bathroom mirror, that in a way that is everything.

And the strangest thing is that *now* she slips from me, as she did not when my father first called with the news, nor during the subsequent days when I told people and received condolences and bouquets, nor during the funeral service itself. Just *now* it happens, not with wrenching cramps, not with the spying of blood, but a visceral desertion nonetheless, like a breath unrooting itself deep in my gut, like a knife sliding backwards out of my chest, and I find myself crying at last.

Catching the reflected image of myself crying, I recall Maynard's funeral: the way Ida's grief was sort of marvelously on display beneath the mulberry tree; the way my grandmother's shone and spilled forth from her face all the day long; and the way my mother hid hers in the dark, homely recess of the pantry. At the time I'd been so certain that if I had to grieve, I'd grieve like Ida, or at least like my grandmother. And here am I, locked in the bathroom, my face, contorted with sobs, every bit as ugly as I had judged my mother's to be when I had come upon her bent and gripping that shelf so long ago.

I wash my face with hot water, feeling oddly good, and slightly transfigured, as after an absorbing sleep, and then I dry my face and pick up the test stick on the back of the toilet for confirmation of what I am by now certain.

"HELLO, BEAUTY," says Hale. He's sitting in the den, a plate on his knees. On the plate are macaroni, lasagna, pot roast, carrot salad, scalloped potatoes, baked ham, and cauliflower. "Have you been crying?"

So help me, I find the kindness in his voice stifling. "No." Although completely irrational, my annoyance is also piqued by the fact that he does not realize I'm pregnant.

"How's your stomach feeling?" he inquires.

"Empty. That looks good, I'm going to get some."

"Share this with me, it's too much." He tugs over a nearby chair. I sit. We take turns with the fork.

The windowpanes are showing twilight. The house has begun to empty. Soon it will be time for Pax to drive us back to the airport. It's beginning to look as though the dreaded exchange between my father and me, which I had thought inevitable, mightn't happen at all. I'm in a muddle, trying to digest what I have just learned for sure, not yet ready to tell Hale—is it because I fear his face will show more worry than happiness?—not sure that my grandmother really has anything left she will prove able to offer me, not sure why I don't feel more relieved at the prospect of this day coming to an end.

"You're quiet," Hale observes.

"I'm eating," I say, eating. "I haven't kept anything down all day. How are you feeling?"

"Much better." He does seem pretty good. And I haven't heard him cough since the church. "How are *you* feeling?"

"I told you. Hungry." Packing a forkful of ham in my mouth.

Why this snappishness with Hale? As soon as I hear myself say it, I want to take it back. I want to make amends, lean in close, and whisper my good news, our good news—but is it good or bad?

The positive test stick is at this moment stuffed down under my mother's T-shirt inside the pocket of my coat, which I tossed back on top of the pile of coats in the bedroom. I think of it, this artifact of hope, this vanguard of probable loss. Its existence makes me happy and despondent. I think of the life it signifies, then remember the strange fact that that life is *inside* me at this moment, being fed ham and potatoes. I feel at once horribly protective of it and horribly at its mercy: will it continue to grow? Or stagnate and desert me? It's this that's the real source of my misplaced anger toward Hale, then. Or not only this. Hale had it right when he told Doris Liu that my mother's death was informing my worry about him. It's everything that serves as a reminder of fragility, of brevity.

"What is it?" asks Hale. Studying my face.

I look at him, look *to* him as though he could make it come out right. "Hale," I whisper, almost an appeal.

"What is it?" Again, and very gently.

But I shake my head, and speak what I have just realized: "I need to find my father before we go."

IN THE KITCHEN I find Pax and Teej, the one eating strawberry rhubarb pie and the other drying dishes at the sink. In fact Teej is now wearing another of my mother's aprons, this one black and printed all over with red chili peppers. Both cousins are chatting away with the several remaining kitchen women.

"We need to go?" asks Pax, looking up as I loom in the doorway.

"Not yet." I glance at the clock. Ten of five. "Fifteen, twenty minutes, okay?"

He nods. "Say the word."

The living room offers up Alvarez but no Grandmother. "Where is she?" I ask him.

He's sitting in the Queen Anne by the fire, and reaches over easily to stoke the embers with the poker as he replies. "I took her upstairs a little while ago, to the spare room. She wanted to lie down for half an hour before we start back."

"Okay. Hey, thanks for coming, you know, for bringing her."

"It's my pleasure."

I give a little laugh.

"No, really. I was flattered when she asked me," he insists. He is really big, Alvarez, in his three-piece suit, his size accentuated by the dainty white coffee cup and saucer now balanced on his knee. But he looks remarkably comfortable, or maybe relaxed is a better word. For a moment he looks to me like the barge on the East River this morning: enviably remote.

"That's sweet."

He shrugs. "It's the truth."

"You have kids, Alvarez?"

He touches his mustache. I think it is a gesture of modesty. "Two. One of each," he adds, anticipating the question. "Seventeen and eleven."

"Nice."

"So," he says, checking his watch, "I'm going to wake her pretty soon. Then I'll go warm up the car while she gets ready. Then, to the airport."

"Okay. Hey, you haven't seen my father, have you?"

"Sorry, no."

"That's okay."

I mount the half flight of stairs connecting the split levels of the ranch house. They are carpeted in beige. The handrail is iron and has some give. I am struck anew, as I am whenever I come, by how radically this house differs from the one I grew up in. The Ashtanga yoga rug hangs in the upstairs hallway. The bathroom door is open, no one inside.

The bedroom door is open as well, and here I guess is where I am expecting to find my father, in retreat, having chosen this room for privacy, perhaps even for proximity to my mother's remaining things—for surely he can't have gotten rid of all her things yet, her clothing, her jewelry. Isn't he at any rate supposed to offer some of that stuff to me?

But the bedroom, too, with its bed still half piled with coats, proves empty of any person. I wander in anyway, open dresser drawers, her jewelry box: yes, all her things are still here. In her underwear drawer I find cosmetics, prescription bottles, perfume bottles; I picture him sweeping it all in here, hastily, haphazardly, in his effort to make the bathroom pristine, to erase from the public areas of the house all evidence of his wife, now deceased. Her oval wooden hairbrush, too, has been dumped in with her underclothes, her sachets and scarves. I take it out, turn it over; long strands of gray-brown hair are entwined within the bristles. Their anachronistic presence strikes me for a second as incredible, miraculously profound. Inside her jewelry box, a tangle of earrings and bracelets and necklaces, a few rings. Her wedding ring. How odd, I think, that she wasn't wearing it Sunday afternoon on her way home from the library. Then I realize it must have been removed after her death, and returned to my father by either the hospital or the crematorium. Not odd, just routine.

The only other room upstairs is the spare room. I have slept there once every year or two of my adult life, on a daybed, normally made up to look like a couch. It's comfortable enough, but small, and even though I never brought Hale on any of my trips to Bovine—even though I had always been vocal about my reluctance to subject him to an in-law visit—it bothered me nevertheless that a single bed is all my parents' house would provide. Now, according to Alvarez, my grandmother lies resting on that bed. I am tempted to knock, to see if she's awake, but think better of it. I'll let Alvarez rouse her; he knows best how to do it, how to approach her if she is disoriented upon waking. The truth is I am still feeling unnerved by the degree to which she seemed changed, earlier, unfocused.

As I am about to go back downstairs, thinking I will have a last look around for my father before giving up (might he have gone out for a drink or something, a drive; might he actually be avoiding me?), I hear a voice coming from behind the spare room door. The doors in this house are hollow-core and easy to hear through, a far cry from the old house in Cambridge with all its heavy oak, and its soundproofed addition, and the noise machine outside my parents' offices. There are no ancient, bare floorboards to creak here; the carpet muffles my footsteps, and I am able to stand right outside the door and listen to what is being said.

"You told her to leave me." It is my father. He is making an accusation, yet he sounds broken-up, impaired, a man who can't lift his gaze to see beyond his own misery.

"Only once." My grandmother's voice carries clearly. "Forty-five years ago. And it took her nearly that long to forgive me."

My father says something garbled.

"What? Speak up, Jeremy."

He obliges with a petulant cry. "I said is that how long it's going to take Beatrice to forgive me?"

I go heavy under the burden of his words.

"But don't you see," says my grandmother slowly, almost pedantically, "that's *your* job. *You* need to forgive yourself."

There is a longish silence. I put one hand on the doorknob. I lay my forehead on the door. My eyes are closed.

Then my father, so low I have to strain to hear, delivers what might either be a confession or a plea: "That's so hard to do."

"Jeremy," says my grandmother severely. "I know."

"It's *hard*."

"I *know*." She sounds almost harsh. "Don't you think I know? Don't you think for years I thought my . . . relief, my reprieve, lay in the hands of others? If Silke would forgive me, if Maynard would understand, if I could just make up for what I'd done by being the perfect mother to Ida. If Sarah would forgive me."

"But Sarah did forgive you."

"But that is not what freed me. Frees me."

I am transfixed, my heart warping, my breath coming shallow. It's as though I'm a child eavesdropping on my parents again, instead of forty-one and eavesdropping on this unlikely pair.

"Marg—" He breaks off. A noise of helplessness.

"What I'm telling you is: don't you put this on Beatrice."

She sounds exactly like herself, not doddery or vague, but Margaret Fourcey to the hilt, and I, her un-guessed-at audience, want to laugh, to rise up clapping, to—how did John once put it?—to fall down and cry.

Behind me, coming up the stair softly for such a large man, is Alvarez. It seems an inopportune moment to cut things short, yet there are planes to catch, I know. We exchange a look; I try to communicate with this look that something momentous is taking place behind the door. Whether Alvarez registers this, I do not know. I back away slightly down the hall and he knocks on the door and enters. I hear him tell my grandmother it's time to go, hear him apologize to my father ("I didn't know anyone else was in here," he says, and I cannot tell from his voice whether this is the truth or a lie), and let her know he's going to start the car. "And," he says, in a lowered voice, "your granddaughter's waiting outside."

So strong was her timbre, so clear her enunciation just a few moments ago, that I am unprepared for the sight of my grand-mother emerging on Alvarez's arm. Her voice had almost made me forget that she is this diminished now, this reedy and attenuated, her hair this gossamer. Yet when she says, "Goodbye, my dear," she grips my fingers with surpassing strength.

"I'll come visit you soon, Grandmother. I'll come to Boston, sometime in the next month."

"I would like that very much." She leans in close to me, as one passing along a secret. "Your father is in there." Tossing a glance over her shoulder. Before she releases my fingers, I swear she gives them a small tug in that direction.

I watch them go down the stairs, my grandmother and her stal-wart squire. It seems funny that earlier I wished for someone fitting that description to escort me to the funeral. I miss Hale. I feel I've hardly seen him today. I think: who cares why I love him, I do, and he loves me, and thank heaven for it. And I'm tired; all at once I can-not wait to sleep with him tonight, to be back on Twelfth Street lying in our own bed, alone together, warm and at peace, neither of us going anywhere for hours and hours at least. That is something to look forward to.

I propel myself toward the doorway. My father is standing at the end of the narrow room, by the window, looking into blackness. One hand is placed on the sill: a rather maidenly pose. If he were a young girl he'd look fetchingly forlorn. He sighs without turning, speaks toward the glass. "I don't know what I'm going to do."

I venture over the threshold a few steps. "Hi . . . I have to leave pretty soon, Dad."

Addressing the window, he says, "I don't know. I really don't. I don't know what I'm going to do." It's a tuneless song. A song sung by an afflicted person, damaged and dumb. Or by a canny person who wishes to broadcast such traits as a defense, a bid for sympathy.

"For God's sake," I say.

His back stiffens.

"God Almighty," I breathe, and close my eyes.

For more than twenty years, my father has operated in one of only two modes with me. Cruel and incisive, as on the last morning of my last visit. Or dotty and ineffectual, as now. I think about the vast range of human experience and behavior, and I think about the stinginess of the slice of the spectrum to which my father has confined himself, and I know that it is not acceptable to me. I am willing to believe that with my mother, his patients, his friends the amateur ornithologists, etc.—even apparently, it transpires, with my grandmother—he has functioned along a fuller bandwidth. Which is great, I suppose, as far as it goes—although it also makes me that much less willing to accept his deficient behavior toward me. In any case, this much is clear: it isn't and never will be all right with me, the choices he's made as a father.

Which is different from hating him.

Which does not preclude compassion.

It's a funny thing about having overheard my grandmother—all that about how it's his job to forgive himself, not mine. She can't have intended this, because I don't see how she could have known I was in the hallway listening, but it has had the effect of letting me off the hook. For all these years, without quite realizing it, I have felt pressure to forgive him, and guilt for withholding this final act of clemency. Now, making my way into the room with him, I feel an unexpected lightness. I go past the little writing desk and the daybed, all the way to where he stands at the window, and put a hand on his shoulder.

He flinches minutely beneath the rough tweed cloth. An animal sort of reaction, the way a barnyard creature will twitch its muscle in automatic response to a fly on its hide. I remove my hand. He says again, as though helpless to stop, "I don't know what I'm going to do."

"Yes you do."

He shakes his head, less an expression of obstinacy than impotence.

"You do, Dad."

"What?"

The words come strangely, as though they are being delivered to me slowly and on time, almost methodically, the way I imagine a nurse handing instruments to a surgeon. There is something equally detached about the way I offer him comfort now. I feel far away. A surgery or a nursery? For the words come also like those of a lull-aby, sung as much to myself as to him. "You're going to be sad," I say. "You're going to miss her. You're going to keep on seeing patients, and meeting with your birders, and recording books for the blind. You're going to see friends, and eat food, and . . . get oil changes . . . buy groceries . . . go to those concerts at the church. Clean your binoculars with your little binocular-cleaning kit. You'll shovel snow, and mow the lawn, and rake the leaves. You'll read, and cook. You'll go on walks."

"I walked with Sarah."

"Yeah, well, now you'll walk without her. Maybe you'll find someone else to walk with."

"No."

"Not right away," I say. And softly, "Maybe after a while."

"How?"

I am aware that he is giving nothing to me, doing nothing for me. He has offered no comfort, no acknowledgment that I may be grieving, too. He is letting me tend entirely to him. His tiny protests, I recognize, are signs that he desires these, my consolations. They are his way of asking for more, of prolonging it.

"I have to go quite soon, Dad. Hale's and my flight," I explain, thwarted and fatigued. I move away from him, toward the door. "I came up to get our coats."

"You and I used to go on walks," my father says as though he hasn't heard me. "Do you remember?"

The utterance surprises me. I study him carefully. Apart, perhaps, from the photographs he'd selected to display on the easels at the church, this is the first indication he's given that he's aware he and I share a past. "Yes."

"We used to go walking on Memorial Drive, when they closed it off on Sundays."

"When Mom would have her headaches." I offer the supplemental detail correctively, in an effort to keep things honest, but if he notices, it doesn't appear to have detracted from the sweetness of the memory. His face has softened; his eyes have gone bright.

"You and I," he says. "You loved to collect those seed balls, those brown seed things."

"You would suggest it. I did it to please you." Another minor correction. Again he seems hardly aware of it.

"And I would tell you stories. Do you remember that?"

"Yes."

"I would tell you stories from the *Odyssey* and the *Iliad*. From Greek myths. You remember?" he repeats.

Outside the window, over his head, hangs a sickle moon, both of its points lethally sharp. But I am seeing the sun, and my father's coppery-locked head towering above me against a backdrop of light-dappled sycamores, a ribbon of brilliant blue water rippling off to his right, the stately old university buildings framing him on the left. He was king to me then.

"Yes," I whisper.

"You would ask for them. You had favorites." He ticks them off with effortless clarity. He is more animated, more present than I've

seen him in a long time. "Atalanta. Circe turning Odysseus's men
into pigs. Athena springing full-grown from the skull of Zeus. I'd
tell them to you on Sundays, by the river."

"Yes. You told me a lot of myths." I take a breath. This is my
opening, my chance. "And you know, Dad," I quaver, feeling my
way, "some of them were terribly self-serving. Some of them got in
the way, really horribly in the way, of you and me having a good, or
a real, relationship, or a relationship, period. Some of them—"

He isn't looking at me. For all I know he may not be hearing me.
I wonder if he even heard my grandmother when she told him it
isn't my job to forgive him.

I have to go, will go, in another minute. But first I want to make
sure to see my father as he is now. A man marked by consequence.
His slouched figure. Barely a trace of the old copper in his crew cut.
His jacket hanging on him in a way that is shapeless, depersonalizing.

My thoughts go to the test stick in my coat pocket, to the
knowledge that soon, in the airport or on the plane, I will hand it
wordlessly to Hale and watch his face while its meaning registers
there. He will react as I did, with delight and apprehension. These
conflicting impulses will flicker over his features, and I will be anxious to manage his response, to telegraph to him even as it is forming, even as his own embryonic feelings about it are still swirling,
that I need for him to respond in a certain way. I will tell him
before he has a chance to speak that I *know* it all may come to
heartache in the end. But isn't that true, I'll say, of all life?

He will look at me and he won't answer right away. He'll think
it over without hurry, and then—not because I have managed his
response but because he trusts me, and is brave—he'll agree, and we'll
do it together, this enormous thing: We'll get our hopes up.

I'm deep in this reverie when my father's voice intrudes. "Some
of them were what?" he is asking. He has turned his gaze from the

pointed moon and directed it at me, or not quite fully at me, with an expression that is somehow both hopeful and defeated. As though waiting for me to say something he knows I never will.

"Some of them," I repeat, and break off. I don't know what I was going to say. I don't even know what meaning it would carry for me to hold him accountable for past deeds now. "Oh, Dad." I am seeing what I have never really seen before, that his tragedy is *his* tragedy, far more than it ever was mine. "Oh, Dad."

Now he does look truly at me, lifting his eyebrows sadly, the odd trace of a smile on his lips. "What is it, Bebe?"

"I just"—all at once, for some reason, I'm having to fight back tears—"I'm so sorry for your loss."

As if a marionette released from its strings, his head bows, his knees buckle, and he sits on the edge of the daybed. I cross the room toward him again, and stop inches away. Never have I been less certain of my role. Until after a prolonged moment his hand lands blindly, mothlike, on my knee; then I bend, with no ambivalence at all, and touch my lips to the velvet back of his head.

ACKNOWLEDGMENTS

Mary Page gave loads of her beautiful intelligence and wisdom to support the writing of this novel; I am so thankful to her. I'm filled with warmest gratitude for my agent Barney Karpfinger, and for Inge De Taeye and Agnes Krup at the Karpfinger Agency. I am grateful for all the good, hard work of my editor, Jill Bialosky, and her assistant, Evan Carver. Dake Ackley first introduced me to the Richard Wilbur poem, and Jutta Handle and Caroline Heller helped me figure out which Rilke translation to use. Betsy Lerner continues to nourish me as a writer, and I think the world of her. Sam Freedman, to whom this book is dedicated, taught me early on, by most graceful example, about following and honoring stories' complexities. Above all I'm thankful for my parents (who couldn't be less like those in this book), and for Reba and Andy, Joe, Rosy and George, and, so much, for Mike.